Aunt Jenny of Sawed Off Corners

... and, The Everlasting Johnsongrass Patch

By Scarlette Hall

NEW FORUMS

NEW FORUMS PRESS INC.

Published in the United States of America
by New Forums Press, Inc.1018 S. Lewis St.
Stillwater, OK 74074
www.newforums.com

Library of Congress Cataloging-in-Publication Data Pending

This book may be ordered in bulk quantities at discount from New Forums Press, Inc., P.O. Box 876, Stillwater, OK 74076 [Federal I.D. No. 73 1123239]. Printed in the United States of America.

ISBN 10: 1-58107-400-X
ISBN 13: 978-1-58107-400-0

Contents

About the Book

In the 1940s, in Caddo County of Oklahoma, there was a rural intersection known as Sawed Off Corners; a name that probably morphed from Sudiff's corner. It was likely an acreage that belonged to someone named Sudiff, in an earlier time. If I recall correctly, it was a designated place for children in that area to catch the bus to school.

The name Sawed Off Corners was suggestive of a place where rough edges are sanded, polished and repurposed for the better. Some people think that nothing of importance happens in those little towns they speed through on their way to a more promising looking place. (In Oklahoma, they'd better watch their speed.) However, good things happen in little out-of-the-way places all over this land. As I drive through small towns all across the country, I often wonder what fine things are taking place there.

I like to research names of people, places and things–especially towns and streets. This story takes place in the Anadarko Basin which has a good supply of oil and gas reserves. The upper layers of soil are also rich and fertile. I chose Sawed Off Corners as an apt name for the place where Tallie Koums experiences some polishing. Her name is taken from the words 'talitha koum' found in the biblical passage where Jesus tells a little girl, seemingly dead, to wake up and get up! Mark 5:41.

Chapter One: Retire? Hoe, Hoe, Hoe

Aunt Jenny Raider wanted to retire, but God wouldn't let her. She argued with Him off and on, pointing out her advanced age, brittle bones, and years of carrying out His assignments from her little spot on earth. Even now, she shook her head as she looked out the screen door and shook her head at His new project — her own tacky-looking, ill-mannered, great niece standing on the entry gate of her farm. She knew the gates of perdition, with their hot hinges about to pop loose, were serious matters to God, but she silently proffered the idea that it was time to let someone else snatch souls off those gates.

She explained again to God that she hoped to quietly tend her flowers and vegetable garden. I want to grow tomatoes larger than Alice Fursby's, not a lot larger, just a little larger, she silently confessed. She glanced sideways to see if Perceived One objected. She knew He wouldn't like the idea, but said it anyway because He knew what she was thinking. She knew He knew, so it was a sort of confession. She waited for a reprimand. None. Just a nudge to get to work.

Working for Him was a privilege, and His plan would be done one way or another. It was best to be in the middle of it rather than against it. She had learned that details might shift around a bit, but He absolutely would not be budged from His will. He didn't budge. Wasn't going to budge. Probably never would budge. She finally concluded that He was going to have work for her to do until her very last breath and when she stepped over into eternity, He would probably have something else for her to do there.

She sighed and resigned herself to the task. Raising her eyebrows high, she focused on Him, reminding Him this was His idea and she would need His help. With that, she opened the screen door of the kitchen and yelled, "TAL—EEE!"

Tallie Koums, her 12 year-old great niece, was still thoughtlessly standing on the rickety old entry gate. Aunt Jenny disapproved of that and a few other things as well. The short shorts with a hole in the rear, the poor posture, the lack of grace, the sullen look on her face, all discerned within the space of a few minutes of Tallie's arrival.

Tallie's dad was Aunt Jenny's nephew and the one who had called for Aunt Jenny's help after he and his wife considered their options. They hoped Tallie might benefit by a change of venue since she wasn't listening to them, and literally begged Aunt Jenny to do what she could to rescue and refine their daughter from poor choices and a hateful attitude. They stressed that they did not want to leave her home during the day while they worked at their hardware store, and she needed more than a baby sitter.

Now, looking at her niece, Aunt Jenny knew something sure needed to be done. A lot more in fact. Nothing about the child indicated she could manage to make proper choices at home for an hour, let alone all summer, and maybe never, God forbid. She only hoped she could bear up under the task regardless of her current infirmities. And sometimes, she was just plain tired of fooling with people.

"Stretch your Isaiah:54 tent pegs, old lady! Here she comes," Aunt Jenny said aloud.

"WHAAAAT!" Tallie yelled back and thought how thin her yell sounded in comparison to her aunt's. The red dust that had been kicked up by her parent's departure drifted over the field in the distance. They were going back to civilization, and she was not.

"COME H'YEAR!" Her aunt yelled again, but Tallie did not move.

"I am definitely h' year," she mimicked the Okie sound. "I'm right in the middle of nowhere."

Aunt Jenny watched Tallie get off the fence gate taking her own sweet time returning to the house.

"Here," she said, not distorting the word, "take this bucket and run get me a few onions from the barn. They're in the side room, and I'd be pleased for you to wash them off at the well."

There was no smile, no "yes ma'am" from Tallie. She just took the bucket and walked down the path to the barn, absently slapping at the tops of some zinnias with it. Aunt Jenny watched with raised eyebrows and changed her mind about what to fix for supper.

Tallie let the screen door slam when she returned with the onions. Aunt Jenny winced ever so slightly but managed a nod of thanks while stirring the contents of a stew pot.

"What are you cooking?" Tallie asked, suddenly aware of her hunger.

"I'm boiling squash to go with some cornbread and leftover pinto beans and some fresh radishes and those onions you brought up."

"I don't like squash." Tallie said.

"Is that a fact? Aunt Jenny replied, unconcerned.

"I don't like radishes either. Bleck!" Tallie said, snarling her nose.

"How sad for you. You have an uneducated palate." Aunt Jenny poured the yellow cubes of squash into a bowl and basted them with more than a bit of fresh, homemade butter. "You can set the table while I take up the cornbread. Use any of those dishes you like from the china hutch."

Aunt Jenny heard two thuds and a couple of ping and rolled her eyes to the ceiling in a silent plea. There sat two carelessly placed plates with a fork thrown in the middle of each. Aunt Jenny stared at the table working her jaw until her partial plate hurt her gums.

"Didn't your mama teach you how to set a table?" she said more sharply than she intended, knowing full well that her mom always set a pleasant table.

Tallie shrugged. "Yeah, but it's just the two of us. Who cares?"

"I care! " Aunt Jenny exclaimed. Now try again and see if you can't make a proper job of it."

Tallie tilted her head, let her shoulders sag, and with exaggerated mocking, dramatically acted like a persnickety person, she reset the table just so.

"That's much better," Aunt Jenny said, as gently as possible. Dinner was her favorite meal of the day and she was loath to have it ruined by sitting at a carelessly set table across from a piece of ulcer bait.

Tallie sat down and immediately helped herself to a big piece of hot cornbread with one hand and reached for the butter with the other. Aunt Jenny grabbed Tallie's hand in mid air.

"Just a minute,if you please," she said and began to thank God for the food. With dramatics of her own, she raised her eyebrows hard enough to push her hairline backward and loudly promised God they would not waste a bite of it. Then she passed the butter to Tallie.

Tallie dished some of everything onto her plate and ate what she pleased, leaving the rest bitten and scattered. Aunt Jenny, on the other hand, cleaned her plate and even mopped up the juices with a bit of bread.

"What are we going to do after supper?" Tallie asked.

"The dishes," her aunt replied.

"The dishes. Great. Then what?"

"I reckon we'll sit on the porch where it's cooler and snap beans."

"How exciting!" Tallie whispered, but her aunt heard it.

"It can be," Aunt Jenny managed to say matter of factly. Control was returning to her –the bracing effect of a good dinner.

Tallie rolled her eyes. Perhaps her aunt had pulled her hair up into such a tight little knot over the years that it had done something to her brains.

"Are you done eating?" Aunt Jenny asked, looking hard at Tallie's plate.

"Yeah. I don't want the rest of that. I told you I didn't like squash or radishes."

"Then you shouldn't have put it on your plate. And, Tallie, I'd be pleased if you wouldn't say 'yeah' for 'yes'. It sounds like someone calling up the dogs."

"I've never heard anyone call dogs by saying 'yeah'. Normal people just say, 'Here, Spot', or something like that. And another thing, I've never heard anyone yell 'h'year' either."

"Is that a fact? Maybe they don't know that 'h'year' is a heap easier to holler than 'here'," Aunt Jenny said while putting the leftovers in the refrigerator. She shut the door carefully and polished the handle with a t-towel. It had taken a long time to save the money, but she got the best– the top of the line with a side freezer. She turned to her niece to instruct her on the dish washing chores.

"I'll dry and you can wash since you don't know where things go yet. You will find hot water on the stove and soap in a jar under the cabinet.," Aunt Jenny said and went to wipe crumbs from the old ball and claw dining table remembering the many meals that rested on it.

"If we had everything that had ever been set on this old table, we'd sure have a heap of good eating." She grimaced from a pain in her wrist as she reached too far to remove the last crumb. My mother always kept a white cloth on the table," Aunt Jenny continued. Anything else was tacky to her notion, but I find this white oilcloth right easy to keep. Saves on my 'lectric since I don't have to iron it," she said and turned to look at her niece.

Tallie was standing on one leg, one foot perched on top of the other, while lazily dragging the dishrag over a plate. Daydreaming. Not listening until she gave her niece a sharp poke in the back with the forefinger.

"Ow! Tallie squawked. "What's the deal?"

"Stand on two feet. You don't want to look lazy. And quit fiddling around. We don't want to be in here all night, do we? And make sure to scrub those dishes good. I don't care to eat today's grease tomorrow."

"Is there anything else?" Tallie asked

"Yes. While you're at it, look for a square soap bubble."

"What? That's stupid! There's no such thing as a square soap bubble."

"How do you know there isn't? You haven't bothered to look."

"I've never heard of one and neither has anyone else," Tallie responded. And I don't care if I ever do, she thought to herself, shifting her weight to both feet. She's lived alone too long. She may be losing it. I'm going to tell Mother.

When the last pan was washed, Tallie yanked the plug and watched the bubbles disappear, a little relieved that they were all sure-enough round.

"Where does this water go?" Tallie asked.

"Into a barrel outside. After it settles, I pour it on my plants."

Aunt Jenny pulled a half-bushel of beans into the middle of the floor and another pain shot through her right wrist. She used her foot to scoot the basket toward the screen door.

"Here," she said, when Tallie hung the dishrag up, "You take a hold of that side and let's carry these on out to the porch." Aunt Jenny handed Tallie a big metal bowl for the beans and pointed to an old bucket at her feet.

"Save the trimmings to the bucket to feed to the chickens. God doesn't cotton to waste," she said, deftly snapping the tender beans, reaching for another handful before Tallie finished her first few. These are right nice. That is something I'm excited about. No bug bites in them. Not limber nor tough like some I've had", she said quickly snapping the beans and grabbing another handful.

Tallie stepped up her pace, snapping fast as she could, but Aunt Jenny's hand beat hers to the basket again and again.

"Yes, snapping these beans is a pure pleasure, although I thought my bones would snap before I got them all planted, she chuckled. I studied on that and decided God invented work for a whole host of reasons; the main reason, lately, to keep me limber in my old age. Then there is the sheer wonder of it all."

Once again, Tallie was skeptical about her aunt's mental acuity. Bean snapping, the excitement of the evening? Wonderful? Not to Tallie, who thought she might need to keep an eye on the old gal.

Then Aunt Jenny stopped and said, "Lookie here". She held up a long green bean, snapped it in half with eyes shut. Take it. Yours will be the first eyes to see the insides of this bean. Think about that. You're seeing something no one else has ever seen but God, Himself. Isn't that a lick?"

Tallie warily took the bean. "I see it," she said.

"No you don't. Not yet. Yooooou don't see it yet, Missy. But maybe one day you will." Tallie again wondered about her aunt's mind. Anyone finding bean guts exciting is totally weird. She really has lived alone one year too many.

"How long have you lived here? Tallie asked, "I mean, by yourself."

"Thirty year this spring." Tallie thought it sounded like a prison sentence and she wondered if saying 'year' made it seem shorter.

"I've lived here most of my life. I was born in this very house, part of it anyway. The folks added the east rooms in '49 and screened in the back porch the following year. Hard to believe it's been that long."

"Why didn't they add plumbing and a bathroom?" Tallie asked.

"Water shortages. The well was nigh on to dry. We weren't sure there would be enough to make the expense of plumbing worth it. And speaking of the which, let's put these beans in the icebox and splash a little water on ourselves. It's about my bedtime."

Nine-thirty. Tallie went upstairs, changed into a sleep shirt, kicked her jean shorts across the floor toward a tapestry covered dressing bench and flopped onto the bed. She shoved the embroidered, long-fringed counterpane to the foot of the bed with her feet. Only nine-dang-it-thirty! With fifty-nine more days to go. She stared at the ceiling, overcome with a wave of boredom. I don't know if I can stand it. And if I do, what will I say when people ask me how I spent my vacation? That I looked at bean guts and hunted for square soap bubbles?

Tears gathered in her eyes. Worse than the boredom was the outrage of her dad. His disapproval and condemnation of her. It was like he had disowned her which was totally uncalled for to her mind. He yelled at her, seemed to go to pieces berating her for saying she was bored. He used the meanest word, the worst word she ever heard him say on her. "Blasted!" Even worse, "DAD-blasted". She fell as she recalled his rant.

"Since you're so blasted, so dad-blasted bored all the time, you can be bored at Aunt Jenny's. I'm not putting up with that word again in this house. Maybe sixty days in Sawed Off Corners will knock some sense into you."

He had slammed the door and scarcely spoke to her again. Even the very day they dropped her off, they hugged Aunt Jenny, then her dad turned and gave her a stern stare and they left.

It stabbed her every time she thought of his loud outburst. It was like a mad fit or something and totally unreasonable. And being in time-out at Aunt Jenny's for the whole summer was totally out of line.

Talley continued to pick at the parts of the situation. He thinks Aunt Jenny is wonderful, and I think she is as weird as a three-legged duck. Anyone with half a brain knows soap bubbles are round. Tallie yawned. They are round, but they aren't all round when they're stacked, she remembered. Their tops are round, but their bottoms aren't.

They are round in reverse! And they can't ever be square because, she yawned again, because air isn't square and they are full of air and air doesn't have a shape except when it is in something. Aren't air atoms round? Then why is a box square if it has round air atoms in it?

A slight puff of air moved the curtains. She rolled over to face the window. Now that old aunt of his is driving me nuts with her goofy ideas. It's all a bunch of beans, she sighed.

~~~~~~~~~~~~~~

The smell of sausage and cinnamon awakened Tallie. It was barely light outside. The promise of something delicious to eat caused her to yank on a pair of shorts and hurry downstairs to a table set with a big bouquet of zinnias, fried apples in cinnamon, sausages, hot biscuits, and scrambled eggs. Aunt Jenny came to the table carrying another plate.

"Here you go," she said. "Here is your plate."

Tallie's eyes grew large. It held one helping of squash and three radishes—the leftovers from her supper.

"Well," Aunt Jenny said. Let's say grace before you start eating this morning."

But Tallie interrupted.

"Why is this old squash on my plate?" She asked.

"We don't waste anything here. You eat what you take out at my house," Aunt Jenny said and began to ask the blessing.

Tallie didn't listen to her aunt's prayer. She was wondering how to make a quick end the squash, deciding the best way was to swallow it down as fast as she could. When her aunt said 'amen' she did. She opened her mouth and crammed the mushy stuff in, chewed it twice and swallowed once, then did the same with the radishes. They stung her tongue but gratefully, took the taste of the squash with them.

"That's a girl!" Aunt Jenny said. "Now, how about something else? Try some of these eggs. They are good and fresh."

Tallie selected a small bite of the eggs. Leftover eggs for lunch was a gagging idea, but fried apples might not be so bad. She took plenty of those.

When breakfast was finished and the dishes done, Tallie wandered outside. She sat on the porch with one leg thrown over the arm of a wicker chair and chewed on the end of her long ponytail. Boringest place in the world she decided for the umpteenth time.

Picking at her circumstances again, she decided that she was quite old enough to have stayed at home by herself whi'e both her parents took inventory of their hardware business. They must have some other reason, especially her dad, to be sending her off for the whole summer. Who would drive 200 miles from St. Louis to do something like that? What is the real reason, she wondered.

There must be a stronger reason to drive 200 miles just to dump me off in the boring country for a whole boring summer. They've gotten picky, lately. Picky about my room, my posture, my time on the telephone. They gripe about everything I do or say. Nothing suits them anymore. Whatever they are mad about,it must be more than me saying I was bored. I sure don't deserve having my whole summer ruined just for that. They don't like my friends much. Especially Amy.

She pierced one of my ears, but couldn't stand to do the other one. I didn't think it was such a big deal that my ear got infected and swelled up. The hole grew shut and got well when the doc gave me penicillin.

Maybe it was because I wore Amy's bikini to the Country Club pool. It wasn't as skimpy as Amy's. It was because of her thong bikini that got us kicked out, and h'year I am, she mimicked.

Muffled sounds drew her away from her own musings to see what her aunt was doing in the kitchen.

Aunt Jenny, red in the face from the heat, was tightening up the lids on some jars.

"Interesting, right?' " Aunt Jenny said between short puffs bearing down on the lid.

"What's interesting?" She said to her aunt who looked like an aged, lady wrestler putting a hammer lock on a jar of beans.

"We call these things 'fruit jars' even when they are full of beans. Did you ever think about that? Fruit has a broader term, you know. Whatever comes out of a seed is a fruit, you see. Life itself is a seed that comes from God who planted it in the earth to carry out a plan He had in mind even before the creation."

"Really? I've never thought about that," Tallie said and didn't find it very interesting either.

"If you put your mind to it, I'll bet you could think of lots of things we call one thing when it is really something else."

How about 'dad-blasted', she thought but said, "I'm not in the vocabulary mood."

Aunt Jenny looked up and mopped her forehead with the tail of her apron. "Your dobbers sure are down this morning. What's the matter with you?"

"There is nothing to do here but sit on your boring porch."

Aunt Jenny's eyes widened with a sudden flash of understanding from the One she perceived to be with her at all times. It was strong and clear that He'd had enough of the word "boredom" reaching his ears. The cup of boredom was up to the brim and spilling over, and needed tending to and right now! Authority rose up in her so strongly, her backbone snapped to military attention.

"Boredom? Did you say 'boredom'? Lah! There is plenty to do, Aunt Jenny said forcefully. Get a hoe from the shed and get to chopping on that Johnsongrass out in the north corner of my garden."

"That's not what I call something to do. I mean, there is nothing interesting or fun to do out here."

"You'll find a good deal of fun and interesting things to do,once you get that grass patch chopped. And another thing, I'm not in the entertainment business. So get to chopping, and do a right smart job. I'll give you until noon to get it done."

"What if I'm not done by noon?"

"Then I'll give you to six o'clock."

Tallie took the hoe and headed for the garden. She groaned aloud when she saw the thick Johnsongrass higher than her head. It looked like a forest, yet there was not another weed to be seen in the rest of the garden. She stared at it and took a whack.

The stalk of Johnsongrass rattled but stood firm. She whacked again, and again, lick after lick before a stalk finally fell. Sweat gathered on her face and trickled down in itchy paths to places difficult to scratch. The gnats swarmed like little clouds. Now and then, a few peeled out of formation and landed around her eyes and the corners of her mouth.

A sweat bee joined the attack, stinging her behind the right knee first, then darting quickly for a taste of her left calf. Tallie slapped at the bee. It retreated unharmed as the gnats staged another attack. She fought them from her eyes and continued to chop away at the stubborn stalks. The bee returned and bit her twice more on the legs while she was busy wiping the whining swarm of gnats out of her eyes, snorting to keep from sucking one up her nose. She slung her hair around to keep the gnats at bay and waited for the bee. It zipped and hovered as if looking for the choicest spot. Tallie stood still and watched it carefully descend. Just as it touched the back of her leg, she slapped it to mush. The gnats retreated as well.

The sun rose higher and higher and so did a blister on her hand. After a few more blows with the hoe, the blister burst. Tallie headed for the house, thirsty and in considerable misery.

"Are you finished," Aunt Jenny asked.

"No, but I can't chop anymore. I got a nasty blister."

Aunt Jenny took her hand and looked at it.

"Nonsense. I'll put a bandage on it and you can use my gloves. I always use them if I have to chop for very long, especially before my callouses get built up. Here's a cool drink of water before you take to it again."

Tallie glared at Aunt Jenny, but drank it down in four gulps and left for the Johnsongrass patch, deliberately letting the screen door slam behind her. Aunt Jenny's grin was almost wicked as Tallie stomped off to the garden with that heavy, old hoe.

The sun was mercilessly hot and the ground mercilessly hard. The hoe vibrated in her hands when it connected with the hard dirt or with a particularly stubborn stalk. She tried pulling the stalks out by hand, but landed on her rump with nothing to show for the effort except for two pieces of leaves. Furiously, she took up the hoe again, whacking wildly this way and that, slashing her way into the thickest growth. Suddenly, she stopped.

Something moved near her foot. She paused. Something moved again among the shadows on the hot ground. A snake. A huge, long snake! With a shriek, she threw the hoe and ran a high-stepping, gee-haw route out of the garden.

Aunt Jenny was at the back step of the house shaking a rag rug when Tallie came running, screaming "Sna-a-ke! It's huge'."

"What sort of snake is it?" Aunt Jenny calmly asked.

"A big one. A great big one! Long! Really long!" She flung her arms wide.

"No, what *kind*? What color?"

"I don't know," Tallie answered breathlessly. Brown or black. Ugly and Huge! It wasn't a grass snake. I know that much. I think it had some white marks on it. I'm sure it was poisonous."

"Were the eyes elliptical or round?"

"Eyes? EYES! Elliptical! Round? I don't know! I didn't look! I didn't take a mugshot and I didn't Mirandize it! It's a snake! Snakes have fangs and fangs have poison in them! They are dangerous!

"You were too busy inventing a new dance coming out of that garden to know what kind you saw. But I imagine it was just the bull snake. It's here most of the time, though it's usually in the barn, and I'm glad to have it around. Bull snakes eat rats and mice that help themselves to my grain. Bull snakes are harmless if you don't bother them."

"I don't care what it was. I'm not going back out there."

"Nonsense. Just keep your eyes open and pay attention to where you're stepping and chopping. Now is the best time to go back. That snake will be off to some quieter spot by now, I imagine."

Aunt Jenny put her hand over her mouth to hide a smile as Tallie forced herself back to the garden. "Boring indeed," Aunt Jenny said half aloud. "We'll just see about that. Well done, God, that was a hoot!"

Tallie chopped Johnsongrass until noon. After lunch, Aunt Jenny sent her to carry what she had chopped to the barnyard for the cow. Tallie craned her neck over the load of grass just in case that snake was around. After she dumped the last load, Aunt Jenny sent her to the garden again. This time, it was to kill squash bugs by picking them off the plants and dropping them into a coffee can containing coal oil.

Tallie's head was baking in the hot afternoon sun. She had refused to wear the straw hat Aunt Jenny offered. She thought of her friends who were probably at the Country Club pool, lying in the hot sun, trying to get a tan. Sunbathing seemed a little silly to her at the moment, sitting on her haunches by the prickly leafed squashes, sweat forming in her hair. Timidly, she reached for a squash bug. She had not thought to ask if they would bite.

Surely they have a way to bite, if they eat squash, she thought. It's a dumb bug that eats squash, she decided. Quickly, she grabbed one and dropped it into the can. Killing it gave her a shiver of guilt, but she continued with the onerous chore. Her knees ached. Sweat ran down her back. One little cloud finally drifted between her and the hot sun bringing a brief relief. She stood up to rest her legs.

"Squatting gets old, doesn't it?" Aunt Jenny said. She was carrying three buckets, stepping over the bean rows on her way to the tomatoes. "Aren't you about finished?" She asked.

"I have three squash bushes left to do," Tallie answered.

"Don't you think it is interesting that a squash bug knows squash from other things? How does it know what to eat? They do get on other things from time to time, but you wouldn't think a bug had any sense, would you?"

"If it eats squash, it doesn't have any sense, or its taste buds are dead," Tallie answered.

Aunt Jenny laughed.

"Think about it, Tallie. There's something right interesting in that.

"Maybe they're called squash bugs because they mostly eat squash. Maybe if they ate bananas," Tallie said, "they'd be called banana bugs."

"Is that a fact? Do you think people might be known by that, too—by what they feed on?"

"Well, you know", Tallie answered, "some kids at my school eat only vegetables and they are called vegetarians. Meat eaters are called carnivores. I learned that in third grade when we studied dinosaurs."

"That's a start."

"I don't know of any others."

"Keep thinking, Aunt Jenny said.

"Some people eat junk food. They are called junk food junkies."

"What do intelligent people feed on?"

"They eat books. They're called bookworms," Tallie laughed, but her aunt didn't and again, Tallie thought her aunt was peculiar to take so seriously what people eat.

"Now, you're thinking. And go a step further. What do people eat when they aren't eating food? Aunt Jenny didn't wait for an answer. She moved from the tomatoes to pick a row of beans and continued to list things that needed doing.

"When you're done picking bugs, get on the other end of this row so we can finish picking these beans right quick like. I either missed some or they grew overnight."

Tallie was amazed how her aunt could straddle a row of beans and stoop from the waist to pick. When she tried to do that, she felt her heart beating in her ears.

"What are you going to do with so many beans, anyway?" Tallie asked.

"Tomorrow is Saturday. I'm going to take some of them to the Trade Fair. I've canned about all I need for winter. Have you got anything you want to take to trade?"

"No. I don't. I didn't bring anything but clothes."

"Do you want to shop for anything in town? I do a little shopping after I do my trading–which includes selling things."

"I would like to get some candy bars, for sure."

"Did you bring some money?"

"No. Mom said I shouldn't."

"She did, did she? I reckon if you want some spending money, you'll have to work out a "way to get it yourself."

"Myself? What about all this work I've done in your garden? Wouldn't that be worth something to you?"

"Oh my, yes. But I'm gladly furnishing room and board, gas to town and back all the time you're here, but spending money is for you to figure out"

"What can I sell at the Trade Fair? If I took anything off this farm, you'd say you own it and I don't have any money to buy it from you."

"Generate your brain. Think about it," Aunt Jenny said. She moved on down the bean row whispering to herself about seeds she plants that seem a long time sprouting".

"That means I'll have to find something on nobody's land that somebody would want to buy. If somebody wanted it, they'd already have taken it," Tallie yelled. "That's what I think," she yelled again.

Aunt Jenny put her hands to her back, stood up, and pushed her stomach out. "That's the last bean for today. Let's go t'house and have some iced tea and a fried pie. I'll wash these vegetables while you clean the dirt off the hoe and put it back where it belongs."

She was putting ice in the glasses when Tallie opened the screen door.

"Wash up," she said, "and I do mean 'up'. Hands up to the elbows,face plumb up into the edge of your hair and behind your ears."

When Tallie sat down, she gulped the tea and gobbled one of the fried pies. It tasted wonderful, and she asked what kind it was.

"Rhubarb," her aunt replied.

"Rhubarb! I've never had that before. It's pretty good."

"I put strawberry juice in mine, and a little lemon. Here's a peach one. Want some?"

Tallie took it even though she was getting full, reasoning that she would not mind eating it for breakfast, if necessary.

"We need to wash this little dab of dishes up, Tallie. If I don't, the little black ants will take us over. You can dry. When we get done, you can run to the well and fill the water bucket."

Tallie was not used to washing up every dish after use. At home, she piled them in the sink or on the counter until her mom put them in the dishwasher.

"I don't see why you can't have indoor plumbing. You don't use that much water by yourself."

"I've thought plenty about it. That's why I had this sink put in. I have been saving up for plumbing and I'm getting real close."

"You've lived here thirty years and you're just now getting close to plumbing this place?"

"I hope. I've never minded going to the well for water until this past winter. I like that old well and its windmill. When it screeks, I know the wind is up or changing."

Aunt Jenny silently recalled falling on the ice, knocking herself out, waking up with a broken wrist,her body covered in sleet and chilled to the bone. She suddenly knew the value of two things: a telephone and indoor plumbing. It was days before she was able to get the pickup out of the barn, let alone negotiate miles of snow to town. So she wrapped her wrist tightly with wide strips of an old girdle, and made a sling for her arm from an old t-towel. It healed all right, but pained her some, yet. Knowing it could just as easily have been a broken hip, she got telephone service as quickly as possible. Besides, she reasoned, somebody else might have an emergency and need her. This new understanding caused her to set aside an earlier judgment that the telephone is an instrument of the devil. As for the plumbing, she was getting close by saving back a little each week from the Trade Fair sales. It was in a secret place. As for her little nest egg at the bank, she wouldn't touch it. It was for something really important such as taxes or hospital bills, or catastrophes--not plumbing.

Tallie's arms quivered carrying the bucket of water. She set it on the cabinet and went to sit in the porch swing, happy to have some free time. She thought about going to town; a nice change and something to look forward to, but she could not imagine what to take to the Trade Fair. Aunt Jenny had certainly made it plain that she wasn't going to give her any spending money and she had not received any from her parents before they left. She suspected that it was on purpose, part of her punishment.

"Tallie, run down to the mailbox, will you, please?" Aunt Jenny called from the kitchen.

"End of free time", Tallie whispered to herself, concluding that chores and infinity were about the same thing around here.

Tallie walked barefoot down the drive past the half acre of zinnias and periwinkles. Standing in warm sand that came up over her feet, she took the contents from the mailbox. There was a newspaper, yesterday's and quite thin, plus two items that looked like ads. She closed the lid to the mailbox which was nearly engulfed by bushes. Something red caught her eye. Little plums. Sand plums, the source of the jam they always received at Christmas time. Both sides of the road had those bushes and they were full of plums. She smiled.

Aunt Jenny was pressing a dress when Tallie returned with the mail.

"Say," Tallie asked, "who owns the land across the road?"

"I do," her aunt said," at least for now."

"Who owns the road?"

"The county."

"Where does the county road end and your land begin?"

"My fences are right on my boundary lines. The county owns a few feet on either side of the road. It's called an easement.

"Really? Well, here's your mail, I gotta go up to my room and do some stuff." She dashed upstairs before her aunt could quiz her about her sudden interest in the road. She opened the closet door and dumped her shoes out of a tote bag. She peeked out the door to make sure her aunt was not around and made a mad dash for the plum bushes, picking the sack full.

After supper, Tallie and her aunt sat on the front porch in the wicker rockers, The breeze couldn't have carried another fragrance. Aunt Jenny read the paper, sometimes moving her lips and sometimes talking back at what she read.

"What time are we going to town tomorrow?" Tallie asked.

"About seven o'clock. Town people don't get out too early. Why? Are you anxious to get to town because you're bored way off out here, are you?"

"That's not why I asked," Tallie said.

"Bored. I don't grasp that notion."

"Bored is when you can't think of something to do," Tallie explained.

"I call that ignorance."

"What if you can think of something to do and it turns out to be blah?"

"That amounts to poor judgment."

"What if it is something you don't want to do but have to do?"

"That sounds like duty," Aunt Jenny said.

"What if it is something you don't want to do because it isn't interesting, but you have to do your duty?"

"It is still ignorance. Duty needs doing for a good reason. Find out what that is. Then figure a way to do it that is more gratifying. The Bible says to do all our doings as if unto Him, because it pleases

Him. His burden is light. So I usually hunt for something to enjoy or to look forward to because of the finished work."

"What about picking beans? Next to chopping Johnsongrass, that is the most boring thing I've done all summer." Tallie avered.

"Not to me. I get something new to think about nearly every time I pick beans."

"Such as?" Tallie asked.

"Well, today, I was studying on why some of them curl up on the ends."

"Their chromosomes tell them to curl," Tallie said.

"Think of that! A chromysewn. Reckon how that works?"

"It's in their genetic code. I saw stuff about that on TV."

"I do declare. A genetic code in a bean. Reckon how it got in there? Was it during the garden story in Genesis?"

"I guess so," Tallie shrugged. "God probably did it."

"That's where a good deal of my thinking takes me. That's why I thank Him for my beans, curly ones and all. Genetic code! Isn't that a lick. That's a good one. Why, Tallie you're just plumb interesting. But another thing I wondered on today is how does a bean know when to stop growing? Why doesn't one go wild every now and then and grow as long as a-body's leg? I can kindly figure how they commence to grow. But knowing when to stop? That had me bested until you came up with that code talking notion."

"It's just in their genetic code, like a recipe, a program code doesn't mess up," Tallie explained.

"Isn't that something?" She grinned and wondered if the Presbyterians had ever thought of using that genetic code to back up their predestination doctrine, them being programmed from the beginning and all.

"What other stuff have you learned from beans? You said you get lots of stuff studying beans."

"Lands! You don't have time to sit here and listen to all I've learned from beans, Missy."

"I have time to hear at least one thing," Tallie said, keenly aware that there was nothing else whatsoever to do.

"Well, nature and all things in nature— people, beans, and all living things—they respond to how they're treated. I have also learned that too much of anything is a harm, even good things like fertilizer and rain. But beans are sturdy little rascals and, with a little care, they'll come back out of troubled times and produce. Just takes a little tending and a little praying."

Tallie looked over the porch rail at the zinnia patch. Several flowers with broken necks hung their wilted heads beside the path to the well. They would never make a seed. Suddenly, she was a little sorry she had been so careless with the bucket.

"So what you do," Tallie said, "is dream up stuff to think about. Like yesterday when you were washing jars, you wondered about bubbles being round, right?"

"Lah, no. I thought of that years ago when I was about your age. But I still think about it now and again. And I've wondered what happens to a bubble when it breaks."

Tallie yawned. "It just splatters," she said.

"Just splatters, huh? Do you think it is really that simple? What happens to the splatters?" Aunt Jenny paused a moment, then added, "Speaking of bubbles, there is a bucket of warm water in the tub by the lilac bushes. I drew it for you this morning. It's about time we get cleaned up for bed. You'll find a rag and some soap sitting on the footboard. Save some of the water in the bucket to rinse with when you're through soaping. And when you're done, throw the water on the bushes."

"You mean I have to bathe all over in one little old bucket of water? Out here in the yard!"

"If you want a tub bath, you'll have to draw your own water tomorrow. Four buckets ought to do it, and if you draw it early in the day, it'll be warmed up by bedtime."

Tallie undressed behind the lilac bush and hung her clothes on the branches. It was embarrassing and even a little scary-to bathe outside. What would she do if a car came down the road? "This is flat prehistoric!" she said and hurried as fast as she could. She dumped the water as told and tiptoed on the footboard to the flagstone walk.

"Carry that wash rag on up to your room to wipe your feet last thing before you get in bed," Aunt Jenny said. She patted her niece's head and went to take her turn behind the lilac bush.

Tallie wiped her feet, spread the rag on the iron bed rail and peeked under the bed. The plums were still there. She lay back with a flop and thought about renegade beans growing long as a-body's leg, maybe longer, long enough, to push a hole right through a house all the way to a dishpan full of bubbles which burst and fly off. Little specks of what? Flying off to where. Mongolia? How silly! She dismissed the goofy thinking and fell asleep.

Downstairs, Aunt Jenny lay on clean sheets and pillowcases that smelled of sunshine and thought of beans and bubbles. How fragile are the bubbles, but what a tough job they do.

"Lord, you teach me so much," she whispered. Bubbles are like prayers, don't you think, Lord? The water is like Yourself, and soap is made of ashes and discarded fat, things that are unwanted, but can be a blessing when turned into soap. You have provided a way for cleansing body and soul. I must be a vessel full of soap and water. You agitated me to make prayer bubbles, fragile and splattered out there, lost to all eyes but Yours. Aunt Jenny smiled in the dark. That would sound absolutely silly to anyone but You, Lord. Right?

Now what about the beans? I'm concerned about that little bean upstairs. Help me to weed gently. And Lord, what on earth is a genetic code? Is it really a recipe? Or is it like Morse code? If she has one, please watch over every little dot and dash, and bless those whatchamacallit things– Chromosomes. Now, if You don't have anything else to discuss, I think I'll go to sleep.

What? Oh yes. I forgot her plums. Bless those, too, since she is learning how to start from scratch. I thought she never would catch on. I believe we're making a little headway. Been fun today. See You in the morning."

Chapter Two: Pulled Plums and Pulled Ponytail

Tallie awoke to the rooster's crowing and the mixed aromas of coffee and hot biscuits. No matter how early she awoke, her aunt was always up, had fed the chickens, gathered the eggs, drawn fresh water, and had breakfast cooking. Tallie wondered if she got up in the dark.

"Well, you decided to get up, I see." Aunt Jenny said.

"That loud mouth rooster woke me up."

"Old Jube can holler, can't he? He thinks the barnyard is his. Crows over it every morning like he's some kind of king in charge." Aunt Jenny pulled a Pyrex dish of biscuits from the oven.

"He's no king. He's just mean. He flapped his wings and charged at me when I went to the barn for onions."

"Did he scare you?"

"A little. But I threw a rock at him and he left me alone. He's like some dogs down the street at home. They growl and bark at me when I ride my bike past them. I haven't done anything to make them do it either."

"Call Old Jube by his name next time, and try throwing some corn to him. You might try that with those dogs, too, only don't use corn," she laughed. "Now, if you'll fetch the butter from the refrigerator we'll eat."

Aunt Jenny asked the blessing and passed the biscuits to Tallie who was wondering if she ought to tell her aunt about the plums. She couldn't decide why she had kept them a secret, actually, except maybe for fear of some protest. Surely her aunt wouldn't object; after all, she said the plums were on public land. Anyway, it was kind of nice to have a little secret all to herself for a little while, some business all her own.

"I want you to wear a dress to town today. No shorts and no jeans."

"Mama told me you didn't like shorts or pants. She said you think real ladies wear dresses, most of the time."

"There are some dresses I don't care for either. Dresses don't make a lady, but a lady in a proper dress is welcome most everywhere. It commands respect, too."

"I guess you are telling me to get these shorts off?"

"If you want to go to town with me, you will."

Tallie changed into a sleeveless dress immediately after breakfast. She slipped past her aunt with the sack full of plums and concealed them between other items her aunt had already loaded into the pickup.

Out of the drive and onto the dirt road, the pickup swayed over alternating areas of washouts and patches of sand. Aunt Jenny whispered to herself now and again, and Tallie wondered if she were coaching the pickup down the road or praying about it.

"Watch those eggs, Missy."

Tallie checked a box containing dozens of eggs in paper mache crates on the floorboard.

"So far, so good," Tallie reported, holding the box steady between her feet. The windows were down. The air felt good and the bumpy ride made her burp.

~~~~~~~~~~~~

The Trade Fair was held in a simple structure on the edge of town. The town of Sawed-Off Corners had been called Sudiff Corners after an early merchant-settler in the area. Eventually, the name morphed into one currently used The building in which the trade Fair was held amounted to a roof with three open sides. It was filled with portable booths, many of which were nicely decorated while others were quite plain. All were filled with things to be traded or sold. On the north end of the pavilion was a permanent wall behind a concession counter managed by two, chubby ladies of the Sawed-Off Corners Home and Garden Club.

Tallie oriented herself to the surroundings as she helped Aunt Jenny carry eggs, beans, squash, fresh onions, and tomatoes to her booth.

"What is in that tote bag?" Aunt Jenny asked as she nodded toward the bag Tallie was carrying.

Tallie swallowed. "Plums," she said,quietly.

"Plums. Is that a fact?"

"Yes, that is absolutely a fact. And they were on public property. Free to anyone, so I hope to sell them."

"That was a right smart idea!" Aunt Jenny said with a smile. Tallie felt a wave of relief and embraced a bit of confirmation due to her Aunt's approval.

"You need to set a price, Tally. Start high and come down as the day goes on and customers fall off. If you don't sell out, you can take them home and make jam to sell, or try to trade them for something."

"How much should I charge to start with?"

Aunt Jenny took Tallie's face between her hands and said, "If I weren't here, Missy, how would you figure that out? They are your plums. How would you decide?"

"See what others are charging for things like mine?"

"That's a start. Now what do you think?"

Tallie smiled. "I think I'd better take a look around."

Tallie found apples, obviously not local ones, at forty cents a pound, and strawberries at ninety cents a pint. She was amazed by the variety of things for sale. Pictures, jewelry, hand tooled saddles, homemade aprons and pot holders, little wooden boxes, crocheted collars, tatted pillow cases, and handmade quilts. Those were really expensive. One booth was full of local honey and sorghum syrup. There were booths with jams, breads, and pies by the slice or the whole. There were even farm tools and antiques for sale. Tallie paused at the honey which had something in it she had never actually seen before. Beeswax. While wondering why anyone would stick that stuff in the honey, someone yanked her ponytail. She turned and yelled 'Hey!'at two teenage boys who were sauntering on as if they hadn't done a thing.

One of the boys said, "You know what's under a ponytail, don't you?" Both boys laughed loudly.

"Jerks!" Tallie yelled. "Hick jerks!" She yelled again, but they kept on going and laughed all the harder.

Tallie turned sharply and headed back to her booth wishing she could have thought of something to say to those hateful hicks, something that would have knocked the grins off their silly faces. She retrieved her plums from under the counter and kicked the box back under the shelf.

"What's all that flouncing around about?" Aunt Jenny asked.

"One of your local hoodlums pulled my ponytail and made a stupid joke about it."

"I'm not too surprised. Pay no mind. What price are you putting on the plums?"

"A dollar a quart. I saw some on the other side for seventy-five cents."

"What makes you think you'll get a dollar for yours?"

"Advertising helps. But as dad says advertising costs, so I'm charging for that." Tallie folded a paper sack and made a sign.

CUTE PLUMS FRESH AS DEW

YOU SELECT. $1.00/qt.

Aunt Jenny looked at her sign. "I don't think I have ever seen a cute plum, but it's an idea."

Tallie put her hands on her hips in feigned defiance. "And I've never seen a square soap bubble either, but if I said I had one, people would probably come to see for themselves. So they can come look to see if my plums are cute. They are round and fat which makes them cute to me."

Aunt Jenny grinned and asked, "What are you going to put them in once someone buys them?"

"Golly! I don't know. What can I do?" Tallie wailed in a wee voice.

"You can find some used, plastic berry baskets in the back of the truck. They are in the storage unit with battery cables and such. They will be dusty, but you can tend to that. I used to sell blackberries in those but I don't anymore."

The crowd grew. Townspeople flowed in, chatting and milling around. One lady carrying a toy poodle bought two quarts of Tallie's plums. Another lady with nylons rolled down to her sneakers was taking forever to hand pick a quart for herself.

"I'd buy them cheaper plums at that other stall, but his'n is already boxed. Pro'lly has wormy or shriveldy ones on the bottom," said the lady in the sneakers.

Aunt Jenny's tomatoes sold like lightning. Tallie was impressed and also at how many people knew her aunt. Introductions were made and Tallie made an effort to remember their names. Her dad said it was important to call your customers by name. It worked! Her plums began to sell.

Out of the crowd a woman waved back and came her way. She did not appear to be one of the locals, and following right behind her was another lady. Tallie assumed they were together since the first lady said something over her shoulder to the second lady as they came toward her.

"Oh, Maudie, look. They really are cute plums. I haven't had sand plum jam in years. Let's get some and make jam."

Tallie looked the woman over carefully. "May I help you?" She said, trying her best to sound like a haughty adult.

"I would like some of your plums. Maudie will attend to it. We are on our way home from the Gulf," she said, and wound her fingers through the numerous gold chains around her neck, "taking our time when we happened to see this quaint little place, Sawed-Off Corners, and this quaint little market of yours."

"Where do you live?" Tallie asked.

"Denver, at least in the summer. In winter, we go to Fiji or some other warm place. Do you like living in this little village?"

"No, I don't. I didn't come here on purpose, I was abandoned here."

"Good heavens! Maudie, that's enough plums. We need to go," she said and handed Tallie five dollars for two quarts of plums.

Tallie watched the woman push her way through the crowd. "Snob", she mouthed to herself.

"What did you learn from that?" Aunt Jenny asked.

"She was dressed like a lady."

"But?"

"She was a stuck-up phony and wanted me to be impressed. She called us "quaint". What is that supposed to mean?"

"Countrified. Uninformed. Just exactly what she was at one time, most likely. Takes more than a dress to make a lady. Now, how many plums do you have left, Missy?"

"I've got about a pint and a........Hey! Someone has stolen my plums."

Tallie whirled around and saw one of the boys who pulled her ponytail scurrying through the pavilion. She ran after him. He stuck his hand in a sack and threw a plum at her and took off again.

"Somebody stop him'" She yelled. "He's got my plums!"

Several people noticed and were more amused than concerned. They merely smiled at the chase.

"Stop him!" She yelled again, but no one bothered until he ran into the parking lot. Finally, a man grabbed him.

"Better give her back her plums," he said quietly but firmly. "I don't think she takes to teasing much."

The boy grinned like it was all a big joke, shoved the plums into the man's hands, and took off again just before Tallie got close enough to swing at him.

"Thanks," she said to the man. He was wearing a badge of some sort and she was glad. Are you going to arrest him, I hope?"

"He was teasing you. Boys will do that."

"Well, I don't like it. Somebody should teach him some manners."

"I reckon someone should. Are you okay?" He smiled at her and handed her the plums.

"Yes, thank you. Do you give out tickets for offenses like his?"

"No, Miss, but if I did, I'd sure have a lot to do," the officer replied with laughter.

"Whatever, but you might think about it. The little hoodlum hick needs help. Someone should make him pay for this. Anyway, thanks again."

Back at the booth, Aunt Jenny explained that the man who returned the plums could have been one of the Trade Fair officials.

"They make sure everything runs smoothly and do the latching up when the trading is done." Then changing the subject, "So, Missy, I reckon I'm about sold out. How about you? Are you sold out?"

"All but this last pint of plums. I made eight dollars. More than I ever did baby sitting."

"You might think about trading the rest of those plums for

something. Go ahead on and look around while I tear down and pack my belongings."

Tallie was not sure what kind of exchange she could get for a pint of plums, surely not much, but decided to see what kind of deal she could make. Since many vendors were already gone for the day, she hurried over to look again at the beeswax honey when a stack of books caught her eye. One of the books had a big, ugly snake on the front. The vendor was an older man wearing a suit like a gas station attendant might wear and a soiled baseball cap advertising Casey's Custom Pellet Fertilizer on the front. He shifted a wad of tobacco in his jaw.

"Them plums and a dollar bill'll getcha that whole box of books. I'm tard a luggin''em around"

"Deal," Tallie said, already figuring that she could read what she pleased of the books, keep what she pleased, and sell some another day if she pleased. Proud of herself, she returned to help Aunt Jenny load up.

So many of the people milling around in the parking lot came over to greet her aunt, called her aunt by name, and called each other by name which suggested to Tallie that her aunt was not only popular, but she might also know the boys that pestered her today.

"I'll bet you know who those stupid boys were today."

"What's that?" Aunt Jenny asked while concentrating on pulling herself into the driver's seat of the truck.

"Those boys! Those jerks that pulled my hair."

"Oh. I don't know which one pulled your hair, but the one that ran off with your plums looked, for all the world, like Tom Sawyer."

"Tom Sawyer! Was his little friend, Huckleberry Finn?"

"I didn't notice who was with Tom," she said, digging into her purse for the keys.

"He was real tall and had red hair."

"Could have been Bandit."

"Those are some weird names. No wonder they're so dorky."

Aunt Jenny suggested they get a bite to eat at the Dairy King before they went to the grocery store. She wasn't about to tell Tallie that someone called "Noodle" and "Hub" Gant owned the Dairy

King. However, she did tell Tallie that they needed to get home and get prepared for Sunday.

"What do you mean?" Tallie asked. "What do you have to do to get ready for Sunday?"

"We'll be going to church, the Country Lane Community Church, and we always have dinner on the grounds after the services. We'll want to take something real nice. What can you cook?" she asked Tallie.

"Anything that goes in the microwave, and you don't have one."

"Heaven forbid! You're in for a cooking lesson when we get home. Why, I'd imagine you'd be cooking up most anything by now."

"Cooking is messy and boring, but not as boring as hoeing," she hastily added.

Aunt Jenny ordered the double burger specials, then asked, "Have you ever tried to create the most marvelous, mouth-watering dish anyone can imagine? From scratch? All by yourself? Something so good a-body would crawl across Texas to take a bite? "

"Nope. Never have."

"Is that a fact?"

"I wouldn't even know how to start if I had. Besides, how can you beat one of these burgers?" Tallie could barely talk through her stuffed cheeks. It was as if she couldn't eat it fast enough.

"Think about something you already like, something you're hungry for. Then add to it, subtract from it, stretch it, fill it, and so on until you get a fine idea. In Psalm 103, it says that He fills our mouths with good things. I notice and yours is certainly full. While there may be other interpretations put on that verse, I do believe it applies to my kitchen as well. So I expect you to come up with a fine idea by the time we get home. Look at that hamburger you are eating. Somebody had to invent it at one time or another. Think about it."

Tallie decided lots of ancient people had stuffed meat between pieces of bread. A hamburger wasn't anything completely new. Most fast cuisines she could recall had some kind of food wrapped in bread. Then she recalled something she had heard.

"Solomon said there is nothing new under the sun, so I can't invent any new dish."

"Then rediscover an old one. Put your own interpretation on it. It'll be new to you," Aunt Jenny said. She pulled a shopping list out of her purse and laid it on the seat. It wasn't a long list: Flour, sugar, cocoa, jar lids. No canned goods except for pineapple. No meat items except for wieners or tuna. Meats came with lease payments from farmers who used her property for grazing from time to time. A box of crackers, yes, but no bread. She made her own.

Up and down the aisles of the grocery store, Tallie pushed the cart and followed her aunt and thought of things she liked. Pizza, Chocolate pie, hotdogs with chili, macaroni and cheese, chicken-fried steak. Those things were seldom served at home in St. Louis anymore since her mom had decided they were going to eat lean and green and learn to love it. Neither did she have any experience fixing her list of her forbidden favorite foods. Seventh graders only learned pudding and scrambled eggs.

All the way home in the bouncing pickup, Tallie thought and thought along the lines of Aunt Jenny's suggestions of bending, stretching, adding, to come up with a new dish. She thought of flattening steaks, stacking them like waffles. Nah. Roll them? Hmmm. Maybe. Maybe roll something inside them? Peas? No, that would look like green slime gushing out when you cut it. Squash? Yuck! That would really look sick oozing out of a rolled up steak. Like a dirty diaper, she thought and laughed out loud.

"What is so funny?" Aunt Jenny asked.

"A squash rolled up in a steak."

"It's a thought, and that beats none a-tall."

"What do you think goes with steak?" Tallie asked.

"Gravy and potatoes are hard to beat."

"I want to roll something up inside a steak. Maybe a little potato."

"And let it swim in some delicious gravy. I like that idea," Aunt Jenny said. "I do believe you're onto something."

As soon as they unloaded the pickup, Tallie gathered some potatoes from the barn. Aunt Jenny was already making her own concoction, a favorite which her friends called "Fat Man's Misery." It consisted of alternate layers of creamy chocolate and fluffy vanilla pudding in a nut crust, covered with a thick topping of whipped cream sweetened with brown sugar.

Tallie peeled the potatoes, the biggest and the best she could find. Aunt Jenny told her if she selected the biggest and the best, the biggest and the best would always be left. At Aunt Jenny's suggestion, she split and parboiled them in salt water before rolling them up in the floured, and seasoned, steaks.

The meat rolls smelled good browning in the skillet. Aunt Jenny coached her through the gravy making, but when it was poured over the meat, Tallie frowned.

"What's the matter now?" Aunt Jenny asked.

"It smells good but it, well, it just looks all brown."

"Then give it some color. Get a carrot. Slice it right thin like. Run it around in some butter in that skillet until it is tender then scatter it over your dish. Then in the morning when we warm your dish, you can mince a few green onion tops for garnish. That ought to spark it up a bit."

Tallie was pleased with the finished product and placed it in the oven to bake.

"What are you going to call that concoction?" Aunt Jenny asked.

"I don't know. Chicken Fried Surprise? Mom sure wouldn't like that name. She never makes anything with the word 'surprise' in the title, nor would she ever order any dish from a menu that had that 'surprise' in its name."

By the time the kitchen was cleaned up, Tallie was tired of thinking about names. She got her box of books and sat on the porch with Aunt Jenny where it was cooler. The snake book was full of pictures, one uglier than next, but no picture exactly like the snake she saw in the garden. However, she had not memorized how it looked and hoped to never see it again.

Since inventory of their hardware store was one of the excuses her parents used to leave her at Aunt Jenny's, Tallie decided to take her own inventory of the rest of the contents of the box. Perhaps she could figure out how she might make a profit from her goods.

There was a copy of O'Henry's short stories, whoever he was; two McGuffey readers and a geology textbook. In one of the McGuffey readers was an old piece of paper with a sketch of a cowboy on a horse in the middle of a hard rain. She decided someone had been drawing when they were supposed to be reading their lesson. It made her smile. She would keep it.

"I forgot to spend any of my money today, except for this box of old books," Tallie said.

"You can spend some tomorrow when the offering plate comes around at church. You might ought to decide how much of your earnings you want to share with the Lord."

"How much do you give?" Tallie asked. "I've never had to decide before. Mom always gave me some change to drop in."

Aunt Jenny thumbed through the Bible and came to a stopping place. "Listen to this," She said.

And they brought the coin. And He saith unto them, Whose is this image and superscription? And they said unto Him, Caesar's. And Jesus answering said unto them, Render to Caesar the things that are Caesar's, and to God the things that are God's.

Aunt Jenny looked at Tallie and asked, "What do you make of that?"

"Caesar had his mug stuck on all the money?" Tallie inquired.

Aunt Jenny gave a positive nod and said, "But you need to think some more. An offering to God should not be a tip."

The end of the day left Tallie more ready for bed than she had ever been at home and it was only 9:30. She didn't care. She yawned, fluffed the pillow and stretched out on the bed. South breezes cooled the room. Another thing Aunt Jenny did not have was air conditioning– just corner windows on both sides of the room.

I have seven dollars left from my plums. That makes me plum rich, she thought. How's that for Okie talk? She laughed quietly. I can afford to give an offering since I'm so rich. If Jesus said to give Caesar the things that have Caesar's face on them, then what am I supposed to give? Maybe I should give some of the plums like the ancient Hebrews. They brought stuff from their fields. Those wild plums were nobody's except maybe God's. But I sold some, so I can and should give something.

Tallie was tired and her eyes closed. "What kind of offering does He want?" She slept and dreamed of the offering plate being passed.

"What are you giving, Aunt Jenny? What goes in the plate?" Her aunt took a leap into the plate which suddenly grew huge and spun wildly!

"Aunt Jenny! Why are you sitting in the offering plate?"

"Rendering, child! Rendering!" Aunt Jenny shouted 'woo hoo' as she and the plate disappeared into a cloud.

Chapter Three: Beer Bottle Eyes and Wiggly Seed

Old Jube hadn't even crowed yet when Tallie's eyes popped open. It was dark out, but there was a light on downstairs. She quietly slipped out of her room. There sat Aunt Jenny, her head bowed over the Bible, her lips moving like they often did during the day. Tallie realized that her aunt was praying and probably had been all those other times, too, not just talking to herself to keep her head straight. A squeaky stair caused Aunt Jenny to look up.

"Well, you beat Old Jube up this morning. I like to get my soul woke up good before he sets to hollering for the sun and his breakfast."

Tallie was not sure what she expected to find her aunt doing before daylight, but she had not expected to find her praying. She felt ashamed, like she had peeped through a keyhole or something.

Aunt Jenny put the Bible up and suggested they get on with their have-to chores. Some things have to be done, she explained, whether it was Sunday or not and sent Tallie out to gather the eggs and feed the chickens, and reminded her to pull a few green onions for her dish.

"I'll be out in a little bit to do the milking," she said, "then we'll eat and get ourselves together and get on over to the church."

The church was located two miles south and one mile west of Aunt Jenny's place. Tallie steeled herself for another boring church service and the dinner to follow with a bunch of strangers. Dinner on the grounds? She had never heard of such a thing.

When Tallie saw the church grounds, they were not like any familiar to her. The church, a white frame building, stood in a grove of black walnut trees. There was a graveled parking area on the side. Attached to the main part of the church was a rectangular structure like a large screened-in porch surrounded by a brick patio. On the patio stood large pots of bright pink petunias between several wrought-iron benches. Along the main church building were crepe myrtle trees and lilac bushes higher than her head.

"Jenny Raider," a woman called and headed in their direction as soon as they exited the pickup. "Where have you been?"

"That's Alice Fursby," Aunt Jenny quietly explained to Tallie, "and she knows everybody and all their business, and what she merely suspects, she adds to. So mind what you say."

"Well, Alice, we've been kindly busy," Aunt Jenny said, taking their covered dishes out of the truck. By the way, this is my niece, Tallie. And Tallie, this is Mrs. Floyd Fursby. Tallie is now twelve years old. John and Ellen's Koums' daughter."

"John, your nephew who has that big hardware store in Missouri.

"That's the one," Aunt Jenny replied.

"Hi there, Punkin. Will you be staying a while?"

"Yeah—ess," "Tallie said, catching her mistake just as Aunt Jenny's eyebrows flew up.

"Isn't she the cutest little thing?" Alice commented while turning toward Aunt Jenny. "Here, let me help you carry that stuff, Jenny. I just plain worry myself to death about your wrist."

"Well don't. Death can plainly wait. My wrist is fine. It's still attached and doing what it's supposed to be doing."

"You'd never let on if it was falling off twice a day. All you Raiders are like that. Tough as nails or pretending to be. Me, I don't pretend to be born to anything but shade and chiffon. I know I'm delicate," Alice said, then sniffed at the dish she was carrying. "What yummy thing am I smelling right through this t-towel?"

"That's something Tallie cooked up. Better ask her."

When Alice Fursby looked at her for an answer, Tallie stammered a moment and called it Polley Steak.

"Never heard of it," Alice said. "Must be something you all eat in Missouri."

Tallie decided to be honest. "No. It is something I made up yesterday with Aunt Jenny's help, so I don't know if anyone else in Missouri eats it or not."

"I knew you were smart. I could tell by looking in your eyes." Alice paused, squinted, stuck her chin out as she bent over and stared into Tallie's eyes. "Your eyes! They are the oddest color. The color of, of, beer bottles!"

"Bite your tongue, Alice Fursby," Aunt Jenny said. "This is Sunday. And whenever did you become so familiar with beer bottles?"

"One sees those bottles along the road from time to time, Jenny," but Aunt Jenny, not listening, opened the screen door to the dining hall and let it slam behind her. Tallie was surprised but followed her into a dining hall where women were arranging their items on a long table. Aunt Jenny suggested Tallie might like to go outside and get acquainted before church started.

Several boys and girls were milling around, but they were mostly younger. Cars were still arriving. She watched, hoping someone her age, someone she might like, would show up.

The crunching noise of gravel on the driveway which meandered through a large copse of trees from the main road to the church, announced the arrival of another vehicle. Tallie watched hopefully. The door opened. A family exited and Tallie froze in her tracks. Tom Sawyer. The dorky jerk that pulled her hair. If he saw her, she could not tell. He went immediately to the trunk of their car to help unload. Tallie positioned herself behind a tree and peeked around it enough to keep him in view.

"Oh, no! " she said under her breath. The man who got out of that same car was the one who had stopped Tom from running off with her plums. She heard Tom call him 'Dad'. She reddened recalling how she had referred to that man's son as a stupid jerk needing to be taught manners. Quickly, she dashed back to the dining hall to lose herself among the women there.

"Tallie, did you meet some of the folks? Aunt Jenny asked.

"Not yet."

"Come on, and I'll introduce you around to everyone."

"No, that's all right, I don't mind. Please don't."

"You're a funny one. I would think you'd be anxious to be with some of the kids your own age for a change."

Aunt Jenny scrutinized her knowing something was not exactly right, but left the matter alone for the time being and headed back to the kitchen to check the oven temperature quickly as the church bell rang.

Tallie felt 'saved by the bell' and stayed close to her aunt as they entered the sanctuary. There were no pew cushions on the homemade, slatted benches. The song books were the paper backed sort. There was a piano and Alice Fursby was playing it. It was the loudest, liveliest playing she had ever heard in church. The people's singing matched Alice's playing, decibel for decibel. The song was about sunshine and rain, and when it ended, it was time for prayer, and everyone remained standing.

The pray-er began by saying, "Oh, kind and loving Heavenly Father, we ask you to hear our prayers today."

"Oh, yes,1" Someone else said right out loud. Tallie jumped.

"Yes Lord, hear us," said another person.

Those spontaneous additions did not seem to bother the man who was praying at all, and as the man continued, several others jumped in to echo or add to what the man prayed. He continued to pray for what seemed quite a while to Tallie. She got tired of holding her neck down.

After the prayer, there was another loud song about bringing in the sheaves. Tallie was not really sure what a sheave was, but decided it had something to do with grain. When the song ended, several men got up to pass the offering plates.

Then a crazy thought: Would her aunt sit in it? She smothered an urge to giggle with a cough. Back to the rendering unto God. How much? Tallie was curious about how much money her aunt made at the Fair and how much she would render to the Lord. When the plate came, Tallie dropped in a dollar and passed the plate to her aunt who placed an envelope on top of her dollar. She would never know what her aunt gave due to the secrecy afforded by the envelope. However, she was relieved that nothing in her weird dream came to pass.

"Good Sunday morning to you!" Said the minister.

"And to you, Pastor," replied the congregation. Tallie jumped again, wishing she could get used to these people speaking aloud in church.

This minister, which everyone seems to refer to as Pastor, was not like the one at her church. He was not dressed in a robe. His gray hair was not plastered down enough to hold every hair in place. She could tell that he had tried hard to make it stay down, but it was wiry and curly and looked uncontrollable. Neither did she expect such a big voice from such a medium-sized man. His voice dominated the room, even above the noisy water cooler.

"I had a good message all ready to bring you this morning, but the Lord changed my mind yesterday. It came to me while I was plowing the peanuts. I could see my Mrs. in the garden picking beans. I planted the peanuts as you know, and she planted the beans, you see.

Over and over, I heard the Lord say, 'You reap what you sow.' In other words, what we fling out is going to come back. (He paused) Multiplied!"

He paused again and leaned on the lectern which looked like a wooden music stand made of a horizontal slab of stained wood, highly polished atop a creamy white, vertical post. Tallie couldn't see any sermon notes nor even a Bible on the lectern in danger of being pushed off as he leaned on it.

"Floyd", the minister called. "Did you ever plant a peanut and get a bean?"

"Naw sir. Never have," Floyd answered.

"Will, what did you plant in your south field?"

"Wheat," answered Will.

"Wheat, you say. What did you get?"

"A right fair stand of wheat."

"What if you had planted the sack that said 'wheat' on it? You wouldn't a-got wheat 'ner sacks, would you? The life, you see, is in the seed, not in the sack with the printed word on it for the whole world to see. Seed with the very life essence in it had to be planted and seed begets the plant it came from to commence with, don't you see? That little seed won't do much in the sack. It has to get out of there and into the ground."

The Minister's voice softened. He grinned a little. "Then it lays there awhile, kindly quiet-like, drinking some water from the soil, feeling kindly warm from the sun it can't even see yet, and then something happens. The minister raised his hands and did a little jig. "It swells up and wiggles around and puts out little roots!" he said as he shook his left leg then his right.

"The little thing has come alive! It's growing, The roots grab a-holt of the earth and the little seed wiggles around some more, and a little shoot starts poking its head up through all the soil into the air and the sunlight. Lookie there! A whole new world than dirt! That little shoot leans in the direction of the sun, the very thing that was warming it all along.

I was sitting on that tractor having myself a good time by then. I got thinking we are all like the soil. We are made of dust, so to speak, but here's the truth. The word of God is the seed. His seed gets His seed back in kind. Multiplied. His word gets planted in our soil and gets what He intended at harvest time—fruit and seed." The minister paused; thought a bit and pulled a small bible from his hip pocket and held it up.

"I reckon we could carry this seed sack around till kingdom come. But it is just a sack containing seed that won't grow until planted inside a soul. My soul, or your soul. If planted, we will get a terrific crop of everlasting life, purpose, and good, orderly direction. It's a matter of planting this seed. Then we'll grow and bend toward His light. He'll tell us when to gee or haw, and that sure takes the worry out of things for me. It's some deal, folks, and it's a daily deal, simply because He wants the pleasure of our company today as well as forevermore. If you want the pleasure of His company now and forever, you are welcome to come forward or stand up and tell us so at this time."

Tallie realized that she had heard every word of the sermon, a first for her, and she felt sorry that no one was going down or standing up to take advantage of the offer. The Minister made a final statement that he would be there all afternoon if anyone wanted to talk to him or had any questions. Then he prayed and dismissed the congregation. Some exited to the patio and others went on into the dining hall, but the minister stayed behind picking up and returning strewn song books to their racks.

Tallie looked at the minister. He looked concerned. With her mind still on the sermon, she turned and ran soundly into a tall man.

"Whoa!" said the man who was standing near her aunt.

"Sorry," Tallie said.

"Tallie, this man you just slap ran into is Sheriff Sawyer, and this young man right here is his son, Tom," Aunt Jenny explained.

Tom smiled, but to Tallie,it was a great big, cocky grin. Nevertheless, she managed to politely say hello. Tom just kept smiling.

Sheriff Sawyer finally prompted, "Thomas?" Then Tom said 'hi', but Tallie narrowed her eyes at him and did not respond. When she had given him a bit of a hard stare, she turned her eyes to her aunt.

"Tallie is spending some time with me this summer," Aunt Jenny said to the sheriff.

The sheriff looked at Tallie more closely. "I believe I saw you yesterday. Weren't you the one chasing Tom?"

"The only reason I was chasing him was because he had my plums," Tallie said, "and that is the only reason I was chasing him."

The sheriff smiled a little. "Well, we hope you come to enjoy it here, don't we, Tom?"

"Sure, Dad," Tom replied and put his hands in his hip pockets, but kept looking at Tallie until, thankfully, Aunt Jenny led her away to help in the dining hall.

Tallie had never seen such a variety of food except in a big cafeteria. The ladies were scooting things around trying to make room on the long buffet table for all the dishes they brought. Tallie uncovered the steak casserole and placed it among platters of fried chicken, meat loaf, pork chops, sliced ham, and barbecued beef. Aunt Jenny was slicing fresh tomatoes. Alice Fursby, lading ice into paper cups, enlisted Tallie to fill them with tea, lemonade, and water.

When all was ready, the Preacher said the blessing and all the men lined up to eat first.

Tallie was surprised and also starving. The women stood by and kept heaping the platters with reserves from the side tables and kitchen ovens. They laughed and chatted and acted like they did not mind waiting at all. So Tallie stayed at her place keeping the drink table supplied until she was joined by another girl who introduced herself as Mary John. Tallie explained she was visiting Aunt Jenny. They continued to chat as they worked the beverage table.

"Do the men always eat first?" Tallie asked.

"For all my sixteen years they have."

"Why?"

"Custom and to honor our men, I guess. And it's kind of nice to get them fed and out of the way so we can linger over our own plates. Besides, I think it's fun to see what the men choose to eat, don't you?"

"I never noticed. Is that really fun? Tallie asked.

"It is to me. I'm practicing my dishes on all these men. I like to cook and try out my recipes on them. I notice what the old ones like and especially the young ones, not that I plan on marrying any of them, but I do believe in being smart about what they like."

"So cooking is your fun thing," Tallie remarked.

"I like it lots better than ironing, don't you?"

"I haven't ever cooked much, but I like it lots better than hoeing for sure."

Mary John laughed and smiled knowingly. Tallie decided she liked this Mary John person, but the sight of Tom Sawyer coming toward the drink table immediately quashed the small amount of joy Tallie had experienced. She turned her back and pretended to be busy with the ice chests until he selected his own beverage and did not turn around again until she heard a man speak to her.

"You must be Jenny Raider's niece," said the minister, holding a plate of food. "She told me you were coming to visit. I'm John Hay, pastor of this outfit. Most folks just call me Pastor." He took a glass of ice tea.

"Hi. Nice to meet you, Pastor." Tallie replied thinking that he looked less sad now.

"Aunt Jenny said you made this steak roll. It looks real good."

"Thank you. I hope it is," Tallie answered.

"I'm not so sure about this pile of squash though" he said, directing his eyes to Mary John. "I'll eat all I can stand of it and then I'll rub the rest of it in your hair, Daughter."

Tallie looked at the squash swimming around in some sort of soupy looking goo and decided it probably would make a better shampoo than food.

"I'll bet Tallie likes it," Mary John told her dad. Pastor Hay laughed at her sassy pretence and walked off to find a place to sit. He was the last of the men in line, which was the signal for the women and children to fill their plates.

Mary John began to explain about her squash dish saying, "The county fair is in September, and I plan to enter a squash dish in the

Original Recipes division. You can taste some and tell me what you think."

"I haven't eaten much squash," Tallie said.

"Well, that's great! You won't be expecting anything special."

"For sure," Tallie half whispered. Resigning herself to tasting some of the stuff, she took a small portion and placed it where it would not touch anything else on her plate.

When they sat down, Mary John smiled great big and said, "Well? Try it."

Tallie took a small taste and swallowed it like an oyster.

"So?" Mary John waited.

"It is much better than plain stewed squash," Tallie said.

Mary John was elated. "I knew you would like it."

Tallie tried to smile. She put the rest of the squash in her mouth along with a bite of cornbread muffin and swallowed quickly. Mary John kept looking at her. Tallie, feeling bound to say something more added, "And it goes down well with this cornbread, too," she said, noting that Mary John had not taken any of the steak roll. Very little of it had been sampled. She was disappointed.

"Dad said you brought some kind of a steak roll. I didn't get any, but I think I will try some. "

"You don't have to. You might not like it. No one has taken very much of it," Tallie said, even though she had taken some of it herself and was pleased with the results.

"Don't look now, but I think that is what Tom and some of those guys are getting for seconds. Looks like the word has gotten around about what is good. "

"He would probably put on a gagging act if he knew I cooked it."

"I'm going to tell him you made that good stuff."

"No!" Tallie begged. "Please don't," she said and briefly explained what happened at the Trade Fair.

"All the more reason," Mary John said and proceeded to the buffet table.

In no time at all, Tom held on to his throat pretending to choke. Tallie turned her red face to the opposite wall and stayed turned until Mary John spoke to her.

"I fixed him. He was good and embarrassed."

"Him? I'm the embarrassed one.

"Tom has been lowered a notch just the same. You didn't see him spit it out, did you? He ate it, and what's more, he liked it. That is the best kind of pay-back," Mary John explained.

Although Tallie felt uncomfortable about the whole incident, she was, nevertheless, pleased that people were going back for more.

Pies, cakes, watermelons, and hand-cranked ice cream disappeared quickly from the dessert table. Aunt Jenny's famous dessert was completely cleaned out. Women circulated among the tables pouring more iced tea and coffee. People sat and visited for a while. Eventually, they began to leave the dining room. Some went outside to play horseshoes and others to play various instruments they had brought.

There were two guitars, one mandolin, one violin, a harmonica, and a tambourine. The players passed the instruments around in a sort of musical game of tag. So many seemed to be able to play, at least a little, on most of the instruments and some were quite talented.

Tallie was impressed by the sounds. She went out to observe and listen.

Those who weren't playing were singing, except for some small children running around the grounds in their own game of tag. She watched the children darting around, grabbing each other, and falling down all over each other giggling and squealing. Whap! Something hit her on the head.

"Ow!" she said and looked up. Tom Sawyer. He had tapped her with a tambourine and was grinning down at her. She had been tagged right in front of everybody and was expected to join in on the song in progress.

"Come on, Tallie! Give it a try," Aunt Jenny called. She pantomimed how to hit the instrument on the heel of her hand.

"I can't play this thing, " Tallie protested.

Mary John, standing next to Aunt Jenny yelled, "Sure you can. Just mark time."

Others began to urge her by saying things like Go for it! Come on! Have fun!

Tallie decided she would ruin their fun if she didn't make a try, and for a few measures, she was able to keep up a steady beat. Then she saw Tom bend over and laugh after saying something to one of his buddies and missed a beat. Her ears burned with embarrassment.

A lady playing the mandolin nodded the time to her, urging her back into the game. Tallie played a little more and tagged her Aunt Jenny.

Aunt Jenny stretched her neck up, tilted her head and tapped and rattled the tambourine producing sheng-click-a-shengs with syncopated rhythms rising right out of the soul. The people all clapped when she banged the thing on her elbow and then her hip and heel. They whooped and cheered her skills.

"Aunt Jenny can sure rattle that thing. She's been playing it for years, but You did all right," Mary John said to Tallie. "Those boys don't mean any harm. You're new here and that makes it fun for them to have a new somebody to tease. Just laugh at them and hold your head up. Don't take it so seriously."

"Thanks," Tallie said.

"Sure. You're alright," Mary John continued. "I know what it's like to feel out of place. Someone is always making a big deal out of me being a preacher's kid; but you didn't, and you are the first one that hasn't. You never even mentioned it."

Mary John and Tallie sat side by side in the shade and listened to the music until people began to pick up their belongings and little ones napping on blankets. After hugs and handshakes, they began to leave.

Pastor Hay patted Tallie on the back. "That was good steak, young'un. Glad to have you visiting us," he said.

Tallie thanked him and thought of that again when she lay in bed that evening. The pastor said he was glad she was there and maybe he was. He might have just been doing his job. Maybe not. He seemed to mean it. But all that playing! Everyone playing all those instruments expected me to be able to play, too, like it was normal or something. I wish I could play something, especially that tambourine. I wish I could have played it so good that Tom Sawyer would have fallen backwards from surprise. But he didn't.

That's the big gap. It didn't happen. The big gap between what I can do and what I'd like to do is more like a canyon. I don't have any talents or skills. I don't know one thing I can do well enough to be asked to do it. The closest I have come to doing something good is that steak dish. Even the Preacher said it was good. As Aunt Jenny would say, "At least it was something." No one fell over backwards with awe, but they didn't spit it out either.

With that, she relaxed and her eyes began to droop. The next thing she saw was a sack wiggling to music. Seeds began to march out of the sack and she tried to catch up with them, but her legs bogged down in cold, heavy mud.

"Wait! Wait! Don't leave me! Let me go with you," she called.

"You cannot play a song you do not know," the seeds sang in mocking harmony. Suddenly a bright light flashed in the distance. The seeds ran toward the light. The light flashed a code warning them to run hard before the light went out. She cried for them to wait but they disappeared into the light which also disappeared. She was left floating in blackness.

"Help!" Tallie yelled, but no sound would come out. "Help me, somebody. Somebody please help me!"

Chapter Four: Old Okies Learnt to Pray--is how they got to be old.

Tallie gasped and sat straight up in bed pulling a wad of choking covers away from her neck. It took a moment to remember where she was.

Horrible dream! she thought to herself, glad to be awake. She shivered from the effect and breathed deeply. It was only dawn and already the air was thick with humidity and heat. She dressed in her coolest sun dress and went down to breakfast.

Aunt Jenny mopped perspiration from her nose and eyes before she passed a hot cake to Tallie.

"It's going to be a scorcher today. It's a wonder Old Janet didn't give cottage cheese this morning." Then she asked Tallie to say the blessing.

"Me?"

"Yes, you."

"Aw—"

"Do it."

Tallie paused and began.

"Jesus, bless these hot cakes and send some cool air today. Amen."

"That was a prayer?" Aunt Jenny asked. "Sounded more like orders to me. There is such a thing as spiritual manners. You don't butt into the throne room and slap down your do-it list. You enter His courts with praise and thanksgiving."

"That sounds like a snow job to me."

"It certainly is not a snow job provided you're honest. You can't butter up God like you're buttering up that pancake."

"I was honest. I didn't say anything I didn't mean. Some cooler air is definitely needed in this place." Tallie's elbows were on the table. Her fork swang and dangled high in the air while she chewed and talked.

"You entered His throne room with about as much decorum as you're displaying at this table. Put those elbows down and listen to me. God inhabits praise. That means He lives in it. You enter His courts with praise and thanksgiving. Praise is God's doorbell. If you can't ring His doorbell, you have to stand outside hollering and wondering if you're being heard. As For thanksgiving– that amounts to giving Him credit for being your source of life and the supply it takes to live it! It amounts to knowing something about His track record."

"Okay. Okay. I'm sorry." Tallie wondered what was eating her aunt, the heat?

"You need to tell God you are sorry, not me. "

"If I did, do you think God would send us an air conditioner today?"

"He heeds an honest cry, but not a disrespectful one. Hot or not, we have plenty to do today. First, these dishes, then pump the horse tank full. It's low and there isn't enough wind to drive the windmill. The fence must be down somewhere, too. I had to hunt up Old Janet before I could milk her. So, I think we had better take the pickup truck and hunt where the fence is down and fix it. You might as well draw up some bath water, too. Do that first while I get this house swept up. This afternoon, we'll both hoe the corn and pick the green beans and squash."

"Good night!" Tallie declared.

"It will be by the time we're finished."

Not a breeze stirred. Tallie carried a bucket of water in each hand. Her arms quivered and the bails cut into her palms. She slung her hair to ward off a cloud of the gnats. After three trips to the well, the tub was full enough for a bath. Two more trips filled the needs for the kitchen. Next, she pumped the horse tank full counting the strokes. At fifty-two, her shoulder blades felt like they were tied together with barbed wire.

Tallie concluded, as she pumped, that her aunt could not possibly think of something wonderful about pumping and carrying all this water. It's boring, she thought, it's painful, and it's absolutely stupid to have to pump water in the twentieth century. Nothing is fun nor wonderful about this. Nothing could make this job pleasant—unless—she paused and thought, unless this handle was Tom Sawyer's neck. She giggled a little. Then she laughed aloud and stuck her head into the water tank up to her shoulders just for the pure love of cooling off. She tossed her head and her, long, wet hair landed heavily against her neck and back. Cool droplets of water felt good running down her skin. She sat on the edge of the horse tank dangling her legs in the tank water. The locusts in the trees were loud as buzz saws. Grasshoppers chewing on weeds stared at her from fixed eyes.

"Too bad we can't eat weeds like you guys instead of pulling and hoeing them. Wouldn't it be wonderful if I could sic you guys onto the garden weeds. You're eating in the wrong patch, dummies," she said and returned to the house.

Aunt Jenny was at the back of the house loading fence posts into the pickup, "Get your shoes on and get some gloves from the back porch," she called. "You'll need them if we have to fix fence. We'll have to stretch this barbed wire and maybe dig a few holes for these post."

'These post.' What kind of talk is that? Tallie wondered as she went to get gloves and shoes on. Okie farm talk, she guessed. When Tallie came back all suited up for the fence fixing, Aunt Jenny asked Tallie to do the driving while she did the navigating.

"Me? Drive? I don't have a driver's license. I've never driven anything but my bicycle, except once when Dad let me ease the car up the driveway closer to the garage door."

"You don't need a license to drive in my pasture. Here, I'll show you how the gears work."

Tallie learned the position of the gears including one called "low-low" or "grandma" for getting out of mud and climbing steep places. The hard part was coordinating the clutch and the accelerator. She moved the seat up as close as she could but still had to stretch to reach the pedals. On the first several tries, the truck lurched and died.

"You drive about like you pray," Aunt Jenny said, pushing her bonnet back off her nose. "Try again and let off the clutch slowly as you gently push on the gas pedal." She used her hands to illustrate the actions.

After one more small lurch, the truck growled, slipped into low gear, and began bouncing over rough places causing Tallie to briefly lose touch with the pedals. She stretched her neck way up high to see over the steering wheel, and stretched her legs as hard as she could to keep her feet on the pedals while guiding the machine around stumps and bushes.

"Be watching for a rock outcropping the other side of that grove," Aunt Jenny instructed.

Tallie veered carefully around it enjoying the whole new experience of driving a stick-shift pickup truck. Aunt Jenny was craning her neck, as well, watching the fence for a breach, and when she saw it, she hollered, "There it is!"

"There's where Old Janet got out. See it? Park under that shade tree and we'll get to fixing the fence."

The old fence post was broken and the wires were tangled. Her aunt took wire cutters to free the broken post, and gave Tallie the job of using the post hole diggers which looked like a giant pair of salad tongs. The whole idea, she learned, was to slam them into the hard dirt, spread the handles and tweeze out enough dirt to make a hole for the new post. Tallie jammed the diggers into the ground over and over. The muscles between her shoulders stung, but she kept at it.

When Aunt Jenny determined the hole was deep enough, they planted a new post. Tallie pulled the wire and held it in place while Aunt Jenny hammered the u-shaped 'steeples' securely over the wire. The so-called steeples were actually staples. Tallie knew that because her dad sold them. It also pleased her that she knew a little something about this fence-fixing business.

When the dirt was packed and the wire attached to the post, Aunt Jenny wiggled it to make sure it was properly installed. Satisfied, she nodded her approval.

"What is next?" Tallie wanted to know.'

"Let's go ahead and look at the rest of the fence while we're this far."

"Do you want to drive?" Tallie asked, trying not to look too excited about getting to drive again.

"No, you go a-head on. You need practice." Aunt Jenny rubbed the right lower part of her back and loaded the tools in the back of the truck. "Old Janet may have more than one back door."

Tallie eased the truck along wondering why her aunt let her do the driving. She could watch for the downed fence as well as her aunt who was fanning herself with her bonnet, which was not anything new, but she was frowning and working her lips around like she had tasted something sour.

"Whew! It is hotter than a two-dollar pistol at a rat shoot," Aunt Jenny said, fanning harder than ever. Tallie looked down to see if the heater might be on.

"Watch out for the ditch," Aunt Jenny said. Tallie slammed on the brakes so hard her aunt fell against the dashboard.

"I don't see a ditch!" Tallie exclaimed, trembling, nearly yelling.

"You can't daydream and drive at the same time, Missy. The ditch is up a-ways. I didn't mean it was right here."

"You yelled 'ditch' so I stopped."

"I see you did. Now go on up this way, easy like, and take to the right so's you can cross that ditch. It's just a washed out place, but you have to pay attention. There's a pond just beyond that. We'll stop there. I want to tend to it while I'm out here."

"Pond? I didn't know you had a pond."

"There's a heap you don't know."

Tallie negotiated the ditch very slowly and brought the truck to rest under a tree near a fairly large pond. Aunt Jenny remarked about the water being down; got a bucket of fertilizer pellets from the back of the truck and began to broadcast them into the water.

"Why are you doing that?" Tallie asked.

"It keeps algae growing for the little fishes and such to eat, and the shade from the algae stops the plants growing on the bottom from taking over. The pond stays cleaner and healthier that-a-way."

Tallie threw a handful of pellets. Some bugs on top of the water scurried away.

"What are these bugs on top of the water?"

"Those are skaters. Some even call them Jesus bugs."

"There sure are a lot of them. Why don't they sink?"

"There's a film on the water and they skate on it. They don't come no more near to sinking than we do on dirt."

"Wish we could go swimming. It sure would cool us off. I'll bet all my friends are at the country club pool right now."

"Look over there." Aunt Jenny threw a shower of pellets in the water. Several snakes swam away to the far side. "Those are water snakes, fairly harmless, but occasionally there will be a water moccasin. Those, you have to be careful of. They are quite poisonous. Do you still want to go in?

"Heck no! There's snakes all over this place. How do you stand snakes all over the place?

"I simply watch where I'm stepping," she said, smiling briefly, recollecting Tallie's dance out of the garden. Then she wet her handkerchief in the pond water, dabbed her face with it and hung it around her neck before ambling slowly back to the pickup.

Tallie drove carefully down the rest of the fence line on the way home and parked under the shade of a large pecan tree growing between the house and barn. The sound of the truck doors slamming caused Old Jube to fly upon the fence and flap his wings over his hen harem, all of which were breathing with their mouths open watching Tallie and Aunt Jenny unload the spare posts and the tools.

"Put some fresh water out for those chickens and I'll see what I can do about some lunch. When you come to the house, remove a couple of buckets full of water out of the bathtub, and pour the rest on the lilac bush. You can drag the tub to the back porch and store it inside.

"Pour it out? What do you mean, pour it out? I just drew it this morning." Tallie exclaimed.

"Just do as I say. I have a notion we'd better pan bathe tonight. Whatever you do," Aunt Jenny pointed her finger right at Tallie, "get that tub in the house."

Tallie wondered if her aunt was making up work to do like in the army, dig a ditch and fill it up. She saw that in a movie once. Tallie bailed a bucket of water from the horse tank for the chickens.

Jube flapped his wings and flew in her direction. Tallie grabbed a big cow chip.

"If you come any nearer, you old snot wad, I'll hit you right in the head with this."

Jube pranced around with his head cocked to one side. Tallie eased past him, half dropping and half throwing the chip as close to him as she dared on the way to the trough. Jube stood his distance while she poured water out for him and his flock. As an afterthought, she went into the barn, got a handful of grain and tossed it in Jube's direction. He waited until she was nearly to the house before he ate any which made Tallie chuckle to herself.

"You're a problem. You should have been named Tom. You old trouble maker. Oh yes", she said, reminding herself she turned to her next chore, the tub business."

Tallie emptied the tub and pulled it around to the back but when she tried to open the screen, it was stuck. Several times she tugged with no luck. Nothing to do but to go around and try to unstick if from the inside. She dropped the tub and kicked a stray weed. It was so hot she thought she could smell the dirt cooking.

Waves of heat were curling distant images. Nothing was stirring. Even the birds were holed up in the shade somewhere. A horn honked from the road as she rounded the front of the house, startling her. The mail carrier. He waved and put something in the box. Rolls of red dust powdered the banks of the road as he drove away.

Tallie went to the mailbox walking carefully in the hot sand so it would not get in her shoes. She found a summer catalog, a newspaper and, oh, wonderful day! A letter from her best friend, Amy. She opened it and began to read on her way back to the house. Engrossed in the letter, Tallie opened the screen door and let it slam. Aunt Jenny frowned.

"Go out and come in again without slamming the door, please, letting doors slam is rude and smacks of a lack of grace," said her aunt.

"Thttt," Tallie quietly noiseed through her teeth, but did as told.

Aunt Jenny breathed deeply, continuing to stir the contents in the mixing bowl before her.

Why am I so short with that child today? she wondered. Am I disappointed that she hasn't said one thing about the Sunday activities.,"

The door closed quietly, Tallie sat down at the table, picked up one of the egg salad sandwiches and began to munch as she read.

"Tallie Kooms!' Lay that letter down and wait for me to be seated before you take to your plate like a hog to slops. Lands! We haven't even asked the blessing yet."

"Well excu-oose me" Tallie threw the letter across the table. "I'm sick and tired of all that phony bull."

Aunt Jenny felt the bile rise in her again, but settled herself and tried to speak softly. Her eyes were squinted down hard on Tallie when she said, "It may take real effort, conscious effort for you to be mannerly and caring. But as long as you are here, you do it. Now, you sit down and say grace, and I don't give a rip how phony it feels to you, Missy. You understand?"

Those muted words were fired like bullets from a silencer, and Tallie wilted under the effect.

"Lord, Aunt Jenny has me doing this grace bit again. Ple-e-ease bless this food and send us a cool breeze. Thank you."

Aunt Jenny reached into a cabinet and withdrew an old, black, oscillating, electric fan. "Maybe this will help a little."

Gently, the curtains at the south window of the kitchen fluttered. Aunt Jenny looked up when the cool air from the window mixed with the air from the fan. Aunt Jenny raised her eyebrows and whispered to herself--it's here.

"Look out there," she said to Tallie and pointed to a cloud bank building up in the south. "The lord may be answering your prayer right quick like."

"Those clouds were going to form anyway," Tallie said.

"How do you reckon that?"

Tallie sighed and rolled her eyes. "When conditions are right, clouds form."

"Then how come the conditions got right?"

Tallie didn't know. She didn't want to think about it either. Another gust of wind blew through the kitchen window. Aunt Jenny got up and lowered it some.

"Looks like we might get some rain, maybe even hail. Why don't you put the truck in the barn just in case."

Tallie swallowed the last of her tea, keeping a chunk of ice in her mouth. She took the keys from a hook by the door and went out being more careful not to let the door slam this time. The clouds were rolling over themselves, she noticed, punching themselves up higher and higher.

Aunt Jenny joined her on the porch. For a few moments, they watched in silence. Then the breeze stopped. The air was dead still. The whole place, sky and dirt and all between it had a greenish cast and a heavy silence. No insect noises. No birds in sight.

"Hurry," Aunt Jenny urged. "I don't like the looks nor the feel of this."

Tallie ran to the truck. Dark clouds piled over her head. She opened the door and put the key in the ignition, pumped the accelerator and turned the key. The motor gave a little growl. Again and again she tried. The growl of the motor got weaker and weaker.

"Start! Dang it!," she said, then she noticed the strong smell of gasoline. "Come on," she demanded and jammed the accelerator to the floor, turning the key at the same time. There was a sputter and a jerk followed by a cloud of black smoke, but the engine started. Tallie gunned it a few times to make sure it would stay started. Gritting her teeth, she let the clutch out slowly and edged the truck into the barn.

A blast of cold wind swished across her hot face. She shivered, closed the barn door, and ran toward the house. Mean looking clouds were heaving upwards and outwards causing hot and cold currents to whip around in all directions at once. It was eerie. She lunged for the screen door and ran in, caring little whether it slammed or not. Aunt Jenny was closing the windows and did not seem to care about the screen door, either.

"Is there a tornado coming?" Tallie asked.

"It's real possible."

"Have you ever seen one?"

"Yes. Several. And I don't care to see another one."

"Is this what it's like before one hits?"

"Sometimes. Could be we'll get no more than a hard rain, maybe some hail, maybe nothing but wind. Sudden storms are hard to predict. We'll simply have to wait and see."

"What if a tornado hits us? Aren't we supposed to go into a closet or something?" Tallie asked.

"We'll get in the pantry if it looks too bad. It's built stouter and leads to a little root cellar I don't use much. We can get down in it if we have to. Underground is best."

Bah-boom!! Tallie jumped wide-eyed and searched her aunt's serious countenance for some comfort or guidance.

"All I wanted was some cooler air—not a storm," Tallie pitifully squeaked out her confession.

"That may be, but it's announcing itself all the same," her aunt said calmly.

The wind picked up and, what once was a flirting blast of wind, became a continuous gale. Both of them stood at the screen door and watched the trees twist and bow before the wild winds. The zinnias were almost horizontal to the ground from the outflow of a downburst of wind. A stray paper sack from some unknown source, spiraled and jerked upwards into the sky before it dived to the earth again. Thunder rumbled constantly and occasionally boomed.

"There it is!" Aunt Jenny hollered. "Tornado! Not on the ground yet. Get in the pantry. Quick!" she said, shoving Tallie in that direction.

Tallie never obeyed anyone so fast in all her life, not lingering one second to see the thing. The sound of the wind changed to an ominous roar. Aunt Jenny drew the pantry door shut behind them. Both were startled upon hearing a wham-clunk followed by a scraping sound from the back side of the house.

"Oh,oh! What in the world was that?" Aunt Jenny asked.

"Maybe it was the roof. Maybe we should go on down into that root cellar!" Tallie said urgently.

Aunt Jenny agreed. She opened the floor lid to the cellar and ducked inside catching a mass of cobwebs in the face. She shuddered and wiped them away. Tallie saw the dark hole and was fearful of following, but pushed her fear aside and in she went.

"I didn't think to bring a flashlight," Aunt Jenny said. "Let's sit here on the steps and not go down there where we can't see. I think the worst has passed. But you never know until you take a look."

Tallie sat on a step and held on to her aunt's waist while trembling and listening to the sound of the storm's roar. Aunt Jenny held on to her niece as the house groaned and seemed to swell and sag simultaneously. More volleys of thunder caused them to jump again and again.

"My ears popped," Tallie said, clutching her aunt harder. Is this place going to crash down on top of us or blow the house away?"

"No. Even if it did, we'd be all right down here. Tornadoes are like big vacuum cleaners causing a change in the air pressure. That's why your ears popped," she answered and ever so slightly patted Tallie's shoulders until the sound of wind was followed by a loud attack of hail.

"NOOOOO!" Aunt Jenny yelled. She leaped out of the root cellar and ran to the back porch with more surprising agility than Tallie could have expected.

"Oh, Lord! NO! Not my tomatoes!" she cried through the screen door.

But the hail came down like machine gun fire and was followed by a torrential downpour of rain so hard it dug gullies in the well-tilled soil. Aunt Jenny stood like a stele staring at a garden she could barely see for the heavy rain and the tears in her eyes.

Rivulets rushed across the yard and detoured around the house. A tin can caught in the path of the current was rapidly filling up with mud. Branches were scattered about. Then almost as quickly as the storm arrived, it departed. Water dripped like ticking clocks from the roof.

Aunt Jenny sighed and walked to the front porch. The flowers were stripped of leaves and broken down. Petals, like confetti, covered the ground.

"As for man," she whispered, "His days are as grass; as a flower of the field, so he flourisheth. For the wind passeth over it and it is gone,' and the place thereof shall know it no more."

Tallie had other thoughts, and spoke them aloud. "Fat lot of good it did to pull all those weeds out of that garden and carry water to that flower bed. Everything is shredded. Absolutely shredded."

"No, not all for nothing, but it saddens me. Truly does."

"That is what I'm saying, a fat lot of good. Now you got nothing!" I've lost gardens before."

Tallie shook her head knowing her aunt would find some excuse to go on weeding a wrecked garden. Things did look pretty sad, she decided and asked, "Will you have to buy vegetables now that the garden is shot?"

"We'll look at it closer in the morning when it isn't so muddy and see if anything is left."

"What if nothing is there? What will you take to the Trade Fair next Saturday?"

"I don't know yet. Maybe nothing, but God provides."

"Why didn't God keep the hail off your garden? You asked Him. I heard you ask Him."

"Maybe He is coming back before Saturday and I won't need anything to trade. Who knows what He is up to? Either way, that's His business."

The phone rang. It was Pastor Hay checking to see if they were safe and how much damage was done. Tallie gave the receiver to her aunt and went upstairs thinking a bath would feel so good. Then she recalled the bathtub. She peeked out the window where she had left it. It was gone. Maybe she could find it tomorrow before her aunt missed it. The storm ruining everything was like getting a zero on all that hard work she had done. It was sad working so hard for nothing, and sad looking at the destruction.

Everything looked so vandalized. The loss of the garden meant Aunt Jenny would have no income for her little extra needs. The bathtub was gone. Everybody needs a bathtub.

Tallie felt guilty again for praying for cool air. Shoot! She hadn't even felt like she was really praying. She merely said a few words and didn't even really think about God hearing what she said, and if He did, she only wanted some cooler air--not a storm. The loss of the tub, though, was her own fault. She could not shake the guilt of that and dreaded when her aunt would find out.

She could hear her aunt talking to Pastor Hay about his fields. Pastor Hay's wheat fields! He did all that preaching about all the farmers raising all that stuff. What if all of them were wiped out by the hail? Tears came to her eyes, but she refused to let them spill.

People may not eat all winter just because of my stupid half-prayer for cool air.

"I can't even pray right. I can't do anything right," she said to herself. Her throat tightened and the tears spilled over in stinging gushes.

She wanted to do something to make things better, but what? She certainly could not replant all the wheat fields. Her few dollars from selling plums certainly wouldn't be any help, but she could offer them to her aunt. She could buy a few groceries– maybe. And maybe she could sell the books she had traded for too, that is, unless nobody else had wanted them in the first place.

I'm so tired of being wrong. She silently wailed in misery due to perceived shortcomings. I'm so sick and tired of being so dad blasted wrong all the time. God! She silently screamed. Help me do something right, and I mean it this time. I really, really do."

Having poured out her soul as earnestly as she ever had in her life, Tallie went downstairs to face her aunt and tell her about the tub, but her aunt looked so sad and tired, she could not bring herself to add to the misery. When it came time to get ready for bed, she dreaded her aunt going to the back porch to wash her feet in a nonexistent bathtub. Great was her relief when Aunt Jenny went to the washstand in the kitchen and simply mopped her face and feet for bed.

Tallie called good night and climbed the stairs to bed. First thing tomorrow, as soon as she could slip away from the house, Tallie resolved to search for the tub.

She stretched out on the bed and wondered what lessons her aunt might be learning from the storm. What lessons could anyone learn from a stupid, destructive storm? Don't farm? Raise cattle instead? At least, cows can head for shelter when it gets bad. She had never heard of hail killing cows, but she guessed it could if big enough. Even dumb, fence-jumping Janet was under the eaves of the barn when I drove the truck in, she recalled.

As for any good coming from a storm, what could it be? Water? Cooler air?" She felt a wave of guilt again. Maybe Janet isn't so dumb. Cows eat weeds instead of pulling them. She yawned. Cows turn weeds into milk. That's pretty smart, she thought and began to doze and dream.

Janet was standing in the corner of a boxing ring. Old Jube had on a bow tie. He jumped the ropes into the boxing ring and pulled down a microphone. "And in this corner is Old Janet! The winner!" he crowed. "And in the opposing corner is the loser, Tallie. Boo! Boo! Tallie is the loser.

Tallie! Tallie!"

Tallie awoke with a jerk and sat straight up in bed. It was pitch dark.

"Tallie! Tal- EEEEEE!" her aunt called.

Chapter Five: Mud and Guts and Ruts

"What! What?" Tallie yelled. Not waiting for the answer as she took the stairs two at a time to get to her aunt.

"Child. I'm sick. I am so sick" Aunt Jenny said, "Pull That chamber pot out from under the bed." She asked, as she sat on the edge of the bed and worked her lips like she had earlier that day. "And get a paper sack. Hurry!"

Tallie got a sack from the back porch and returned to see her aunt sweating and pale.

"Help me up," Aunt Jenny groaned. "I've got to get on that chamber pot."

"Uh-ulk!" A dry heave. Tallie put the sack between her aunt's knees.

"What is the matter? Do you have diarrhea? A stomach ache or what?"

"It's my stomach and when I toss my cookies, I sometimes dampen myself."

"You mean you do this often? Get sick to your stomach?"

"I've had a bout or two, lately. Usually it passes fairly quickly but for some reason, it's hanging on tonight."

"What causes it?"

"I don't know. Maybe that egg salad was too ripe."

"I ate egg salad and I'm not sick."

"Ulp, ulp, OH. Uuh, uuh, arrrgh!" Up came more of the greenish, stringy goo.

Tallie ran for another sack and a wet washcloth and asked, "Are you hurting, or are you just nauseous?"

"At my age, everything hurts. You get to where you pay no attention to it." Aunt Jenny wiped her face and tried to smile, but it was a lame effort. Waves of nausea overtook her and the resulting volume was increasing.

"I'm going to call your doctor and ask him what to do," Tallie said.

"No, no. This'll pass. Besides, he'll be asleep."

"I don't care if he is asleep."

Aunt Jenny grabbed the sack and began to heave again.

"See? It isn't passing. I'm going to call a doctor. Maybe he'll tell me to give you some Alka Seltzer or something," Tallie said, already looking through the phone directory. She found only one doctor listed. Aunt Jenny was too busy throwing up again to protest the call.

"Dr. Gilbert? This is Tallie Kooms." A pause was followed by a louder repeat of her name, "Tallie Kooms! I'm Jenny Raider's niece. Aunt Jenny is sick. She is vomiting a lot."...."No, it's runny, ... Just a sec, I'll ask her."

"Aunt Jenny, he wants to know where you hurt?"

"Stomach and right up under my shoulder blade."

Tallie reported the answer, listened, then said, "We had egg salad, but I'm not sick. Can't I give her some Alka Seltzer?" She listened and then said, "Now? Me? It's 4:45 in the morning. Why can't you come out here? (pause) Oh! Oh! All right. We're coming."

Tallie explained that there could be a real problem and the doctor wanted them to get to the hospital right away.

"I don't know whether I can drive or not," Aunt Jenny replied.

"I'll call Pastor Hay." Tallie said.

"No, you won't; 'twould do no good. He said that the bridge is out over to his place. Go pull the truck around, and I'll see what I can do."

Tallie quickly put on some clothes and ran in the dark to the barn. An unseen washout in the dirt caused her to misstep and fall. Her knee was bleeding and stinging, but she hurried on and pulled the barn door open wide. The chickens in the coop-next to the barn squawked. Something flew out of the loft, swooshing close to her head.

"Get!" she hollered at it, and got into the truck. "I've got no time to be polite, God. Make this thing start. Please, God," she said, turning the ignition.

Errr, errr, orrr," the motor growled.

"What's the deal here?" She stomped the accelerator again while turning the key.

Errr-rrr-orrr.

"Okay! Okay! Thanks to You for seeds, sheaves, and thinking lessons. Praise, praise, praise, and thank You by the millions. I need help here and it isn't for me—it's for her! Won't you do it for her? Please!"

Tallie pleaded from some new place out of her soul, and tried the ignition again. The engine caught. She raced the motor to be sure it would keep running.

Gooden-gooden, the motor sounded smoothly when the accelerator was pressed.

"Thanks. For sure. I mean it," she said.

Tallie parked the truck as close to the porch as she could and hurried to get her aunt. The doctor said her aunt's symptoms could be the result of any number of things: ulcer, appendicitis, heart attack, gallbladder trouble, twisted bowel, or just severe gas; but it was imperative that he examine her right away. He made it very clear that he did not diagnose over the telephone, nor did he intend to make a trip in the middle of the night to a farm five miles away from emergency hospital equipment and laboratory services. If her aunt had allowed her to call, it must be serious and a one-way trip was the fastest way to get her attended to and attended to properly.

Tallie realized he made sense, but she did not like his bossy tone.

Aunt Jenny was at the wash basin trying to bathe again and putting on talcum powder. She asked Tallie to get her nice, blue print dress out of the closet.

"No! You don't have time for all of that. The doctor said to hurry. Here are your house shoes. Stick your arm in this robe and let's go."

"I don't know when I've gone a night without a bath and sure as I do, something like this happens," Aunt Jenny mumbled, "and this is the sorriest gown I own." She fretted and every move she made was an effort. "Get my purse out of the closet. My Medicare card is in it."

Tallie got the purse and some extra paper sacks, too, just in case. Aunt Jenny, pale as paste, leaned on Tallie's shoulder all the way to the truck. Tallie boosted her up under the steering wheel with great effort.

"I can't drive. I just can't!" she said laying her head down on the steering wheel. "Oh, Lord, I'm going to throw up, she said and began to cry.

Tallie ached at the crying and shoved a sack under her face as she threw up again. The smell made Tallie gag.

"Help me back into the house, I can't drive. I'll wreck us for sure. I'd rather die here than in a ditch."

"No. Scoot over and lay down. I'll drive," Tallie ordered, thinking of the causes: Ruptured appendix, Twisted bowel, Heart attack!

Aunt Jenny moved over and lay in the seat, too weak and too sick to care.

Tallie held her lower lip in her teeth anxiously starting the engine. It kicked right off to her relief, but then there were new problems. The road was a total layer of mud crisscrossed by washouts. The going was slow. When she thought she could speed up, the back end of the truck fishtailed causing her aunt to have dry heaves. Aunt Jenny let small groans escape every time Tallie hit a rough, washed area. A smooth spot was up ahead. She was glad and thought she would try to go a little faster. The truck slid sideways causing the rear wheels to end up in the bar ditch. Stricken with fear, Tallie gunned the motor unwittingly digging into the muck deeper and deeper.

"Shift," Aunt Jenny said weakly.

"Do what?"

"Shift into four wheel. Grandma gear on the lower right side."

"Right! Got it!" Tallie said.

The wheels grabbed into the mud and held a firm track out the ditch, but her legs were shaking so badly it was hard to keep her feet on the pedals. The added sense of security afforded by the four-wheel drive enabled her to recoup her courage to guide the truck through the muddier, low places. She was breathing easier until she realized there was a bridge between her and the highway. Once again, panic flooded her gut. What if it was out?

Silently, Tallie prayed again. God, praises to You. I'm praising You, not a real long praise, because that bridge is coming up and because Aunt Jenny said that You don't think it is a snow job and that I should do that. She said You live in praise, whatever that means. I'm praying for her. Don't let her die, and help me cross that bridge.

The truck slid sideways again and the wheel spun a bit before grabbing. Aunt Jenny groaned and went into dry heaves. To make matters worse, there was no moon nor any stars shining making it difficult to see what lay ahead.

"I'm sorry," Tallie said to her groaning aunt, "but I can't see very far to miss the bumps."

"Put on the brights."

"How?"

"Button on the floor board at the left."

Tallie stretched with her left leg feeling for it with her foot. When she found it, she pushed down hard rounding a curve in the road at the same time. There was the bridge and it looked intact, but what if it fell from under them? She felt she had no choice and since it was a short bridge, she would do what she had seen in the movies—gun the motor and fly across. The lights of town glimmered in the distance urging her on. She stepped down harder on the accelerator, pressed her lips tight, and gripped the steering wheel with great resolve. She slammed her foot to the floor board, held it down and blasted across, bouncing down, soundly on the far side.

"Tallie?" Her aunt spoke weakly and tried to sit up.

"It's okay. We're nearly there." She repeated 'nearly there' over and over in her mind.

The highway felt like velvet after the miserable, muddy road. She passed some houses, a grocery store, a service station, and then realized she did not know where the hospital was.

"Where is the hospital, Aunt Jenny?"

"Where are you now?"

"I don't know. I can't see any street signs, but there is a stoplight up ahead."

"Make a right turn at the light."

When she got close to the stoplight, there was a blue sign on the side of the street with the word 'Hospital, 2 blocks' over an arrow pointing to the right. Two blocks later, she pulled into the parking lane right by the door. A nurse with a wheelchair came out the door like she was expecting them. A second nurse was holding the hospital doors open. A car pulled up nose to nose with the truck. A man jumped out and started snapping orders. Apparently the doctor.

"Hurry up." he yelled as he opened the door on Aunt Jenny's side of the truck.

Tallie stood on the sidelines and watched them load her aunt into the wheelchair and followed behind them up the ramp and into the hospital waiting room.

"You stay here," Dr. Gilbert ordered Tallie as they ran down the long, green tiled corridor with her aunt slumped over in a wheelchair.

Tallie stood alone watching them go. The doctor barked some orders and slammed-pushed his way through a set of double doors. Tallie kept staring down the hallway until her own feelings returned. Her knee began to sting, her eyes felt gritty, and her legs weighed a ton. She sighed and walked back to the muddy truck to get her aunt's purse and the car keys. It was lighter outside now, but not daylight.

There was nothing to do but wait. Tallie went back into the hospital waiting area and sat on a plastic, green sofa. She leaned her head back and closed her eyes to keep from crying.

"God, I thank You for helping us to cross that bridge. Please let her live. She was sick all day. I'm sure that's why she was so grumpy. I know that now. I won't complain about being bored anymore. I'm sorry if I made her sicker by upsetting her. I'm sorry I lost her bathtub, and I'm sorry for my smartalec request for cool air. I hope You didn't beat her poor tomatoes to death just to teach me a lesson. I don't understand that. I just don't, but I don't care if I never do, if You will let her live. I'll forget about the tomatoes if you will." She closed her eyes and almost slept until someone called her name.

"Tallie?"

Tallie's whole body jerked at the sound.

"What is it? Is she dead?"

Sheriff Sawyer stood before her. "I just saw the truck out front. Is who dead? What's going on here?"

Tallie told him what had taken place, careful not to mention that she had driven the truck without a license.

"I'm amazed she could drive—her being that sick," he said, discerning the look on Tallie's face. "I reckon she had a little help from you getting here. "

"Yes, she did. I drove her. And I don't care if you put me in jail. Do it and see if I care. And what's more, I would do it all again."

Sheriff Sawyer laughed. "You're something. A little like her, I think. Aunt Jenny Raider, The Generator. We all call her that, but not to her face." He laughed quietly, again. "Has Doc said what the problem is yet?"

"No. He told me to get out of the way and hasn't come back."

"I'll see if I can find out what's going on. You wait here. I'll be right back."

When the sheriff returned, some nurse Tallie did not see earlier came back with him and told her that her aunt was in surgery for what was probably an acute, gangrenous gallbladder. She also said something about probable cholecystitis and cholelithiasis—a bunch of long words meaning stones and infection along with gangrene. She stated, with no detectable signs of sympathy, that gallbladder surgery was not a difficult operation, Furthermore, her aunt had a good, strong heartbeat and all was going smoothly. Then she looked at her watch, did an about face and marched back to the front desk.

"I think she likes to try to scare us, saying all those long words," the sheriff said, grinning," but we ain't, are we? Aunt Jenny will be just fine. There is nothing to do but wait, so why don't we go get some breakfast?"

"I'd rather stay here for now, but thanks anyway," Tallie answered.

He said he would be back and on his way out, he asked the nurse to get Tallie something to eat from the kitchen.

Tallie ate a bowl of watery oatmeal and curled up on the couch. The tasteless food felt good in her stomach and she fell asleep. This time, there were no dreams, just a good sleep until she was roused by the desk nurse loudly answering a ringing phone.

A man in denim jeans and cowboy boots sat in front of Tallie. One foot rested on his knee, and his fingers were laced together in his lap.

"Good morning." The voice belonged to Pastor Hay.

Tallie's mind cleared enough to realize that the 'Pastor might have awful news, else why was he here?

"Is my aunt—is she gone?"

"No. She's in the recovery room."

"Why didn't you wake me up?"

"I figured you needed the sleep."

"Is she doing okay?"

"Far as I know she is. It'd take a heap more than a nasty gallbladder to take Jenny Raider out."

"How did you get here? Aunt Jenny said the bridge to your place was out."

"It is out. I rode in on Brownie, my horse. Sheriff Sawyer called me this morning before daylight. He said you all were down here."

"I wish they'd tell me something or let me see her."

"I saw her. There's a little window in the door back there. She is resting and rid of a nasty gallbladder. She'll be up and around in no time a'tall, the doc says."

"How much time is that?"

"If all goes well, she can go home in four or five days, most likely."

"What do you mean—if all goes well?"

"The doc is a dandy surgeon, but it depends on how fast that wound heals. She is a little older than she used to be. Doc won't let her leave until he is sure she is on the mend. Now what about you? We would like for you to come stay with us awhile."

"I don't think so. I don't want to leave Aunt Jenny. It's, it's. It's my...I'm the one who..."

"You think It's your fault she got sick? Is that what you're thinking? Child, her gallbladder acted up long before now. She's real fortunate you were there to help her."

"But you don't understand. I prayed for cool air, not even a real prayer really, just popping off. And a storm came and everybody's crops were wiped out. And the bathtub blew away, and the hail came, and Aunt Jenny prayed for her tomatoes, but they got pounded anyway, and my manners got on her nerves, and I got bored doing all those farm chores she gets such a large charge doing. She even has to get up early to pray, I guess because she is old and chores are hard and things are so bad. Yesterday, she was feeling really bad. She was hurting too much to drive around the fence rows, so she let me drive, partly because she was feeling bad, and partly because she was trying to give me something special to do. Then she got real picky about slamming the screen door, and I got real snotty. I just don't understand seeds and bubbles, and I don't care if I am the first one to see the insides of a bean's guts, and I just plain get on her nerves! And— and— Tallie choked back the tears.

Pastor Hay raised his eyebrows. "Whoa now. That's a big load you've toted. And you're right, I don't understand what all you two have had to deal with, but I can tell you this much. You're worn out, but your aunt is going to be fine. She's going to be fine partly because of you. That's a big part. The sheriff told me what all you did for her."

The Pastor leaned forward, his arms on his knees. "Tell you what", he said, "let's go see if she's awake yet." Then he laughed a bit and rubbed his chin. "I doubt that you or anyone else can jump on her nerves hard enough to cause her any harm. I purely can't imagine that. How about it? Let's go see if we can visit her for a moment."

Aunt Jenny lay under a sheet; her dry lips were partly open. A tube ran from her arm to a bottle on a metal stand. Tallie stood by the bed. As if Aunt Jenny knew someone was there, her eyes parted briefly. She tried to smile and closed her eyes again. She whispered Tallie's name and drifted back into sleep. Tallie took Aunt Jenny's hand and held it and was struck by the thinness of the skin, all worn off in the garden dirt and dishwater, Tallie thought.

"She looks awful. I think you should pray or something," Tallie said. "That's what you're supposed to do, isn't it? Isn't that your job?"

"Nope, it's my privilege. He studied Tallie briefly, then opened his mouth to pray.

"Wait!" Tallie interrupted and pointed to Aunt Jenny. "She says to start out with praise. God lives in it, whatever that means, but I can tell you for sure, it's like using keys to start up a motor. And don't do a snow job on God either. He won't like that."

"She says that, does she?" Pastor Hay smiled. "I'll give it my best."

The pastor stood at the foot of the bed. With a half-smile and eyes wide open, he placed his hands on Aunt Jenny's feet and began to talk to God.

"Heavenly Father, Your names are as powerful and awesome as they are loving, beautiful, and gentle. I know Your names and You know mine. Thank you for that honor. You said to lay hands on those sick among us and to pray for them. You are Jehovah Rapha, God of our healing. Aunt Jenny is Your servant, Lord. Let Your healing word and light flow, restoring her health quickly to the advantageous service she renders for Your kingdom. I've a notion that you two are up to something. So by the name above all names, Lord Jesus, restore Jenny Raider, I pray. I'm much obliged. Amen."

Tallie looked at her aunt and decided that she looked better and seemed to be sleeping more soundly.

"Thanks," she said.

"Tallie, you ought to come stay with us until your Aunt Jenny can go home. Some of us can go over with you to tend to her place and bring you in to see her every day."

"I don't know."

"Have you a better plan?"

"No. But I want to call my parents first. And I can't just leave her here alone."

"She'd rest better knowing things are being tended to at home and that you are being taken care of by responsible adults she knows well. That is the best you can do for her right now."

"Yeah. I mean yes, she would want the chores done. She'd never skip one, for sure. I'll call my parents from Aunt Jenny's house."

Doc Gilbert was standing in the foyer talking to Sheriff Sawyer about Aunt Jenny;

"It's fortunate for her that we did not delay so much as a few hours. However, she's basically healthy. Comes in each September for a checkup. I'll probably be able to dismiss her about next Saturday, possibly, providing she has someone to stay with her," the doctor said.

Tallie walked up in time to hear what the doctor said. "I'm staying with her."

"And who are you?" asked the doctor.

Tallie wasn't sure she liked him.

"I'm the one who called you last night. I'm her niece."

Pastor Hay intervened.

"Doc, this is her niece come to spend some time this summer. She drove that truck over some mighty rough terrain last night to get Aunt Jenny in here so's you could operate."

"Oh. Hm-m-m. Well. You did the right thing," Doc said and patted Tallie's head, but Tallie pulled away. "Understand this. I'm not about to let her out of here until I'm satisfied she can function on her own or has adequate nursing care at her disposal," he said, "but right now, everything looks good. I did a good job and made sure of it." Then he shook hands with the man and went down the hallway.

The nurse called Tallie to the front desk to relate Aunt Jenny's insurance information. While the nurse made photocopies of the information, Tallie wrote the home telephone numbers of the Pastor and Aunt Jenny for the nurses to have in case her aunt needed anything or got sicker or something.

"Young lady," the sheriff said, "It would be a good idea to run the truck through the car wash before all that mud bakes on it. Then Pastor Hay can take you home in it."

"But what about the horse?" Tallie asked.

"Tom rode Brownie home a couple of hours ago," Pastor Hay replied, "so let's get going. There isn't anything worthwhile we can do sitting in here."

"What about the bridge? Didn't you say it was out?" Tallie asked.

Sheriff Sawyer explained that a road crew was out there working on it right now. Then he gave Tallie a little pat on the shoulders and said he'd better get back to the office.

Tallie fell asleep in the truck on the way to the car wash and did not wake up until Pastor Hay stopped in Aunt Jenny's driveway. Tallie roused and rubbed her eyes which felt like they were made of sandpaper.

"I'll feed and water the stock. You get whatever it is you'll need from the house. I reckon you'd better latch up the doors when you're through in case the weather decides to act up again," Pastor said.

Tallie packed for herself and also got some gowns for her aunt. Latch up in case of bad weather? At home, she thought, we latch up in case someone wants to latch on to all our stuff. Thinking of home, she remembered to call her parents.

Tallie told them about Aunt Jenny's operation assuring them that all was well, and that she would be staying at the Hay's house until Aunt Jenny came home. She carefully avoided any talk about how they got to the hospital.

"No, I'm at Aunt Jenny's right now getting her gowns and latching up. That's what they call it here. It means locking up the house.

Pastor Hay brought me out here. Do you know him? Oh, good just a minute, I'll get him."

Tallie called the pastor to the telephone.

"Hello? Well, nice to hear your voice, too. Yes, it has been quite awhile. Oh, she's a little tired, I think, but tough," and laughed. "I know it's hard not to come on down, but everything will work out. Mary John and Tallie will take the bit and harness. No, no trouble at all. We're glad to have her come stay at our house. Sure, we'll let you know if there's any change at all. I know you'd come and we'll call if we need you. Yes. The Lord keep you. Yes, she's right here," said the Pastor and handed the phone to Tallie.

"Mom?...I'm okay....I will. Mom! ...I'm fine. Yeah, uh yes. I will call you tomorrow. Bye."

"Ready?" Pastor asked.

"All but the latching up," she replied.

The pastor surveyed the crops and storm damage as they rode along and Tallie stared out the window on the passenger side thinking that her mom had sounded like she really meant it when she said she loved her. She even acted like she would like to come down and help, but she isn't for some mysterious reason other than that inventory excuse.

The Pastor repeated his suggestion that Mary John could come over with her to get the mail and help tend to all the chores, and he would make sure she got to see her aunt every day.

They rode in silence for a bit. The pastor took a serious look at her and asked if she was all right.

"I'm okay."

"Are you willing to settle for 'okay'?"

"I guess. I don't know. Okay is okay, isn't it? Who cares?

"You think you are in this situation alone?"

"No. You're here helping me do all this stuff."

"But you act like it's all up to you. I'm guessing that is the way you feel at the moment?"

"Sorta. I'm down here by myself and my parents aren't coming."

"Do you like putting up with that lone-ness?

"I gotta. No one can get in my skin and do it for me."

"Wouldn't it be something if someone could jump in your skin and help you figure out what to do with all your stuff?"

"You mean Jesus, don't you?" That wasn't hard to guess, she thought.

"Kind of. It's actually the job description of the Holy Spirit sent by Jesus. He is the designated helper. It's a matter of doing a couple of things like admitting you aren't a very good boss-god. Once you resign from being your own god, the Holy Spirit is available as your personal helper and guide. He wants to be involved but He won't come to you unless you really mean it. I can tell you He is interested in doing more than just pulling your shirt tail off the barbed wire fence. Many people go through life disconnected, just okay, because no one ever tells them where to plug in. Well, that is my job. That is what I do. I'd be derelict in duty if I didn't tell you where your help is. "

"So you think I'm not plugged in?" Tallie asked.

"Do you think your Aunt Jenny is?"

"She's plugged into something, all right. She gets turned on by beans and dishwater bubbles."

Pastor laughed. "She would. I've suspected for years that she and the Lord have some kind of unique something going on."

"I wonder if she hasn't gone a little 'off' being out here by herself all the time."

"She's never alone. And you don't have to be alone either. She has given herself entirely into God's care and most of us come around to see her regularly. She's not alone, physically or spiritually. It's a hoot and a real adventure," he said. Smiling, he pushed his straw hat back and scratched his head.

"I've joined the church. I joined when I was in fifth grade."

"When you join the church, that's what you join. When you join Jesus that's another thing. That is when you get plugged in.

Tallie was quietly thinking this preacher was like no other one she had ever known. It was as if he could see her mind. She was beginning to be a little uncomfortable with the conversation when he explained that such talk often makes people coil up inside themselves which was normal.

By then, they neared the bridge and the road crew. Tallie was glad when he pulled over and left her alone while he went to talk to the workers. She looked down the road toward the Hay's house.

"Rats!" she said aloud, recalling that Tom Sawyer was there waiting for a ride back to town. He's in for it if he says even one word to me," she thought.

Chapter Six: Bathtub Hunting on Horseback

Mrs. Hay took Tallie underwing, doctoring her knee, then into the Kitchen for vegetable soup, chicken sandwiches, and a slice of chocolate cake still warmish from the oven. The Pastor came in, kissed his wife, and sat down at the table. There was a question and answer session about Aunt Jenny, then the Pastor took the hands of Tallie and his wife and asked the blessing. Tallie quit chewing, hoping no one noticed. When the amen was said, Tallie took another big bite of the sandwich. Mrs. Hay smiled, patted Tallie, and went into another part of the house to finish vacuuming.

"Hey, Hay!" The screen door slammed. Tallie looked up with a jerk. It was Tom Sawyer.

"Ho, Tom. Smelled the food, did you?" the pastor asked.

"All the way past the barn, and it must be good by the looks of balloon cheeks over there," Tom said.

"Help yourself, son, there's plates over by the stove."

"Miz H. fed me once, but I could use another slice of that cake." Tom bounced his eyebrows up and down a couple of times and proceeded to cut a large slice, glancing at Tallie, flashing his teasing grin.

Tallie's mouth was so full of food she could scarcely chew, and for the sudden lack of spit, couldn't swallow it either. Finally, she took a small sip of water to wet the bulk. It hurt her throat all the way down when she swallowed. Tom acted like he knew just exactly what was going on and was thoroughly enjoying her misery—the snot. He took a mincey, little bite of his cake, relished it slowly and licked the icing off the fork, staring at Tallie with that know-it-all grin. Then suddenly serious, he turned to the pastor.

"So what's the deal with Aunt Jenny"

"Gallbladder. Doc Gilbert took it out. She's doing right well. Resting good when we left. I appreciate your bringing Brownie back and missing ball practice."

"No sweat. Coach understood. Besides, the field is too wet anyway. We'll get in a practice before the game."

"When is that game coming up?" asked the pastor.

"Next Wednesday."

Tallie was glad they were talking and leaving her out of it.

"How's that knuckleball?" Pastor Hay inquired.

"Perfect."

"It had better be. Barbershop talk has it that the Boggy Creek pitcher has a long, strong arm. They aren't short on hitters, neither. What do you think about that?"

"I think we'll see about that next Wednesday night," Tom answered.

Preacher Hay smiled and wiped his mouth.

"Let's see how perfect that knuckleball is. I have a ball around here some'ers, or did you bring yours?"

"Does ten pounds of flour make a big biscuit?" was Tom's retort.

When they left, Tallie put the dishes in the sink and walked to the back porch wondering where Mary John was. Something flew out of the cellar and landed with a plop causing her to jump. A wad of mud. Out flew another.

"Mary John?" she called down the steps.

"I'm down here."

"What are you doing down there?" Tallie asked.

"Shoveling mud. It is all my fault. I left the cellar door open and it came in pretty bad. I'll be up in a minute."

After a few scraping noises, Mary John emerged from the cellar carrying a bucket and shovel and said, "So, you had a pretty rough night, I hear."

"Sort of. But I'm okay."

"What happened? I want to know every detail," Mary John said.

Tallie followed along to the horse tank telling her the story while Mary John cleaned up the shovel and bucket; followed Mary John to the kitchen where she washed her hands; then to the table where Tallie finished the last of the story while Mary John ate a piece of cake.

"You done good, Tallie. Were you scared? I would have been, " Mary John admitted.

"Yes, I was kinda scared the whole time, but I nearly freaked out when we got to that old bridge near the highway. I was scared the flood had washed the legs loose and it could fall over."

"Anyone would have been scared, and you can't always tell if some of these old county bridges will hold. Makes me shiver to think about it."

Mrs. Hay interrupted their talk and gave instructions to let Tallie get a nice hot shower and a nap, as Tallie must be 'plumb wore out'.

Worn out or not, Tallie followed Mrs. Hay to Mary John's room. The neatness of the room struck her. Nothing was out of place. A little vase of ox-eye daisies filled a pitcher on the dresser which complemented the wallpaper of tiny lavender flowers on a creamy white background. Tallie thought of her own room in St. Louis. Her walls were covered in what she considered "cool" posters, a dresser overflowing with stuff she never bothered to throw away, drawers full of unmatched socks, wadded up underwear and unfolded T-shirts. Her mom had declared that she could live in that mess if she wanted, but she was not going to clean it again because the last time she had, it took thirty minutes just to get the junk off the floor so she could run the vacuum.

Tallie was careful in this room to fold her clothes and place them in her small tote bag. She climbed into the bed. It felt good. It smelled good. It felt okay to lie down a bit. Just okay? Pastor Hay says there's more than okay. She smiled a little at her accidental rhyme and continued it. This whole room is a bouquet, that's okay. Her eyelids closed. A tub flew through the air, end over end with daisies falling out. Not okay! She ran for the tub. Gallstones fell like hail, pelting her head.   A-l-o-n-e, the wind howled, No clothes on. The bridge is gone. H-e-y, you don't know the way. That's not o-k-a-y. A large black cloud shaped like a vacuum cleaner dipped out of the sky and chased her as she ran with heavy legs. It lunged toward her to suck her into everlasting oblivion. Tallie jerked awake.

"Stop it!" she said to nothing in particular and fluffed her pillow. I don't want to be alone, but I am, she thought.

"Jesus, I don't want to be alone or just okay. I really don't," she said. A few tired tears fell onto the pillow. She slept again, quietly.

Mrs. Hay was sitting on the floor pinning a hem in a dress Mary John had on when Tallie came in from her nap.

"Come on in here, Tallie. How was your nap?" Mrs. Hay asked.

"It was okay," Tallie said. Pastor Hay turned down the corner of the newspaper he was reading and looked straight at Tallie. Tallie looked away from him.

"Did I get any calls from the hospital?" Tallie asked.

"No. But no news is good news. We'll go in 'dreckly' and see her, Punkin," Mrs. Hay responded.

Tallie wondered what time 'dreckly' was. Tom Sawyer was sitting across the room watching a baseball game on TV and barely glanced in her direction. Good, she thought, and sat down on the couch as far away from him as possible.

Pastor Hay shook a crease out of the newspaper.

"Listen to this," he said. "It says here that two men in Lincoln County fleeced local residents for a sum in excess of $7,000 operating a gas-leak repair scheme while posing as employees of a local gas company." Pastor Hay shook his head and continued, "Authorities believe the same two men may have been involved in other fraudulent schemes, preying mainly on elderly citizens." He put his glasses down on the coffee table and shook his head again. We need to be as wise as serpents and as harmless as doves in times like these."

Mary John asked, "Exactly how are we supposed to do that?"

"It means," he said, "to be street-wise. Be a jump ahead in knowledge. Pay attention to what is happening. Anticipate it. A snake knows what is going on around him. He flips that old tongue out there and gathers all kinds of information. It knows what it can swallow and what it can't. Snakes are quiet. Don't draw much attention to themselves. That's why it's a surprise when you run onto one. But you take a dove, now, it makes no trouble for nobody. Some say they mate for life. It's loyal, you see? Doves fly a straight course, unlike tweety birds that dip and dive and tweet and chirp. Even dove wings make a particular sound as they fly. Doves are cool-headed when the heat is on. They avoid danger without attacking by using their instincts. For us, that would be our spiritual wits, I'm figuring.

"Why, John Hay! I had no idea you had such a wealth of knowledge about doves, Mrs. Hay said. I'm impressed," she emoted while they laughed at her dramatics.

" You mean for us to watch out and be cool, right, Pastor?" Tom said.

"I reckon that sums it up, Tom, but you're going to have to stretch out your message if you ever make a preacher."

"No way. I'm not going to preach. I don't mean nothing against you, but preaching isn't for me."

"I said as much myself,once."

Mary John turned at her mom's command through a mouth full of pins and said, "Tom, you have the streetwise part down pretty good. How are you doing on the dove part?"

"Be still," Mrs. Hay chided her daughter. You're squirming like a convicted sinner."

"Do you want me to hold her still for Miz H.? Tom teased.

"No," Mrs. Hay said and put the last pin in the hem. I'm done here. It's time for you kids to get ready to go into town. I want to see Aunt Jenny and I know Tallie does, too."

———------------------------------

Jenny Raider was groggy but awake when they arrived. Flowers lined the window sill and a long bench beneath it. Some had been bought and some were from people's gardens.

"What is this I hear about you," Mrs. Hay asked, smiling down at Aunt Jenny.

"I threw a shoe, I reckon."

"Lord have mercy! I see you did, and look," Mrs. Hay pointed toward the door. "Tallie's here. She brought your things in, too."

"Sure enough?" Aunt Jenny whispered through a dry throat.

"She sure did. Nobody told her. She thought of her own self. And she's been anxious to see you all day, too. Doc said we could only come in one or two at a time. I'll let them come on in a spell."

Aunt Jenny smiled weakly. "She got me here you know. She did good, didn't she?"

"Yes, she did. You have a right to be proud of her."

Aunt Jenny drew a deep breath and relaxed a bit. Tallie came into the room carrying a paper sack and walked quietly over to the bedside.

"Hi," Tallie said timidly. She set the sack on the bed table and bumped a bottle of something that fell over and when she picked it up and looked at it she was astonished.

"Yuck! What is that?"

Aunt Jenny winced and tried not to laugh.

"Those are my gallstones, Missy."

"What are they doing in here? They're nasty looking."

"Doc brought 'em."

"That figures," Tallie said. He took them out, let him keep them. Pastor and Mrs. Hay brought flowers. They picked them themselves."

"Doc picked these stones for me. They're ugly, all right, but I'm sure glad they are over there in that jar. Besides, I think he wants me to know he was spot on about his diagnosis."

Pastor Hay had appeared and stood quietly against the door jamb.

"Doc wanted to show her he didn't dive in there for nothing."

"Come on in, Preacher," Aunt Jenny called. "Did you lose your crops?"

"We got a little damage, but we'll be alright. You've got your own crop in here what with all these flowers. Have you had lots of company this afternoon?"

"No, not that I know of. The nurse brought most of these in. But Alice Fursby got past the desk and came in a-while ago. Seems like her sister had this same operation back in '49 and like to never got over it. Then she told the nurses up front that they should "give me vinegar baths.""

"That sounds like Alice. Aches and pains are her specialty. It really is too bad she didn't finish nursing school. But on the other hand, I reckon the Lord knew where He wanted Alice and where He didn't want her."

Aunt Jenny laughed and winced a little when the stitches grabbed. But the pastor didn't mind the wince. Laughter is good like a medicine, and might save her from painful adhesions.

"Mary John has something for you if you are up to her company. I'll let her come on in if you'd like," he said.

Thanks for coming, Pastor. Send her in here. I'd purely love to see that child."

Mary John came in with a cellophane bag tied in a big pink bow.

"I brought you these peppermints. Doc Gilbert's nurse said you could have some by tomorrow."

"Oh good! They're one of my favorites."

"I'll wait with my folks and let you and Tallie visit some more. The nurse said not to wear you out."

When Mary John left, Tallie asked her aunt if she was really all right.

"Why sure. Are you?"

"I'm okay. Pastor and I took care of things at the farm. Sheriff Sawyer told me to run the truck through the car wash so it's all clean, now."

Aunt Jenny frowned. "I hate to be such a burden on everyone."

"No, don't say that. They act like they are really glad to be doing stuff."

"They are. Knowing them as I do, I'm sure of it. It's my pride rarin' up. It's hard to be here flat on my back and let everyone else do all the doing. Pride is an old beast."

"If I do the chores at your place, and help out at the Hay's house, then maybe you won't feel like we're imposing on them. Mrs. Hay always has leftovers she throws to the pigs, so don't worry too much that I'm eating up their food."

"No, I'm not worried about that a bit. I'm glad you are staying with them. Be sure to be right tidy and leave things like you found them."

"I will."

"Are you sure you're alright?" Aunt Jenny asked.

"I'm okay. I talked to Mom this afternoon, too. She'll be calling you tomorrow, and...well, I'd better go."

Aunt Jenny smiled a little. Tallie said goodbye again, and walked down the hall wondering what tomorrow held for both of them. Whatever tomorrow held, there was one thing she definitely intended to do—-find that bathtub!

The next morning at breakfast, the Hays decided that Mary John and Tallie should ride the horses over to do the chores at Aunt

Jenny's each day. It would be good for the horses and free up the cars for other uses.

Pastor Hay never knew when he might be called out for something and might need a vehicle. Mary John had explained to her that sometimes people called him in the middle of the night, and not to be alarmed if the phone rang at such times. Sometimes people picked her dad's name out of a phone book to come help them with a flat tire, or want money for gas to get to the next town where, supposedly, their dear old granny was waiting to see them before she died. She said there were times when her dad told them he had two dollars on him and would be glad to use it to buy the gas, and not only that, he would offer to follow them over there so he could pray for granny. That is when they hung up.

Thus, the main reason to go on horseback was to leave cars available in case someone was truly in need of the pastor's help. Tallie was afraid of horses even though she had never ridden, but was determined not to show any fear. It was important to her to do the chores for her aunt, and most of all, she was flat-out determined to look for the lost bathtub.

Mary John led a bare-backed mare to the porch, stood on the steps, grabbed the horse's mane and hopped on. Pastor Hay put a bridle and bit on Brownie and handed the reins to Tallie, expecting her to follow Mary John's example of mounting up without a saddle and stirrups. It astounded Tallie that all these country people assumed everyone else could do the things they do, such as ride horses and play instruments. She wondered what they'd ask her to do next, butcher a hog and chew the hides for shoes? Determinedly, she did as shown and mounted the horse that looked back at her like he knew she was a blooming novice.

Brownie had a mind of his own. He stood flat-footed and would not move, even though she pulled on the reins. Brownie was not interested in being seen transporting this dumb city cluck anywhere. He swung his long tail lazily at a fly and stood there playing like he was dumb as a stump. Pastor Hay slapped him on the rump which prompted the horse to move on in line and catch up with Mary John. Nevertheless, he shifted into a gait so slow and bouncy that Tallie had to hold onto the mane for fear of falling off.

"See you later, Daddy," Mary John said, she slowed her mare into a gentle walk. Brownie settled down and followed the mare. Tallie watched Mary John pull the reins in the direction of the gate. Tallie did, too, but Brownie stooped to chew some of the Johnsongrass by the mailbox. She timidly pulled the reins. Brownie shook his head in protest. Tallie pulled with more of a jerk and he finally started down the road and moved alongside the mare. The two horses walked along with their heads bobbing in unison. Tallie relaxed a little.

"I'll bet you are bored to bits out here," Mary John said, only it was more like a pronouncement.

"I have never been so bored..." Tallie noticed her answer may have slightly offended her new friend and quickly added, "but I was bored at home, too. My summer plans got all changed up without me having any say in it. And it is different at home. I'm too busy to notice now. It's different here than at home where I could call my friends and just talk or go do something."

"What is it like in St. Louis? I mean, what do you and your friends do for fun there?"

"We watch tv, go swimming, eat pizza, go to the mall or the zoo, stuff like that. "

"I live in a zoo! Mary John laughed and patted the mare's neck. We have to go thirty miles to the next town to go to the movies or to a real pizza place. But you can get pizza at the Dairy King or the restaurant in the motel. We like to get pizza there after baseball games. Tom's pitching in the game tonight, and I know for a fact we'll be there. Maybe we can get pizza afterward."

"I'll probably stay with Aunt Jenny while you guys are at the game. I'm not too crazy about baseball anyway."

"Nor Tom Sawyer either," Mary John laughed. "He really bugs you."

"He thinks he's cute, and I don't."

"But he is cute, Tallie. He can be a smart aleck at times and teases people a lot, but he is smart, real smart. The teachers put him in special independent courses they ordered from the university."

"La-ti-dah".

Mary John laughed at Tallie's response.

"Really, he's not so bad. He isn't afraid of work, and he hopes to get a baseball scholarship when he goes to college after his senior year. He makes all A's, even in the hardest of subjects."

"Well, goody for him. My grades were not so good last year," Tallie admitted.

"What happened?"

"I don't know, just boring stuff. I think those grades are why I got stuck here for the summer. My parents said they had to inventory the store, and Mom was going to work more hours this summer and didn't want to leave me at home by myself. But I'm smart enough to know inventory doesn't take all summer, and she only works full time when an employee goes on vacation. We've only got two employees. It doesn't take Einstein to figure I'm being punished. It's 'time out' for the entire summer!"

"I'm glad you came, whatever the reason. I see the same people all the time. It's a rut. I even know what they're going to say most of the time. We all wear the same things and do the same things. What are they wearing in St. Louis?"

By the time Tallie finished with the fashions and the ins-and-outs of life in St. Louis, they were entering the driveway of Aunt Jenny's house.

They divided up the chores and quickly went to work. Mary John fed and milked Janet. Tallie fed the chickens. Together they pumped water into the horse tank for the cow and carried water to the chicken troughs. Mary John gathered the eggs while Tallie picked up the mail and looked at the damage to the garden. When Mary John had stowed the washed eggs in the refrigerator, she helped Tallie reset and retie a few ragged tomato vines to their stakes. They pulled weeds and shored dirt up around the green bean stalks, even though a majority of the blooms and branches were gone. The onions weren't to be seen, but Mary John said the bulbs would grow and stay okay in the ground for quite awhile. Some of the corn was standing, and the squash, to Tallie's disgust, was doing well. They picked some to take back to the Hays.

Tallie made some peanut butter sandwiches for lunch. While they ate, she began to understand that these country people sized up other people according to how hard and how well they worked. It was that little comment Mary John made about Tom not being afraid of work—even though he lived in town and was smart, he was not afraid to get his hands dirty and do hard work. It seemed to impress them that anyone from town could or would work. Such things as riding horses and playing instruments were simply expected to be done the same as chores like rural kids did. Tallie also figured out that smart wasn't fully smart to them unless you could use your hands as well as your brains.

"What is next?" Mary John asked, wadding up her napkin.

"I think we're through except for one thing. Aunt Jenny's bathtub blew away during the storm and I need to look for it. It blew out over the fence and into the pasture somewhere, I think. Do we have time to look for it?"

"Sure. We can ride out that way on the horses," Mary John said.

They rode slowly through the brush in all directions. Tallie could tell that Mary John was tired of looking when she began to ask questions such as: Just exactly where did it fall? How far did it go? Did you see it fall?

Tallie explained that she did not see where it landed but suggested they look through one more thicket, and if it was not in there, she would look for it another time.

Dismounting Brownie, Tallie shoved her way into a brushy area which was higher than her head. She waded deeper into the branches figuring the tub couldn't possibly have fallen through such tightly woven bushes. Pausing a moment, she decided there was no use to try to go through to the other side. Something tickled her ankle. She looked down. A tarantula was raking at her with its front legs. Tallie squealed at the top of her lungs. The horses shied and Mary John fought to hold them in check. Tallie threw her hands up before her face and tore out of the thicket.

"What's the matter?" Mary John yelled.

"Tarantula! A huge, hairy tarantula!"

"Oh, I thought you'd been bitten by a rabid skunk or something. Are you alright?"

"I'm fine except for a slight heart attack. Let's get out of here. I don't know where that stupid bathtub is," Tallie said and shivered again from fright. She grabbed the mane and hoisted herself upon old Brownie's broad back, safe from crawling things on the ground.

The sun was hot. The wind was hot. The road was baked and blown dry. They rode along quietly swatting an occasional horsefly.

Mary John asked, "Did you make all these crooked ruts?"

"I probably did."

Tallie thought about that night again and began to wonder about some things.

"You know what I think?" Tallie asked.

"What?"

"I think Aunt Jenny knew she was sick and needed me to practice driving just in case."

"Maybe. Maybe not. Maybe the Lord knew and made sure you could drive. He watches over His people."

"Her garden sure took a beating. He didn't watch over that. She asked Him to protect her tomatoes, but they're pretty shot."

"Sometimes," Mary John said, "God says 'no' to things and overrides our prayers, but Daddy says it is for a good reason whether we ever know it or not."

"What is the big deal about keeping reasons secret? Why doesn't God let people in on things?"

" Sometimes He does tell us. Maybe other times it's because we need the chance to trust Him and discover Him for ourselves, or maybe we'd miss out on the adventure of living and so would God. Shoot! I don't know. Ask Him yourself," Mary John said. It rankled her when people assumed she should know all about God and everything in the Bible because she was the pastor's daughter.

"Your dad said stuff about God being an adventure. I always thought God was more interested in rules than fun. If you keep His rules, He keeps you from having fun."

"The only thing I know of that God likes to keep us away from is the devil's booby traps. Sin always hurts somebody and God doesn't like that. He likes for us to have fun and be healthy and enjoy each other and do interesting things. I also think He is going to make it up to us for the stings we have to take because of other people's sins, and I bet He is thinking up some colorful ways to take revenge on our enemies and on all little bitty mean people.'

"What do you do for fun when you are all by yourself or doing some boring thing like hoeing the garden?" Tallie asked to change the subject.

Mary John grinned and thought a moment before answering.

"I guess the most common thing I do is yodel."

"You're kidding'"

Mary John let out a peal of yodeled notes and laughed. Tallie was amazed.

"How do you do that?"

Mary John pointed to her throat and wiggled her finger.

"You have to control your Adam's apple, and make it jump just right while you use your tongue to punctuate the sounds. Like this, "Oh-de-oh-de-ay. Now you try it."

Tallie looked sideways at Mary John and shook her head 'no'.

"Oh, come on. Have some fun. No one can hear us but the horses."

"No, I'd rather not," Tallie said. "I'd probably sound like my aunt's rooster."

"Do you like to sing?"

"I took choral singing in school," Tallie said, "but I didn't learn any yodeling.

"Do you know *Don't Fence Me In*?"

"Never heard of it, but it sounds like a song old Janet would like."

"I'll teach it to you and you can sing it to Janet the next time you have to milk."

Mary John wasn't the least bit shy about singing. She sang so strongly and confidently that Tallie soon began to feel comfortable enough to join in. By the time they crossed the mended bridge, Tallie was singing full voice, oblivious to the heat, all cares momentarily forgotten. She took the melody and Mary John yodeled in accompaniment. Tallie had never sung out like that at school. She had done as little as it took to get by, but now discovered what fun it was to let go and sing out, mistakes and all.

"You have a rich, alto voice, Tallie," Mary John said. "Did you know that? You ought to sing often and keep it exercised."

"I really don't sing much."

"Well, I'm telling you, you should," Mary John said, "because you have a real distinct sound, and you catch on quick. This time, you take the alto and I'll take the melody. Let's see how low you can sing with that bass voice of yours."

Mrs. Hay heard the girls singing and called her husband to listen. He walked onto the porch.

"Listen to that, "will you," Pastor exclaimed. "Mary John has that child singing right out."

"That's a good thing," Mrs. said. "She needs to loosen up a little, I think. She acts so knotted up somehow."

Pastor Hay patted his wife on the back. "You're the one with the gift of discernment."

"Oh, John, that's just common sense."

"I know. The Lord's common sense. But you are the one that picked up on that inner tenseness natural like. All I see is a sad little sheep on the other side of the fence singing with a happy little sheep on this side of the fence. Little sheep making friends."

Mrs. Hay playfully slapped her husband with a dish towel and told him they had better hurry up and get around if they were going to town.

While the Hays family went to the baseball game, Tallie stayed with her aunt who was sitting up in bed. Aunt Jenny reported that she had eaten and even walked a few steps. Tallie was encouraged by the news. Aunt Jenny, on the other hand, noticed that Tallie was brown from the sun, and something else–something she could not quite name, a good thing, and she was grateful.

Tallie reported on the damaged garden, and quickly added the good news that some of the plants were still producing, hoping good news would take the edge off bad news. Aunt Jenny was unphased by her report.

"There's always a remnant," Aunt Jenny replied. Tallie wondered what that was supposed to mean.

Doc Gilbert stuck his head in the door. "I see you haven't run off yet," he said to his favorite patient.

"I decided to stay for supper, Doc. I have an i-dee you're the only doc in the state that orders cornbread and greens for your patients."

"You won't be having that for a few days, yet. I'm on the way to the ball game and if I were to let you eat that, I'd have to be back here in no time to tend to you. He bent over to look at her wound. Boy! That's good work," he said and patted his own shoulder.

"Of course it is. I asked for it to be," she sassed. Then in a more sober voice said, "I'm grateful for those skilled hands of yours." She paused a moment then added, "And you're still my favorite Doc."

"Ha!" He blurted. "Easily said. I'm the only doc in town." He pulled the gown together. "But you're still my favorite patient."

"That's because I let you dissect those dead toads on my kitchen table when you were a kid, right?" Aunt Jenny laughed.

"Maybe, or the time I hit that rabbit with the tractor and you handed me a sewing basket and a hand ax. 'Take your pick', you said. Remember that?" Doc asked.

"I certainly do! You cheated us out of meat for supper."

They laughed together, except Tallie who sat in a chair at the foot of the bed, totally unseen and left out of the conversation. Finally Doc asked who the kid-o was.

Aunt Jenny explained Tallie's kinship connections and explained that Tallie would be able to take over any nursing duties when dismissed on Friday.

"Friday?" Doc said. "Did I say Friday, Tillie?"

"My name is Tallie. And no, you didn't say Friday, but I hope you do."

Doc Gilbert turned to Tallie and pointed his finger down at her.

"When she does leave here, " he said, "she must not climb long flights of stairs nor lift anything heavier than a glass of water until I examine her and say otherwise. Is that clear? She should walk ten to fifteen steps 3 to 4 times a day. Got that? And in the shade!"

Tallie looked at him without responding. He stared her over good and obviously found her wanting of any worth whatsoever.

"Listen, Aunt Jen", he continued, "we've got some good LNs that can stay with you when you leave here. Your insurance will cover it."

"Tallie can look after me. I don't want some stranger nosing around in my house," she said rather forcefully.

Aunt Jenny was as serious as a hog on ice and he knew it.

"Well, whatever. But don't expect to go home prior to Saturday," he said vying for the upper hand. Having reestablished himself as the authority, he patted her arm, kissed her forehead and left.

Tallie listened to the doctor's footsteps until she could hear them no more, then said, "He's an old know-it-all ."

"You have lots to learn yet, Missy. He just about does know it all, and could be running more than one famous hospital back east, but chose to stay here. He said they have plenty of me back there but this town has only one of me. AND, he's letting you stay here way past visiting hours. As for his lack of attention to you, his patients come first to the sacrifice of manners sometimes. Now, how about watering some of those plants folks have sent?

~~~~~~~~~~~~

On the way home, Tallie got to hear all about the baseball game which, it seemed, Tom won single-handedly. 'Tom Sawyer this' and' Tom Sawyer that'. His head must be as big as a blimp, she decided. He'll be so buttered up he can't stand up. Maybe she would not have to be near him again for a while.

"Tom is coming out tomorrow to help me stack hay," the pastor said to Mrs. Hay. "It won't hurt for him to keep that pitching arm of his limbered up."

"I'm glad you said something. I like to know when there is another mouth to count for supper," Mrs. Hay replied.

Tallie groaned inwardly. He can have my supper, she thought.

Mrs. Hay went on to plan the rest of the week out loud.

"You girls need to pick blackberries by Friday. We can take some to the Trade Fair on Saturday. And I expect Aunt Jenny will be coming home, according to Doc. We'll save some berries for a pie for her. I'm amazed the berries weathered the storm so well."

"Aunt Jenny said that God always leaves a remnant," Tallie said. "Whatever that means."

Pastor Hay banged his hand on the steering wheel.

"That's it! That is what I needed to hear. Thank you, God!"

Tallie was in the dark about what the Pastor meant, but Mrs. Hay and Mary John seemed to understand, and when she went to bed that evening, she wondered about the ' remnant' remark as well as what to take to the Trade fair, and also anticipated that Tom Sawyer was sure to be a big fat nuisance tomorrow. Cocky over his big fat win. To be ready for that, she went to sleep making up answers to every smart aleck thing he might say.

"Don't, fence me in," she sang in her sleep, swinging on Aunt Jenny's gate. The gate snapped shut. Tallie was on the outside. She pulled and yanked. Tarantulas mocked, "Remnant! Remnant!" and crawled in masses about-her feet.

"Don't fence me out," pleaded a voice from nowhere. "I can't open the gate!" she cried, trying to climb over it. A horsefly the size of a real horse swooped at her. She lost her grip and fell toward the high-pitched chittering of thousands of furry spiders. Immediately, she jerked awake, and gladly to the smell of coffee and bacon. It was good to be awake from the too-realistic dream. She washed her face, pulled her hair up to the crown of her head in a ponytail and went to the kitchen.

At home, she ate dry cereal, maybe a piece of toast, or a leftover piece of pizza in contrast to the Hay's family table which was loaded with home-canned peaches, hot biscuits, bacon, scrambled eggs, oatmeal with raisins, several kinds of jelly, fried potatoes, and cream gravy. It was as if they had never heard of cholesterol or calories. Yet, none of them were fat.

Pastor Hay read Psalm 3. Tallie soon learned that he read some portion of the Bible aloud every morning and asked the Word to be blessed to them along with the nutrition in the food.

"Speaking of nutrition," Tallie said, "what do you think about cholesterol?"

"That's fat in the bloodstream, isn't it?" Maggie Hay answered. "I never have thought much about it, have you, John?"

"I've read on it a bit..." Pastor Hay paused and buttered a biscuit and smothered it with gravy ... but I've never worried about it. I reckon activity burns up extra fat. An occasional fast takes care of the rest. In fact, I occasionally have to squirt a little oil on a rusty bolt to loosen it up."

"Meaning what, Daddy?" Mary John asked.

"Meaning my old joints need a little buttering now and then." Pastor Hay took a bite of food and chewed slowly, as if in defiance to the notion that anything could be wrong with the Lord's butter. "

"The way I see it, we eat what we grow, which looks and tastes like what it was when God made it. If it hasn't changed much in the processing, I trust it to serve my body as it ought. The Bible says we oughtn't to overdo anything. That's the part I have to watch. Last Thanksgiving the TV said cranberries cause cancer. According to them, the Pilgrims should have died off." The pastor grinned and added, Shoot! We'd have to quit eating altogether if we cut out everything they find fault with. Pass me another biscuit, Mama, and something to oil it with, please."

"There comes Tom, Mrs. Hay said loudly. " If any of you want another biscuit, better get one now."

"I heard that", Tom said. He made sure the screen door was shut and sat down at the table.

Mrs. Hay put a plate before him and told him there was another pan of biscuits in the oven. Just to show it was so, she took them out and placed them before him.

"Eat all you want," she said, "and if that is not enough, I'll make some more."

Tallie swallowed the last of her milk and excused herself to go to her aunt's house to do the chores. Mary John said she would get the horses.

While Mary John milked Old Janet, Tallie watered and fed the chickens and looked the garden over. She picked a few squash and cucumbers and stored them in the refrigerator. Next she ran upstairs to look in the box of books she had traded for, selected three and wrapped them up in a scarf to carry to the Trade Fair. Then she sacked up some squash to sell just in case other people lost theirs in the storm. That way they would not be wasted, nor would she be obliged to eat them.

Once the chores were done, the girls went to look over the pasture one more time for the old bathtub. Tallie knew that Mary John thought it was a waste of time from her comments.

"That tub may be in the next county, Tallie, if it flew off as high and as far as you say; and probably bent out of shape when it landed. Tornadoes can carry a cow to the next county.

"Could be, but, I just felt like I should try to find it. I'll meet you on the road after I shut the gate, " Tallie remarked and looked for tarantulas when she slid off the back of Brownie to lock the gate.

It seemed silly, too, to lock a gate anyone could easily crawl over but she did it anyway and trotted Brownie up to where Mary John waited in the shade of some blackjack trees.

"Do you want to sing *Don't Fence Me In*? Mary John asked.

"Let's sing something else, okay?"

"How about—uh—'Ragtime Cowboy Joe?"

"Never heard of it," Tallie said. "It must be old."

"It is. But it's a classic and I like it. Jump in when you're ready."

Tallie was not in the mood to sing, but the lively tune soon melted her mood. She sang along with Mary John, even identifying with the out-of-place cowboy who wasn't bowlegged nor tan like most cowboys were.

"If you like ragtime, let's try some scat," Mary John suggested.

"Scat?"

"It's like singing without words. Like this: a-dat-ċa-do-dazat. Like lazy yodeling. No bouncing the Adam's apple. Let's try it," she said, starting another tune.

"I know that one. It's the horsefly's national anthem, Tallie said. '*The Sting*' by Scott Joplin."

Tallie did her best to scat, amazed at all the things Mary John could think of to do. They sang scat all the way home, even in the barn while they used curry brushes on the horses.

After the animals were turned into the pasture, Mrs. Hay put Mary John to work in the kitchen and sent Tallie to sweep porches and to bring in the clean sheets and towels from the clothes line.

The laundry smelled so good to Tallie. She had never folded things that hung outside on a line to dry before this summer. Next, she took a broom and began to sweep the porch which wrapped the entire house. She hummed as she swept her way around to the back side of the house. Since no one was around, she decided to quietly practice yodeling.

"Oh-DEE-oh." She coughed and tried again, a little louder. "Oh-DEE-Ay," she warbled. An awful noise. Tallie rubbed her throat and tried even harder to create the yodelling stacatto with her voice. A sudden rip of loud laughter caused her to jump and whirl around. She knew it was Tom before she saw him. He came onto the back porch.

"You jerk! You smart aleck country clod!" she yelled.

The more she hollered at him, the more he laughed. He put his hand over his mouth and tried to quit, but could not.

"Shut up! Shut up!" she screamed and whacked him right in the face with the straw end of the broom. He immediately bent double with his hands to his face.

"My eye!" he moaned. "You've put my eye out!"

Tallie saw blood on his cheek.

"Oh God!" she whimpered and threw the broom into the yard. She ran around the house and down the road, crying and running until she had to stop to get her breath. It made her sick to her stomach to think of what she had done to him. She cried, some more over the horrible thing she had done. It made her so ill, she fell to her hands and knees and threw up.

How she wished she could undo what she had done! Her hair stuck to her sweaty face. She pushed it back, stood up, and walked down the road toward Aunt Jenny's house with great effort, sobbing deeply as she went.. She recalled again and again the horror of seeing the blood running down his cheek. It made her so weak and dizzy with fright, her knees buckled and she fell down on the side of the road.

"Oh, God! Oh, God! His eye! She wailed aloud. I've put his eye out! What have I done! she cried over and over in her mind, trembling and sobbing. He will never get to be a pitcher again! He won't get a baseball scholarship. I've ruined his life. "

The sound of hoofbeats finally penetrated her grieving. It was Tom coming her way on Brownie. Tallie rose up, deftly jumped the fence and raced into the pasture. Tom secured Brownie to a fence post and chased Tallie on foot, finally getting close enough to grab the back of her blouse. She went into hysterics, screaming.

"What is the matter with you?" Tom said, shaking her. "Knock it off! He said as she looked up at him.

A wash of relief ran all through her being when she saw that he had suffered no more than a slight scratch above his eye. Realizing he had not been seriously hurt all along, anger flew all over her, and she drew back, full force, to slap him. Tom grabbed her arm and doubled it behind her.

"What is the matter with you? Are you on dope or something?" He hollered right in her face.

"I should slap your jaws off! You are the only dope I've ever been around!" She yelled back. And I don't like your jokes, you—you—stupid stuck-on-yourself hick! Dope? How could you even think such a stupid thing?"

"What do you expect? You can't take a joke. You're paranoid. You hide behind trees at church, you can't keep straight time on a simple tambourine. I figured you'd been sent here to come off something."

"Well you figured all wrong, smart boy." Tallie's eyes filled with tears and spilled over. Tom let go of her arm and looked away. He took a big breath, and let it out slowly.

"The Mrs. said for me to find you and get you back to the house for dinner. We'd better go," he said quietly.

Tallie walked across the pasture behind Tom. He crossed the barbed wire fence and easily hoisted himself onto Brownie. When Tallie crossed the fence, he reached his hand down to help her onto the horse behind him.

"I can walk," she said. Tom threw up both hands."Look," he said, "they're waiting on us. Get up here." He reached down and pulled Tallie up and told her to hold on to his waist.

"No thanks," she said.

Tom reached back and pulled her hands up to his waist. "Hold on! ... and lighten up and shut up. You take yourself too seriously."

His admonition stung and confused her. Her parents had often accused her of not being serious enough. She decided that it made no difference what she did—it was wrong in someone's eyes. Heck with them all!

Chapter Seven: Blackberries, Greenbacks, and a Straw Broom

When Tallie visited her aunt that evening, Tom's criticism continued to haunt her. She wanted to talk to Aunt Jenny about it, but couldn't seem to work it into their conversation. Aunt Jenny was also restless and while she didn't exactly fuss, she expressed again and again what she needed to do at home; how good her own bed would feel especially without the noise of trucks and trains, and how she'd like some food with a little seasoning to it.

On the way home, Mrs. Hay said she, soo, had noticed the fussy restlessness of Aunt Jenny. She assured Tallie that it was a sign that Aunt Jenny was feeling better.

"As you well know," Mrs. Hay said, "Aunt Jenny didn't care whether she was lying on a floor or a feather bed when you brought her in. Eating was the farthest thing from her mind. Now, she wants seasoning in her food and her own bed. That is a good sign she is getting well. You can make her a berry cobbler tomorrow. That will please her."

"I don't know how to make a cobbler."

"Mary John will show you tomorrow. There's really nothing to it. It's easy. You girls will just have to pick the berries first."

Tallie silently mocked their assumptions. Sure it's easy! They think everything is easy and anyone can do it. It's easier to go buy one. Maggie Hay parked the car and looked at the moon. There were three rings around it which could mean rain. That could make some difference in the berry picking she thought and decided she would asked her husband's opinion. After a quick rundown on Aunt Jenny's condition she did just that.

"Do you think it will rain tomorrow, John?" she asked her husband.

"It could. I do feel better that Tom and I got the hay stacked.

You might want to watch the forecast. They do get it right once in a while," he laughed, "but his Hay is going to hit the hay."

"You're tired from trying to keep up with young Tom, and foolish to try to. Confession is good for the soul. Admit it. You overdid it, didn't you, Reverend?" Maggie poked her husband for added emphasis.

"Now Mama, I may not work as fast, but I work smarter and longer than most of the young ones."

"Pooh!" Mrs. Hay said to him and turned to Mary John to ask if she knew where that bottle of Rawleigh liniment might be.

"I didn't know we had any," Mary John said.

"Speaking of medicine, I put some antibacterial ointment on Tom's face," the Pastor said. When I asked him about that scratch over his eye, he said a wild cat scratched him. Reckon?"

The ensuing silence was heavy. Tallie figited but finally spoke.

"I hit him in the face with the broom."

No one responded.

She added. "I hit him with the straw end. I didn't mean to hurt him. I hit him with the straw end because I thought the handle would be worse."

"Was it worth it--hitting him?" asked the pastor.

"What do you mean?" Tallie asked. "He asked for it."

"What did it cost you, and what did you get? Don't answer, just think about that," said the Pastor.

Tallie thought about it all right. She couldn't sleep. All she understood was that once again, she had incurred disapproval. Tired of rolling around and around in the bed, she quietly walked through the house to the front porch.

"Oh! Sorry. I thought you all were going to bed" she said to the pastor who was sitting on the porch spring eating a bowl of Jell-O while his wife clipped coupons from the newspaper. Tallie turned to leave.

"Want some?" he asked.

"No. No, thanks. I'm not hungry."

"You're having trouble sleeping, I reckon."

"A little."

"Me too. Sore joints" the pastor said.

"But I suspect your problem is bad dreams,right?" Mrs. Hay interjected.

"Sometimes. Real goofy stuff ever since I got to Aunt Jenny's."

"The Lord sometimes stirs me with a dream", the pastor said. I used to have some pretty wild dreams when I was about your age: Things chasing me, snakes chasing me, running from danger with heavy legs, falling off high places."

"Me, too," Tallie said and watched the pastor lick the back of his spoon.

"I have a notion that dreams of that sort are caused by needs. A need is a hunger, and we haven't identified what our real hunger is, so the dream is trying to help us get the answer," said the Pastor.

"I dreamed of spiders trying to crawl on me last night," Tallie said, "and I've dreamed of gates being shut and wind storms, and being left behind."

"It's not easy being your age. You haven't been alive long enough to have a great deal of experience in living. It takes time to get some understanding. I remember when I was about your age, I felt like everyone nagged me, felt like I couldn't tie my shoelaces to suit anyone."

"I know all about that." Tallie said.

"Inside, I thought I was a pretty good Joe, but no one else seemed to think so."

"Me, too," Tallie sighed. "I didn't want to hurt Tom, but he was making fun of me and I couldn't stand it, so I hit him." The pastor looked at her but made no remark about her comment and went on with his own experiences.

"I had a run-in with my ball coach when I was a boy. He benched me, and things went from bad to worse that summer. I wound up hating the human race and decided to let my ball coach and my dad go to thunderation. That's when Dad sent me over to Aunt Jenny's to work. You didn't know that, did you, Mamma? "

"I'll declare! No, sir, I didn't." Mrs. Hay remarked.

"Well it's the truth. She used to raise crops in that pasture behind her house, and when I wasn't chopping cotton and corn, I had to chop Johnsongrass out of the corner of the garden. That was the worst stuff I ever tackled."

Mrs. Hay laughed, and so did Tallie.

"Me, too, Tallie admitted. She has me out there nearly every day chopping that stuff. It grows back overnight."

The pastor smiled knowingly. "Anyway, before summer was over, I got down on my knees in that high stand of grass and told God I was at the end of my string and He could take over from here on out. I told Him I was a little scared, a lot angry, and tired of trying to please the world."

"What happened then?"

"A right good number of things, but He took over. And you know what? I have had only one person to please ever since. A lot of burdensome junk lined up like ducks and flew south. Things aren't always easy, but I have an easiness inside--a peacefulness that sure is nice.

"Really?" Tallie asked.

"Maybe God is trying to get through to you in those dreams, Tallie, Mrs. Hay said. You are a beloved part of His creation. You might as well get on your knees and save yourself a bunch of misery by turning yourself over to Him. It's that simple, but it is all up to you. I have done that. Everyone in this house has as well as most of the church. I was terribly shy. Still a thumbsucker in first grade that grew into a teenager with a gap between her front teeth. I did not want anyone to come very near to me or look at me. Trusting God was one of the hardest things I ever had to do. First, I confessed my fears to God. Then one day, I presented myself to him publicly at church. My knees were shaking but I did it." She picked up the pastor's empty bowl and spoon and, without looking at either of them, said they'd better call it a day.

In the bedroom, Tallie stared at the ceiling and thought about their conversation. It seemed foolish not to give God a real chance, she decided. She knelt and looked out the window at the night sky.

"God, help me," she whispered. "I'm a seed, aren't I? Will You please open the gate to me? Will You plant me? Will You please plug me in and glue me together? Even if no one else likes me, I hope You will learn to like me. She felt tears coming and let them fall. I'm sorry I hit Tom. I feel like I'm on the outside looking in and I hate it.

I used to be sort of smart, but I don't know if I am any more. I feel pretty stupid. Do You take care of all that kind of stuff? I hope so? But even if You don't, even if I'm bored, even if my life falls apart or is totally boring, I want You to be the one in charge. I mean it; I really mean it. Amen."

She got off her knees feeling empty, but somehow better. Pastor had said that God leads people into adventures and she wondered if He was planning any for her.

Friday was fun for Tallie. She had never been blackberry picking before. Mary John explained several things about berry picking, such as wearing long sleeved shirts and rubbing sulfur powder from ankles to ears, not missing any of the 'little cracks and crevices' to avoid chigger bites which are extremely itchy. By mid-morning, two white, enameled buckets wagged at their sides on the way to the berry vines. Mary John said the berry bushes had come from Aunt Jenny's place several years ago when she said she had to cut back on caring for so many of them, and that it was the favorite berry of the Raider family. Mary John also explained that she preferred not to put berries into a tin bucket because the rough surface would bruise and scrape the fruit and give them a tinny taste.

Even though the vines occasionally managed to grab their clothes and scratch them through their shirts, and the gnats came to do their warting, the girls paid little attention as they filled their buckets and sometimes, their mouths. Tallie decided it was best not to mention gnats or vine scrapes. Complaining and whining wasn't heard at the Hay's place.

When the buckets were about halfway full, Mary John suggested they see who could fill their bucket first. It was to be a race while yodeling with the stipulation that they must yodel without stopping, or the race would be forfeited.

Tallie simply sang the yodeling syllables at first, picking the plump berries as fast as she could, thrusting her arms among the vines with as much expertise as possible to keep from getting scraped by the briars. As her confidence increased, she attempted to truly yodel, pushing away the memory of Tom's laughter. She experimented at bouncing the notes with her Adam's apple. Loudly and horribly, she struggled to find the right technique. Mary John's own yodeling faltered and she fought for control, but the laughter finally broke through. Tallie kept on squawking and wailing away until her bucket was heaped with berries.

It was the first time in her life that she had won any sort of race, and it felt good. It felt good, too, to win on someone else's turf by their rules, and to laugh deep and hard about the whole thing. Picking berries for a cobbler to celebrate her aunt's homecoming was fun, but that was Mrs. Hay's idea. Tallie had a couple of ideas of her very own to pursue.

~~~~~~~~~~~~~~

On Saturday morning, Tallie's first waking thoughts were of the best and most important thing for Aunt Jenny's homecoming. She and Mary John had worked to get everything ready, but one last thing remained.

"God, please help me. I need a bathtub." She earnestly whispered the prayer on her knees before dressing, before going down the hall to help do all that needed to be done prior to going to town.

Mary John decided to help Tallie sell squash in Aunt Jenny's booth at the Trade Fair as well as some of her own blackberries packaged neatly into little boxes decorated with calico bows. A good thing since people came by in droves to ask about Aunt Jenny. Tallie got tired of telling the same story wishing she had written it all out with copies to distribute. Most of the people had been to see her aunt, but wanted to hear the whole story, just the same. The whole town seemed to be comparing notes. If Tallie skipped a detail they had heard third-hand, they pressed for verification.

Mary John was glad for the inquirers and did a brisk business selling berries. The hail damage caused produce to be higher in price. Even jams and jellies went as fast as people could place them on the counter. Tallie, however, had not sold one book and very little squash. Mary John suggested that customers seemed to like the smaller squash better than the big ones, but that big ones could be used in cakes, breads, and for stuffing, if they had the recipes.

"Why don't you write out a recipe then, and I'll find some cards and copy some after I make a phone call, okay?" Tallie asked and without waiting for an answer, she hurried away to call the hardware store.

"Do you have one of those old-fashioned, metal bathtubs?" she asked. The voice replied that they had not stocked those in twenty years and doubted that one could even be ordered anymore.

Momentarily, she thought she would cry, but then an idea came to her. How much does a regular, modern bathtub cost?" she asked. "Oh!" she exclaimed., "Do you have anything cheaper? ...I see. On sale already? ...No. I just wanted to check. Thanks."

Six dollars was not buying any bathtub today. She needed ninety-seven more. Tallie returned to the booth. Mary John had sold all but three rather large squash using the recipes. The berries were gone long ago. Tallie thanked her and suggested they go shut down.

"No, let's wait a little bit," Mary John said. "I'll go look around and who knows, maybe I can shoo someone over to buy the rest of your squash."

Tallie stood the books upright next to the remaining squash hoping to attract a potential buyer. The pencil drawing inside the geology book fluttered to the floor. She propped it up against the wall hoping it might bring a dollar. It was a good drawing. Meanwhile, she opened the book on snakes trying to look engrossed to entice others to browse the books.

"You like that book?" a child's voice asked.

"I sure do," Tallie responded.

"I did-dent. It gave me nightmares."

"You'd better not stand here looking at it then, little kid."

The little boy ran off and Tallie's hunch that the books had been around a long time was confirmed. She sighed, gathered up the books from sheer embarrassment, and ducked under the counter to hide them.

"Say! Is anyone here?" It was a heavy, masculine voice.

Tallie scrambled from under the counter. "Yes. May I help you?" Tallie asked the well-rounded, middle-aged man.

"Possibly. That's a nice pencil drawing you have there. Is it for sale?"

Tallie looked him over carefully. He looked prosperous enough and seemed in the buying mood since he carried several parcels. She thought about asking ten dollars for the drawing and if he balked, she would come down to five.

"I like that picture," she began. "I'm not really sure I want to sell it, but we've had some unexpected expenses due to a recent storm and I thought I might sell if the price is right."

"What kind of price do you have in mind?" he asked with a smile. He shifted his feet and seemed to be in a hurry..

"How about nine-fifty? I don't think that's too much to ask for it," she said.

"Do you mind if I look at it?" He fidgeted some more.

Scared of losing her customer, she quickly countered her own offer. "I'll take nine and throw in the squash."

"Will you take a check?" he asked.

"We usually deal in cash around here, but if you have a driver's license with a picture on it, I guess it will be okay." Tallie had already decided to sic Sheriff Sawyer onto him if the check was bad, and wished she knew where his car was so she could get his license plate number. Tallie had the odd feeling that he could read her mind because he was grinning as he wrote the check. Over the customer's head, she saw Tom Sawyer and it looked like he was coming her way. Yes! It was. She snatched the check up from the counter and pushed the squash and drawing toward the man who seemed equally glad to be done with his shopping as he hurried away.

Tom was definitely making his way toward her, stopping now and then exchanging words with some of the people who were milling around the pavilion. Tallie turned her back quickly to engage in an overdone version of busyness, packing and tidying. She sure didn't want him to think she was anticipating his visit.

"Is that a witch? Surely not. She doesn't have a broom," Tom said, and he walked right on by.

"That makes it your lucky day, doesn't it?" She shouted at his back.

Everything was packed and ready to be loaded when Mary John returned.

"Oh, good. You sold all your squash," she said.

"I really didn't sell it, I sold a drawing and threw the squash in as a come-on."

"Let's figure up how much we got." Mary John said and poured coins and dollars from a pint jar.

Tallie handed Mary John the old purse she used, told her how much she had in it at the beginning of the day, and asked her to sort it all out while she carried the boxes to the Hay's car.

"Oh, Wow! Mary John exclaimed. "What a day!"

"You can say that again," Tallie mumbled, trying to look over the large boxes in her arms. A whole nine dollars and something, right?"

"Nine? And then some, unless I can't read. This check says nine-hundred dollars."

Tallie dropped the boxes and grabbed the check. "This must be a joke or a mistake or something. Find the sheriff. Maybe he can catch this... thief," she looked at the name on the check, "this Mr. Jorbison."

But Mr. Jorbison had disappeared. Mary John brought Sheriff Sawyer back to speak to Tallie and suggested that she take the check to the bank as soon as possible and have it verified. Mary John found her parents in the crowd outside the pavilion and told them about the check. The pastor agreed they should do what Sheriff Sawyer said. He chuckled at the news of the big check.

Tallie and Mary John loaded their empty boxes into the Hay's car and they all drove immediately to the bank. Tallie prepared herself for the loss of both the squash and the picture. She handed the check to the cashier and asked him to call the out-of-town bank to see if it would bounce. The cashier disappeared into a private office for three minutes or less, but it seemed much longer to her before he reappeared. When he did, he was expressionless.

"Do you want to cash this now or deposit it? He asked.

Tallie felt light headed and tingly.

"It is a good check? No lie?" She asked.

The clerk smiled and repeated "No lie. It is not a forgery, and we've never had a Jorbison check bounce at this bank."

"I want the cash, please."

Tallie ran, hopping and skipping, to the car waving the cash to the cheers of the Hay family.

"Isn't it something how the Lord provides?" the Pastor remarked to Tallie.

"He provided a long time ago, then. I've had that picture ever since I first came to the Trade Fair." She went on to explain that it was hidden in an old geology book in a box of books no one else wanted to buy.

"He'll give thee treasures, hidden treasures of the darkness." quoted Pastor Hay.

Tallie looked at the Pastor wondering what in the world he was talking about.

"There is always a blessed remnant," the pastor said.

Tallie had no idea what he was saying and wondered if anyone else understood what he was talking about.

Mary John grabbed the back of the seat and leaned close to her dad's ear. "This wouldn't have to be the only treasure, would it? I mean, God might have something else for the remnant, right?"

"Yea, verily!" Pastor said, "But what fun to find out if this is one, Daughter. It's like being a bird dog following his nose."

Tallie held nine one-hundred dollar bills and stared at them.

"I'll de-clare!" Mrs. Hay said.

"What are you going to buy first?" Mary John asked.

Tallie folded one of the bills and placed it in her billfold.

"That one is for a rainy day," she explained. It was the Hays family's turn to be mystified by what she meant.

"What are you going to buy? A new dress? A TV?" Mary John asked again.

"Nope. I'm going to buy a bathtub." Let them laugh, she thought. It was then she explained about the tub to Mary John's parents and how hard they had searched but no tub was found.

"Maybe you will please help me get it out to Aunt Jenny's. We can use her truck to haul it", Tallie suggested.

Mrs. Hay frowned.

"Honey, I don't think they even make those any more. You might get a little round one, but Aunt Jenny couldn't get down in it too well, I'd think."

"I know that. I'm going to get a real one. And I'm going to hook a hose to it to drain the water into something. That way, Aunt Jenny can use the tub until she gets her house plumbed, if you all will take me over to the appliance store."

Tallie picked out a gleaming white, claw-footed tub and six decorative, daisy-shaped foot grippers for the bottom to prevent falls on the slick surface. When the owners heard it was for Aunt Jenny's homecoming, they added a fluffy, white, bath rug for free. Pastor Hay selected a good length of rubber hose and suggested he go with one of the plumbers who would haul everything to the farm and get it installed all in one trip.

"You girls can go on and do your shopping before you pick up Aunt Jenny. That will give us time to get it done before you get there," Pastor said.

It seemed to Tallie that Mary John and Mrs. Hay took forever to poke around buying fabric and browsing the clothing racks, and lollygagging through the grocery store even though she knew that Pastor Hay and the delivery man needed time to get the tub in place before they arrived home.

Tallie was anxious that the homecoming would be a success. She checked her memory.

Yes, she gave the house key to the pastor. Yes, she told him where to put the tub and hoped he would remember; and everything else had been done little by little all last week. The cobbler was made. Then finally, after a lot of shopping and very little buying, they went to collect Aunt Jenny who was already dressed and sitting in a chair in her room.

The nurse insisted on pushing her to the car in a wheelchair. Aunt Jenny balked and protested only to give in when the nurse said it was hospital policy and if she wanted to go home, she had better sit down. Mrs. Hay and Mary John loaded the flowers and Tallie carried her aunt's personal things. Aunt Jenny sat in the back seat drinking in the country as if she had been gone a year.

"I'll tell you for sure," she said,"I don't know how townsfolk sleep. Something toots, clangs, screeches, or whistles every two minutes. I love the quiet of the country."

"Oh, I reckon town folk get used to it," Mrs. Hay said. "My cousin complains about the noise every time she visits us. The roosters crow before sun up, the dogs yap at things in the night. Why, I remember the first time she came here, she stepped onto the porch and a tree full of locusts began to sing. Alfred Hitchcock would have been proud of her. She threw her hands over her head and screamed and ran back inside like they were after her. And we really don't notice them much, do we?"

Aunt Jenny sat back and folded her arms. "I'll take the background music of the locusts over revving motors and squealing tires any day. A garbage truck backed up right under my window every morning at ten a.m. Beep, beep. I don't think I'd ever get used to all that racket in town. Not to change the subject, but where is the pastor? I hope someone isn't bad sick."

Mrs. Hay grinned and nudged Tallie." He's out to your place opening up the house so it will be nice and cool and aired by the time you get there. And there was a little chore he wanted to do for you."

Aunt Jenny frowned a little wondering if Tallie had not properly done the chores.

"Aunt Jenny, guess what." Tallie quickly interrupted. "We sold out this morning."

"What did you find to sell after that awful storm? Hailstones? Or my gallstones?" she asked and laughed.

"We had blackberries," Mary John said, "and Tallie kept just enough for you a cobbler pie. She even made it all by herself."

"You showed me how," Tallie quickly added.

"Praise be! My mouth is a-watering already." Aunt Jenny wondered if her garden had enough produce to keep her the rest of the summer and asked how bad off the garden was, thinking that Tallie might have tried to cover up the extent of the damage.

Tallie told her, again, that the squash was still growing, that some of the beans had bloomed but the grasshoppers were chewing on the leaves, that two of the tomato plants were surviving, and the onions were doing all right and making larger bulbs in the ground.

"It pays to can a little extra on good years. I'll eat this winter," Aunt Jenny said.

When Mrs. Hay headed the sedan through the open gate and down the horseshoe drive, Aunt Jenny stuck her head out the window as far as she could lean, assessing everything she could see.

"Look at that! Look at that!" Aunt Jenny pointed toward the flower bed in the middle of the horseshoe drive. "Who did that? Did you do that, Maggie?"

"No. Tallie did. I didn't see it until yesterday when I delivered the cobbler. The flower project was her own idea and she fixed it up all up by herself." -

Aunt Jenny looked at the flower bed where Tallie had hit the zinnias with the water bucket. All the flowers ruined by the hail had been removed. The good ones had been watered and cultivated. Three geraniums surrounding a small rose bush had been added. The surviving flowers looked like orphans compared to what used to be there, but a new start was better than nothing.

"How wonderful! How beautiful!" Aunt Jenny exclaimed. When they parked the car, she went over for a closer look, leaning down to touch them gently.

"I got the geraniums and rose starter from Mrs. Hay," Tallie said.

"She paid me," Maggie said, "and insisted on it, Aunt Jenny. I have quite a few flowers in pots, but I can't put out much of anything like that in my beds. The dogs wallow them down and what they don't wallow, they dig up. But that rose there is a root start from my big white bush and it needed to be moved anyway." Maggie Hay watched Aunt Jenny gently shake Tallie by the shoulders, called her a little toot and hugged her close, and kissed the top of Tallie's head.

"You'd better get on in and sit down, Aunt Jenny," Tallie said. "I'll help unload your stuff."

Aunt Jenny walked slowly toward the house and noticed the delivery van parked in the back. "Whose truck is that? I was so busy looking at the flowers I didn't even see it."

Mary John grinned and said that her daddy came out in it.

"What on earth is he up to?" Aunt Jenny asked. She put her hands on her knees and slowly walked up the steps with Tallie's help. If I'm seeing right, that's the truck from Gate's Hardware & Appliance," Aunt Jenny said and stopped on the porch to let her hand drag across the wicker rocker. How good it was to touch the things of home, she thought, reaching the screen door. Inside her own kitchen, she unconsciously took a deep breath and let it out slowly, ridding herself of a week's worth of townish miasma and hospital disinfectant.

"Oh, look," she said, seeing the vase of fresh wild flowers on the table. "It looks so pretty and clean here. So fresh. Not at all like it has been shut up for a week. I half expected the field mice to have taken the place over– them and the cobwebs."

The noise of the van leaving coincided with the pastor peeking his head through the curtains that separated the back porch from the kitchen. "Come and see," he said.

"Did the storm pull the screen door off the hinges back there?" Aunt Jenny asked.

"You'll have to come and see." The Pastor stepped into the kitchen, bowed and pointed to the curtains.

Aunt Jenny used some dramatics of her own as she looked sideways at the others for a hint of what was waiting behind the curtains. She raised her eyebrows even higher, pursed her lips , and stepped slowly to the curtain. . She stood still and hesitated while she relished the mystery and stretched the anticipation of all of them as much as she could before carefully opening the curtains to the back porch.

"Look at that! Of all things! Isn't that a lick? Praise be! Who's anointed head got that fine idea?" Aunt Jenny clapped her hands over her mouth and then to her chest. "How wonderful, Pastor," she said, turning to thank him.

"No, not I. This was Tallie's anointed idea. All I did was talk to the plumber and help do some lifting."

"Did you really think all this up by yourself?" she asked Tallie.

"I thought of a real bathtub, but I never thought of putting a water spigot in a barrel and on a stand like that. That's as big a surprise to me as it is to you," Tallie answered.

"Look," the pastor said and began to show how they had put a hole in the rain barrel and fitted it with a faucet to turn the water on and off. A small piece of hose was attached to the drain which could be coiled and tucked under the bathtub when not in use. The barrel could hold extra water in winter as well, or be filled from town if the well went dry.

"That's the fanciest workings I ever saw," Aunt Jenny said.

"Well," the pastor replied scratching his unruly hair, "I don't know about that, but it'll do until you get a better rigging."

Maggie Hay insisted Aunt Jenny had stood up long enough and insisted she rest in a chair.

"You're going to have to fight the urge not to overdo while you're recovering," Mrs. Hay said.

"I can tell that a-ready, Miz Maggie. And I'm forgetting my manners. Let me offer you some of that cobbler I've been hearing about and something cool to drink. Tallie, could you do the honors? And serve it on the porch, please. I've been shut up like a pill in a box far too long. I want to eat my cobbler and enjoy my new flowers and the outdoors all at the same time."

Tallie served her aunt the finest portion she could, which was the one with the crispier, buttery, sugary top and added lots of rich juice from the filling. Aunt Jenny looked at it skeptically and back at Tallie before taking a bite. She tasted it slowly and seemed to study the flavors and texture. She swallowed while Tallie waited in anticipation.

"It's fittin', girls. Real fittin'. In fact, you've no idea how good this tastes to me. Lord have Mercy! Is this ever good."

Mary John nudged Tallie in the ribs to second the declaration, and Tallie was relieved that her efforts had been acceptable. In fact, she felt good about all that she had done to make her aunt's homecoming pleasant. But when the Hay family left, she noticed her aunt droop wearily against the back of the wicker rocker.

"Why don't you go rest a little bit like the doctor said. I'll get a head start on the chores," Tallie said. Aunt Jenny made no objection.

Jube flapped his wings and strutted when Tallie entered the barnyard. He dashed in her direction twice, careful not to get too close to her.

"Jube, you think you're a royal rooster because you look like one, but you're really a tacky turkey. I have to feed you first just like those women at the church feeding the men first, just to get them fed and out the way." She laughed.

After the chickens were fed and fresh water poured in the

trough, she put hay in old Janet's bin. Finally, she filled and carried two buckets of water back to the house where she discovered her aunt sound asleep.

Tallie quietly set a kettle on to boil and went to the garden where she found two tomatoes, a big batch of squash, several cucumbers, and the first picking of a few okra pods which, she discovered, had to be cut from the stalk with a knife. By the time she returned to the kitchen, her hands and arms were burning and stinging like a million microscopic ant bites. She tried washing her arms but the stinging persisted, so she prayed.

"God help me. I've been poisoned by something." and even though she was concerned how long it might last or if it would make her sick or cause her to break out in sores, she went on washing the vegetables to cook for supper. She had seen her mom fry okra and remembered that besides salt and pepper, it should be dredged in cornmeal mixed with a dab of cornstarch. The fragrance of frying okra summoned Aunt Jenny from sleep and to the kitchen. Tallie was rubbing her arms while trying to set the table.

"Are your arms bothering you?" Aunt Jenny asked.

"I think I've been poisoned by something."

"Have you ever picked okra before?"

"No. Mom buys ours at the grocery."

"When you pick okra, you'd best wear a long-sleeved shirt and gloves. Okra and peaches, too, are good to make a-body sting. It takes an hour or more for it to wear off of its ownself, but you can take some of that cucumber rind and smear it over your skin. That'll help."

Tallie rubbed herself with the cucumber rinds, relieved to know it was not something serious nor would it last long.

When they sat down to dinner, Aunt Jenny asked Tallie what they should take to the church dinner.

"Church dinner! You can't go to church."

"I don't know why not. I've been dismissed from the hospital and it's not like having to do a day's laundry on the scrub board to sit in church. So, let's decide."

"I have no idea what to take. "I'm not even sure you should go. I think I'll call your doctor and ask him."

"He won't care what we take to the church dinner," Aunt Jenny replied.

"That isn't what I meant, and you know it."Aunt Jenny smiled a bit. " I was just being smart. I want to go and if I get tired, well, we'll come home."

"Or if I decide we should come home. I don't want any more nights like that other one that landed you in the hospital, okay?"

"Okay. I'll try not to be a burden or cause you any fright. Now, what is handy around here that we can stir up into something good?"

"There is squash and plenty of it. A few onions, but the only meat that is thawed is a little bacon," Tallie said.

Aunt Jenny thought a bit. "I have some bell peppers frozen up. The more I think about what is handy, the more it sounds like a pan of cornbread dressing. What do you think?"

"Squash doesn't sound like dressing to me."

"Tallie, people put everything in the world in dressing. Why, I even heard of someone finding a dishrag in it one time...not on purpose though."

"Yuck! That sounds like something from the Three Stooges." Then she remembered chasing a bite of Mary John's squash with cornbread.

Her aunt went to the cabinet and found the Caddo County Cookbook which she suggested they follow as long as they did not overload it with small cubes of squash. Tallie silently seconded the latter idea.

"Savory Summer dressing. That's the very thing," Aunt Jenny said. Let's get it made."

"I'll do it and you can tell me how, okay? Besides, I thought you might like to try out your new bathtub while I cook."

"I don't think you can imagine how grand a gift that is to me. I'd never have thought of rigging up the water supply like that. I'm even thinking of getting a hot water heater and some plumbing after I see what my medical bills are." Well", she said, pushing herself up from the table, "If you can handle it in here, I think I'll go try out that new tub."

The sweet smelling bubble bath and warm water were a pure pleasure and she sat in the tub the whole time Tallie prepared the squash dish. Every now and then, Tallie ran to the back porch for a consultation. The casserole smelled good as it baked. A good sign, they decided and when it came out of the oven, they were pleased with the looks.

"What is that?" Aunt Jenny asked when Tallie pulled out a second, smaller dish.

"That is our taste-tester dish. I'll make something else if this doesn't taste right. Here, you try it."

Aunt Jenny took a bite and gave Tallie no visible or audible clues as to its worth.

"Well?" Tallie asked.

"You try it and see what you think."

Tallie timidly took a bite. "It's not too bad, is it?"

"No," Aunt Jenny said,"and tomorrow, it will be even better. Dressing gets better as it ages."

"I hope so," Tallie replied.

"Tallie," Aunt Jenny asked quietly, "how did you happen to come by enough money for that tub. It is a wonderful gift, but I cannot help but be curious."

Tallie explained about the drawing she sold.

"And," she added, "I have the rest of the money upstairs. I didn't think to ask how much it would cost to get the real plumbing done. I was only thinking about getting the tub. It was my fault the other one blew away, and Mary John and I have ridden horses all over this place looking for it. We can't find it anywhere."

"Why do you think it was your fault that the old tub blew away?"

"I couldn't open the screen door. It was stuck. So I left the tub to go inside to try to open the door. On my way around the house, the mailman honked and I went out there. Then I got all involved in reading my mail and forgot the tub was in the backyard"

"That's purely understandable. And I'm glad it blew off. I might never have gotten rid of it myself. It's easy to get set in one's way. You have more than made up for the loss of that old tub. As for the plumbing, I'll manage that," and she gave Tallie a big hug.

"How will you manage? The garden is pretty shot. You don't have very much stuff to sell."

"I've lived long enough to know that God makes a way. I'll have all that I need. To tell you the truth, He even throws in a few extras just to let me know He can. No, I've learned there is always a remnant, a seed, something to prime the pump so to speak, and it multiplies and suffices. Sometimes, I have to look or hunt, or reach hard, but I get it right on time. And speaking of time, we'd better get to bed. I'm looking forward to tomorrow."

Tallie lay in bed and decided that the new tub was really nice, but also realized that she would miss bathing outside by the lilac bushes. I mean, really. Who did she know that had ever had such an experience? You couldn't get by with that in St. Louis.

What was that? Her Aunt Jenny talking? Praying, she guessed, and yawned and went to sleep, presently dreaming she was holding onto a piece of cloth imprinted with lilacs. The cloth grew long, changed to green then to very black velvet. It undulated and flowed down the stairs, out the back door, down the steps into the yard and out of sight.

Chapter Eight: Milking: a Cow, a Hat, and a Long Prayer

Jube's crowing awakened Tallie, a reminder that the chores would have to be done all by herself. As usual, her aunt was already in the kitchen drinking coffee but still in her nightgown, something Tallie had never seen before. Usually, she put on the dress she had worn the evening before, did her morning chores, and then freshened up just before lunch time. Saving all her strength for church, Tallie decided. She asked her aunt if she was planning on cooking something for breakfast.

"No, just a little toast. I know that if I started lifting more than I should, I might rip a stitch and you'd be just as ripped to boot."

"Good thinking," Tallie said and nodded her approval.

"That's my line, Missy."

Tallie repressed a smile and went to draw water, gather eggs, feed chickens, and then to confront Janet. Janet rolled her brown eyes around and stared back.

"You expect to be milked, don't you? Well, we're both in for a treat." Tallie reluctantly pulled the short stool in place with her foot, hesitating to sit down. Janet swung her head around munching a wad of hay and stared at Tallie with a look of disdain and impatience.

"Okay, okay! Don't act so snooty," Tallie responded. She placed a bucket under Janet's distended udder and sat down.

"This is disgusting," she muttered and made herself take hold of one of the teats. She pulled. Nothing. She pulled again. Nothing. Janet swished her tail right into Tallie's face. Tallie grimaced and dodged while pulling on the teats with both hands. Again, Janet swished her tail and slapped Tallie soundly in the face.

"That's enough of that!" Tallie yelled and got up from the stool. She took a piece of twine and tied a monkey wrench to Janet's tail.

"Now, try swinging that around, you bossy old bag." Satisfied that she had solved the tail problem, Tallie began to actually obtain some milk for her efforts. She was proud of the good amount that was collecting in the silver bucket. The very moment she smiled with pride, Janet lifted her tail, monkey wrench and all, and let go a gush of urine that splashed into the milk as well as on Tallie who jumped and screamed.

Janet shied, stuck her foot in the milk bucket and hit Tallie in the head with the wrench, all at the same time. Tallie pushed on Janet to make her take her foot out of the bucket but Janet wouldn't budge. Tallie's head was throbbing in pain, and the small amount of patience she had was stretched to the limit.

"If you don't get your foot out of there, I'm going to bite your leg!" Tallie yelled. She slapped Janet hard as she could on the rump with the palm of her hand and got a broken blood vessel in the process, but Janet withdrew her foot. Tallie poured out the urinized milk dreading to tell her aunt what happened.

Aunt Jenny was not in the kitchen but had eaten and left some toast on the table for Tallie. Tallie looked at the knot on her forehead in a mirror over the washstand. She bathed it in cool water, sighed and sat down to eat the cold toast.

"What do you think?" Aunt Jenny stood in the doorway to the kitchen pointing to the brim of a very large, white, lacy hat garnished with a great variety of flowers and bows.

Tallie stared. If her aunt had appeared in a mohawk hair cut, it would not have startled her any more than that hat.

"Well?" Aunt Jenny asked again.

"It sure is—interesting—-and—-uh—colorful."

"Good! That is the very effect I was after."

"Do you mean you are really and truly going to wear that today?"

"Certainly. I'm celebrating. These flowers and ribbons are off the bouquets folks sent me. I want to squeeze all the good out of them I can, so I pinned them on my hat." Suddenly, Aunt Jenny forgot her hat and squinted her eyes at Tallie. "What in the world have you done to your forehead?"

"I got it milking, but I'm okay. Janet hit me with her tail and then she stepped in the milk bucket, so we don't have any milk. I hope that's not a problem."

"Since when did you learn to milk?"

"Since this morning."

"Great Day! I was going to call Claude Worth to come do that while we were at church."

"Who is Claude Worth?" Tallie asked.

"He is my tenant just north of here on the other side of the road. Well, so be it. I'm just as glad not to call him. You'd better go up and get ready or we'll be late. I'm going to let you drive us this morning and we don't want to go too fast. Oh, that reminds me. Sheriff Sawyer came to see me in the hospital and gave me an emergency permit for you to use till I feel like doing the driving."

Tallie went to dress. "Not go too fast? She doesn't remember going over that bridge, I guess."

Aunt Jenny was the center of attention, hat and all—especially the hat. Even Alice Fursby was more interested in the hat than in rehashing the gallbladder operation or giving out medical advice. Tallie smiled. Finally, she understood the hidden reason for wearing the elaborate thing. It derailed Alice and all the others who wanted her to relive the hospital event. Nor did she want to hear long stories from others who'd been hospitalized. Her intention was to honor everyone that came to see her in the hospital. Tallie stood back and watched her aunt in rare form entertaining the crowd.

"These daisies were from the Thompsons. This big bow was on the zinnias Judy Jenkins brought. She grows the sweetest dwarf zinnias I ever--. Oh those? They are called sweet William, and this is mock orange. I put it on the side so that every time I turn my head, I can smell the fragrance....Sure, take a big sniff. Isn't that lovely? Joyce Parks sent that in a mixed bouquet. I know she selected every single flower herself because she has such good taste. This big, pink rose is from Maggie Hay's garden. I just love the delicate color. Yes, that big, silver bow with the glitter was on a basket of French fries from Noodle and Hub."

Tallie laughed quietly to herself. She knew that her aunt had not been allowed to eat those greasy French fries. The nurses ate them. Then, Aunt Jenny called Tallie's name, and when she looked, Alice Fursby was headed in her direction and Aunt Jenny right behind her.

"Good morning, Tallie," Alice said. "You've been a good little nurse to hear your aunt tell it. If you need any help, now, you be sure to give me a —--what on earth! What have you done to yourself?" Alice asked. She grabbed Tallie's face and rubbed the knot which had swollen to some size above her left eye. "How on earth did you do that, child?"

"She's not a child, Alice. She drove me here this morning on an emergency permit, and you know the sheriff wouldn't allow a child at the wheel."

"Did you bump yourself while driving that bouncy old truck?" Alice asked, her brows knitted together in concern.

"No. I was milking when it happened."

"Oh?" Alice was puzzled and eager for more details, but Tallie quickly excused herself.

"Alice, let her be. I didn't ask her, but I think she tried doing what many a first-time milker has tried," Aunt Jenny quietly said.

"Oh, do tell!" Alice exclaimed. She delighted in being a confidante, especially since it was not something Aunt Jenny often afforded her. "You mean she weighted the cow's tail?"

"I reckon, or cut the hair off of it. I haven't looked at Janet yet. But a weighted tail or a nekked tail can raise a hearty knot."

They laughed together which also pleased Alice as much as carrying both casseroles to the kitchen. In fact, Alice couldn't remember anyone else ever getting to carry any of Aunt Jenny's dishes to the kitchen before. It was nice to be doing one's part. Then Aunt Jenny gave an unintended little laugh after glancing at Alice.

"What's so funny?" Alice asked.

"On, nothing. I was just thinking," Aunt Jenny said, actually amused at Alice parading to the dining hall with the casseroles. Alice laughed too, supposing that Jenny was picturing her cow with no hair on its tail.

Tallie hung around the church keeping an eye out for Tom Sawyer, but he was nowhere to be seen, which was okay, she told herself as her aunt called and motioned for her to come inside. When they took their places in the pew, Tallie began to meditate on what her aunt had said about the Lord's providing.

Had He? Does He always give back to people something that gets taken from them, maybe even something better or different from that which was lost? Had He? What about the bathtub? Neither of us has gone without access to one during the whole ordeal. And the remaining garden produce, and that old hat filled with flowers and bows sitting on a head that was too sick to even hold up a hat last week, what about all of that? How much of that was gotten by our own efforts and how much of it was from the Lord?

She thought back over the coincidence of the drawing being in that old book that had been bought, sold, and traded all over Sawed Off Corners. Did anyone bother to examine the books?

And if that tub had not blown away, I doubt I would have spent any of my money on a bathtub for her. The garden, too, is coming back enough to keep her in vegetables to eat and maybe a few extra to sell. That's too many coincidences, she thought.

Pastor Hay called the meeting together with an opening prayer, and when the singing was over, the offering plate was passed. Tallie placed an envelope in it and thought her aunt was almost smiling. It was kind of fun for a change to let her guess at what was being put in the plate, especially since it didn't rattle like a little dab of change. Then more seriously, Tallie reminded God that her aunt didn't have any proper plumbing. Alice Fursby finished the offertory solo with an improvised flourish. The Pastor thanked her and leaned over the little book-stand of a pulpit.

"We sure had us a storm, didn't we? Any damage out to your place, Will?" asked the Pastor.

"Some."

"Lose anything?"

"A good many green pecans blew off the trees."

"Are all of them gone?"

"No, sir. A few are still hanging on," Will replied. "There's a remnant, then?"

"I reckon that's right."

Pastor Hay shifted his gaze to Floyd Fursby.

"How about out to your place, Floyd?"

"We're missing a few shingles on the barn and part of the wife's garden is washed out in places."

"Some of this and part of that. Not all of it. Maybe those shingles had worked loose over the years; maybe they'd got old and wore out and needed replacing. Flood water gone wild usually takes a few good plants with it, but not all. Same is true of the wind. There seems to always be a remnant. How many of you have seed stored up for fall planting?"

Every farmer raised a hand, but just briefly and not too high.

"How many of you with businesses see to it that you put by a little for the lean times so's you can meet expenses. And those of you with salaried jobs, don't you try to keep a little something in reserve? Heads nodded.

"That old rule about not eating your seed corn must have been learnt from God. He always sees that there is a remnant. He provides from generation to generation. For instance, He commenced with eight seeds after the Great Flood. Noah and his Mrs., his three boys and their wives. Then as far as I can tell, God might have got plumb down to one seed by the time Abraham came along. I can't know for sure, and probably there were others but anyhow, He started up a new thing with Abraham and made provision for Abe's seed forever, including his spiritual seed.

"God began to plant toward His kingdom again. Abraham and Sarah had a son and that son got two, and one of those got twelve sons. Then, old Abraham, he cut a contract with God. Or actually, God cut one with him, and God was good, for His part down through the generations even if Abe's descendants didn't always keep their part.

"Genesis XII. Look there, if you will. God promises to bless Abraham, and bless all those that bless Abraham and curse all those that curse Abraham, but through Abraham all the people of the earth are to be blessed.

"Now, folks, that is a reckoning of the original seed and original seed gets original seed as you recall in our previous studies. Original seed is powerful and resistant to disease. Hybrid stuff plays out after a while. God is the keeper of His original seed and He watches over it, tends it. He promised to do that very thing. The original seed can be found in God's remnant. If you're glad for God's provision, say so."

Amens were loud and clear. Then Pastor Hay turned to several other passages in the Bible and read about remnants and explained as well as he was able to understand it himself.

Tallie was giving her full attention when he said, "There will be a remnant and according to Isaiah, chapter fifty-five, verse thirteen, we'll never have to chop another weed, not one weed in that day. There won't be any out there trying to take over and choke out the remnant of the originals.

Tallie could have shouted out loud and nearly did. She was amazed that the talking-back-to-the-pastor kind of congregation didn't shout. However, the Pastor said that corn seed got corn and spiritual seeds got spiritual things, that one should plant toward what one wanted to reap. Finally, her wondering about all that remnant talk was satisfied.

"Now, it is good," said the Pastor, "to know who His remnant is. One time, Elijah had no notion that God had a seed left in all the world but himself. He was convinced that he was all alone and the heathens were after his hide and fully intended to nail it to Jezebel's barn door. But God surprised Elijah with the news that He had seven thousand seed in reserve. That must have gotten Elijah's attention. It should have comforted the prophet that he wasn't in the fight by himself. We don't always know who they are, do we?. Remnants come in many forms–even His people, don't you see?

"It is not good to think you are all alone when, in fact, you aren't. So, the Pastor raised his hand and gave a command. "Remnant, stand up! If you see a new seed among yourselves this morning, give them a hug or a handshake. Take notice of the new seed among you. Encourage each other. Stand up and behold ye the seed of God. You're a-looking at His remnant specifically chosen by Him for these days. A special group. A set-apart people, chosen from the foundation of the world! WOO HOO! he shouted. Lord have mercy! What a blessing! I'll dance on that all week, Praise God! What a mighty God we serve!"

Tallie stood up and Aunt Jenny stood proudly beside her placing her arm around Tallie's shoulders, and mercifully, not looking at her. Tallie was so afraid of crying if her aunt looked at her. The congregation began clapping and shouting amens, milling about, laughing and talking.

Alice Fursby made the piano fairly jump as she pounded out *Walk in the Sunlight* with Godly gusto. Pastor Hay shook Will Thompson's hand. Tallie was surprised that Mr. Thompson was a new seed. Then the Pastor came to Tallie. He took her face in his hands and smiled at her. Her eyes filled up with tears she could not control. One spilled over and ran down the back of his hand. He smiled at her and caught the other tears with his thumbs.

"I'm not sad," Tallie said.

"I know when I see the spill-over of an inward baptism. It's a grand day and I'd purely like to know the adventures that wait before you. Let me in on a few of them, will you?" He shook his head in wonderment and gave Aunt Jenny a pat on the shoulder as he moved on through the congregation.

Tallie was mostly in a daze as others came to greet her. Mary John hugged her, Alice Fursby squeezed and pumped her hand until Tallie was embarrassed from the attention. Fortunately, Pastor Hay called everyone back to their seats for a closing prayer.

"Thanks be to God," he said, "for the new seed and for the provision through the ages that reaches down to this very day to provide for Will and Tallie– as well as the rest of the seed You, Lord, have planted in this place. Thank you for the remnant of our present crops in the fields and gardens, for Aunt Jenny's recovery and her lovely hat, for the safety of us all through the storm. Bless your food provisions which we are about to enjoy and the hands that prepared it. I ask You to enjoy it with us. Bless it to our health, fellowship, and all service we do in Your name. Amen. Now, the rest of you will have to run to beat me to the dining hall. I'm particularly hungry today."

Tallie and Mary John took their usual places at the beverage table filling glasses with ice, pouring drinks, and setting out cups for coffee.

"Where's Tom Sawyer?" Tallie asked.

"I don't know," Mary John replied, "but sometimes he spends the night with some of his buddies. They go camping or fishing, or to Oklahoma City just to mess around. You can ask the sheriff if you're really interested."

"No, I'm not that interested."

Mary John smiled and asked, "See that guy over there?"

"Where?"

"By the door, silly. The tall one in the blue plaid shirt, the red-head with the dark brown eyes."

"Dark brown eyes? I can't see the color of his eyes from here."

"He's cute, isn't he?" Mary John didn't need a second opinion. Her mind was clearly made up on that.

"He's tall enough to be cute someplace. Who is he?" Tallie asked.

"That's Banta, but everybody calls him 'Bandit'. He is the star of our high school basketball team, and called 'Bandit' because he is great at stealing the ball from the other team."

"Banta. That certainly is different. I've never heard it before."

"It was his mother's maiden name. The Thompsons have been coming to our church some this past year. Maybe they will be coming often now that Mr. Thompson has made his decision. Bandit is really popular at school. He's a senior this year."

"You're a sophomore, right?" Tallie asked.

"Right, and he scarcely knows I'm alive. Sh-h-h! Here he comes.""Hiiiii, Bandit,"Mary John said, drawing out the sugary-toned greeting.

(Tallie rolled her eyes, incredulous at Mary John's behavior.)

"H'lo, uh, uh, Mary John."

(Tallie thought his relief at getting her name right was obvious.)

"What beverage may I serve you today, Bandit?" Mary John asked.

(Bring on the bread, the butter is thick in here.)

"I dunno. What do you recommend?"

(He doesn't care as long as it's wet. Can't she see that?)

"Lemonade," Mary John said. "It has vitamin C which is good for the respiratory system."

(...and scurvy. Tallie coughed to hide a giggle.)

"Really? Well, uh, that's great. Thanks," he said and moved on while Mary John stared after him until Tallie nudged her in the back.

"Did you hear that, Tallie? He remembered my name."

"He said it right out loud and I heard him." Tallie was not about to point out that her necklace pendant had her name engraved on it. Instead,Tallie asked her if she had brought something to serve today.

"I brought blackberry cobbler and my own version of au gratin potatoes. Did you notice whether Banta had some?"

"No. I couldn't see if he did or not. But he had that big plate of food covered up with fried chicken."

"Fried chicken, huh? I just happen to have a wonderful recipe for batter-fried chicken. I think I'll bring that next time."

"Maybe you can figure a way to write your name on each piece, too, so Bandit will know who fried it."

"You are so smart! That's a great idea, Tallie."

"I was just kidding."

"Well, I'm not. Maybe I can brand my chicken somehow. Daddy has some old branding irons in the barn somewhere. I'll figure out something."

Tallie poured two glasses of tea and suggested they fill their own plates because she was starved. Mary John broke out of her own world of thought for a moment and looked at Tallie.

"I'll bet you *are* hungry. It has been a big day for you. On Sundays, I am hungrier and everything tastes better than at any other time. And when you've been specially involved, it makes you starved, or just the blistering opposite. Don't you get hungry when you go to church on Sunday?"

Tallie thought of the times she watched the clock in church just waiting to get home for lunch and answered, "I guess I do. I just wanted to go home and eat. I hadn't done anything special to make me hungry."

"I don't know what the deal is, I just know that church makes me hungry. Maybe God knows what it's all about. Once when Jesus was hungry He sent his disciples off to buy some food, and when they got back, He had experienced so much fulfillment ministering to someone that He didn't care if He ate or not. I haven't gotten to that place yet, but Daddy has. Sometimes he's starved, like today, and other times he could care less about food. Spiritual business can take a lot out of a person. It also takes a lot of courage to announce publicly what you and God have worked out privately. I know. I've been there, and I was starving afterward. So let's eat.

"I'm ready!" Tallie replied.

"And how on earth did you get that nasty knot on your head?"

Tallie and Aunt Jenny left earlier than usual, not staying for the fellowship nor the second round of dessert. They took leave ladened with leftovers from those wanting to help out during Aunt Jenny's recovery.

Aunt Jenny took off her hat and rested her head against the back of the seat in the pickup. When they arrived home, she changed into a shapeless house dress and rested on the front porch in her rocker reading all the back newspapers and mail. Tallie put the food away and went to the well for fresh water before she joined her aunt on the porch.

"What do you think?" Aunt Jenny asked.

"About what?"

"About being a part of the remnant," she said, still looking at the newspaper.

"Right now, I feel empty and a little bit sad."

"You're right on course, then. You've said goodbye to bad rubbish, which makes it reasonable for you to feel some loss. It left a hole that needs filling. And while you have had some in-filling already, some things will continue to need filling, to be dug up or pruned and the infillings and new growth will continue as He proceeds to care for you, all of your life, with your cooperation of course."

"What am I being filled with?"

"Wisdom. Peace. Things we can't even guess at. This is a vulnerable time for you, so be careful. It's real easy to get the sags about now."

"How am I supposed to keep from getting the sags?"

"You don't fully keep from getting them, you overcome them. Read the Bible— a lot. Ask for help. Practice overcoming it. Determine yourself to learn something from ugly events that land in your territory. Pick a verse and quote it against the ugly thing. Even Jesus started his defense declaring "It is written.." But whatever you observe or do, lay the Biblical pattern on it and if it doesn't match, something is off. And of course, pray lots–all the time, in fact."

"All of the time? I have to go to school and do regular stuff like eat and sleep. How can I pray all the time?"

"You've always got thoughts in your head. Turn those into conversational prayers. Ask for wisdom as you study, safety as you travel. All such as that. Prayer gets to be as natural as breathing once you start to practice. It spills out natural like and sometimes when it shouldn't. I remember going to the picture show once, and one of the characters was about to be hurt, I said, 'Oh, God! Help that man!' I felt a little silly, but that's how natural it gets to be. I say things to Him like, 'God, it's time to pick beans.' Then once in a while, He'll show me something special about the subject of our conversation."

"That's why you talk about bubbles and beans." Tallie said.

"The beans and bubbles were right before me to learn from. I reckon if I were fixing flats at a filling station in Oshkosh, he'd find a way to teach me something. I don't know what all he'll put before you to learn from, but you'll learn and you will grow wiser."

"And what will I do with all this wisdom I'll be getting?"

"Who knows. It's your future. You will mess up now and then, and you won't always get your way, but on your worst day—you're a royal princess in the household of the Most High. That never changes. My advice is that you read the Bible to keep spiritually sharp."

"Is that why you read your Bible every day?"

"That is part of the reason. It's also one way the Lord and I talk to each other."

"He talks to you?" Tallie asked.

"Sometimes it's just a word in the Bible that gets my attention, like the word 'remnant'. I was reading along and *'remnant'* took my interest. I was glad I studied on it since Pastor Hay preached on it this morning."

"When I was staying over there, I told him you said there is always a remnant, and he got really excited and said, 'That's it' That's it!' "

Aunt Jenny smiled. "Is that a fact?" It must have been the hook God wanted to hang His message on this morning. It brought Will Thompson to his feet sure enough, and you, too."

"I dreamed about a remnant the other night, but it was a cloth remnant."

" Maybe your dream prepared you to hear what was said this morning", Aunt Jenny said and shook the folds out of the paper like she didn't want to talk any more at the moment, so Tallie dropped the subject and looked through the old geology book for a while. The colored pictures of rocks were the most interesting to her.

"What do you see in that book?" Aunt Jenny asked.

"There are lots of different colors of rocks."

"Look up," Aunt Jenny said. "What do you see?"

"The sun is going down."

"And?"

"There are lots of colors in the sky, just like in the pictures of these rocks."

"What did you say?"

"Colors in the rock and in the sky."

"In the rocks?"   .

"Yes. The prettiest colors are on the inside. The rocks look dull until you cut into them and then the colors really show up."

"Is that a fact? There's your first lesson in wisdom. You ought to be able to think on that for days. What you glean, store. It's bound to come in handy one way or another."

"What do you think?" Tallie asked her aunt who began to chuckle.

"Me? I think I'm going to put my gown on for bed. I've read enough of this colorful paper to last me a while. And I think I'll study about colored rocks before I go to sleep."

"How will you line colored rocks up with the Bible?" Tallie asked.

"There's a good deal about colors and rocks in the Bible–enough to keep me busy with thinking for quite a spell."

"Such as?"

"Joseph had a coat of many colors, Lydia was the maker of purple cloth, Jesus is the rock, eagles nest on rocks, a house built on a rock can outlast a storm, and so on."

Then her aunt got quiet as she appeared to be seriously pondering something for a moment. When she looked up, she told Tallie to latch up the door.

Tallie was a little puzzled. She had never been asked to lock the door nor had she known her aunt to ever lock it when they were in the house.

"Why?"

"I guess all that foolishness in the newspaper has put me in the notion. Just do it, please."

Tallie wondered only momentarily about it and did as asked on her way up to bed. Other things were of more concern at the moment, such as what adventures awaited her and if she would even know one if she were in the middle of it. And what about the stuff she was supposed to learn from– the stuff before her like remnants, seeds, rocks and colors? How could any of that be important? Nothing of any particular significance came to mind. When she lay on the bed, she thought she heard someone talking.

She listened carefully for a moment and decided it was Aunt Jenny praying a little louder than usual. Tallie yawned and tried, again, to gain wisdom. She pondered on how to use cloth remnants and what one can do with seeds. People wear cloth remnants; plant seeds or eat them; collect rocks or climb them or wear them. Some jewels are simply rocks all cleaned up. There are rock walls and rock houses. She yawned and decided there wasn't any wisdom in any of that. They were common things.

Common. What could all those common things have in common? she wondered. Maybe what they have in common is that they are all common and don't have anything in common." Then she smiled. "Oh, yes, they do. They are my lessons and that is what they have in common." She then made an important decision and fell asleep.

––––––––––––––––––––––––

After morning chores were done, Tallie walked into the pasture to find the rock outcropping. She didn't think it would be hard to find, having nearly run into it with the truck. Besides, she intended to carry out her decision to collect some rocks. It might be that some of those rocks were valuable. Maybe that old geology book would help her identify a valuable find, Then she could sell them at the Trade Fair. It made no difference to her that she had $700 in cash. She simply did not want to go to the Trade Fair empty handed. It wouldn't be any fun. She picked up several small rocks and put them in a bucket, some from the rock outcropping, and others that looked appealing on her way back to the house. She was engrossed in her rock gathering until a whorl of dust rising on the road got her attention. A car? The postman? Tallie wondered and stepped up her pace, A car. It pulled slowly pulled into their drive. Tallie set the bucket of rocks down on the porch, it was not the postman. Quickly, she went to the screen door and called to her aunt.

"Someone is here."

"Who is it?" Aunt Jenny asked.

"I don't know. Two men."

Aunt Jenny left the Daisy churn on the table, wiped her hands and walked casually to the porch. The two men in dark suits exited a blue sedan. They both looked to be about fifty years old to Tallie and about thirty to Aunt Jenny.

"Good morning! Nice day!" said the first man to exit the car.

"Yes, indeed," Aunt Jenny responded. Immediately, Tallie knew that something was 'off' even though her aunt smiled and greeted the men.

"Nice place you have here," he said looking all around. He glanced at Aunt Jenny, then at the sedan and back again.

"It is, thanks to the Lord," Aunt Jenny said. "May I help you in some way? Are you lost?"

"No, no. We've come on a special errand, you might say." Then the man stepped boldly up onto the porch and Aunt Jenny took a step boldly toward him.

"Is that a fact? What sort of special errand?" Aunt Jenny asked.

"We're on an errand of mercy," said the first man, motioning for the second man to join him as he continued his spiel. During the last storm, there was heavy damage to the chapel on the Indian reservation. It was nearly ruined. All the families who live there have pitched in and made these genuine buffalo-hide Bible bookmarks. For a contribution of $25.00 or more to this cause, we'll give a bookmark as a token of our appreciation.

"Aunt Jenny—," Tallie started.

"Don't interrupt," Aunt Jenny said sternly. She took the bookmark and examined it more closely.

"What exactly happened to that chapel?" Aunt Jenny asked.

"Blew the roof off. Just blew it right off," said the first man jesticuling with both hands. Aunt Jenny raised her eyebrows at the comment. It seemed to encourage him and he continued with more animation.

"Yes, it was a bad storm, all right. One of the walls gave way. He paused as if seeing the thing in his mind, and continued. It was bad, bad. There was other damage, too. Cracks for instance. Sad thing for those poor Indians who built that little place of worship with their bare hands and piggy banks. Sad. Sad. It had stood the test of time for years and years. A landmark, you might say. Now it's just laying there about to be lost forever for the lack of money to repair it." He shook his head in despair.

"That's right," said the second, thinner man. "Those poor, old Indians are counting on the good people of this area to help them in their worthy cause. You have a place to worship next Sunday, I presume."

"Yes, I do," Aunt Jenny replied.

"How would you feel if it had been blown away?" the second man asked.

"I'd want to replace it as soon as possible." Aunt Jenny said, acting as if she were proud of herself with such a fine answer.

"That's precisely my point, lady. Most of your good neighbors have been really helpful, too. Mrs. Fursby, for one. And by the way, here's a letter of endorsement with your sheriff's name to verify our cause."

"But Aunt Jenny," Tallie protested again only to be fairly shoved into the house by her aunt who also told her to go inside and stay there until she was finished visiting with the gentlemen.

"I'm always glad to give something to a good cause." She turned and spoke through the screen door to Tallie to bring her purse. When Tallie handed it to her, she snatched the purse and motioned Tallie back inside as she slammed the door and handed the men twenty-five dollars.

"Now then, gentlemen, since this is for such a good cause, I do want us to have prayer. You fellows kneel down here before me and I'll pray. Are all the donations you have collected so far in that box with the bookmarks?" Aunt Jenny asked the second man who was still standing holding the box.

"Yes. Why?" asked the first man.

"He needs to get over here and hold it up so's I can pray over it, too," Aunt Jenny said.

The second man approached warily with the box. The first man yanked on the second man's coat tail and he knelt before Aunt Jenny, box and all.

Aunt Jenny stood above the two men, extended her hands over their heads and began to pray. Loudly and slowly, she prayed.

"L-o-r-d. Lord. L—o—r—d, what a blessing to know You personally and to know that You loved us so much that You gave your Son that whosoever--any old whosoever, any old scudder, anywhere, at any time, who fits Your proper description of all whosoevers— and I believe it means that whosoever believeth on Him should not perish, but have everlasting life. Oh, yes, Lord, and how I praise You for Your personal care, care You exercise by watching over Your own people, the Indians, and the rest of us, even the little bitty nobodies who might be up to no good, but will eventually be somebodies up to good things. Thank You for watching and seeing. You promised that whatsoever the Godly do would prosper and return Godly gains."

Tallie opened one eyelid and peeked out the screen door at the two men who seemed to be favoring their knees, shifting back and forth to ease their misery. The thin man's arms were quivering from holding the box so high. Then she looked at her aunt who was resting a hand on each man's shoulder, and Tallie was almost certain she was pressing down just a little.

"We ask," her aunt continued, "that you prosper Your cause. I thank You that You promised whatsoever we ask of the Father God, our Lord Almighty, in the name of Your precious Son, Jesus, that it will be done. You've promised that what we bind on earth will be bound in heaven, and what we loose on Earth or the moon or even on Mars will be loosed in heaven; that what we bless will be blessed, and what we curse will be cursed something fierce. I know Your word is true and that You watch over it to perform it. I've seen You perform it. Lord, I could stand here and praise You with testimonies for hours on how perfectly You perform Your promises."

Tallie's eyes flew open. Was she going to? One of the men loosened his collar with his index finger, and the other one squirmed and uttered a pitiful little squeak.

"Nevertheless," Aunt Jenny continued, "I am absolutely delighted to give to You and to You alone some of Your blessing to me. I ask now that not one nickel, nay, not so much as one penny of this be wasted. Most importantly, I ask a particular blessing, a special blessing on these offerings, and I ask that if one red cent is used for anything other than Your purpose for our poor old Indian brethren, may that offender be dogged by the hounds of hell fire to the day of his repentance and a righting of all his wrongs, and conversely, may the blessing be doubled on those who use this money to further Your cause. I so pray. Amen," Aunt Jenny said, pushing down on their shoulders a little more before she released her hold.

"AMEN!" The men said.

Aunt Jenny folded her hands and smiled very genuinely at them. The two men slowly stood up, rubbing their knees and shaking the kinks out of their legs. Aunt Jenny asked the men if they'd like to go down to the well and draw themselves a drink of water, but they very rapidly declined.

"Nope. We thank you but we have to get on with our work," the first man said, backing away.

"Here, I forgot to give you this bookmark. Take two. Maybe that girl would like to have one," he said. He stretched his arm way out to hand her the markers and turned over Tallie's bucket of rocks as he ran to the sedan where the other man was revving the engine. Aunt Jenny waved goodbye and saw them clear out of the gate before she let Tallie out of the kitchen.

"Aunt Jenny,—" Tallie began gathering the bucket of rocks.

"Yes?"

"Mama said there aren't any Indian reservations in Oklahoma."

"There aren't."

"Then why did you give them $25.00?

"I didn't give it to them. I gave it to the Lord's work.

"What Lord's work?"

"We may never know, but it's a hoot! An absolute hoot to do what I'm led."

"Even that praying? That was some prayer. Did you mean it?"

"I meant every word of it."

"Even that stuff about the hell-hounds of fire? What was all that about?"

"I don't know, Tallie. It just seemed like the thing to say. And you know what? I don't think they were used to being on their knees, do you?"

"That one man was really squirming."

"Was he really? Ha! What a delight. I'm glad I kept them down for a while." Aunt Jenny put her arm around Tallie's shoulder.

"That wasn't a letter from Sheriff Sawyer was it?" Tallie declared more than asked.

"No. No indeed. His signature is on your temporary permit. Take a look at it. Besides, the Sheriff has no such authority nor would he endorse those men on his own. He runs for office and that sort of thing could be misconstrued against him if anyone ever did decide to run against him. What I'm wondering is could they be the same men who've been pulling tricks elsewhere in the state like I've been reading about in the papers. Only this trick wasn't thought out very well at all. Maybe they think whoever lives outside the city limits has limited brains."

"Well, we did get some high-dollar bookmarks out of it," Tallie replied.

"That's another deal. Those Indians must have sent the genuine plastic buffalo hides to Taiwan to be made into bookmarks. The label says so."

Tallie laughed and then was serious again. Twenty-five dollars was a lot of money for her aunt to lose, and she decided to remind her.

"You knew those men were not telling the truth so why did you give it to them?."

"I invested it. I did what I understood was right to do. Now, I'd better get back to the churn before the cream sours." Aunt Jenny sat down to finish churning but to Tallie, it was more like she had dropped down.

"Are you all right?" Tallie asked.

"I'm fine enough. I just get to thinking of other things I wish I could be doing instead of what I am doing."

"Such as?"

"Cleaning out that hen house for one. It needs it bad and the droppings should be mixed with compost or soil and spread on the flower bed. The laundry basket is overflowing. And the windmill needs greasing something fierce. Every time you turn it on, my hair stands up. It makes a screech. Tornado damage most likely. It's not the enjoyable little squeak which I enjoy when it catches the wind. Something needs oiling or tightening or both. And my hoe handle is working loose. The blade needs sharpening. The porch needs painting. The curtains need to be pulled and shook and washed. I need to put up some pickles, clean out the cabinets. The list goes on and on. And all that is on top of the daily chores."

"I'm doing the daily ones," Tallie said, "and I can do some of those other ones. Besides, in a few days, you might feel like doing some of those things a little at a time," Tallie replied to her aunt who just sighed and said nothing.

After lunch, Tallie wanted to go rock hunting again, but when she was sure her aunt was asleep, she headed for the hen house. She had never been in it in the heat of the day, and it was full of ripe manure which literally took Tallie's breath. She wondered if the chickens could smell it. It was thick and the broom she brought was woefully inadequate. She needed a shovel and the wheelbarrow and wished she had a fire hose.

First, she knocked the excess off the roosting rafters with the broom handle. Droppings fell into her hair and shirt. Disgusting as it was, she knew it would happen over and over until she got finished with the job. It wouldn't do to run to the horse tank to wash until the job was done. So she squared her shoulders, shook her hair out and kept at it.

She wondered what Amy and the rest of her friends in St. Louis was doing, and what they would say if they knew what she was doing. Suddenly, she swelled full to bursting with loneliness. Maybe her friends were at the movies or eating pizza or talking on the phone. It was a safe bet that none of them were doing what she was doing, and they probably didn't care what she was doing. The lonely feeling weighed on her and settled into her chest.

She gritted her teeth, scooped a big, slimy batch of dung with the shovel and tossed it into the wheelbarrow, raking out what stuck with a trowel from the barn. She shook what she could out of her hair and took off her shoes. No use ruining them, she thought, tossing them out the door. Her stomach churned but she shoveled and scooped the mess trying to decide whether to breathe through her mouth or her nose.

She finally decided to work as fast as she could so she wouldn't have to breathe the fumes any longer than necessary, but wished she had not taken off her shoes. The feel of the goo on her feet and between her toes was bad as the smell, and quite slick. After this load, she was going to wash her feet and put her shoes back on. Taking a deep reach into one of the scooped piles, she slid and fell face forward into all that lay beneath her. For a moment, she thought she would cry. Then she did.

"This must be the sags Aunt Jenny warned me of. Help me, God. What shall I do? Praise You? Like when You helped me start the truck? I don't feel much like it. Look at me. I'm filthy! It stinks in here!"

Even so, she began to make herself think of things she should be grateful for, such as the eggs that came from the hens, but just the eggs, not the stuff she was shoveling. Aunt Jenny got only forty-five cents a dozen for eggs, and right now, that didn't seem like enough for all the effort it takes to tend to chickens and clean their mess and water and feed them with bought chicken feed. One thing for sure, she would never eat another egg without remembering this day.

Three loads had been mixed with compost and dumped on the flower bed when she was backing out of the hen house with the fourth load. Someone said, 'Hey', causing Tallie to jump.

Oh, no! It was Tom Sawyer, she realized and collected herself. She turned and faced him, filth and all.

It took him a moment to say anything. All he could do was stand and stare at her with stunned respect that she would tackle such a chore. Tallie, on the other hand, was totally embarrassed but took a stance and didn't move, just in case he had any smart remarks.

"Dad dropped me off here on his way over to the Fursby's place. He said Aunt Jenny might need some heavy work done. So, I'm here. How can I help?" He asked. He casually tossed away the big rocks he had picked up when he heard noises in the chicken house.

"Well, you're too late for the worst of it, but you can scrape out that last load and help me get some fresh straw from the barn for the floor." ...and remembering he had sort of volunteered, she added... "if you want to."

By the time she had dumped the wheelbarrow and washed her arms and legs at the horse tank, Tom had cleaned the wheelbarrow and spread straw on the hen house floor. He went to the horse tank, ducked his head and arms into the water and flung back his hair.

"I raised those wooden shutters on the sides of the hen house," he said. "They need to be kept open to cool and air the place. I reckon Aunt Jenny closed them when the storm came."

"No, she didn't. They must have blown shut and she hasn't been out here that I know of." Tallie felt stupid that she didn't think of opening them herself. "I didn't think of that. In fact, I forgot the hen house even had shutters."

Tom thought she was daring him to make any more remarks. He shook the excess water off his arms and ran his fingers through his hair like a makeshift comb. He glanced at her while thinking she was a touchy little twit. Real touchy, but had plenty of admirable grit.

"Sorry," Tallie said, "we don't keep towels down here."

"No big deal. It feels cooler this way."

"Does my aunt know you're here?" Tallie asked, looking at the ground first and then the sky. Anything to keep from looking straight at him too much.

"I tapped on the door, but no one answered."

"She was asleep when I left. Maybe she's awake by now. We'd better go see," Tallie said and led the way up the path.

Aunt Jenny was on the porch shucking a bucket of corn. Tallie frowned and said, "I thought you were going to rest."

"I did. Hi! Tom. Come on up here and let me look at you."

"Hi, Aunt Jenny. It looks like you're doing all right."

"Getting better. Getting lots better, " she answered.

Tom sat down on the step at Aunt Jenny's feet and explained about his dad dropping him off to do some chores.

"Your niece has already cleaned the hen house. All I did was open the shutters and put down some straw."

"Oh, wonderful. I know it needed it and I thank you both for tending to that. How would you kids like a soda pop?"

Tallie's eyes lit up. She didn't know they even had any in the house. Taking an ear of corn, she began shucking and pulling out the silks. Tom followed suit.

"Dad said he issued a temporary driver's license for you. "

"That's what my Aunt Jenny said. It's in the pickup glove box."

"Not everyone can step into a four-wheel vehicle with a compound shift and drive it."

"Aunt Jenny showed me the morning she got sick."

"Still it was gutsy of you driving those roads in the dark and the hard rain knowing they would be in bad shape."

"I didn't have time to think about that, and I didn't do a very good job either. I went off the road once, and I was scared, real scared to tell the truth."

"You slid off the road?"

"I did, and my legs were shaking like crazy. Finally, Aunt Jenny quit vomiting long enough to tell me to shift into 'grandma', and I did and gunned it as hard as I could."

Tom laughed then asked, "How old are you, anyway?"

"Thirteen," she said solemnly.

Tom was surprised. She looked more like eleven to him and decided it was because she was so tiny.

Tallie sat quietly and shucked the corn. Today was her birthday and no one knew or even remembered. No package from her mom and dad. Not even a phone call. Some birthday. It was enough to give anybody the sags. She took a sip of the pop Aunt Jenny handed her and went to the barn to throw the corn shucks into Janet's trough. It was hard not to cry again, but she held it back knowing her face would swell and turn red.

Tom finished his pop and climbed up on the windmill with an oil can and some tools to make minor repairs. Tallie went on with her own chores, mulching the remaining chicken manure into the compost pile for the flower beds and garden. She watered the plants by hand from the barrel that drained the kitchen sink. It seemed like endless trips in the hot sun carrying water to both gardens, and when that was done, she would have to carry water to the house. Tom beat her to that chore. She found the buckets filled and in place in the kitchen and he was sitting on the porch filing the hoe.

Tallie was grateful for that bit of help and went to the mailbox to see if there just might be something there for her. Nothing. Ads and yesterday's Sunday paper. She kicked at the sand and walked back to the house so deep in thought she almost didn't hear Sheriff Sawyer drive up next to her and stop.

"Hey, Little 'un. Want a ride up to the porch?"

"That's okay, I'll be up in a sec." She had hoped that even this late in the day, there would be a card or a call from her parents or some of her friends. No one remembered. No one at all. She kicked the dirt again and continued on to the house.

"Yeah, two of them," Tallie heard the sheriff say to her aunt in the kitchen.

"Are you talking about those two con men?" Tallie asked.

Aunt Jenny shot Tallie a warning glance and said, "Yes, you remember? Those men I read about in the newspaper. The sheriff says we should be careful if they come around here and not to be taken in by their high jinks."

"They could be dangerous," the sheriff said. "I got a profile on them after Alice Fursby called. They were affiliated with some two-bit, east coast gang years ago called the Hellhounds. That bunch was known to set people's hair on fire for the fun of it."

Tallie's eyebrows flew upward. "That explains—"

"Explains why we will be locking up at night for a while," her aunt interrupted, "and why the sheriff is warning all of us to be careful."

"Well, I don't want to unduly alarm you ladies. They're probably a couple of cheap cons. But knowing their connection to gangs, it pays to be careful. Alice said the two men were soliciting donations for some cause or other. She told them they would have to go out across the field where Floyd was mowing and ask him if she should donate. At that point they made some excuse and left. What galls me is they're using my name in the deal." .

"No one would buy that trick, Hank Sawyer. We all know you better than that," Aunt Jenny said.

"I hope you're right. But I think I'll leave Tom with you ladies for a night or two until I can locate those yay-hoos. The highway patrol has been alerted by my office that these solicitors are wanted for questioning. Meanwhile, you two are the only ones out here without a big dog or a man around. Tom is a good-sized boy and he carries a pager in his pocket. He's to use it if any strangers show up. Then me and some of my men will take it from there. "

The sheriff went down to the well to speak to Tom and left. Tallie got the buckets to go milk Janet, but her aunt stopped her and said she'd have Tom do it and insisted that Tallie take a bath and that it would be a good idea to wash her smelly hair as well. But first,Tallie set some of the leftovers from Sunday out of the freezer to thaw for supper to keep her aunt from doing a bunch of cooking.

After the bath, Tallie did feel a little bit better. She certainly did smell better according to Aunt Jenny who told her to set the table while she freshened up a bit herself.

Tallie was not sure how she felt about Tom staying there overnight or about those con men. If she had been back in St. Louis, she would not have thought twice about someone ripping someone off. She saw it on TV all the time. It was stuff that happened to other people, people remote from her; just like they were simply part of a TV show called "The News" and no different than the fiction that came on before or after "The News." Now, it comes close to real news as she and her aunt were assigned a bodyguard–such as he was.

Tom knocked at the screen door lightly before coming in. He had found a way to clean up, too. The well she guessed. His dad must have left him some extra clothes.

"Tom," Tallie quietly said, while setting the table, "those men—they were here today."

"I know."

"You do?" She thought for a moment, then continued, "I can't figure out why Aunt Jenny didn't say something to your dad."

"Who can figure Aunt Jenny's thinking?"

"Right, but how did you know those men were here?"

"Will Thompson called Dad. Those men showed up over at his place and said that Aunt Jenny had donated generously. He called my dad to see if he had really given them his okay. That's mainly why dad sent me out here, that, and to help out with the chores," and gave a short laugh. "But when I got here and neither of you were in the house, I thought something was up for sure. I stood around a little bit and when I heard noises from the hen house, I picked up a couple of rocks and went to investigate. I had no idea what could be in there. I saw your shoes and a nasty looking shovel. Thinking something was wrong, I eased up closer. Then you backed out of there looking like someone had mopped the floor with you," he raised his hands, "no offense intended."

"I guess I did look pretty bad."

"Dad said those two guys might have sized you two up as easy marks for later,and without so much as a dog for protection. So I guess that makes me the watchdog."

"She gave those goons $25.00. Can you believe that?"

"She's got her own way of doing things. We're all used to that. She's as independent as a stray cat and just as tough."

"That's for sure. She had those two men kneeling and leaned on them and prayed over them until they squirmed."

Tom laughed. "She would. Man, that's her alright."

"S-h-h! Here she comes," Tallie warned.

Tom and Aunt Jenny did most of the talking during supper, talking about the windmill, gardening, and baseball. Tallie wasn't very hungry. They seemed very happy to just talk between themselves and did little to include her. Her birthday was drawing to a close, and not even a call from her mom.

"I've never eaten anything like this," Tom said, "What, is it?"

Aunt Jenny told him it was cornbread dressing with squash in it and that Tallie had thought it up as a good way to eat squash since they'd had it boiled, baked, and fried for weeks. Tallie watched Tom's face but could not decide if he liked it very much or not. And sagging a little more, she decided she could care less if he did. Besides, he was quite at home with Aunt Jenny. They could talk about baseball and leave her out of it for all she cared.

Instead of listening to them, Tallie recalled last year when she had a slumber party with five other girls on her twelfth birthday. During the night, they heard noises on the lawn and slipped out the window of her bedroom in their skimpy, babydoll pj's to see what was going on, holding on to each other, whispering, scared, trying not to giggle. It was some of the boys who knew about the slumber party and were toilet papering the trees and bushes in front of her house. It was a wild scene when they scared the boys and chased them off. Lots of squealing, everyone running around and falling down in the dewy grass.

She remembered her dad flying out of the house in his boxers and a baseball bat causing more squeals when he came to investigate. What a night! She had felt like she was part of that group at last– Amy and her four friends. She sighed as Tom and Aunt Jenny pushed their chairs under the table.

Tallie volunteered to clean the kitchen and they let her. That hurt even more, although they did bring their plates to the sink before they went out on the porch. When she finished, she sat back down at the table with her geology book. She was not interested in going out on the porch to hear them gab about their little stuff.

The sun had just gone down when she thought she heard a car coming down the road. She went to the south window and looked. It was! Horrors! It had no headlights on. Quickly, she went to the screen door.

"Tom, a car is coming and doesn't have any lights on. Do you think it could be those men?"

"You go back inside and I'll watch," he said.

The car slowed to a stop as someone opened the gate and slowly turned in the drive. Tom sent Aunt Jenny into the kitchen telling them to stay out of sight. Tallie scrambled to the back porch to find something to use for a weapon.

"Tallie!" Tom yelled.

Every hair on Tallie's head knotted in her scalp. She ran to the front porch clutching a broom.

"Happy birthday to you, happy birthday to you," sang a whole yard full of people. "Surprise!" they yelled. It was the Thompsons, the Hays, the Sawyers, some of Tom's friends from the baseball team and two of Mary John's girlfriends.

Ice cream freezers appeared along with two big birthday cakes, one chocolate, one coconut, gallons of punch, and tables and lawn chairs out of the back of their cars and pickups. The ladies set up tables with decorative paper cloths.

Tallie turned to her aunt who was pulling out a stash of paper cups. Aunt Jenny smiled a little. "Well? Go on out there and shut the screen," she said. "You're letting the flies in."

"Put that broom down, girl. Please!" Tom yelled, "before you put someone's eye out."

Aunt Jenny urged Tallie off the steps to blow out the candles on the cakes so the people could be served. A cheer went up as the last candle went out, and the totally wonderful, disorganized party began.

While some ate, others played instruments. The men played catch with the boys and sometimes, with the girls. There was even a contest at the horse tank to see who could hold their heads under the water longest, but only the boys did that.

"Whose idea was this?" Tallie asked Mary John, "Yours?"

"I don't know who started it, but the word got around. It's fun, isn't it? I made the coconut cake. Everyone eats chocolate all the time. I wanted to fix something else. It's my newest find. Buttermilk sheet cake. Like it?"

"It's wonderful!" Tallie enthusiastically declared and meant it as Mary John's mom called for everyone to gather around to watch Tallie open her presents which had appeared on the porch undetected.

There was a T-shirt from the baseball team autographed by all the players and a baseball cap with 'Sawed Off Corners' stitched across the top. Tallie put the cap on causing the team members to cheer. The next box she lifted to her lap was heavy. It contained a Ryrie Study Bible with the date of her belly-button birthday and her spiritual birthday listed in the front. There was an inscription signed by pastor and Mrs. Hay on the inside cover: To commemorate the most wonderful day of your life. Tallie felt her eyes fill with happy tears.

Mary John and her friends' gift consisted of a very nice bottle of perfumed bath oil. One of the boys must have said something to his teammates about the gift since they all guffawed and would not tell anyone else what was so funny. One of Mary John's friends called them uncouth. Tom asked the girl to spell that word and the girl replied, "Y-O-U." Tom bowed to her while all laughed.

The Thompsons gave her a three-pound box of chocolates in a box shaped like the state of Oklahoma with the state seal on the lid. Tallie was surprised that they even got her a gift. She barely knew them and told them how nice that was. Mr. Thompson said the gift was meant to commemorate the fact that Tallie and he share the same spiritual birthday. Tallie grinned, opened the box and told him to have the first piece. Even Sheriff Sawyer and his wife, Geneva, gave her a present.

Tallie laughed when she opened it. A wanted poster with her name in bold letters at the top above her latest, most horrible school picture. On the bottom in small print it read: To remember your 13th birthday in Sawed Off Corners. You are always wanted here.

Last of all was a gift from Aunt Jenny in a large box wrapped in funny papers and tied with a huge, blue bow. She could not imagine how or when her aunt had managed to shop for her. Tallie peeled through the layers of the wrappings. There it was, the most lovely, white-eyelet sundress she had ever seen. Tiers and tiers of ruffles fell from the shoulders to the hem over a made-in pink petticoat with a white lace ruffle on the hem. The girls 'oohed' and the boys whistled.

Tallie looked at her aunt for a long time and then asked, "How did you--" but her aunt put her finger to her lips and winked. Tallie's eyes could not contain the tears as she ran and hugged her aunt who told her to put her gifts in the house.

Aunt Jenny watched Tallie gather the new treasures and put them inside and remembered the fun she had getting Doc Gilbert to do her shopping for her. He did have good taste even if it was expensive, and it was too bad he couldn't be here, but some little tyke was needing his appendix out.

Pastor Hay and Will began playing the Virginia Reel. The sheriff took Tallie by the arm and declared it didn't matter if she had ever heard of that dance or not. If she could play follow-the-leader, she could dance the Virginia Reel. He flung his legs out in a fancy prance. Tallie laughed out loud and from way down deep for the second time all summer. Someone was throwing confetti on them every time they skipped up and down the row of dancers. It was fun. Delightful fun. Immediately after the reel, someone said, Name Game. Pastor, you're 'it'. Tallie had no idea what was coming next.

The Pastor began to play a lively tune and sang:
I know a gal who's now thirteen, dances the reel just like a queen.

"Tallie!" the crowd replied and someone told her to make a rhyme without breaking the rhythm of the song.

I know a lady who has a hat, bows piled high, now think of that.

"Aunt Jenny!" they all said.

Aunt Jenny smoothed her apron while the pastor played what they called the thinking chorus, then she began.

I know a boy who's baseball crazy, works real hard and ain't a bit lazy."

"Tom!"

Tom rubbed his chest and took a big bite of ice cream and sang with his mouth full.

Whoever made this peach ice cream? I could eat it till I bust a seam.

"Geneva!" They cheered her and her famous peach ice cream.

Geneva covered her face with her hands, composed herself, and sang:

I know one who's richer than gold. Tends his sheep and never grows old. "

"Jesus! Praise God! Hallelujah!" they all shouted.

The pastor nodded to Will and they played the ending flourish on the game.

"Well said and well sung," the Pastor said. He laid his guitar aside, gathered them all in a circle for prayer and thanked God for the good day. He went around the circle laying his hands on each person, called them by name, and asked a particular blessing on each and all. Tallie thought he was very brave to do that since they would know whether it would come to pass or not.

For Tallie, the Pastor asked God to give her a fine purpose with many interesting adventures and a long, godly life. For Aunt Jenny, he prayed for health and all needs met. Hugs and good wishes were expressed as they all departed.

Going to sleep was hard that night, not only because Tom was bunking on a cot on the porch, but because she was reliving the wonderful party and wondering what surprise her mom and dad had for her. Aunt Jenny said they told her they had something for her when she came home, but it was not something that could be mailed. As for the party, it certainly was much better than a mere slumber party. Confetti in her hair was more fun than toilet paper in the trees. Then she recalled earlier in the day, she had had chicken manure in her hair, and she had had the sags. They were gone.

"God, did you do that? Did you tell all those people to throw a party for me? Who thought that up? Did you do that? You did, didn't You? Thanks", she whispered. "It was fun. Real fun. I guess that means You answered my hen house prayer and kept me from staying in the sags. What is next? The rocks?"

Chapter Nine: The Trees, the Rocks, The Renter

Tallie yawned and stretched. The sun was high and a strange odor captured her attention. Quickly, she dressed, pausing only long enough to admire her frilly new frock hanging in the closet still wondering how Aunt Jenny had managed it. There was that odor again.

The closer she got downstairs, the stronger and more constant it became. Turpentine? She followed the odor, as well as the voices, to the front porch. Tom had painted half the front porch already and Aunt Jenny was arguing about the other half.

"I'll paint that side later," she said. "If you paint it all now, we'll have to use the back door all day."

"This is quick-dry paint. It'll be dry in four or five hours. By noon," Tom insisted. " I can put the porch furniture under the shade tree."

Tallie backed away from the screen door to let them fuss it out and made herself a piece of toast to go with a slice of ham which someone had left on the back of the stove. She didn't realize she had slept so late. It was already seven o'clock.

"Well, birthday girl," Aunt Jenny said, coming into the kitchen. "You really slept late this morning. Janet has already been milked and I gathered the eggs, but there is something I want you to do since Tom insists on painting that whole porch floor today."

"Hoe the garden?" Tallie asked.

"No. I want you to drive me up the north road a-ways."

"What for?"

"I haven't been up that way for some time, and there are things I want to see up there."

Tallie was a little puzzled, but it was not a chore she minded. Aunt Jenny told Tom they would be back 'dreckly'. After Tallie boosted her aunt into the truck, she drove slowly on the north road which was sandy and canopied by big trees. Aunt Jenny held her head up high observing the fence for any sign of damage. In the distance on the left was a ramshackle structure of a once fine house. The nearer they came, the more she could see it. Trash was scattered around the yard. A stray dog lay in the shade of a gutted car body. A slanting screen door was barely hanging on its hinges.

"Does anyone live there?" Tallie asked.

"Claude Worth. Some call him Worthless Clod. This place gets worse and worse. Stop a minute and let me take a look."

"How long has he lived there?" Tallie asked.

"I rented this house to him over two year ago."

"Two years ago?" Tallie emphasized the plural.

"That's right. Two year ago last month," Aunt Jenny said, emphasizing the singular.

"You mean this is your property?"

"It is. I lease the pasture to Will Thompson and he runs a few head of cattle on it. Has for years. He told me last night I ought to come take a look at this place. When Claude moved in here, it was in pretty good shape. All it needed was some paint. I even gave him money to buy the paint and two months free rent to do it or have it done." Aunt Jenny shook her head in disbelief..

"Have you owned it for a long time?"

"That house was built by my Uncle Ted and Aunt Tallie. She's the one you are named for. Aunt Tallie would turn over in her grave if she could see this place." Pointing toward some trees, she said, "Aunt Tallie planted those big pear trees in 1919, and those peach trees in 1945. I guess I'll have to see about getting someone to cut those dead limbs out. It makes me sick to see how Claude has let this place go to ruination."

The climbing rose by the rusty mailbox was nearly lost in the weeds. The wind gusted and a piece of newspaper tumbled across the front porch and came to rest against a pile of junk. Aunt Jenny sighed and continued to survey the mess.

"That tree over there by the well was planted in 1976."

"That was the year I was born," Tallie remarked.

"That's why she planted it, and because you were her namesake and the centennial year. You were the centennial baby."

"I didn't know that."

"Well, that's the way she remembered and commemorated events in her life. When you were named for her, she found the finest tree she could and planted it over by the well. I was here the day she put that skinny little stick in the ground. She said it was from good stock even though it had no more than three leaves to soak up the sun and flap in the wind. She was old and that was the last tree she ever planted. She recited Psalm One over that stick and called it Little Tallie's tree. She didn't live too much longer after that."

Tallie could not have sorted her thoughts just then, nor could she describe her feelings. Below her level of awareness, she began to realize she had roots running deep in inheritance, branches for duration, foliage and fruit for the season, and a sense of importance and belonging.

"I knew I was named for Daddy's great-aunt, but I didn't know anything about the pecan tree."

"She planted it where she could see it from her kitchen window."

"Do those other trees stand for something?"

"Oh yes. The pear trees are for the year Uncle Ted Koums returned from World War I. Then in 1945, the Raider nephews came home from World War II. We all had a big reunion right there in that front yard and she planted those peach trees. Your granddaddy, Layford Koums was there that day. We were all there: the Raiders and the Koums and she planted a peach tree for all the boys. Uncle Layford always called them her 'peace' trees. Pretty soon, it became the 'peace orchard' to the rest of us as well."

"I was wondering," Tallie said, "how you remembered the dates those trees were planted. I had trouble memorizing dates of all that stuff in history class. What about those trees around the house? Do they have a special meaning?"

"Aunt Tallie planted trees around the house when they built it back at the turn of the century. A few of them have been replaced, except for that big oak. The ones there on the north, were all planted in a row, were put there right after the dust bowl as a windbreak. If you could see it, they go down the back and join up with another big shelter belt across the north pasture. Those are native blackjack oaks and have replaced themselves as the years have progressed. The cedars have grown up there on their own. But that old oak went in shortly after they moved here. She brought the sapling with her from North Carolina off her mama's place. Every year, I expect to see it toppled over from old age or from a storm, but it's still hanging on to the ground."

"Like you, huh?" Tallie teased.

"I reckon. I sure played in it when I was little, and we've grown old together, you might say."

"How come the peace trees and the pear trees haven't died?"

"Lord, only knows, child. By all rights, they should've, but there they are to this day. She didn't plant trees when anyone died, just tombstones. Death, to her, was just a matter of being transplanted. Her trees were about life and the joy of living it. So there you are."

Tallie looked closer at the pecan tree planted for her and asked, "What is that wad of stuff in the branches?"

"Webworms. That tree needs spraying. Claude hasn't done one thing to keep this place nice. He hasn't paid his rent for the last three months, either," Aunt Jenny said.

"Is he out of work or something?"

"No, he has a good job at the filling station. I can pert-near guess why he doesn't have fifty dollars for his rent. They cut his 'lectric off last month according to Alice Fursby. The man has problems and whatever they are, they've been added to by those brown whiskey bottles you see all over the yard. Sometimes, I swear I can smell that stuff clear up to my house. Let's go home."

Tallie turned the truck around and asked her aunt what she planned to do about that Claude person. When her aunt said she hadn't made up her mind yet, Tallie suggested she tell him to pay up and get out. Taking a last look before the house was out of sight, Tallie saw the barest portion of a blue car sticking out from behind the house.

"Why don't you take his car from him for the rent?"

"Then how would he get to work?" Aunt Jenny asked. "Besides, I wouldn't have that little, yellow thing. What would I do with some little, fancy sports car? He sure is crazy about it. Keeps it all slicked up and tuned up. Too bad he doesn't apply some of that elbow grease to the rent house."

Tallie knew that it physically pained her aunt to see the place in such a sorry state and said nothing more on the way home. Aunt Jenny moved slowly up to the steps of the house. When she saw the second half of the porch painted, she cheered up a bit and did not seem to mind going around the house to the back door. Tallie went the opposite direction and yelled for Tom.

"Yeah!" he yelled from somewhere.

"Don't 'yeah' to me, just come h'year," Tallie called back.

When Tom came into view, she motioned him to follow her away from the house then told him, "I think those con men are down at Claude Worth's."

"Are you sure?"

"I'm pretty sure it's them. I could partly see a blue car sticking out from behind the house. Claude Worth has a yellow car. Do you think we should tell your dad?

"Yeah, I'd better let him know that something is different down there. I'll go call him."

"Aunt Jenny will hear you." Tallie protested.

"Right. I'll punch the beeper. He'll be here lickety-split."

And he was.

Tallie expected him to arrive with the siren going. Instead, he arrived slowly and quietly up the drive.

"What's up, Son?"

"Tallie thinks she saw a blue car behind Claude Worth's house. It could be those con men that were conning Aunt Jenny."

"I'll drive down that way and check it out. You kids stick close to the house."

Tallie sat down on the porch step by her bucket of rocks. Tom looked concerned and she assumed it was for his dad's safety. She was glad her dad wasn't a sheriff having to stick his nose into suspicious places and wished she knew something to say, but couldn't think of a thing. She sorted through her rocks and kept quiet.

"Dad can handle those two guys," Tom said aloud to no one in particular. "He'll be alright."

To Tallie, that sounded more like something Tom had learned from his mom when the sheriff was up against an iffy situation.

"If he isn't back soon," Tom said with a smart grin, "I'll send you down there with a broom."

"Let up on that broom stuff, will you? I'm tired hearing about that," Tallie said and threw a couple of rocks back into the bucket with extra force.

"You started it," Tom said. The grin was gone. Tallie bristled at the challenge to fuss and decided to go for it.

"You asked for it," she said. "You know you did."

"All I did was laugh that day. You freaked out and started slinging that broom like a crazy woman. That's a major overreaction. And face it, kid, you were funny. Think about it!"

"You snuck up on me and laughed at me at the same time. I was startled. What did you expect? You got what you deserved." Tallie pushed a strand of loose hair out of her face and exhaled the rest of the air she had sucked in to blast him with. "I'm sorry," she said. It was like a reflex or something." She sat down beside the rocks and began to crack them with a hammer, putting the pieces back into the bucket.

Tom stood and stared at her a moment, then said, "Yeah? Well, you'll be glad to know the guys have given me a hard time about that 'cat' scratch."

Tallie took a silent satisfaction that Tom had to take a little of what he liked to dish out, then said, "I told you I was sorry, and I meant it, but I'm not going to say it again. So drop the subject, please."

"Whatever you say. You're the one with the hammer."

"You just can't leave well enough alone, can you? You've just got to open your stupid trap!"

"Okay! I'm sorry, too," he said with a high voice and backed away with his hands in the air. Really," he said more quietly, "I apologize, okay?" Tallie looked at him suspiciously.

"Anyway, what is with the rocks?" he asked.

"I'm studying them."

"What're you learning?"

"Nothing yet. I've just started, but I've got a geology book, and I'm going to find out what kind these are. "

"Geology is interesting. We studied it in ninth grade and I thought it was pretty cool."

"Do you know what kind of rocks these are?" Tallie asked.

"That's a piece of sandstone, and that white one there is gypsum. They're common around here. Gypsum is mined north of here as you go toward Boiling Springs State Park. They use it in a whole lot of industrial products."

"What about this shiny one?" she asked.

Tom took the hammer and began to crack some of the rocks for her. They used the book to identify and sort them, completely engrossed until the sound of a car caused them to anxiously look up. The sheriff had returned.

"There wasn't any blue car down to Claude's place, nor anywhere in the local vicinity," he said.

"But I was sure I saw a car in the back. Did you look in the back of the house?" Tallie asked.

The sheriff replied that he had and that if she did indeed see a blue car, it was gone now.

"Dad, what about Worth? Was he home?"

"I didn't go in the house, but he didn't answer the door and his mail has not been picked up for two, maybe three days. I would need a warrant to go in there unless someone asks me for a wellness check."

Aunt Jenny came to the door causing them to quit talking about the con men.

"I thought I heard a car," she said. Can you have a bite of lunch, Sheriff? It isn't fancy. Just a big pot of ham hocks and beans. You'll have to come around to the back door to get at it. Tom has painted the front porch."

"I'd walk through the back door of Shanghai to get to a bowl of your beans,"

Aunt Jenny disappeared from the screen door and the sheriff cautioned Tallie and Tom not to mention anything about his little investigation to Aunt Jenny yet, but to keep a sharp eye on the comings and goings up and down county road.

After lunch, Aunt Jenny sent Tallie with a can of coal oil to the squash patch and sent Tom to pump the stock tank full of water. The sheriff sat at the table with Aunt Jenny, turning a glass of very sweet tea around and around between his hands.

"How old was I when Sheriff Hadley brought me out here? Thirteen?" he asked.

"Yes. Thirteen going on thirty. Eating nails and burping tacks."

"I guess I was plumb full of sour piss, 'scuse me."

"No. You'd only fooled yourself and your teachers into thinking you were incorrigible. Cussing just so's you'd be kicked out of school early on a hot day, or any other time you took a notion to slouch around. You weren't bad. You were full of fear."

"Yep. I was," he agreed with a quiet laugh. "And I didn't even know I was. I thought I was tough. I recollect cussing you and you just stood there laughing at me."

"Oh, I didn't laugh, did I?"

"You did. You know you did. I was out there chopping that Johnsongrass hard as I could with that dull, guest hoe you keep, and you wouldn't let me stop to listen to the World Series. You told me I could have till noon to finish, and when I didn't get done, you wouldn't let me come in to hear the game."

"Now, wait a minute, Hank Sawyer. You slipped off to the pond to smoke cigarettes and chunk rocks at my calves. That's why you didn't get any chopping done."

"And you hid the radio and made me chop that whole afternoon before I could come to the house for supper. I remember chopping and cursing the English language for the lack of more cuss words. Then when I came through that back door, still cussing, that's when you let me have it with that bucket of slimy, mop water."

"Oh, Hank, that wasn't mop water. I was emptying out the drip pan from under that old, wooden ice box I used to have. When I threw it out the back door, you just happened to run into it, that's all."

"You tell it your way. I'll tell you mine. It was nasty! It stunk. It had bugs in it, as I recall. And you sure laughed. Don't you remember making me sit down on that little dippy, three-legged stool to dry off? And you stood up over me like a giant. There I was squatted down with my knees up to my ears. And you kept questioning me as to why I cussed. You questioned me until I realized that I was cussing because I was afraid. Afraid no one would listen to me unless I cussed. Afraid no one would think I was tough unless I cussed."

"Well? You quit cussing, didn't you? And you carried water and fifty-pound sacks of feed, pitched hay, dug holes, and got strong as an ox. You also ate more pinto beans and ham than anyone I ever fed."

"That is something I'll never forget," he said, "and you know, I don't cuss to this day, not even to a rancorous prisoner. I just tell 'em plain and straight what's what, and so far, it has been enough."

"They know you mean it. Know you aren't afraid. Right-doing carries a power of its own. I know you don't cuss any more, but you get cussed at, don't you, Hank?"

"Yep. And it is a dead giveaway ever'time. They're just scared and weak down inside. Dangerous maybe, but scared and weak all the same."

"If they get too mouthy, call me. I'll bring my mop water."

They laughed deeply.

"You would!" He laughed again and stood to leave telling her that he believed he'd have Tom to stay the night, again. That he would rest easier if Tom stayed with the pager, and said he would return in the morning to take Tom in for ball practice.

Tallie heard the sheriff drive off, before she finished picking all the squash bugs off the vines and filling the bucket with squash. She had learned to pick squash quite small, so she would not have to eat so much of it at a time, and it sold a lot faster as well. The cucumbers needed picking, too, and surprisingly topped off the bucket. She carried them into the kitchen and asked Aunt Jenny what they were going to do with all of the squash and cucumbers.

"Why don't you figure something out?" Aunt Jenny said without looking up from washing the dishes.

"I'd like to figure out something good to cook with the squash."

Aunt Jenny smiled to herself and suggested that Tallie look at the Caddo County Cookbook for an idea.

"What if I don't find something?"

"I have some rat killing of my own to do, so I'm leaving it up to you, Missy."

"What if I make something that tastes just awful?"

"Then we'll be eating something that tastes awful, and we'll eat on it until it is gone. I can promise you that."

"I know, I know. The Lord doesn't bless waste. And, what sort of 'rat killing' are you talking about?"

"Ripping rags for rugs."

Tallie rolled her eyes to the ceiling. It was just like her aunt not to throw away a rag.

She picked up a cookbook and turned to the section on vegetables. There wasn't much in that section that looked interesting, but the dessert section was loaded with recipes. There was even one for a squash pie, but Tallie couldn't see ruining pie with squash nor was she ready to try to make pie crust. At her school, only the eleventh- grade students got to make pie crust in home economics class. The cobbler crust she had made with Mary John's help was not too hard to do since cobbler crusts weren't quite so touchy to make. They could be a little thicker and still be okay.

Turning past the pies, she read about cake and found a recipe calling for riced potatoes, whatever that was. Why not use a riced squash, she wondered. Was it one with rice in it? Tallie hollered from the kitchen, "What is a riced potato?"

"It's a peeled, boiled potato pushed through a rice grater, or a colander," Aunt Jenny called back.

"Can you rice a squash?"

"Not very likely. They're too moist when boiled, but you can grate a raw one right fine."

This time, it was Tallie's turn to smile and Aunt Jenny's turn to roll her eyes toward the ceiling wondering if they would be eating something awful until it was all gone.

"Can I use the oven to bake something?" Tallie asked.

"I reckon so. It's already hot in there."

Tallie gathered the soda, spice, flour, fresh butter, brown sugar, eggs and buttermilk all together on the cabinet. Aunt Jenny listened to the rattle and clatter reminding herself that she asked for it. She had turned the little novice loose in the kitchen and had, thus, bound herself to eat the results. It was an old family rule that if you cook, you'd better give it your best try because it would be eaten. No throwing away food just because you wished you had done a better job.

Aunt Jenny began to pray silently, Lord, I only know of one

time You called a conference, and that was when You were deciding whether to go on ahead and make mankind and put him on the earth. I've an idea it must have been a pretty rough decision and plenty of nerve to turn him loose to on it.. There's one loose in my kitchen, now, making who knows what, and like You, I have to accept the outcome.

"Exactly what does 'cream butter' mean?" Tallie hollered again.

Aunt Jenny silently said, See Lord?

Aloud to Tallie, she answered, "It means to beat it up real soft and fluffy. Use the mixer."

"Oh. Fluff the butter by beating it up good. Why didn't they say that?"

"It's a cook's shorthand to leave out some words. All kinds of work have their own language. Take the word,'wrench'. It's a tool to some folks, but to Doc Gilbert it means a pulled muscle. To my mother, it meant to get the soap out of her washing," she laughed as she went back to ripping up rags, sorting the colors, and silently talking to God.

Your work has its own language too, doesn't it? I'd never thought of that before. Covenant, prayer, bless, love, faith. Especially faith, the power plant of our belief. Those are your working words. And then, there's Your personal and powerful working word 'let'. It boggles my mind to think what it might have been like when You said, 'LET there be light'. Did you pause after you said 'let'? Did You think twice about or relish the anticipation of the thing about to happen? What did it sound like, Your language, Your working-word ripping through all that dark nothingness? Did Your word blast a trail and all the light followed on cue? Or did You say it casually and quietly and the light sweetly flowed in, curling up and around all the corners of this place? Hm-m-m. I can't imagine making light from scratch and using sound to do it. My, My!

Anyway, since Your word does what it says--that is to say--let does the letting. Let's let. Let's let your creative word use the power You built into it. I'm letting that young'un in there use our supplies to learn, and You did the same with Adam. That 'let' word is pretty risky, but then You invented courage, right? It must have been fun to listen to Adam use his words to name all the critters. Did You laugh? I know You had times when You wanted to un-let the letting. I reckon forgiveness is the closest we can come to that on this side of life, Lord. Thanks for teaching me how to un-let the sorry 'letting' I've put into motion back when. I'm glad you haven't decided to un-let us all in a wink. So, let Thy will be done."

"DONE?" Tallie called. Aunt Jenny jumped from her tangled musings.

"What was that?"

"I said, how do you know when a cake is done?"

"You time it by the clock, or stick a toothpick in and check to see if any batter is clinging to it, or pat it on the top gently for firmness."

Tallie decided to pat the top. Solid as a rock. Proudly she tipped the cake onto the cake plate, and the raw middle ran out all over the dish and cabinet. She quickly scooped up what she could, poured it back into the pan and into the oven, and washed the cake plate before anyone saw her mistake. Finally, the cake passed all the doneness tests. She allowed it to cool upside down on the cake plate and frosted it with a simple glaze.

"Come see," she said to her aunt. Aunt Jenny smiled a bit and said, if it tasted as good as it looked, it would be delicious.

Tom came in the back door all sweaty and dusty and asked if he could use the new bathtub. Aunt Jenny took a long look at him and said if he planned to eat at her table, he'd better do just that. He handed her a pail of milk and drew the curtains to the back porch.

Tallie set the table and hoped that Tom did not use up all the warm water, but just in case, she put extra water in the kettle on the back burner of the stove. Next, she put ice in the water glasses and set the little fan on the floor to dispel some of the heat. Aunt Jenny told her to get the marinated cucumbers and some jelly out of the refrigerator which she did and when she set them on the table, she saw Tom on the front porch. He had to be the fastest bath-taker ever, she decided.

Aunt Jenny took the food from the oven and called Tom in to eat. Once again, Tallie felt left out of most of the conversation which was about town people she did not know, and about baseball, of which she knew very little. Her part was to pass this and that and watch them as she ate. Tom ate some of everything and ate everything on his plate. Not like her friends in St. Louis who seemed to take pride in being picky-eaters.

Some wouldn't eat red meat, others wouldn't touch a green bean or an onion. She recalled seeing whole trays of food being dumped into the garbage at the school cafeteria. It never occurred to her nor her friends that there was a lot of work—planting, reaping, processing and transporting and cost to get that food to the cafeteria, just to be dumped by some snotty little snobs. Even those who packed their own food often turned their noses up at the contents.

Sometimes, mothers would bring a pizza to the school for some little group of chums, and it appeared to Tallie they made a big issue of it simply to announce that they were too good and too special to eat the food of the commoners around them. She had proudly been one of those diving into a skinny slice of pizza made at some restaurant, turning her nose up at food prepared in the school cafeteria, and acting picky at other times, even when she was so starved by three o'clock she could have eaten the gum from under her desk. How stupid can anyone be!

It was one thing not to care for a particular food, but quite another to work at it. Thus, she dived into the rest of the squash on her plate to prove she had outgrown the picky-proud behavior as silliness. Naming that behavior for what it was, she felt free of it. While squash was not her favorite food, she could eat it with a certain amount of grace.

Aunt Jenny saw Tom surreptitiously eye the cake. She smiled and said, "Tallie made that cake. Are you up to a slice?"

"I might try some, please," he answered.

Aunt Jenny slid the cake across the table to Tom. Tallie was a little anxious wondering if he would like it. He cut a slice and was about to lift it onto his place, but he hesitated.

Tallie put her hands on her hips. "What's the matter? Are you having second thoughts?"

"No. Well, sorta. I've never had this kind of cake before. It's different ."

"What do you mean 'different'? Tallie asked. "You haven't even tasted it yet." She wondered if he could see the grated squash in it. Tom lifted the slice for them to see.

"Good grief, it's hollow!" Tallie exclaimed.

Aunt Jenny's jaw dropped. "Isn't that a lick?" She said and began to laugh. When Tom looked at Tallie through the missing middle of the cake, Tallie laughed, too. Aunt Jenny told Tallie it was a wonderful trick and they could chink it together with ice cream.

"Chefs in New York City would give their eye-teeth for that recipe. You may never be able to do that again, even if you try," Aunt Jenny said. Tom took a big bite.

"A nice, light texture," he declared, "and very tasty for a tricky cake."

Aunt Jenny liked the flavor of the thin layers and commented that the spices were perfect. Tallie noticed that no one could tell that it contained squash and she was not going to tell them it did.

While Tom helped Tallie with the dishes, Aunt Jenny went to the porch and thought how wonderful the way the cake turned out, tasty and fun, too. And how wonderful not to have to eat some awful concoction for days on end.

"Lord, You are so inventive at answering prayers sometimes," she declared with a whisper. It's heap cooler out here, kids," she called.

Tom walked into the yard. He drew a circle in the dirt, set a tin can in the middle, and began to chunk rocks at it. Aunt Jenny told Tallie that Tom was always throwing at something to keep his arm limber and his eye sharp. Tallie watched, then lost herself in the geology book until time to go to bed. She was glad he didn't run her ragged with more comments about the hollow cake, and as for throwing rocks, well, she would see about doing a little of that herself. He wasn't the only one with arms and sharp eyes.

Tom's dad came to pick him up shortly after breakfast and, as soon as he was gone, Tallie flew through her chores. Aunt Jenny left off pottering in the flower bed when Tallie returned from milking and followed her into the house. Tallie was glad to see her aunt walking around, picking flowers, sticking to light and enjoyable tasks. In fact, Tallie thought her aunt looked much better.

"I think you're getting well fast. You act like you are feeling good today."Aunt Jenny looked pleased.

"I'm feeling tolerable well today, and better ever'day. Soon as you strain that milk, I believe I'll make some butter to sell next Saturday. What are you taking, or are you too rich to bother with trade day?" Tallie took a clean straining cloth to filter the warm milk into quart jars and thought for a moment.

"I'm going to take something," she told her aunt, "but I don't know what." Then she changed the subject and told her aunt she had something she wanted to do and I would like to be away from the house a little bit."

"And what would that be??" Aunt Jenny asked.

"Exploring," Tallie said.

"Where do you plan to explore?"

"Just on your property, okay? You won't try to lift anything or go down the stairs, will you?"

"I'll be just fine, but don't you be foolish. And don't you be gone long or I'll be worried and have to set out a-foot to find you."

Tallie took a bucket and went down the north road. She felt her ears grow hot, not from the sun, but from getting nearer and nearer to Claude Worth's. What if those con men were there right now? What if that Claude person was the boss of all the con men in the state of Oklahoma or something? Maybe they weren't down there at all. Maybe she had just imagined seeing the back end of a blue car. Either way, she was going to investigate.

Kblick. Kblick. The sound of the car doors. Tallie jumped into the ditch and was ready to jump into the dense brush if the car came in her direction. She listened. The car started. Someone revved the engine. She climbed up the ditch into the long grasses and brush on the fence line and listened.

The car was coming her direction. She crawled deeper into the grasses and shrunk herself as small as possible while the car blasted past her, sending dust fogging in all directions. Desperate to know if it was those men, she dared to look up as they sped by. Yes! It was a blue car containing two men, and she knew who they were. When they were out of sight, she walked along the fence row to the house just to look around. That whole bunch was up to something and she was going to look for as many clues as possible.

The whole place looked quiet enough, she thought, just like

any old house she had seen many times along the rural highways. Who could ever imagine what might be going on in some of those old houses that looked empty and deserted? Maybe they were CIA headquarters. Maybe safe houses for informers or defectors. They could be hideouts for wanted criminals and she could be face to face with one of those possibilities herself.

The place looked deserted. No sign of Claude. Braver, she walked down the side of the house stopping to peek around the corner into the back yard. Beer cans. Whiskey bottles. A trash can spilling frozen food cartons and tin cans. Two old shoes lay just beyond the trash. Tallie was about to go on around the corner of the house when one of those old shoes moved. She jumped. Was she imagining things? She looked again more intently and with great caution. Those shoes were attached to the feet and legs of a real body lying flat on the ground under a pile of trash.

Tallie's mind began to race. Had somebody beaten up somebody or shot somebody? Part of her was scared and wanted to leave, but the other part was curious and won out. She crept closer to the feet under the trash pile. Something stunk. Flies scrambled out of her way. Finally, she stood at the feet of whom she assumed was Claude Worth. Drunk. He stunk. Flies swarmed over him wading in splashes of vomit on his shirt and urine on his britches. She forced down a growing gag. She had never seen such a sight. Sympathy and fear vanished. Anger and shocking disgust pushed it all out, robbing her momentarily of any reasoning.

At a loss, Tallie stood there and stared at a fly crawling over Claude's nose. The fly rose briefly and alighted at the corner of Claude's mouth. That fly was going to crawl into that man's mouth! Something had to be done about that filthy fly and that filthy man. She set her bucket down and shooed the fly from Claude's mouth, then she began to pray aloud.

"Lord, is this one of those adventures of Yours? This man is a mess! He's dirty and drunk. Something needs to be done about him. He obviously doesn't care about himself any more. Maybe You can give him a nightmare like you gave me. Give him a doozie. That's just a suggestion, Lord. I'm sure You can think of something. And what am I supposed to do? I can't go home and leave him to the flies, and I can't carry him into the house," she said. She looked around the messy yard. A newspaper flapping in the garbage can gave her an idea. She pulled it out, raked the chicken bones off, picked up two sticks, and made a tent over Claude's face anchoring it with a couple of rocks. Claude never stirred. The screen door squeaked in the wind. Most of the screen wire was loose and bent outwards. Reluctantly, Tallie decided to investigate the inside of the house, and Claude would just have to lie there under his little tent. She had done the best she could.

The kitchen was filthy. Food and dishes were scattered all over the place and had been for some time. A curled up piece of petrified bologna lay atop a slice of molded white bread. Spoons were stuck to the insides of pork-n-bean cans.

"Nasty, filthy mess!" she said aloud. On the cabinet was an unopened bottle of vodka and two bottles of beer, one of which was partially gone. She grabbed the beer and poured both of them down the drain, turning on the tap water to chase out the stink of it. Her eyes opened wide, and for a moment, she was tempted to throw the bottles through the window.

"WATER! Running water!" she said aloud.

Hard core anger spread over her like the ants she stared at on the cabinet. They were everywhere carrying away cargoes of stale Twinkie crumbs.

"Dear God!" She raised her voice in protest. " My aunt has been breaking her back to carry water all these years while that no-paying renter has it at his fingertips and doesn't even bother to USE IT! She grabbed the vodka bottle and proceeded to empty it into the sink. Her eyes narrowed. Her lips tightened. Her chin stuck out in defiance. She set the empty bottles down in the sink ready to tell that slob exactly what she thought, and there he stood. All her blood seemed to rush to her feet in spite of a hammering heart. She watched, his head wobble on his limber, dirty neck.

"Wha'y'doin 'ere?" he demanded, so drunk he could barely stand or talk. "A'ser me! Wha'y doin'? Who th'ell are ya, n' wha'y'want?"

Tallie stood wide eyed, unable to make herself reply. Claude shoved the table across the room with both hands. Tin cans and dishes flew in all directions.

"I—I—came for the rent," she managed to say weakly. "Aunt Jenny sent me for it."

"Nah, sh'di'nt." He looked around the kitchen and saw the empty vodka bottle on the cabinet. He wailed like a wounded animal and looked at Tallie. He weaved and growled a noise only a wild animal would understand.

Tallie was truly scared. He lunged toward the empty bottle. Tallie sprang out of his way. He caught the edge of the cabinet to steady himself and reached for the vodka. Wailing again when only two drops fell on his tongue, he threw the empty bottle through the torn screen door. Tallie flattened her back against the wall and slowly inched her way around the room. Claude knelt on the floor raking contents from under the sink until he found a little brown bottle. He gulped a great portion of it, then twisted around and leaned against the cabinets with his legs sprawled out on the floor.

"Git' G'ouda'ere," he yelled. He lifted the bottle to his lips again.

Tallie stood mesmerized at the sight of him. Suddenly, he was absolutely still, staring blankly at nothing. Was he dead, she wondered? She watched until she saw that his chest was moving ever so slightly with shallow breathing.

At that point, she slipped quietly out the screen door. Feeling safer outside, she finished her rather savage prayer for Claude Worth through the screen.

"God, look at that! I hope You give him exactly what he needs to stop drinking and to pay his rent, and to clean this place up. I hope You do it," she said, raising her voice a little louder, "before he swells up and bursts from all that whiskey; before those flies hatch maggots in his mouth to pick his teeth and eat up his rotten liver!"

Claude fell over to the floor. Tallie lost her nerve and bolted in the direction of Aunt Jenny's house, running all the way to the mailbox before slowing down. She hugged the mailbox like an old friend and waited for her wind to return. It would not do to have to explain to Aunt Jenny why she was out of breath. Neither could she wait too long to rest. Aunt Jenny could be watching her right now, so she retrieved the mail and walked slowly to the house pretending to be interested in yesterday's paper.

"Here is the mail," Tallie announced.

Aunt Jenny shut the refrigerator door and set some cottage cheese on the table.

"Where is your bucket?" she asked.

"Oh, Uh—I left it outside somewhere."

"We'll need some more water pretty soon unless you want to lick your dish clean enough to use in the morning."

Tallie laid the mail on the table and started toward the well. When she figured she was out of sight, she ran hard as she could to Claude's back porch, hoping he was still 'out of it' and that the blue sedan had not returned. She rounded the corner of the house, hopped over the trash, and grabbed the bucket, and ran toward home without stopping. Only this time, she cut through the pasture and crossed the road into the woods, running uphill toward the well where she was supposed to be pumping water.

Tallie splashed her red-hot face with water from the horse tank. When she got her breath, she pumped water from the well, drank some, and went to the house.

"Hot again today, isn't it," Aunt Jenny said. "In fact, I thought we'd have some of those cottage cheese and fruit for dinner so's we won't have to light up the stove. And I think we ort to wait to hoe the garden until it cools down some."

"I don't think you should hoe yet."

"It won't hurt me to get out there and hoe a little."

"Maybe I should call that grouchy Dr. Gilbert and see what he says," Tallie said.

"No, don't bother him. I don't think it would hurt to at least pick a few vegetables, do you?   Soldiers who'd just had appendectomies got right up during World War II. They had to. The enemy was coming and that's how they found out that getting up and walking helped a-body heal faster. Did you know that?"

"No, but you aren't a soldier and if you pick up a hoe, I'm going to call that doctor. Besides, there isn't much to pick. You go look."

Aunt Jenny squinted her eyes and looked across the room at Tallie's red face.

"Come h'year and let me see your face. You look red as a beet." Aunt Jenny felt her face as Tallie protested the examination.

"I'm just hot from hurrying around."

"Hurrying? H-m-m-m. Well, go set the table and we'll sit down and eat a bite of those cheese and pears. That should cool us both off."

Tallie pondered for a moment about her aunt's way of saying things—how she used words such as 'ort' and 'drekly' and now, 'those cheese'. Did her aunt think of cottage cheese as more than one cheese? Who knows, and she certainly wasn't going to ask her.

"Did you always set the table all your life?" Tallie asked. She hoped her aunt would drop the concern for her red face and not quiz her about where she had been all morning.

"I certainly did and will do so when you are gone from here.."

"Why? It's just extra work."

"I like little celebrations," Aunt Jenny said. She raised up her nose as if offended that anyone would question such a thing. "That's what my meal times are, and it is more enjoyable to eat in a nice setting. I don't care for gobble-and-go. Sours the stomach. I like to thank the Lord and take time to taste the flavors of things, because I'm glad I've got something to eat, and I celebrate that."

"You've never had to gobble-and-go? Never had to hurry?"

"A time or two, but not at my house. Once when I took a trip on a Greyhound bus, I didn't have much time between buses. I had to eat fast and I had a sour stomach for hours. It taught me a real good lesson. I never go off anymore without my own sack of fried pork chops or some sandwiches."

"Pork chops!" Tallie said. "Wouldn't you feel silly pulling a pork chop out of a sack and eating it in front of people? Wouldn't they stare?"

"I don't give a raggedy rip what people think. In fact, there were some that offered good money for part of my food."

"Did you sell it?"

"Not a bit of it. But I did share."

Tallie laughed and asked, "What important thing got you on a bus?"

"You. I struck out on that bus to help your mom when you were born."

"I didn't know that. Did you really?"

"I did. I diapered and bathed you and prayed over your little, pudgy, pink body the day you came home from the hospital. And I prayed for your parents, too."

"Does God answer all your prayers?"

"I don't keep track of all of them, but the big ones, the serious ones I keep mindful of and yes, He does. Prayers are stored up in vials in heaven and whether answered 'yes' or 'no', will be poured out on the earth in the last days. Sometimes I don't know whether I pray very rightly or not, so I ask Him to sort my prayers just like I sort beans."

"Another bean lesson." Tallie surmised aloud.

"There's a good'eal to learn from beans. I told you the first time we talked about beans I couldn't tell you all I've learned from them. If a-body knew all there was to know about beans, why, he'd know the secrets of the universe. Most folks don't even think about much of anything, let alone beans. They just gobble their way through life and go on with nary a thought. Gobble and go. Ignoring things. Gulping down the mysteries of the universe with nary a thought. His energy that created that bean is released into energy and health again to run these bodies of ours. We'll be accountable for the use of that energy and health to my notion. So how are you going to use your energy before we spend some on that garden drekly?"

"Oh, fool around with my rock collection maybe."

"Let's get the table cleared. I'm going to lie down for a few minutes and conserve some of my energy," Aunt Jenny said, thinking it would be okay with God.

Tallie thought all that stuff about energy usage was pushing things just a little. God surely wouldn't cut judgment that close. She dumped her rocks on the kitchen table and sorted through them again. She sorted them by sizes, colors, and then arranged some to fit like pieces of a puzzle.

"No one will buy them unless they are worth something," she whispered aloud to herself, "and let's face it, you guys are not valuable. You guys need to be cute or useful or both like my plums to be worth something. So, what can I do to make you cute? People need to smile at you. Then they will like you. That's it! You need to smile.

She picked up a pencil and drew a smile on one of the rocks, a big nose, and some big eyes using the natural contour to suggest the character of the face. Ha! she liked it. She glued it to a fatter rock to make a body. On and on she drew and glued making people shapes until she heard her Aunt moving around her rest time. Tallie was eager wondering what her aunt would say about her little creations.

"Well, now. It looks like we have company in here. That one over there looks a good'eal like Alice Fursby."

"Which one?" Tallie asked.

"That one with the big mouth, or generous mouth, I should say."

"You meant a big mouth. I know you did." Tallie enjoyed ribbing her.

"It's your turn to be honest. Didn't you think of Alice when you drew that face?"

"I'll never tell," Tallie said, grinning.

"Whoa up!"

"Okay. I drew it just to be drawing, but I do think it looks a little bit like Mrs. Fursby."

"And I suppose that one over there with the mole on the jaw just happens to look a little like me?"

"It just happened that way, honestly. I didn't intend to copy anyone's face."

"My next guess is that you plan to offer these for sale, right?"

Tallie nodded. Her aunt said she doubted they would bring much unless they could be of some use other than sitting around gathering dust.

"I don't know what they could be used for except a paper weight," Tallie said.

"Let's think. Holding paper down—"

"Holding paper up!" Tallie raised her arms. "They could hold up recipes or business cards."

"And messages or memos in offices," Aunt Jenny added, "or they could hold grocery lists."

"But they don't have any arms," Tallie said.

"And the little nekked things don't have any clothes either. I have some scraps in my rag rug box that I can't use to any other satisfaction. I'll sort some out for you."

"They need hair, too. Everyone uses yarn for hair, so I think I'll use some embroidery thread or dental floss or twine, but not yarn. As for their arms, maybe a wire frame covered in cloth?"

"Now you're thinking."

"I can get some of those little tiny baskets they use for party favors. Then they could hold junk like pins, buttons, paper clips, and pennies. Little stuff like that."

"Or little dried flowers in the baskets for decoration. Some of those little squeeze-clips could hold papers on some of them, too."

Tallie suddenly lost her enthusiasm. "I don't have any of that stuff and we won't be going to town until Saturday."

"Who says we won't? We haven't been to the laundry since I got home. We'll go tomorrow. I have enough scraps for the clothes. There is enough wire in the tool shed to fashion some arms."

"I'll pay you for it."

"No, just let me pick out one to keep here for myself," her aunt said.

"Deal! And I think I'll copy some recipes for examples."

"There's an idea. And if the recipe was real valuable, like Alice Fursby's blackberry jam cake, it would sell for quite a sum."

"Do you think she would give it to me?"

"Hah! She wouldn't share a recipe for a mud ball, let alone that cake that has her secret ingredient in it."

"I'll use one of my own, the steak rolls I made."

"Too bad you can't tell us all how to make a hollow cake!" Aunt Jenny smiled. "It looks like you'll be getting honey from a rock! Or should I say money from a rock. What a hoot!"

Chapter Ten: Claude's affliction. Alice's secret. God's provision

Tallie's breath grabbed in her throat. So engrossed was she that she did not hear a car pull into the drive. In fact she jumped when someone knocked loudly on the screen door. There stood Claude Worth. Tallie clinched the back of the kitchen chair afraid to open the door. Aunt Jenny peeped into the kitchen, saw Claude and went to get a closer look. She spoke through the screen door.

"Sit down before you fall down, Claude," she said, pointing to a chair on the porch. Tallie will fix us all some tea."

Claude sat down with a flop. Aunt Jenny studied him then quietly asked, "What is it, Claude?"

"I'm—I'm sick. I was trying to call Doc Gilbert, but my phone is cut off."

Loose, baggy skin hung under Claude's eyes. He didn't look at Aunt Jenny when he spoke nor could he control his shaky hands.

"What's ailing you?" she asked.

"Can't sleep. I—I thought Doc could order me some sleeping pills. I get cold and sweaty. When I do fall asleep, I have nightmares. I think I've got the flu or something. You'd better not get too close to me."

"I'm not going to catch what you've got. Tell me about those nightmares. Sometimes it helps if you tell a-body."

"Maggots. Filthy maggots hatching in me, eating on me. Makes my skin crawl like it has a mind of its own." Claude rubbed his arms.

"I'll call Doc. You sit right here on the porch and don't move, sir. You do look a-mite weak.

She went inside and told Tallie to put right much honey in Mr. Worth's tea. Tallie looked puzzled. "He is a sick man," she called over her shoulder.

"He isn't sick, Tallie countered. "He's hung over, that's all. Why didn't you tell him that?"

Aunt Jenny looked sternly at her.

"He knows that, Missy. And what good would it do him? He'd dispute me."

"How could he dispute you? It's obvious!"

"Not to him. It takes time for a-body to get around to owning their faults and weaknesses. Claude is sick, physically, mentally, and spiritually. A-body don't want to admit to weakness, especially not a man. A hang-over amounts to alcohol poisoning. I call that ' physically sick'. So take that tea on out there to him while I call Doc."

Tallie timidly carried the tea to Claude. He muttered thanks without looking at her. The glass shook in his hands and some of the contents spilled.

"Sorry," he muttered, pitifully, finally looking at Tallie. He stared for a moment with squinted, rheumy eyes.

"I know you. I seen you someplace," he said, scrutinizing her face.

"I've been here most of the summer visiting my aunt."

"Naw. I seen you someplace else," he insisted.

Tallie was getting nervous, afraid that he would figure it out any minute. Claude kept staring while Aunt Jenny talked to the doctor.

"No, Doc, I'm fine," Aunt Jenny said. I'm calling about Clause Worth. I think he's ready for help ... yes. Certainly. We'll bring him right on in."

Tallie was relieved when Aunt Jenny returned to the porch and Claude lost interest in trying to figure out why she looked familiar.

"Claude, Doc says we're to bring you right in. He'll get you fixed up," Aunt Jenny said.

"I can drive my own self," Claude replied.

"Let me have your keys, Claude, you might faint or something."

"I don't allow anyone to drive my car," he protested.

"We'll go in my truck. We were going in to do the laundry anyhow. But you better let me have the keys so I can move your car around back. I'll take good care of it." she said, then sent Tallie to fetch the truck.

Claude sat in the middle, slumped over in silence all the way to town. He had a vacant look and smelled like rotten onions. Aunt Jenny led him into the hospital like a child.

Tallie waited in the truck, absently looking at the surroundings when she saw Alice Furshy peek out of a particular store in the distance, exiting quickly when she thought the coast was clear. Tallie grinned.

"I think I just found out the secret ingredient of your famous cake!" she said to herself. She watched Alice walk down the street and disappear around the corner of the bank. The bank's computerized sign read 102-F. Hot. Very hot, she agreed with the sign. Her bare legs were sticking to the vinyl seat. Aunt Jenny came across the parking area fanning herself with a hanky.

"Whew! Let's get our laundry in the machines before we run the rest of our errands."

Tallie started the truck. "What's going to happen to Claude?" she asked.

"Doc put him in bed and gave him something to help with that alcohol poisoning. I don't know what will happen after that."

"Why did you keep the keys to his car?"

"Doc thought it would be best. Why didn't you come on inside where it was cooler when you saw I was going to be there awhile?"

"I don't like hospitals," Tallie said, "and I sure don't like your grouchy doctor. Besides, I think I've found out the secret ingredient in Alice Fursby's cake. I saw her sneaking out of the liquor store. I'll bet she uses liquor in it. What do you bet?"

"She does."

"And you knew it?"

"Known that for years. I've got the recipe. She thinks it's her mother's, but it's your Great-aunt Tallie's version of a recipe made by her Aunt Merrick. There's no telling where Aunt Merrick got it. My guess is she made it herself. Vanilla wasn't a ready article back when. She made blackberry or elderberry wine from what berries she could find any given year. It was legal to make wine and such up to 200 gallons a year for household and medicinal uses.

Aunt never came close to making that much."

"Aunt Merrick. That's a different name."

"Her real name was America, but we called her Aunt Merrick."

Tallie let the subject drop to concentrate on parking the truck at the Speedy-Washateria. They unloaded the dirty clothes as fast as they could, rushing inside where it was cooler. Tallie was anxious to hear the rest of the story. Aunt Jenny sorted and stuffed the clothes into three machines with generous helpings of soap. Tallie followed along, plunking in quarters and starting the washers.

When they sat down to wait for the clothes to wash, Tallie asked, "How did Alice Fursby get it?

"Get what? Oh, the recipe. It was printed years and years ago in our newspaper in an article about Aunt Tallie. Alice's mother cut it out and kept it. I have a scrapbook at the house with the whole article in it. It tells how Aunt Tallie wrote down the recipe from Aunt Merrick who cooked from memory. Aunt Tallie brought it when she came out here to settle. That article also told about Aunt Tallie's commemorative trees and about other activities in those early days.

However, a couple of Carrie Nation's leftover WCTU-ers took exception to the wine she put in that cake, so Aunt Tallie didn't make it for anyone except the family, and precious few of them knew she put wine in it. Aunt Tallie sure didn't want to offend anybody. She said she couldn't for the life of her figure out why they objected to a little wine in her blackberry jam cake yet pour all that whiskey and rum on their own fruitcakes for Christmas."

"I can copy it since it belongs to us, and clip the recipe to my rock people."

"No, you won't., That'd be stealing."

"How could it be? Stealing is when you take someone else's stuff. If everyone brags on that cake, it would help me sell my rock figures."

"You'd be stealing. You'd be stealing Alice Fursby's brags. How else does Alice get any brags?"

"I don't know," Tallie answered. "I haven't heard of any others, except for when she plays the piano for church."

"There you are, then."

"I still think I have a right to do it."

"You may have rights clear to the top steps of the Supreme Court, but I've put my foot on the neck of that idea, and you'd better check with God before you decide any different."

"Yes Ma'am!" Tallie pulled clothes from the washers and worked her own thoughts.

"Have you ever made that cake before?"

"Not in a long time. Don't have to. Alice makes it often enough to satisfy us all. Let's get on over to that bric-a-brac shop and grocery store so we can get home. I want these clothes on the line before dark. I like a little smell of sun in them before I double them up."

At the grocery store,Tallie said, "I bet Mary John will bring fried chicken next Sunday, and you know what, I bet she brands it with her initials."

Aunt Jenny twisted her neck around to look at Tallie and laughed. "What on earth for?"

"So Banta Thompson will know she made it."

"Is that a fact? Are you going to brand your dish, too?" Tallie shrugged and said she hadn't thought of a dish to take yet.

"Name a color," Aunt Jenny said.

"Purple."

"Eggplant, turnips, beets." Aunt Jenny said.

Tallie turned up her nose at all those items.

"Orange," Tallie said, thinking that was safer.

"Oranges, tangerines, apricots, pumpkins," Aunt Jenny said.

"Oranges. That sounds good," Tallie said. "I take fresh fruit and cookies."

"Cookies? What kind? What can we do to gussy them up? "

"Make them bigger? Make them hollow like my cake?" Tallie laughed.

"How can you make a hollow cookie? Aunt Jenny asked, leading her further and further into the thinking process.

"We could dig it out. Or we could bend the edges together so it would have a hollow middle."

"You've got it! A little cookie basket!" She patted Tallie on the shoulder and suggested that she could bake them in muffin tins and fill them with a fluffy custard with fresh fruit on top.

"Would they get soggy? Tallie asked.

"We'll put fruit on at the last minute before we go. There's an old trick that might help, too. Brush the cookie baskets with egg whites to make them moisture proof before you bake them.

"What if this turns out to be a big flop?" Tallie asked.

"Then we'll have to eat it up ourselves. But if you're determined not to waste anything, you'll take pains to make food taste good. Furthermore, don't make up more than you want to eat if it does flop."

When the errands were finished, they hurried home. Tallie could tell that her aunt was tired.

"When are you supposed to see the doctor again?"

"He looked me over after he admitted Claude."

"What did he say?"

"That Claude would be all right."

"No, I mean about you."

"Nothing, except to take it easy. Not to be rearranging the furniture or roofing the barn," Aunt Jenny said. She looked straight ahead while talking, trying to hold her blowing hair in place. The previous animation was absent from her voice.

Tallie felt uneasy but could not figure out why, other than her aunt looked tired. After they arrived home, Tallie insisted on hanging out the clothes. With that done, she returned to the house to get the water buckets and fill them.

"Tal—LEE", Aunt Jenny called. Shivers ran all through Tallie as she bolted to the back porch with her heart in her throat.

"I forgot to bring a towel," she said from the bathtub. "Bathing in this wonderful thing is a pure pleasure."

Tallie let out a slow breath of relief, found a towel, and handed it to her aunt.

"By the way, I made up some cookie dough and some lemon custard while you hung the laundry. Both are chilling in the refrigerator. We can bake up a couple of cookies to experiment with after supper."

The first two cookie baskets stuck to the muffin tins, but the next two came off beautifully. Tallie brushed them with egg whites and put them back in the oven to set the glaze. Next, they put in the cooled custard topped with fruit to test how long it would take before the cookie basket got soggy. During the wait, Tallie put the finishing touches on her rock figures. For some, she made little, copper wire spectacles held up by a tiny pebble nose.

"What do you think?" she asked her aunt.

Aunt Jenny looked them over carefully. Tallie could not tell what she was thinking until she grinned and said that they must wait and see what Sawed Off Corners thought, but she suggested Tallie put a high price on them.

"How high?" Tallie asked.

"Deuteronomy 32:13 high. Read that and ask God to help you decide. Now, what about those cookie baskets?"

Tallie reported that the custard stood fluffy and high; the fruit had oozed a bit, but the basket was unphased.

"Pour a little raw Jell-O in that fruit to keep it from oozing, Missy. That ought to do the trick. Folk's will find them fun to eat, I think." Aunt Jenny yawned, announcing her bedtime.

"Me, too, but I'm going to bathe first," Tallie said.

When finished with her bath, Tallie tiptoed up the stairs avoiding the squeaky space she had come to know so well. She shut the door softly, and hunted up Deuteronomy 32:13. She liked the thought of all those good things: honey from a rock, oil from a flinty rock, and riding on high places. But wondered how much to charge for the rock people? $32.13? A little high. Should I sell the whole bunch of them for $32.13?

She got a pencil and divided $32.13 by the ten, then by nine and that came out to be an even $3.57. Tallie smiled at the perceived understanding....You don't want me to sell the Alice Fursby figure nor her recipe either. She put the Bible away, pulled the sheet up to her waist, and slept.

A remnant of green carpet unfurled in her dream. Tiny little people walked around on it. A loud noise caused the tiny people to hide themselves in the nap of the green carpet. The carpet turned black, curled upon itself, rolled out the door, and turned green again to the sound of laughter.

"Weird, but okay dream," she said awakening. She scratched her head, yawned and stretched. It was Saturday. The business of the day took precedence over any further thought on the strange dream. There was much to do.

The kitchen was empty but bacon and biscuits were hidden under a t-towel on the cabinet. Tallie stuffed a small biscuit with a slice of bacon and ate it on the way to the barn. Aunt Jenny was throwing grain from her apron to the chickens. Tallie wondered why she didn't use a bucket instead of her apron.

"I've already milked Janet," Aunt Jenny said.

"You are supposed to take it easy," Tallie reminded.

"I am. I haven't moved a stick of furniture, nor put one shingle on the barn, but you can carry the milk in."

Tallie filled up the water bucket and carried both milk and water to the house. Several times, she returned to the well for water to fill the bathtub tank. Her arms didn't quiver like they used to. Old Jube spread his wings and took two flying hops toward her. She scooped some water from the bucket and flung it on him.

"Shoo! You old feather duster."

Jube folded his wings and strutted a few retreating steps. Tallie emptied a pail of water into the trough for the chickens and picked up a small clod of dirt which she let fly at a fence post hitting it square-on sending little pieces of dirt in all directions. Jube squawked. Tallie laughed and went to the house enjoying the feel of the earth under her bare feet.

Aunt Jenny had a dress box full of pot holders, a styrofoam cooler filled with several rounds of fresh butter on ice, five cartons of fresh eggs, as well as several bags of fresh cucumbers and okra ready to go. Tallie loaded her Aunts wares and wondered how her own things would sell. Aunt Jenny's products always sold.

"Hey, Aunt Jenny, do you have a piece of green cloth or something I can display my rock people on? Tallie called in the direction of her aunt's bedroom.

"There is a little green bath mat in the linen closet. Will that do?"

"Like a dream." Tallie smiled to herself and placed the green mat over her box of figurines.

The day was already hot–too hot to roll the windows up to keep the dust out, so Tallie drove very slowly to prevent kicking up any more dust than necessary. It did little good when a car sped past smothering them in great clouds of it. For a moment, it was even difficult to see the road.

"Jerks!" Tallie yelled at them. Aunt Jenny coughed, and fanned herself, obviously disgusted.

"Who was that?" Aunt Jenny asked. "Surely it couldn't have been any of the neighbors."

Tallie pulled off the road and waited for the dirt to settle down. The speeding car rounded the curve ahead allowing Tallie a mere glimpse of a blue sedan before it disappeared from sight. Fear stirred in her, and she gladly waited to continue to town.

In spite of the heat and dust, there were plenty of shoppers and sellers milling around in the pavilion. Many wondering aloud to each other when it was ever going to rain again. The exhaust fans at each end of the pavilion seemed to help a little. Aunt Jenny set her wares out. She smiled at Tallie's rock figures and asked her what price she had decided on.

"Deuteronomy 32:13 suggested that I charge $3.57 each. God priced them."

"You'd better have plenty of pennies on hand or round up your price. I thought you had ten rock figures."

"I do," Tallie replied, "but I left one at home," and she quickly changed the subject.

"I see the Hays over there." She waved across the pavilion to Mary John.

While people stopped to chat with Aunt Jenny, Tallie eyed the area to see who was selling what and what was going the fastest.

Someone had goose feather pillows and hand-tooled horse bridles for sale. There were cantaloupes and watermelons, but not as much fresh produce as before the storm. No one had anything closely resembling her rock people, and most of the business seemed to be taking place at the Home and Garden Club's soft drink counter.

Aunt Jenny's regular customers bought her out right away leaving her free to gad about the other booths. Tallie stayed put. She had lots of lookers but no takers until a well-dressed man approached.

"Hello, there. I'm Fred Jorbison. I bought a sketch from you a few weeks ago, remember?"

"Oh! yes. I remember you."

"And you are...?" he asked.

"I'm Tallie Koums."

"I was hoping you'd have some more of those sketches for sale."

"No, I don't. The one you got was all I had. The only reason I had it, I found it in an old book I'd bought." An awful thought froze Tallie on the inside. "I hope you don't think you paid too much and want your money back."

"No, it was worth every cent. I made a good but fair profit on it, too. Actually, I took a chance on that sketch and it proved to be an authentic Fredrick Remington sketch."

"Does he want it back?"

"No," Mr. Jorbison chuckled. "He was a Western artist during the pioneering days of this country."

"I don't have anymore of his stuff, but I do have these nice rock figures with these little clips. They will hold things like your business card, reminder notes, pictures of family on them. They're originals. I made them. I'm not famous yet, so they only cost $3.57, but when I do get famous, the price will be a lot higher."

Mr. Jorbison kept his business-like composure and looked them over with great care. "That seems a reasonable price for an original. I'll take that one with the mustache, and that lady over there–the one with the apron and white topknot. But please, no squash in the bargain this time, okay?"

Tallie laughed and wrapped the selections carefully. Others stood nearby covertly watching the transaction.

"Here's my business card," he said, "If you run into any more promising art, give me a call."

"Sure," Tallie said and read the card. "You're the first art dealer," she said loudly enough for all to hear, "that I have ever met and I really appreciate your business."

Mr. Jorbison shook her hand and left. His exit was followed by curious stares. While whispers were being exchanged in the aisles, Tallie rearranged her little rock people on the green bath mat. The stare-ers and whisperers waited, for what seemed to them a respectable space of time to pass before they sauntered over to Tallie's display for a closer look. Tallie left Mr. Jorbison's card in plain sight and in a short time, every rock figure was sold.

Aunt Jenny chuckled all the way home over the story. "Isn't that a hoot? All those folk snapping up the latest thing in folk art? Then to herself, she praised God for his adventures.

"Folk art?" Tallie looked at her aunt quizzically.

"That was the rumor being whispered about. Maybe you'd do well to make some more--only not so many, and do them up A+ like. Now think. Expand."

"Make them with long necks?" "Or bigger for a door stop?"

"Shrink it, now."

"Christmas decorations. Valentine's Day. Tiny ones on little mirrors."

"Add--what?" Aunt Jenny continued.

"Voices, furniture, animals."

"Voices?" Aunt Jenny asked.

"I don't know. You said to add, so I did. Hey! What if some hold scriptures? That's like voices.

"Yes! Good one. Let's think some more. What have you learned about rocks? Think on that in your spare time. Add, subtract, expand, contract. Turn things upside down and inside out, and look at them from all angles. You'll get more ideas than you can put together."

"Okay, but you know what? Why don't we do something to your butter and egg containers. You can sell them with or without containers. You could cover the boxes with old wallpaper samples or cloth. Or make some little cloth bags for some of your goods which could be used as gift bags or for something else later. That way, the buyer gets more for the money."

"That's a right fine idea," Aunt Jenny said. " I can use leftover scraps from my hook rugs and quilts. I make some of those in the winter, you know. Some of my quilts bring upwards to S300.00"

As they rode on home in silence, Aunt Jenny mopped her face with a hanky. Tallie kept a close watch on her and decided next time, she would carry a thermos of cool water.

"Stop!" Aunt Jenny said abruptly.

Tallie slammed on the brakes, "What is it?"

"Turn around," Aunt Jenny said, "We've got to go see Claude."

"Claude? Claude! Right now?"

"Yes. Claude, and right now."

"Why?"

"I'm not sure." she said just drive me back to the hospital.

They found Claude in his room. Everything looked okay to Tallie.

"How are you, Claude?" Aunt Jenny asked and before he could answer, she added "and what do you need?"

"A stiff drink," he replied.

"Hush about that. Here, have some of this, " Aunt Jenny said, pouring him a glass of water. He took a few sips and she sat down in a chair beside his bed.

"Tell me about yourself, Claude."

"There's nothing to tell."

"Tell me anyway. I want to know what is going on, and I'm going to sit here until I do."

"I can't sleep much. Nightmares wake me up."

"Do you want me to tell anyone you're in the hospital here?"

"NO! I mean, no, please. I've already had Doc call the filling station. There isn't anyone else to notify. Just keep it to yourself."

"Where did you live before you showed up here?"

"Back east."

"Why come to this little town? Single men usually move away from little towns, not to them. I think you've got troubles."

"Everybody's got troubles, Lady. I got mine."

"I'm waiting, Claude, Out with it."

Claude wrinkled his forehead and sighed. "I had a one-man garage and gas station business back there. I made a decent living, but then I started getting hit, you know—robbed. At first, I figured it was just one of them things— the risk of doing business. I could'a stood it once or twice, but it got to be a regular thing by different members of the same gang, the Hell Hounds. The police did what they could, but they couldn't stay at my place all the time. So the last time they held me up, I was ready for 'em. I'd had it. I put a small booby trap rigged to a timer into the sack to blow up the money, but when they rode off, the main dude sat on the sack and wound up with a hunk of his ugly butt blown off."

"Oh! My stars and garters!" She said, as she cringed and her eyebrows jumped to her hairline at his wording.

"Sorry," Claude apologized.

"Don't be. I didn't expect a pretty story nor pretty words either. Get to the rest of the story."

"Well, booby trapping is against the law, so I never called the police, but I knew those dudes would be after me. I had to get out of there, so I sold off cheap and lit out. I picked the remotest place I could find and still get work."

"You were thinking of lighting out again, weren't you, from this hospital.

" Yes'm. I was hunting my clothes just as you came in. They're after me and they'll run over anyone to get to me. Including you," he said, his eyes wide, popping out from fear.

"Nonsense. You stay put. Doc will take care of you. Besides, how would they know you are here in this hospital?"

"They have their ways. You don't know them like I do."

"Nevertheless, you tell Doc there might be a problem and let him decide what to do. He's a good man. Do exactly what he says do."

Aunt Jenny patted his arm and stood to go. She had forgotten about Tallie standing in the doorway, hearing the whole thing and was concerned that she had heard it. Tallie, on the other hand, was more interested in getting her aunt home to rest, and the sight of home was good to both of them at first.

The downstairs closets, cabinets, and most of the drawers were standing open. Aunt Jenny stood in the living room with her hands on her hips, looking at the mess with disbelief.

"That's it!" Tallie declared, "I'm calling the sheriff."

He told them to go out of the house and wait for him on the porch.

It was mere minutes before Sheriff Sawyer ran up the steps with a furrowed brow; Tom right behind him. Tom stayed with Tallie and Aunt Jenny while his dad made a thorough inspection of the whole house. After a search of the barn and hen house, the sheriff stood next to Claude Worth's car.

"What's this doing here?" he asked Aunt Jenny.

"Claude left it here for me to watch after whilst he's away from his house," she told him.

"I can drive it, Dad," Tom offered, trying not to look too eager.

"No, Son. It could be wired to blow. Whoever was here was looking for some*thing*, or most likely some*one,* since nothing is missing."

Then to Aunt Jenny, he asked. "Do you have any notion what's going on? Because I have a suspicion or two of my own."

"We went to town to see Claude. I might as well tell you, he's in the hospital and thinks someone is after him..."

"...and," Tallie broke in, "there were two men here in a blue sedan wanting donations for some Indian chapel, only I don't think they were for real, and I'm pretty sure I saw them again today. A blue car passed us real fast, but there was so much dirt flying I could barely see it. Maybe they saw Claude's car here."

Sheriff Sawyer went to his patrol car and asked his dispatcher to put him through to the hospital.

"Yeah, Sheriff Sawyer speaking. Get Claude Worth on the phone. Oh? Is that right? How long? What did they look like?...Yeah... Yeah... Got it. Thanks," he said, replacing his radio. He pushed his big Stetson back and rubbed his forehead as he walked to the porch.

"The nurse said she went to take Claude's blood pressure and he wasn't there. Minutes later, two men she didn't know came looking for him. They insisted on going to his room even though she told them he was gone. They said some ugly things and left in a blue four-door sedan."

"What does that mean?" Tallie asked the sheriff.

"I'm not sure yet," he told her. He pulled his Stetson down tight and said, "Tom, call the station to send a tow truck for Claude's car. I don't want this thing out here. It could attract trouble. I'm impounding it and it'll be safe. You all go in the house, now. Tom, get a hoe handle or a stick of wood and keep it handy and latch the door. I've got another call to make, and then I'll go down to Claude's place and take a look. I should be back before the tow truck comes."

When the sheriff returned, he said he had not found anyone on the place, and only two clues– two different sets of car tracks heading south out of the dirt drive and a past due notice from the electric company. No tire tracks were seen entering Aunt Jenny's drive from north of her house. The trouble had arrived from the south, apparently.

Sheriff Sawyer talked to the tow truck driver, briefly, who nodded several times while he put his gloves on before leaving with the little yellow sports car hooked to his truck by a big heavy chain.

Next, he handed Tom a walkie-talkie, and told Aunt Jenny he wanted to post Tom with them to report any unusual goings on, but another reason was kept to himself. The sheriff knew that even a 'little dog' could give an intruder pause. Besides, it would not hurt Tom any to help out with the chores.

Tallie watched Tom take a milk pail to the barn. Inside, Aunt Jenny was mumbling, putting her things straight again. Tallie went in to help.

"What did you say?" Tallie asked.

"I SAID, I feel like my privacy has been violated. I've been snooped on. Peeked at. Somebody has had their hands on my belongings. I'm so grateful we had the laundry with us. I would have been mortified if they'd prowled through all my dirty underwear and such. I know some folks send their laundry out to be done, but I could never do that. Absolutely couldn't, and won't, as long as I can help it. I can't abide the notion of them peeking at the labels, or checking how well you sew your seams, knowing your petticoats are lacy or plain, and knowing the sizes of everything. Those things aren't anybody's business, and that's a fact. That is why my clothes line is out back of the house."

"What about when you were in the hospital?" Tallie reminded.

"You can be sure there was not a speck of nothing on those hospital gowns and linens I used. When you brought me my own gowns, I hid my used ones in my overnight bag and locked them up."

Tallie changed the subject on purpose. "Since Tom is milking, shall I start supper while you finish putting your drawers in order?"

"Fine," Aunt Jenny replied. "I took out some beef patties this morning. Let's have a hamburger. I've been hungry for one ever so long, and it was too hot to sit in the truck and eat one at Noodle and Hub's place. I'm tired of those leftovers, aren't you?"

"Okay by me," Tallie said.

"I hope you can find a fresh tomato and onion out of the garden. There's pickles in the refrigerator. Put out plenty of those. I've got pickles running out of my ears. Tom likes them. Oh, and make at least two burgers for him. He is hollow legged."

Tallie thought it was no wonder Tom likes to stay with Aunt Jenny, she sure takes note of his preferences. Even at dinner Tallie noticed, again, the ease with which they swapped stories. Tom's pranks with the baseball team were often punctuated by Aunt Jenny's laughter, especially the one about the little Vaseline ads that they taped to the baseballs prior to the game since greasy balls had been outlawed. What was funny about that? The coach made the boys take them off and, after the game, someone had vaselined the doorknobs in the locker room. Tom suspected the coach since he was the only one not anxious to get in there.

Tallie thought Aunt Jenny should know none of that was very funny, certainly not funny enough to warrant all that amount of laughter. Aunt Jenny acted like she had never heard of such an outrageous thing. Tallie sat quietly and listened since she didn't have any stories to swap, and wondered what she had done all her life that she had no stories interesting enough to share.

After supper, Tom stuck some sticks in the piles of dirt and chunked rocks at them while listening to a baseball game on the radio Aunt Jenny plugged in on the porch. Sometimes, he put 3 sticks in the ground, carried 3 stones, spun on his toes to see if he could hit all three in rapid fire.

"When I was a young girl," Aunt Jenny said leaning over to Tallie, "I could out-chunk nearly any boy in this county. Are you any good at it?"

"I hit a post this morning."

"Tom," Aunt Jenny called, "teach this gal to chunk." Then to Tallie she said, "I'm going to get my crochet, but I'll be back to see how you do."

Tom came to the porch slowly, tossing a rock up and catching it with ease.

"Want to try one?"

"I guess so," Tallie said. She threw at the closest stick, came close, but missed.

"Follow through and point at the target when you let the rock fly," he instructed. "Move a little closer. We can have you back off as you get the hang of it." When she was set, he told her to draw an imaginary bead to the stick.

"Draw a bead? What the heck does that mean?" Tallie asked.

"Make a mental line between your eye and that stick. See it re-e-al clear, then mark a spot on that stick and don't take your eyes off it. And when you're ready, let that rock fly down that imaginary line, and point to the spot you're aiming at until the rock lands."

"Gotcha!" Tallie said and did as told. She hit the stick easily. At Tom's direction, she backed up and tried again. He kept coaching her with a quiet voice, just like the golf announcers on TV.

"See?" he said and smiled slightly. "It's a matter of concentration and the follow through form."

Tallie threw again. "All right!" she said. Feeling confident, she let another rock fly and missed.

"You can't get cocky," Tom said, "You've gotta stay sharp. Forget about the last shot. Make every move count in sequence for this shot."

Tallie chewed her lower lip in concentration and threw again with success. Restraining all inclinations to gloat, she did allow herself to smile just a little. After successfully hitting the targets five times in a row, Tom had her move back several more paces. From there, she only hit two of five targets. Tallie threw her hands up.

"Don't give up now," Tom said, "You need to keep at it if you're serious."

"That's right, Missy," Aunt Jenny hollered from the porch. "You're making a right good showing and with a little practice, there's no telling how good you might be. But I think we need to snuff the wick in the next little bit, kids, or you two won't stay awake in church tomorrow."

Tallie put the custard and fruit into separate containers and the cookie cups into a basket lined with a tea towel. At the last minute, she went upstairs to dress.

Aunt Jenny was returning from the horse tank with a large vase of water when Tallie came down the stairs in her new birthday dress. For the first time in her life, Tallie felt rather pretty.

In the middle of the garden, Tom held a large vase while Aunt Jenny arranged the flowers in it.

"That will have to do. I hope they hold their heads up long enough to decorate the table," Aunt Jenny remarked. Turning toward the house, they saw Tallie on the porch. Both of them paused for a moment, affirming that she looked good in the dress even though neither of them said a word. Tallie repressed a smile and collected the baskets of food from the porch.

"Tom," Tallie called, "would you please drive today? I have to hold this basket in my lap."

Tom looked at her again, just long enough not to stare.

"Sure." His voice broke. "No problem."

Tallie repressed another smile.

"That's a good idea, Missy," Aunt Jenny said. "Climb up there in the middle and give me a hand up, will you please."

Tallie reached for Aunt Jenny's hand and when they were all settled in, Aunt Jenny said, "Not too fast, now, Tom. What isn't ruts is holes and sand on this road. I do wish the county office would send a grader to smooth it out a bit."

"Yes'm," he answered, driving at a snail's pace and asked "Are you all going to stay all afternoon?"

"We'll see," Aunt Jenny answered.

"You might want to. I helped Pastor Hay hook up the water cooler in the dining hall. Mrs. Fursby called and said it was about time to do that."

Aunt Jenny leaned across Tallie to talk to Tom. "Alice never could take the heat with much grace, nor the cold either. She says it's due to her 'poor circl-ation.'"

Tom laughed. "Mamma said she doesn't move fast enough to circulate much air, let alone any blood."

"Tom!" Aunt Jenny said in feigned astonishment. "You oughtn't told that on your mama."

Tom laughed again. "Mrs. Fursby seems fragile."

"Fragile, my foot! She's tough as a boot. She just don't let on, that's all." Aunt Jenny sat back in place and patted Tallie on the knee. "How are those cookie cups riding, gal?"

Tallie peeked into the basket. "So far, so good."

"Cookie cups? Cups? Tom asked.

"Yes, cups. You'll see them at lunch," Tallie remarked.

"Did you make them?"

"Aunt Jenny and I both worked on them, but you don't have to eat any."

"You really go in for hollow food, don't you?" He teased.

"I wasn't aware that you were keeping up with the stuff I make," she said.

Tom grinned.

"Why, next to baseball," Aunt Jenny put in, "food is the first thing on his mind."

"Maybe," Tom replied, eyeing the turn-off to the church. He swerved the truck just sharply enough to cause Tallie to have to lean against him. He smiled and watched Tallie hold onto the cookie basket and listened to her tell him to take it easy and not be showing off. He laughed and parked the truck in the shade. When everything was unloaded, he joined a group of males outside the dining hall.

Tallie and Mary John were instructed to start pouring ice water and lemonade early since it was 90 degrees in the shade.

"Lah, me," Alice Fusby said, coming in the door wearing a wide-brimmed lacy, straw hat with a huge, purple, polka-dotted bow. I'm ever so grateful that they got the air hooked up. I knew it was going to be hot. All sorts of meanness and revolutions break out in hot weather. People don't do such foolishness when it's freezing cold. They're too busy hunting a stove to back up to."

She took a glass of ice water and sat down next to Aunt Jenny. Tallie perceived that she was waiting for someone to comment on her new hat, and Aunt Jenny in particular.

"The only thing that breaks out in hot weather in Sawed Off Corners is the blooming heat rash, Alice," Aunt Jenny said.

"You know the best thing for that, don't you? Rub yourself with cornstarch real good and," she whispered to Aunt Jenny loudly enough for all to hear, "put plenty where the elastic in your under-wear touches your skin ."

Mary John punched Tallie. Both tried to keep a straight face, but began to shake with silent laughter. To avoid spewing lemonade, Tallie bolted for the door with her hand over her mouth.

"Is that child sick, Jenny?" Alice asked. "She's at that funny age, you know."

"No, I don't know. And she isn't sick. She's worked in the hot sun all summer and hasn't thrown up a-tall. Drink your water, Alice, she is just fine," Aunt Jenny said, staring after Tallie. Then she turned back and said, "Tell me about that hat of yours, Alice. Is there a story to go with it?"

Tallie went past the church all the way to the road to get control of her laughter. Mary John was only a moment behind and together, they broke out afresh in laughter, holding their sides and wiping the tears. Suddenly, Tallie's face fell.

"What is it?" Mary John asked.

"It's that blue sedan. It's coming. See it? Go get the sheriff, quick!"

Sheriff Sawyer casually walked out of the church yard to his car and motioned for Tallie to go back to the church. He slowly headed down the road. The pastor sounded the bell for services, and Tallie was torn between returning to safety inside the church or to keeping an eye on the sheriff and the blue sedan. Tom and Mary John rigorously motioned for her to come, so she did.

"Isn't anyone going to help the sheriff?" She asked. "He's by himself against those criminals!"

"Dad radioed for help," Tom assured her. "You all need to go inside. Will Thompson is going to follow Dad in a minute. I'll climb that walnut tree. If I think they need help, I'll yell."

"Come on," Mary John said and took Tallie by the hand. "Tom has that thing-a-ma-jig and can talk to his dad and the deputies, too."

People were seating themselves in the pews as usual, unalarmed at the departure of the sheriff and the absence of Mr. Thompson. This was not the first time the sheriff had been called away, thus, no one was upset but Tallie. She tried to get her aunt to sit in the back row.

"What on earth for?" her aunt responded and told her to sit down.

This is my Father's world; I rest me in the thought was the first line of the first hymn and it sailed right over Tallie's head making no impression whatsoever. She was too busy worrying about the imminent danger arriving while everyone else simply sat there singing. She fidgeted during prayer. Aunt Jenny zapped her with a quizzical look. It helped her to sit more still. However, she strained her ears for sounds from outside, half expecting to hear gunfire any moment.

When the congregation stood for the next song, she looked back hoping to see Tom and the sheriff, but they weren't there.

She wanted to peek out the door ever so badly, or warn people, or something. If those men have silencers on their guns, she thought, we'd never hear them shoot the sheriff. The congregation sang *Farther along, we'll know all about it.* Tallie thought there is stuff they should know right now.

Pastor Hay stood up and began preaching. Tallie listened a minute but could not contain herself any longer. She raised her hand like a student in school.

"What is it, Tallie? Pastor asked, causing the whole congregation to look at her. It was extremely embarrassing, but she felt driven to share her concerns.

"I think the sheriff is in danger and Tom is out there in a tree, and Mr. Thompson is out there somewhere, too. I think we should go out there and help them, or pray, or something. It isn't right to sit here singing songs when they need us."

The pastor asked Floyd to look out the door and see if anyone needs any help. Then he thanked Tallie and asked her to lead out in prayer.

"ME?" she squeaked.

"Yes, I think you are the appropriate one since this matter is troubling you."

Tallie said, "Lord," and then went blank.

"Go ahead, Tallie," the pastor urged. "It isn't unnatural for opposing forces to try to keep us hog-tied when we seek God's attention."

"Lord," she said, refusing to be hog-tied by any enemy, "thanks for listening and taking care of things all this week. And now, there is some other stuff going on and I'm not sure just what. So take care of the sheriff, Mr. Thompson, and Tom and all those who are out there helping. Please don't let anyone get hurt. Thank You. Amen."

"Amen," the Pastor said. He opened the Bible to Psalm Ninety-One, and read it to the congregation, only he never looked at it. This Psalm is a good, old Psalm. It warms me in the wintriest times and shades me in the warmest times. This Psalm is a treasure map describing a secret place. Do you Know where it is? he asked. (Many shook their heads 'no'.)

"I got to wondering about it and studying on it. I sometimes think God likes a little mystery, too. It's right fun following the clues and all. So I was reading here, the other day, about the Ark of the Covenant, and there are two critters called cherubim that spread their wings over that ark.

They're hovering over a place called 'The Mercy Seat', which is where God focused Himself to dwell in the olden times. That's a picture of what's in heaven. He had to give those early followers something to set their eyes on and to experience so they could remember it all. That's my calculation. I don't claim to have the last word, but it makes as much sense to me as what any other commentator has to say on it. This is my understanding. If it isn't spelled out in the Bible, the rest is a guess and a good one if it doesn't contradict the word itself.

"That Mercy Seat was a visible place where certain ones could talk to God directly. Now you know as well as I, God wasn't stuck in that ark-box. He only focused Himself to meet with the people in that place. The Hebrews kept that ark in a tent called a tabernacle. They used a tent since they were marching around trying to get to the Promised Land. After they got there, it took a while before Solomon built a great temple and put the ark inside, in a special place called the Holy of Holies.

"The ark was back behind a heavy drape that hung from ceiling to floor; but when Jesus died, that drape was mysteriously ripped from top to bottom. That was a sign, to my notion, that Jesus intended that any of us, anytime, anywhere, could call on Him and He would give His immediate attention. No one can keep blood-bought citizens of his kingdom from talking to Him personal like. That, my friends, that right there is what I call a 'comfort zone'.

" If you're on a worldly hotseat and need out from under the devil's breath, run to the Mercy Seat. The angels of the Lord will fan you. If the world is giving you the cold shoulder, icy stares, or your heart is cold from lack of love, run to the Mercy Seat and enjoy the Lord's assurance. Right there is where we adjust our spiritual thermostat. All of us should read Hebrews the ninth chapter this week along with this Psalm and bask awhile in the Lord's comforts."

At the pastor's signal, Alice Fursby played *Blessed Assurance*. Mary John got Tallie's attention and pointed to the back of the church. There sat Floyd Fursby, Tom, Sheriff Sawyer, Mr. Thompson, and the two men from the blue sedan. Tallie was stunned and had a mind full of questions marks.

Pastor Hay announced that visitors were present and invited them to stay for Sunday dinner. Tallie's question marks became exclamation points. The sheriff himself escorted those men to the dining hall like they were a couple of good buddies.

"Hey," Tom called to Tallie, "Thanks for the prayer you said."

"You heard me? Clear out in the tree?"

"No, I was on the back pew."

"All of you? The whole time?" She asked to nods of 'yes.' That's embarrassing! I embarrassed myself and prayed for nothing. That's stupid."

"Praying is never stupid, and what you did took spiritual grit."

"I hate looking stupid, gritty or not."

"You want to talk about looking stupid? That's your birthday dress and it looks nice on you. But Aunt Jenny wanted to put some extra lace on the underskirt ruffles. She had me buy 10 yards of lace and bring it out to her. Those ladies in the shop really gigged me.'Was I taking up sewing? Enrolled in Home Ec? And just what are you sewing that lace on, Tom?' he minced and mimicked in a falsetto voice. But when she sent me back for some pink ribbon, I had my mother get it."

Suddenly, Tallie knew how Aunt Jenny felt about people knowing all about her underwear. Picturing the whole scene, she couldn't help but laugh.

"Did she put all that lace on there?" Tom asked.

"This isn't show and tell, Tom, but thanks for the trouble. We need to go to the kitchen," she said. When she saw the two men from the blue sedan were talking to the sheriff in the dining hall, Tallie hesitated to enter.

"I still don't think we're safe–any of us– and I'd like to know what is going on," she said to Tom.

"Dad'll find out. Besides, there's only two of them and a whole bunch of us."

Tallie took her place at the beverage table hoping that the sheriff had thought to frisk those men. At her back was a big refrigerator.

If those criminals suddenly pulled guns and started blasting, she would open the door and get behind it.

"What's up?" Mary John asked and cut her eyes in the direction of the visitors.

"Who knows? I haven't found out anything yet, have you?"

"Nope. Why don't you flat out ask those guys when they come through the line—who are you and what are you doing here?" Mary John suggested.

"Not me! It might make them nervous and trigger happy. Shhh! Here they come."

Tallie moved closer to the refrigerator door, just in case, but couldn't help looking at their plates first. There was a big chicken breast branded with an 'M'. Mary John had actually branded her chicken pieces and Tallie could not help but stare incredulously.

"Interesting chicken, isn't it?" the first man said.

"Yes. Yes it is," Tallie mumbled and dropped her face to concentrate on pouring drinks.

"You're the one that stays with the elderly lady, the praying lady, aren't you?"

Tallie stuck her chin up and looked at him squarely. "She's older and she prays, but she isn't exactly elderly."

"Correction accepted," he said. Both men thanked the girls for the tea, smiled and left them.

Mary John watched the men nod and speak to others as they moved through the crowd looking for a place to sit.

"Those guys don't seem so bad to me," said Mary John. " They talk nice and polite."

"They're good at fooling people because they are con artists. I don't trust them. They aren't who they claim to be, raising funds for some church that doesn't even exist. They're phonies."

Mary John shrugged and quickly lost all interest in the strangers. Banta was coming her way. When he asked for lemonade, Mary John heaped his glass with ice and smiled politely, especially when she noticed the branded chicken on his plate.

"Did you fry this chicken? I figured it might be your brand."

"I did, and it'll be the best chicken you ever ate."

"That good, huh?"

"You can try some from those other platters, if you don't believe me," she said.

Banta smiled and said he believed he'd stick to what he got, and in three steps his long legs hauled him across the room to a table.

"How do you know that's the best chicken he'll ever eat?" Tallie asked.

"Because we grew those chickens, and I know they were fed right, and they aren't all mucked up with dyes and chemicals, and because they haven't been frozen and thawed nine times between here and their old homeland. Besides, a little exaggeration in advertising is to be expected, see?"

"I thought there was some kind of law about truth in advertising," Tallie remarked.

"There is. Look at that," she said, looking at Banta " His cheeks were full and he gave the OK sign to Mary John.

"Told you!" Mary John said.

"Let's go get some of it so I can decide," Tallie suggested. "The guys would laugh at me if I talked to them like you do."

"That's because you aren't me. You'll have to find your own methods," she said, nudging Tallie.

Tallie smiled, but decided she did not ever want to do 'methods' on anyone, and certainly not on some goofy guy.

"I think you need to start thinking about things, Tallie. What are you going to talk about with the boys? What are you going to have going for you as a future wife?"

"That sounds like bait and I'm not fishing. As for talking to guys, I do, sometimes. I talk about whatever is going on. I'm not going to sit around and make up stuff to say to anybody. Most guys I know are smart-offs. I'm not interested in talking to smart-offs."

"I saw you talking to Tom. Is he still as big of a smart-off as you thought when you first came?"

"He can be okay at times," Tallie admitted and changed the subject on purpose. "By the way, your chicken was really good. Let's get some dessert."

"Oh look at those tarts!" Mary John's eyes lit up causing Tallie to smile. Mary John noticed the pleased look on Tallie's face.

"Are those yours? Did you make those?" she asked.

"Aunt Jenny and I did, but mostly it was her."

"That's a neat idea. I'm proud of you."

"Thanks," Tallie said, thankful to be off the subject of boys.

"Tom keeps looking over here at you, Tallie," Mary John pointed out.

Tallie looked up. Tom was looking at her. He grinned and then looked back at his dad and the two men. In a moment, the two men stood, shook hands with the pastor, nodded to the sheriff and left. That's when Tom got up and walked in her direction.

"Here he comes, Tallie," Mary John said as if Tallie wasn't fully aware of it.

Tom turned a chair around backwards and straddled it. "You'll never believe it," he said to the girls.

"Never believe what?" Mary John asked.

"Catch this. Those two men," he explained, weren't really fundraisers."

"Well, really." Tallie tossed her head and sent her ponytail flying back from her shoulders with a sarcastic jerk. I already told you that, and now they're going off scot free. Your dad should have arrested them."

"No, listen. It's really something. Those men are two university professors, researchers working on a study about small town society. They have researched different groups, sometimes for corporations, sometimes for articles for magazines. And anyway, those guys were researching whether people in rural towns were more gullible or more trusting than in big city areas and whether they are more generous or more stingy than people in the metropolitan areas. They took newspapers from various towns to decide which towns and cities they would use to test their comparison study. So when they read about the storm, they got this idea to come collect funds for a fake cause. They made up that story and made up the letter from Dad. Then they began outside of town in the farming areas thinking it would cause the least suspicion and least commotion. HA! They sure learned something different about that. They went out to the Fursby's and then to Aunt Jenny's."

"That was a mistake, I'll bet," Mary John said, leaning across the table toward Tom with more interest as he continued.

"You know it. See that larger guy? That's Dr. Alwort. He has arthritis in his left knee. He said he thought he'd die from kneeling while Aunt Jenny prayed on and on over her check and the collections they claimed to have before she let him up off that porch."

Mary John giggled.

"Why were they hiding down at Claude's?" Tallie asked, seriously. It wasn't funny to her.

"That's another deal. They had asked at the gas station about their car engine sounding funny, like the timing was off. Whoever was on duty told him Claude would be the one to see about that, only he wasn't at work and told him how to find Claude's place. So they went out there right after they left Aunt Jenny's. Claude was pretty well lit but took a look at the motor. They hit him for a donation. Claude said he didn't have any money and they'd better pay for the car repairs up front if they expected him to do the fixing. They said they would pay half now and half when he got finished. Claude agreed, only he passed out before he did any of the work. So they left, but stopped by Will Thompson's place for a donation on the way.

They hung out in town trying to get their car fixed but no one could get to it fast enough to suit them so they went back out to Claude's the next day and he was sober enough to do something. They paid him and left."

"I knew they were down there," Tallie said, and more than once."

"But here's the kicker," Tom continued. "They said Aunt Jenny prayed about the hell hounds chasing them down if they were dishonest. These guys knew about some dudes called Hounds of Hell, or maybe hell hounds. Anyway a biker gang. They had studied gang behavior as grad students back East and tried to question some of the members, but the leader—some mean 'mogumbus' mumbling something about missing part of his behind got so mad about their nosing around, he crashed his bike through their motel window and threatened to take their scalps for a peculiar use if they didn't bug off."

"That sounds a little wild to me," Mary John said.

"I'm not sure I believe a bit of it," Tallie said, "It's too stupid to believe."

"I'm just telling you what they said. Think what you want. They said after Claude got their car fixed, the money they had collected was missing. They wondered if Claude took it. So they went back to check.. They found Claude, lit as usual, but no money.

"Since they were there, they asked him if he had ever heard the Hounds of Hell. They said Aunt Jenny mentioned them, so maybe Claude knew them as well. Old Claude went nuts. Grabbed a tire tool and threatened to tear their heads off and told them to go tell the Hell Hounds they'd get the same thing if he ever saw one of them. That's when they left, lickitey-split only looking back to see Claude falling over the garbage cans when he tried to run after them. As for the missing donation money, it showed up later in their car trunk under some of their stuff."

Tom finished and sat quietly relishing his report before Tallie broke his moment with her question.

"Why did they come out here today? Have you wondered about that?" she asked,

"I reckon they wanted to make things right. They wanted to give the money back to Aunt Jenny and to square up with Dad."

"They should give her money back—with interest if you ask me," Tallie replied.

Tom told her that Aunt Jenny wouldn't take the money back, that she said to plow the seed into what God intended, and Pastor said he would give it to the nearest mission for Indians. There was one near Riverside Indian School and he knew the pastor there.

"Then who the heck ransacked Aunt Jenny's house?" Tallie demanded. "No one has any answer to that, and I think those two men are leaving something out of the story."

"I don't think so. That mystery is still out there." Tom said quietly and thoughtfully.

"Then your story may not be the whole story on these two men, right? I'm going to ask your dad right now to arrest them on suspicion of unlawful entry before they have time to get away."

Tallie marched over to the sheriff and asked, "Did you find out who ransacked Aunt Jenny's house? Did you question those men about it?"

Sheriff Sawyer pulled back a chair for Tallie. "Here," He said, "git down so I don't break my neck looking up at you."

Tallie sat down on the edge of the chair and leaned forward.

"Well?" she asked.

"Yes. I questioned them as to their whereabouts as of last Friday. I asked that question first thing this morning."

Tallie started to speak, but the sheriff held up his hand to quieten her. "And," he continued, "I double checked their story. They were in Boggy Creek all day taking surveys for one of their articles and speaking to the Downtown Merchants Group during their noon meal. The motel there had them registered, had records of their phone calls and the time they were placed. Bonnie waited on them for breakfast at the Main Street Cafe. So I can pretty well account for their comings and goings the whole day over there. They couldn't have been the ones to prowl Aunt Jenny's house."

"Then who did?" Tallie asked.

"I'm checking it and I have a gut feeling."

"Someone passed us going ninety-to-nothing on the road to town last Saturday. I'm pretty sure it was those guys. It was a blue car."

"Lots of folks have blue cars. Could you see who was in it?"

Tallie dropped her head. "No, not really."

"Well, we'll find out what the deal is," the sheriff said and patted her on the shoulder.

"I hope you do. Some creep is still walking around out there and could be planning a return trip to our house."

"Be sure and latch up at night and call if you see or hear anything suspicious at all. I have some extra eyes working in the area since that incident. We'll get 'em."

Tallie sighed. The sheriff stood, patted Tallie's arm, and ambled toward the door. She was not comfortable with the idea that someone was still at large. It was hard for her to tell how much importance he gave to the matter in spite of what he said.

When Tallie asked her aunt who the prowler could be, she displayed very little concern and continued to dish out seconds on desserts saying that it would all come out in the wash. Dismissing the subject, she pointed to their cookie tarts which had disappeared down to four—–faster than ice cream in August.

Bandit's long arm reached between Tallie and her aunt for another cookie tart. "Good stuff," he said to them both.

"Help yourself," Aunt Jenny said even though he had already done so, then she nudged Tallie. "Look out. You're liable to take Mary John's beau, but consider the fact you'd have to climb a ladder to look him in the eye."

Tallie made a face at the idea. "Mary John will make somebody a good hired hand. She thinks boys want a good cook with a strong back."

"She's nearer to the truth of it than most girls. What do you think the boys look for?"

"A beauty queen with a big bank account."

"And you? What assets do you look for in the boys?"

"I'm not lookin'. Most of them do what they can to make each other laugh. They spike their dopey hair, wear their baseball caps backwards to match their brains, slam locker doors, talk loud, bump into everyone they can, and give corny answers to the teacher's questions.

Aunt Jenny chuckled. "That will change, Missy. Go on out yonder now, and visit while I gather up our belongings. We'll be leaving in a little bit."

Tallie went outside and sat down next to Pastor and Mrs. Hay. He smiled and said, "What you did today in the meeting was good."

"It was embarrassing and all for nothing."

"No, no.. Wait a minute. Maybe you needed the exercise in faith. You may have prayed after the fact, but don't you think God knew you were going to pray? You have to do as led. Everyone here understands that. I've prayed after the fact. Perhaps God says, 'John Hay's going to pray, so let's get the thing tended to now.'"

"You did the loving thing," Mrs. Hay added, "and that is always acceptable. Perhaps if you had not prayed, those men might have backed out of coming to own up to what they were doing. The little dab of money they collected might have caused harm in some way. Who knows?" Tallie listened, but she still felt a little silly.

The Pastor' wife sensed her lack of peace.

"You were needed this morning; needed all the time you've been here, or you'd be somewhere else. We'd all be somewhere else if we weren't needed here," his wife said.

Tallie looked at them, not sure she bought into all they said, but knew they believed it. Their comments sounded like a summary of a long and weighty study into which few had ever waded.

"Thanks," she said quietly.

"It's an adventure, sometimes a mysterious one, but never dull," Pastor added.

"That's a fact!" Tallie replied.

Pastor and Mrs. Hay laughed. Mrs. said she was beginning to sound like Aunt Jenny.

Geneva Sawyer dropped a tambourine onto Tallie's lap. "Your turn," she said, "I've got to gather up my dishes."

"Go on," the Pastor encouraged.

Mary John called out, "Come on, Tallie. Come help me sing."

Tallie picked up the tambourine and went to stand by Mary John. When they began to sing *Don't Fence Me In*, Mary John sang loud and strong. Tallie recalled the horseback rides, the way old Brownie smelled, the shimmering heat distorting the image of the pastures while cooking the red dirt, the smell of Johnsongrass, and the rhythmic sway of Brownie plodding along bobbing his head. Little by little, Tallie's timbre rose to match Mary John's.

Aunt Jenny looked through the screen of the dining hall. Alice Fursby came up beside her.

"Why, Jenny! You never told me what a talent that child has. Does she take voice lessons up there in St. Louis? How long has she been singing?"

"Hush up, Alice, and listen. This is all new to me, as well."

The song was followed by a spot of silence, then with whoops and clapping, the crowd yelled for more.

"Jenny, you know who she sounds like?" Alice asked.

"I do. Sounds just exactly like her Great Aunt Tallie."

"I haven't heard singing like that since we were girls eating blackberry jam cake on your Aunt's front porch. It's wonderful." Alice said, crossing her arms on her chest.

"Maybe, but she hasn't done p-squat with that tambourine yet," Aunt Jenny blurted.

"Hush yourself, Jenny Raider! I'm ashamed of you. It won't send you to hell to brag on that child a little."

To Aunt Jenny's look of dismissal, Alice looked right back. She wrinkled her chin and said in defiance, "Well, I'm going to brag on her whether you do or not. Kids need a little encouragement. You ought to do some of that while she's here."

Aunt Jenny watched Alice smother Tallie with a big hug, knowing Tallie would smell like a quart of White Magnolia cologne after Alice was through with that bear hug. She caught Tallie's eye and gave her a smile and a sly wink. Forgive me for tricking Alice, she silently asked the Perceived One. It is just so easy to do, I am ashamed of myself.

Several others personally complimented Tallie and after some small talk and goodbyeing, the people began to depart. Tallie thought again about the prowler who might be lying in wait. She was grateful that Tom gave her the pager before he left.

"You're awfully quiet," Aunt Jenny said. "What's on your mind?"

"Nothing really. I'm just trying to drive around some of the deeper ruts in the road. Did you know the Hays let Bandit take Mary John home in his car?"

"He seems like a nice boy. Are you jealous?"

"Heck no."

"Is that a fact? Well, it's time Mary John sat on the porch with someone besides her folks and the dogs. One of these days, it'll be your turn. It's been an interesting day all around, hasn't it? Take those professors. Wasn't that a lick?"

"I'd like to see them go to jail. That's the lick I'd like to see. I don't trust them. And I still wonder who was in the house, don't you? Even the sheriff said we'd better latch up the doors until we find out."

"I guess we'd better do what he advises."

Tallie parked the truck and helped Aunt Jenny step out and onto the porch. She unloaded their dishes, changed clothes and went to the barn to milk the cow.

As she milked, she pondered what her aunt said about her 'turn coming'. It meant boy friends, obviously. Maybe that will be okay someday—some distant day. She realized the boys had never run after her like they did Amy and some of the other girls. Amy had been kissed under the fire escape at recess in the second grade. She recalled the only boy that ever chased her in grade school had green teeth and a runny nose. She was glad when he moved to another town. None of the boys she knew gave her any special notice except on test day when they wanted to copy her answers. Sometimes, she let them see wrong answers before she went back to change them. That was the last of the copying by the little cheaters.

Tallie set the milk aside and went to pump water. When the bucket was full, she pumped a handful and splashed her face. The sun was going down splashing colors of flaming orange against lavender. A slight breeze blew her hair and cooled, her damp face.

"God, why do I feel this way, barely seen or tolerated by people around me? It's like I've intruded on the world of others who seem to have it all together."

There was not a lot she had against boys, nor for them either. That seemed to be the same way they considered her, too, she realized. What am I doing here in the boondocks of Oklahoma, five miles from that little one-taxi town? She silently asked again.

Aloud, she asked, "Is there an actual someday for me? Will anyone ever tell me I'm nice and want me around? What is wrong with me? How many times will I have these sags? I thought once You and I got together, everything would straighten up."

She sighed again, flicked a gnat off the foam on the milk, lifted both buckets easily and returned to the house.

"The straining rags are on the clothesline," Aunt Jenny said. She could see Tallie's dobbers were down. "It has been a nice day," Aunt Jenny continued, "but once in a while, a nice time can leave you with an emptiness when it's over. That's a natural thing on this side of heaven. There is a little thread of sorrow that wiggles through feast days here that won't be present in heaven."

Tallie looked up sharply, but said nothing as her aunt continued.

"Everyone senses it to one degree or another, but not everyone knows it is biblical. Being aware of it is usually enough to shuck it off and get glad about something again, like getting home and taking off your shoes and nylons."

Tallie laughed. She was so used to going barefoot now, she kicked off her shoes at every opportunity.

"Let's go soak our feet in a pan of water on the porch and eat a snack before we go to bed. There's no telling what tomorrow holds" Aunt Jenny suggested.

Tallie wondered what the night held, not tomorrow. She remembered to latch the door and read Psalm Ninety-One before she went to sleep. It mentioned that God would *cover thee with, with His feathers.* She laughed. Her pillow was filled with feathers. It also said not to be afraid of the terror of the night. Comforted, she slept.

~~~~~~~~~~~~

Tallie's hair stuck to her damp face. The sun wasn't up and already it was a hot day. Janet had disappeared again. Maybe it was too much to hope that she'd run off for good. Tallie walked through the pasture, dewy weeds slapping at her bare legs, hunting for the cow. Gnats buzzed. She brushed them away and passed between two small trees. A curtain of sticky spider webs engulfed her face. She shrieked and backed up. Her skin puckered like it was trying to crawl to the top of her head—elevator skin.

"To heck with you, Janet," she said. "Do her own thing. You can swing that big, old bag of milk around until it petrifies. I'm going to feed the chickens. You can drag that bag home when you are good and ready."

Tallie flung open the barn gate, slammed a coffee can into a fifty-pound sack of scratch, threw it into the feed troughs, then, off she went to the well for a drink of water.

"Maw-w-w-w. Maw-w-w-w-w,"

Tallie looked up from the pump and there stood Janet demanding attention. Tallie purposely pumped the water more slowly.

"You can just wait, Sister."

She ducked her whole head under the pump and gave the handle a big pull. The cool water felt so pleasant on her head, she pumped some onto her legs. It had not been a good idea to go through the pasture in a short, thin gown and shower thongs.

Reluctantly, Tallie herded Janet into the milking stall. There was a small cut on the lower side of Janet's leg. Gnats were crawling all over it causing the cow to stomp and kick to rid herself of the pests. Suddenly sympathetic, Tallie poured cool water on the leg and dosed the wound with some thick, smelly, tar-colored salve from the storage room. By the time the milking was done, the sun was well up and blazing hot. The breeze was up, too, like a hot breath.

"What kept you so long?" Aunt Jenny asked, taking the breakfast from the oven.

"Janet wasn't in the barnyard again and when she did show up, her leg was cut. I put some of that salve from the store room on it. She was stomping so bad I couldn't milk, and she finally calmed down when I got the salve on her."

"Good. I use that salve for everything but wallpapering and pie making."

Hot as it was, Tallie enjoyed the full breakfast of sausage, gravy, scrambled eggs and pan toast. She laughed.

"What's so funny?" her aunt asked.

"Some people I know in St. Louis are probably jogging before making a smoothie with a piece of organically grown cantaloupe and skim milk. The joggers should try hunting Janet before breakfast. They could afford to eat a couple of eggs and sausages."

"Speaking of cantaloupes, we've got some coming on. I'll go check dreckly. I need to carry some water to things, especially the tomatoes. They're trying to bear again."

"I'll carry the water," Tallie bossed. "You look at the cantaloupes."

"I might sell some of the melons if there's enough ready. That should make the city joggers happy. But we do need to water before it gets any hotter, else it'll steam the roots. Run on out there in your gown-tail and get started. I'll put on some chicken to cook for later. No sense in keeping this kitchen heated up all day long."

While Tallie watered, Aunt Jenny came to prowl the cantaloupe vines raising them with the hoe satisfied there might be some to market by Saturday. One or two had been terrapin-gnawed and a few had bird pecks. Aunt Jenny retrieved a pile of newspapers from the house and returned to the garden when Tallie spied her.

"What are you doing?" Tallie asked. Her aunt stood up from wrapping a melon in paper.

"I'm hoping the terrapins and birds won't eat through the funnies to get at the goodies," she said. Then with one melon and four ears of corn in her apron, she pointed to the house. "Let's go inside and work. It's a mite hot out here."

Aunt Jenny emptied the contents of her apron on the cabinet. Tallie walked up the stairs to dress. Aunt Jenny watched her niece's ascent. She had grown taller, leaner, firmer, tan as a biscuit with sun streaks in the top of her thick, auburn hair. She carried herself gracefully and quietly. Carrying water buckets gets gracefulness heap faster than dictionaries on the head, she affirmed to herself, but there were other graces yet to be. While Aunt Jenny was considering the graces that were missing, Tallie came down the stairs two at a time.

"Aunt Jenny! There's a blue sedan coming down the road. Quick! Get the broom while I lock the doors. I've got the pager and I'll call the sheriff!"

"Calm down, for pity's sake, and don't you punch that pager just yet."

Tallie punched it anyway when the blue sedan pulled into the drive. A tall, skinny man slowly unfolded himself from the driver's seat and placed a western-styled, straw hat on his head. He stretched and looked over the surroundings, briefly. Tallie's skin began the elevator crawl. He sauntered to the steps and stopped.

"Hello," he called loudly, which is country manners. You could be shot for a prowler or have dogs sic-ed on you if you didn't announce yourself. "Is anyone home?" He hesitated a moment then stepped onto the porch and knocked.

Aunt Jenny set the broom behind the door jamb and spoke through the screen. "What can I do for you?" she asked.

"My name's . Wayne Black, Ma'am. Are you the lady who makes those little rock figurines?"

"I'm Jenny Raider, Mr. Black. My niece makes those. Why do you ask?"

"I'm a rock hound in my spare time, and my wife has a gift shop in Oklahoma City. She bought a couple of those figures from an art dealer who got them in Sawed Off Corners. I asked around and got sent out here. I hope I'm not inconveniencing you showing up like this. I should have called, I guess."

Aunt Jenny exited the kitchen and used her t-towel to remove some imaginary dust off the seat of one of the porch chairs, another example of country manners in action. Tallie eased from behind the screen door.

"This is Mr. Black, Tallie. He bought some of your rock people from that dealer."

"Pleased to meet you," Mr. Black said and stood to shake her hand. "My wife and I like those figurines of yours. They have a lot of personality. Makes us smile every time we look at them.

"Thank you, sir. " Tallie said.

"In fact," he continued, "We were hoping you might have some more for sale. I had some business down this way today, and was hoping I could buy a few now, if possible."

"I've only got one right now," Tallie said. "How many do you want?"

"The wife said she'd like to have twenty to twenty-five if the price was right. This is the height of our tourist season, you know, and she likes to have something a little different from the other shops. We bought the others for $10.00 a piece, but were hoping to best that price by purchasing several."

Tallie grinned at Mr. Jorbison's wheeling and dealing, coughed to keep from laughing, and said, "I can make some more I think."

"Would you take $5.00 each and I'll pick up the shipping?"

"Deal," Tallie said.

"If I were you, I would number or name them, and maybe sign your name on them. Here's Mrs. Black's card and here's mine."

While Mr. Black and Tallie continued to iron out the details of their verbal contract, the sheriff arrived. Aunt Jenny looked at Tallie knowingly, and Tallie shrugged.

"Howdy. Just passing by on patrol this morning." Sheriff Sawyer said, "Would you happen to have a glass of iced tea handy? It's as hot as a two-dollar pistol out there." He smiled, but surreptitiously eyed the stranger.

"Come on up, Sheriff," Aunt Jenny beckoned. She looked sideways at Tallie again. Tallie hurried into the kitchen for the tea and returned in time to hear the sheriff speaking to Mr. Black.

"So you've been here before, have you?"

"Last week. Saturday to be exact," Mr. Black answered, "and I was in this area earlier in the month working from some seismograph maps. They're not the newest, but I had a hunch the government would be working their way over here pretty soon to make some new readings."

"There were some seismographers poking around here last fall," Aunt Jenny remembered.

"That property across the road, does it belong to you, Mrs. Raider?"

"Yes, why?"

"I contract for oil and gas leases which brings me to a matter I want to discuss with you, Mrs. Raider," he said. Then he went on to explain his offer and handed her some papers to look over.

"You can take your time," Mr. Black said. "Call me if you have any questions."

Aunt Jenny wiped her glasses and looked at the potential contract. "What do you think, Hank?" she asked and passed the papers to him.

Sheriff Sawyer looked at them and said, "It looks legal. Includes information about repairing damages that could occur, and payments made to the lessor whether they drill or not. But I'd advise you to have a lawyer take a gander at it."

"How soon do you want an answer, Mr. Black", Aunt Jenny asked.

"I'd like to know in a couple of weeks, if possible, m'am. I'll be in town for a couple of days at the Grove Tree Motel if you decide any sooner than that." Mr. Black graciously shook hands all around and left.

The sheriff watched him go, noting the number of his license plate out of habit. An Oklahoma County tag. Then he turned to Aunt Jenny and said, "It'd be nice to have that money coming in regular-like, wouldn't it? And if they drill, it would be down the hill from you on that other property which wouldn't inconvenience you much."

"I'm going to ask my lawyer about it," Aunt Jenny replied.

"What lawyer?" he countered.

"The one I talk to about all my business; then if necessary, I'll get a second one," she laughed as did the sheriff.

Tallie's stomach growled prompting Aunt Jenny to ask, "Want some lunch, Hank? I've got fresh roasting ears, cantaloupe, fried chicken, and the trimmings."

"That's persuasion enough," the sheriff grinned and rubbed his belly.

"Tallie, you go on in and set the table," Aunt Jenny instructed. Then to the sheriff she said, Tallie punched that button thing and that's why you're out here, I'm guessing."

"Yes'm. She was doing what I told Tom to tell her to do."

"Blue sedan or no, she didn't do what I told her to do, but I'm glad you're here all the same. I don't like monkeying with papers. There's too much paper business these days. Wears me out reading all that little-bitty print with words that can mean first one thing and then the other. And when all strung together, they don't make any sense a-tall."

The sheriff laughed, and said, "You should see the paperwork piled on my desk, Lady. Sometimes, I'm convinced it's a plot from hell to keep us officers tied to our desks instead of doing our jobs."

"Speaking of which, you still don't know who was prowling my house, do you?"

"Not yet," he said. He took off his hat, laid it carefully on the buffet and proceeded to wash up.

"I'd like to take my flyswatter to whoever it was," Aunt Jenny said, causing the sheriff to laugh again.

"I'd like to offer you that chance, but we could both get sued over it, and you'd lose all that big oil money," he laughed some more. Being around her took all the kinks out of a bad day. So did the good food she prayed over.

Aunt Jenny and Tallie spent some time watering the rest of the gardens as the sun set.

"If you got that lease money, you could pipe water to your house, and to the gardens." Tallie suggested. "You could have an indoor commode next to the bathtub, not that you don't have the fanciest outside one I ever saw: wall paper, real seat with a lid, linoleum floor, fresh flowers on that little magazine stand, a brass toilet paper hook. How do you keep it smelling nice?"

" There are several ways. A good dose of fresh dirt, a couple of scoops of lime now and then, or cedar shavings if you can find them. "

Aunt Jenny lifted a partially filled water bucket to the next plant. If she envied anyone anything, it was the town people turning on a hose to water their flowers.

"Anyway, I'm thinking on plumbing the house whether I lease to Mr. Black or not." Silently, she thought it was wondersome. An oil lease, of all things. Then she prayed a two-word prayer–Wisdom, please.

"Take Mr. Black's offer. I did. I don't have anything to lose." Tallie thought for a moment and added, "Well, I guess I could lose the shipping cost and a few supplies if they refused the order."

"See?" Aunt Jenny said. "There's always more to it than you first think for. Besides, there is more for me to consider than you'd think, too. I'm not going to worry about it--we're not supposed to, you know--and I'll give Mr. Black an answer as soon as I get one."

"Tomorrow?" Tallie asked.

"That's cutting it a little close, but we'll see.

Tallie emptied the last of the water in her bucket and said she was going to hunt for more rocks before it gets any darker.

"Alright. I think I'll put some bread on to rise. Don't go off too far nor too long!" her aunt hollered.

Tallie wandered down the road picking up a few small stones with possibilities, crossing over to a rock outcropping in the pasture for larger stones, finally gathering more than she probably would need. Smooth stones would be so nice to have, but were hard to find except near a river. Tallie thought of the bridge over the river she had jumped the night of the gallbladder attack. She thought about that horrible night again. It seemed ages ago. But tonight was a nice evening. Quiet. Real quiet. No birds calling. Odd. No insects either, come to think of it. Something was not right. She stood still, alert and listening,wondering what the deal was.

Uneasily, she turned around and was startled. Something was standing in the shadows a few yards away. It looked like a big dog, only it was skinny and staring at her with his tongue hanging out of his mouth to one side. He wasn't alone, she noted. There were two more standing a few feet from the first.

They weren't dogs, she realized. Maybe coyotes or wolves, but certainly not dogs. Her heart pounded and her skin began its elevator ride. She made herself turn around and took a few steps away from them toward the pasture fence, then stopped and looked back. They were a few yards away, but now closer, spread out and standing still with the lead animal in a crouched position. He crept cautiously, almost imperceptibly, forward.

Some atavistic impulse suddenly rose up on the inside of her. She reached into the bucket, never taking her eyes off the animal, grasped a stone, and let it fly straight at the animal's nose. Bull's eye! They shied, ran in a circle, and backed up still facing her. She quickly followed with two more hitting his cohorts, one on the shoulder and one at the hip. The latter two yipped and ran off several yards, but the first one slipped noiselessly into the shadows. She yelled and charged them, rocking their heels as they turned to run.

"Go home! Get outta here! Git! HYAW!" She yelled and chased until she was sure they were well on the run. Then she cut across the field back to the road, scrambled over the fence and ran to the house faster than she had ever run in her life.

There stood Aunt Jenny on the porch with a rifle at the ready. As soon as Tallie's feet hit the porch, her aunt set the rifle aside and grabbed her up in her arms.

"I saw 'em child, but was afraid to shoot. You were too near the line of fire. I was about to take out across the pasture and fire in the air when you commenced to let them have it with those rocks. You did real good. I'm so proud of you!" Aunt Jenny said and patted and soothed her. "You're okay now."

"I was scared, really scared. What were they? Coyotes? Wolves?"

"Wolves. I haven't seen wolves nor heard of any being in this part of the country since the last big drought. They were lean. Really lean. And hungry. I'll call the farm bureau tomorrow and report it. They need to know about this, if they don't already." She ushered Tallie into the house.

"I think I'll shut the door on the chickens and lock old Janet in the barn tonight. Turn that flood light on, will you? Those wolves could still be hanging around out there with more of them than we saw. Aunt Jenny picked up the rifle.

"I'll go with you," Tallie said rather loudly.

Aunt Jenny smiled. "If your a-coming, bring whatever rocks you have left in that bucket."

"Gottcha! You never know what's going to happen next out here, do you?" Tallie remarked.

A toad hopped out of their way causing Tallie to jump. Aunt Jenny pretended not to notice.

"Some things are predictable enough," she said, "and other things are a complete surprise, but it's never boring."

The chickens fluttered and clucked a bit...not liking to have their sleep interrupted by the noise as the bar was placed across the door. Aunt Jenny shooed Janet into the barn and made sure the side vents were propped open and the screens were holding. Tallie was glad she had shut the barnyard fence earlier to keep her from running off. It may have saved her being supper for the hungry pack out there. That thought for Janet's incidental safety prompted Tallie to see the connections for good outcomes. Even old Janet's wandering ways led to the pen which led to her probably being spared from a wolf attack.

Aunt Jenny held Tallie's hand in the dark as they walked back to the house.

"I thought that wolves and coyotes don't usually attack people," Tallie said.

"They'd have to be hungry to do so, but nothing's carved in stone that says they always do the usual thing."

Aunt Jenny latched the screen door to the house and returned the rifle to its hiding place behind the buffet, wondering if she could hit the broad side of a barn. Perhaps the noise would have been enough, she consoled herself. Simultaneously, she berated herself for letting so much time go by without target practice, and for not having cleaned that rifle in a month of Sundays.

"Well," Aunt Jenny said aloud, "those wolves certainly took my mind off that lease offer for a spell. It's true that today has its own

worries, and I don't have to jump ahead to the concerns of tomorrow."

"Me either. I threw away most of my rocks."

"So be it, I'm really proud you learned how to chunk. It turned
out to be a good thing to know, didn't it? Are you going to thank
Tom for showing you?"

Tallie paused on her way to the bathtub, "I don't know, but I
guess I should."

She leaned back in the tub, relaxing in the warm water. She
thought about her rock figures on the old green bath mat, Mr.
Jorbison happened to buy them, then sold them to Mr. Black who
happened to be in the oil business. Rocks started the whole thing.

This has been my lesson in rocks, she decided, and continued to
muse. Maybe things that seem to merely happen are more guided
than she thought. It might be wise to make up some extra rock
people to sell here, too, and put them on that green bath mat again.
She hoped Mrs. Black has a green cloth to set them on in her shop.
Black and green. Maybe I should study colors.

Tallie dried herself and went to bed wondering about colors.
Maybe I should dress one of my characters in black and green. Why
am I so hung up on black and green? I never dreamed of such a
crazy thing as selling those rock figures to a real gift shop. Dream.
The dream. That is what you're trying to pull out of the back of
my mind. The black material flowing out of the house and turning
green, the black color is for Mr. Black and the oil, and that green
is for the bathmat and the money that will come. That has to be it.
She put her understanding in the hands of God. Should I tell Aunt
Jenny, or let her figure it out? She silently asked the Lord. I suppose
I could tell her my dream and if she puts it together—well, I'll let
that be Your business.

~~~~~~~~~~~~~~

When the two of them were washing dishes the next morning,
Tallie shared her dream as casually as she could and asked, "I wonder if it has some special meaning. What do you think?"

"Some dreams have special meaning and some don't. Does it

suggest anything important to you? Black and green cloth flowing. Could be the wind blowing your sheets off you."

"There was barely a breeze last night. The black cloth that turned green makes me think of Mr. Black and the green money he pays me, and green is the color of the mat my little figures sit on. In my dream, they were tiny figures walking and talking on the green cloth. I wonder if the black cloth also meant he is in his hunt for a black oil lease flowing for you. What do you think.?

"Like I said, I can't say. I'm not disagreeing, mind you, it's just that I can't say." Aunt Jenny, however, had just gotten her own answer from God which lay in Tallie's dream.

Tallie gave up on the dream query and changed the subject. "Can we go to the river bottom, then? I'd like to collect some smooth rocks."

"The river bottom! That's more than halfway to town. I'll think about it but right now, I've a need to call my neighbors and the farm agency about those wolves," she said and folded up her dish towel.

Tallie followed her into the living room. Aunt Jenny sat down at her desk and removed some papers off the top of the telephone directory. She paused and studied one a moment.

"Okay. I'll call these people then we can go to the river bottom. And come to think about it, I need to go to the hospital."

Tallie lurched inwardly. "Are you sick again?"

"No, no. I got a notice from the Medicare folks, and I owe Doc a little dab. Knowing him, he wouldn't bill me until Will Thompson bales the prairie hay off my place this fall. I don't want that bill hanging around like a raveling on my skirt tail all summer. Then if time allows, we can also stop at the river bottom."

"If he hasn't sent you a bill, why pay? Tallie asked.

"He probably wouldn't ever send a bill, but it's the law. This notice from Medicare information tells me what I owe him, and he is supposed to bill all Medicare holders. It's the law unless the person is totally destitute. I can't imagine why everyone in hock up to their gizzards in mortgages for their two-story brick houses, two cars and a boat on the lake would think I'm destitute. I've got a cow, chickens, a truck, a house and land, all paid for years ago, and the Good Lord Provider, who sees after my little financial matters. The last thing I am is destitute," Aunt Jenny said and flipped through the phone book for the number of the farm agency.

"Maybe the Good Lord Provider is trying to provide for you some more with that oil lease," Tallie said, hoping she wasn't pushing her aunt too hard.

"Maybe. And maybe I'm going to have to take charge of a whole crew of rowdy, tobacco-chewing, honky-tonkin' roughnecks, straddling the gates of hell, poking and digging day and night on my property. Lord have mercy! "

"You're going to sign that lease," Tallie said.

"Yes'm. I am."

"OH NO! God help the roughnecks!" Tallie exclaimed.

"Indeed, God. Help them. And I'm sure He will if any come here."

Tallie was squirming to know what made Aunt Jenny change her mind, but didn't ask until they were on the way into town.

"I didn't change my mind about anything. Those seismograph boys have been back and forth across my land ever so many times, and I've studied on it for quite a spell. The only thing I need to be careful of is the lease agreement."

"Then why were you so stewed up about it yesterday?" Tallie asked.

"There's other things to reckon with; other folks involved."

"You mean the roughnecks."

"Them and other things."

Tallie knew her aunt didn't like to talk about her own business to anyone else, but gave in to her curiosity and asked her what she meant by 'other things.'

"I've known for some time that my land lies right in the Anadarko Oil Basin. That means if they drill, or only lease, it is a direct gift from God. I'm not about to refuse His gifts. However, I don't want Aunt Tallie's house or trees disturbed. And, too, I wasn't sure about taking on those men.

She paused for a moment trying to discern how much to say, and just how to say it before continuing. But I've lived here a long time. This is my post, and I know God doesn't send people out here for any length of time a-tall without a reason. They'll come—those roughnecks. And they'll drill. Whether or not they find oil, I can't say. Drilling is only part of the reason they'll be sent out here. That dream of yours helped to remind me it's what flows out of here that counts more than what flows in." Then her aunt gave a little tired laugh and continued.

"I've been feeling a mite too old to monkey with all this foolishness people get into. In fact, I waited to see if I could 'Jonah' out of this next one. But if He insists, He'll provide what I need to fool with all those oil jockeys and whoever else He cares to send out here. I'm commissioned to occupy until He comes, so I might as well learn– at this advanced age– to deal with it and like it best I can."

Tallie asked her aunt if she thought God sent her there for the summer for a particular purpose. Aunt Jenny explained that God rubs people together for a very good reason. It may well be that He put us together for a good reason.

"He takes people like they are and so must I. It's like taking the weather as it comes and dealing with it."

"Whether a person or a tornado, it is all the same to you, right? Tallie asked.

"You might say that." Aunt Jenny smiled and continued, "I do believe I've encountered Miss Squall and Mr. Blustery a few times. But like Pastor said, there is a comfort zone for us." Tired of answering so many personal questions, she told Tallie they needed to get on with their business at hand.

"Yonder is the bridge. Do you want to pick up rocks coming or going, Missy?"

"I'd rather not have to hurry hunting rocks, so let's do it on the way home. That way, we won't be late or get our clothes dirty. I can let you off at the hospital and go buy the things I need at that hobby supply. "

~~~~~~~~~~~~

Doc Gilbert was sitting at his desk reared back in a swivel chair with one foot propped on an opened desk drawer, dictating reports into a recording device when Aunt Jenny peeked around the door. Doc waved her on in and finished a sentence she could not begin to understand.

"How are you doing?" he asked.

"What do mean, 'how am I doing?' Don't you have any confidence in your skill?" She smiled wryly and smoothed imaginary wrinkles from her freshly pressed dress.

"You sound like your old self again. What's up?"

"My old self brought you a cantaloupe from my old garden. You still like them, right?"

Doc Gilbert's turn to smile. He recalled a day every bit as hot or hotter than today when she had put him to chopping that everlasting Johnsongrass out of one corner of an otherwise meticulous garden. He had gotten so hot and hungry before noon, he sneaked over to the cantaloupes and found one just turning ripe enough to eat, cut it open with a pocket knife, and polished it off and buried the rind.

The next morning at breakfast, there was nothing but a dish of cottage cheese on the table. Not his favorite food. Aunt Jenny told him she was trying to find a ripe melon to go with it, but there wasn't any. He recalled their discussion as if it were yesterday, about the missing melon.

"What we don't eat of 'these' cheese for breakfast will be our lunches. I reckon we can make out on that until dinner I was just sure there'd be a melon out there sommers," she said.

"Maybe a terrapin got it," Doc recalled saying.

"Not unless they've taken to carrying knives." She handed him a sack.

They laughed together. He lifted the cantaloupe out and took a whiff of the sweet fragrance it gave.

"Yes, I still like cantaloupe, and I'm more excellent with knives than I ever was back then, but I hope I put them to a better, less nefarious use. AND, I won't eat this one if it's the only one you have," he teased.

Aunt Jenny smiled. "I've got a good but small crop of melon this year. The vines did well considering the hail beating it took. Both Tallie and I dig holes near the roots and fill them up with water. Helps them weather the heat right well. If I can keep the terrapins and crows off, I should have a-plenty."

"You're feeling good, are you? No problems?"

"Me? I am tolerable well. But I'm curious about something. Can you tell me what has become of Claude? I don't want to pry, but I don't know where he is or when he's to come back nor nothing. I've got some business to do about my land and Claude is one loose end holding me back."

"I sent him to a special hospital unit. If you need to get a message to him, I can call."

"Do that, please. Tell him I'm concerned about so many strangers fooling around in these parts, lately. I'd like permission to move his belongings into the storage room at Sipe's filling station. He worked there, as you know. I'd appreciate it, and I'll pay for the call."

"It's a toll free number," Doc said.

Aunt Jenny continued. "How did Claude get to that other hospital? Doesn't the sheriff have that little car of his?"

"Claude was too shaky to drive and likely to run off for another bottle of booze or to parts unknown. So I tapped the volunteers up there to come get him," Doc explained and dialed the toll free number. "I've got to make rounds in a minute. I'll let you talk to him, yourself." He paused for the ring and the answer, frowned, and stood up abruptly.

"No!" he yelled, "I will NOT hold. This is Doctor Gilbert. You put me through to Claude Worth's floor immediately." Remembering Aunt Jenny was in his office, he added "Please," in a quieter tone of voice.

"Claude? This is Doc Gilbert. Aunt Jenny's here in my office and needs to talk to you." Aunt Jenny took the receiver.

"Hello? Claude? You're feeling better, I hope...Good...."

Meanwhile, Tallie paid for her purchases thinking her best find was the glue gun. Outside, she glanced at the big clock on the bank. There was time to get a couple of limeades to go from the drugstore. Aunt Jenny would like that. She shifted her packages and pushed open the heavy glass doors of the drugstore.

It was an old-fashioned place, well air conditioned, a shiny wooden floor, a grill and a soda fountain. She ordered and waited. Someone laughed. Glancing that direction, Tallie saw the most striking girl she had ever seen. She was seated in a booth with Tom

Sawyer. He said something and the girl laughed again—a pleasant, quiet, rich sound as if she had practiced it to an art.

Tallie turned her back to them and looked down at her feet. Dirty, rusty feet inside old, bent-out-of-shape sandals. The clerk set the drinks on the counter, and Tallie pushed some coins across the marble counter, suddenly aware of her hands. Scratches. Chipped nails. Palms marred with stained calluses. She quickly took the drinks and left.

Once outside, she hurried to the truck. It looked dirty, too. Dead grass on the floorboard, red dust on the dashboard. One glance in the rearview mirror was a further insult. Her hair was held back by dopey little barrettes to keep it out of her beer-bottle eyes. That's what Alice Fursby called them, wasn't it? Oddly colored, beer-bottle eyes. She started the truck and backed out more rapidly than she should have. A car honked followed by the squeal of tires. Tallie slammed on the brakes. Her legs and hands shook. It was several moments before she calmed down enough to drive on (very slowly) to the hospital.

Aunt Jenny opened the door and something spilled onto her feet. "What on earth?" she exclaimed.

"Oh no! Those were the limeades I got for us."

Aunt Jenny raked the liquid and ice from the floorboard with her bare hands and climbed into the truck, declaring that she had to get on to the motel and see Mr. Black.

Mr. Black insisted they stay at the motel coffee shop for lunch after the lease papers were signed, but Aunt Jenny declined saying they had too many other things to do. She thanked him politely and exited the coffee shop as fast as possible.

"Why didn't you let him buy our lunch?" Tallie asked.

"Half the town eats there. In no time a-tall, they'd all know my business or be asking me about who that man was that I was seen with. Besides, you've whetted my appetite for a limeade. And I haven't had a drugstore chicken salad sandwich in a coon's age. What about it? Shall we treat ourselves?"

What could Tallie say? She only hoped Tom and that girl were gone. They weren't. The girl was seated in a sporty, little silver car looking up at Tom, and he was bent nearly double trying to talk to her through the window with his arms propped on the top of the low-slung, Cinderella pumpkin.

Tallie parked across the street and hoped her aunt would not ask why. Still playing for time, she fumbled around in her purse for a missing comb, looked into the rearview mirror and raked her bangs into place with her fingers.

Aunt Jenny stood beside the truck. "What in the world are you doing?"

"I'm comin'," Tallie said and together they walked across the street.

"Hi kids," Aunt Jenny called and waved her handkerchief to Tom and the girl, both of whom were in the princess's pumpkin and backing away from the curb. Tallie's insides squirmed. She hung back and let her aunt go ahead of her. Fortunately, they did no more than wave back as they drove away.

"If they had not been in such a hurry, I would have asked them to join us," Aunt Jenny said.

"I'm glad it's just us today," Tallie said, and she meant it with all of her heart.

The drugstore personnel acted like Aunt Jenny was some sort of queen come to visit. It was as if she was doing them a big honor to come eat one of their sandwiches which were toasted in butter on the grill, served with pride and a sliced dill pickle with a mound of potato chips on the side. Every employee in the place, including the pharmacist came to chat. Tallie didn't have to talk much except to respond to the introductions between swallows of food which tasted better than she expected.

"No, no ice cream for me, but how about you, Tallie?" Aunt Jenny asked. "This is my treat, today."

Tallie declined.

"Would you like anything else?" a waitress asked.

Tallie declined again thinking that what she would like is to know where Tom and that girl went, and what they were saying to each other. Did they have some special friendship, and who was she, anyway?

The cashier refused to let Aunt Jenny pay saying, "No charge. Mr. Henry said so."

It was one time Aunt Jenny did not get her way, even after much protesting, so she left a rather large tip instead.

On the way home, Tallie asked her aunt who Mr. Henry was and why he would not let her pay.

"My daddy used to own that drugstore."

"I didn't know that."

Aunt Jenny smiled and Tallie could see her eyes running back through lots of years sorting out what to tell and what to leave out. When it looked like she wasn't going to say anything more, Tallie asked if Aunt Jenny's dad had been a pharmacist.

"No. He sold patented salves, syrups and non-prescription pills for people and animals, but he wasn't a real pharmacist. It was called an apothecary shop back then. He had cosmetics, gift items, perfumes, and even that old soda fountain they've kept all these years. People would come in and buy phosphates and ice cream."

"So who is this Mr. Henry?" Tallie asked.

"He used to work in the drugstore for my dad; even lived in the back of the shop and got interested in pharmacy. Finally he went off to school to study for his license. When he finished, he came back here and pretty much took over the business.

It was a wonderful boon for my aging dad. And when Dad died, he gave the building and the inventory to Mr. Henry in return for a small percent of the net earnings to Mama as long as Mr. Henry owned the store. Then there was some do-hicky paper about if he sold it and blah-blah, and what to do if Mama passed on, but I don't recall all those details. Mama lived a year to the day of Dad's passing and I got a little settlement off her part of the drugstore. So that is who Mr. Henry is and he doesn't charge me out of respect for my dad no matter how much I fuss at him."

Aunt Jenny wondered again if Mr. Henry wasn't the one who deposited cash to her savings account. That account always had a little more in it than she figured.

"He got a good deal, if you ask me," Tallie said.

"Maybe so, but he sure has worked for it. He owns drug stores all over this end of the state and who knows where all else. Turn down Myrtle Street up there, and you can see his house."

The house sat in the middle of an acreage on the edge of town. It was not too large to look homey and welcoming with wide porches hugging the house all the way around the neatly landscaped grounds. A screened-in breezeway joined the house to a guest cottage. In the driveway was a little silver sports car.

"Isn't that the same car that girl was in? The girl Tom was talking to? Tallie asked.

"I can't keep up with Ceidra Henry's cars, but it was a fancy little roller skate of a thing as I recall. Did you see her? She is a pretty girl."

"Yes, I saw her." Tallie drove on by the house.

"She isn't here too much any more," Aunt Jenny continued. "Goes to some private school somewhere. Then she and her mother travel to Europe and Africa and anywhere else they get all puckered up to see. Mr. Henry sticks closer to home tending to business, and too, he's a little older than his Mrs."

Tallie drove out of town and crossed the bridge before Aunt Jenny asked her if she still intended to collect rocks from the river bottom. Tallie said she had to or she would not be able to fill Mr. Black's order on time.

It was hot. The weeds were high. Tallie proceeded toward the riverbed thinking that traveling to Sawed Off Corners and picking up rocks from the river bank sure wasn't anything like traveling to Europe and Africa. Aunt Jenny followed Tallie down the slope to Tallie's surprise.

"What are you doing?" Tallie scolded. "You might slip down the bank."

"I'm going to go a-wading in that creek–something I haven't done in years." She set her shoes aside and stepped into the water while watching Tallie kick over and sort through rocks.

"Well," Aunt Jenny said. "this may not be Europe or Africa, but I'll bet there's folks over in those places who'd like to be here seeing what we're seeing and doing what we are doing, don't you reckon?"

"Maybe, Tallie replied. She stuck out her chin and kicked at the rocks a little harder. A creek is a creek," she added.

"No, it isn't. Think about it." Aunt Jenny swirled a foot through the water. This is this creek. It isn't anywhere else nor in some other country. It's right here and that makes it unique. You can't see this creek in Africa." She waded out a few feet further and stepped into a hole of water up to her shoulders.

"Tallie!" she yelled.

Tallie dropped the bucket of rocks and ran to her aunt who was trying to inch her way across the hole. Every time she moved her feet, the sand shifted and caused her to sink even deeper into the water.

"No." Aunt Jenny quietly squeaked with desperation when Tallie waded toward the edge of the deep hole. "Get a stick."

Tallie flew into the bushes up and down the bank until she found two branches that weren't rotten. One, she handed to her aunt to push against the bottom of the river and the other to pull her to the bank.

"Be careful, Tallie. Don't let me pull you in here. Just a minute. Let me kindly get fixed."

Tallie held on to the branch with all her might and dug her heels into the mud. Aunt Jenny held the branch with her left hand and stabbed around with the second stick until she found a more solid place.

"Ready?" Aunt Jenny asked.

"Ready." Tallie said with her lips drawn tight.

Holding tightly to Tallie's branch, Aunt Jenny gave a big push against the river bed to buoy herself, then letting go of the first branch, she grabbed Tallie's branch with both hands struggling to get at least one knee back upon the edge of the underwater hole.

"I've got you. Get your other knee up if you can" Tallie pleaded.

"I—I'm not sure I can!"

"You have to!" Tallie breathed a prayer. "Hang on. I'm going to pull hard. Ready?" Aunt Jenny nodded. Tallie heaved with all her might. Aunt Jenny landed belly down where she had first begun to wade. Then she laughed and sat up and laughed some more.

"I didn't set out to go a-swimming," she said between the laughter.

Tallie waded to help her up, frowned and said, "That is not funny."'

"I no more saw that hole than I can fly, and I'd about as soon try to fly off a tree branch as to swim."

"You scratched your knees," Tallie said, still unamused.

"They'll mend. Go on and get your rocks. I'm all right now, and one good thing, at least, I'm cool."

Tallie shook her head and went back for her rocks. On the way home, Aunt Jenny chuckled.

"What's so funny now?" Tallie asked.

"I was wondering what I would have done if I had stepped off into that water hole by myself with no one around."

"And?"

"I guess I would have stood on tiptoe until the creek dried up. Can you imagine folks driving by waving, thinking I was just cooling my heels?"

"That's not funny, either!" Tallie said. "You should have seen yourself up to your neck in that water."

"I guess I was a sight. I'm sure glad you were there," she said and patted Tallie's arm. "If you hadn't been there, I'd have had to sein fish in my skirt tail to survive."

"You probably would have, and figured a way to cook them, too."

"Some folks eat raw fish, you know. I'm not wishing for trouble, but if it comes along, the least I can do is grab it by the neck. Wring a lesson from it. I'm thinking. I try to learn what to do with troubles."

"How about not wading without a life vest on?" Tallie answered.

"Good answer", she said. If trouble or problems come around, make them pay off. Don't suffer for nothing. Make it pay off. Learn something from it."

"Like wearing a life vest when you can't swim and you're 70-plus years old and want to go wading?"

"Well, you think about it. You are a princess of the royal household of God. You have a duty to rule over your assigned realm and to learn from doing so. You will make mistakes and step off into a hole now and then, but you'll learn."

While her aunt hung her clothes out to dry, Tallie went to do chores and thought about Ceidra Henry's looks, especially that small mole on her left cheek which made her look so, so very different. Her hair was black and shiny. Her eyes were unusual, too. Lilac. And the lids colored with eyeshadow to match. Ceidra was, well? Exotic looking, she silently decided. Exotic. If you set the two of us on a shelf, I'd be a dirty, old, chipped, beer bottle and she'd be a bottle of exotic, expensive perfume from Patagonia or Egypt or somewhere.

Tallie sighed and carried a pail of milk to the house wondering what to do. What lesson is there in looking like a chipped beer bottle?" she wondered. Ugly is ugly, and beauty is beauty," she told herself, However, she decided to call Mary John to find out more about Ceidra.

As soon as her aunt went to pick fresh flowers for the house, Tallie called Mary John and tried to think of some way to bring up the subject of Ceidra matter-of-factly, but couldn't.

"Hi, Tallie, What's up?"

"I saw someone today named Ceidra. What do you know about her?"

"Gee, I don't see her too much except when she is home from her private school or between trips to Mongolia or somewhere. Why?"

"I've never seen anyone who looks like her."

"She is pretty in an odd sort of way, and people do stare. She has lots of nice clothes and goes to Dallas to get them, too. Gets anything she wants. Where did you see her? I didn't know she was in town."

"I didn't really meet her, I just saw her talking to Tom in the drugstore and wondered who she was. Aunt Jenny told me a little about her dad and all. Does she go to your church?"

"No. She's Presbyterian. They like all that classical music. It's just creepy pipe organ music to me. But she and Tom always get together when she is home and she comes to our church with him pretty often. They've always been really good friends. He teases her a lot and she eats it up, because most guys are— ba-duh, ba-duh—Porky Pig tongue tied around her."

"She really likes Tom and his teasing, huh?" The idea was almost more than Tallie could absorb and changed the subject. "So what is going on with you?"

"Lots. I'm glad you called because I was going to call you and tell you that I'm going to be gone for a whole week. I'm going to attend a special session at Oklahoma State for high school students interested in agricultural or home econ science careers. Isn't that great? They sent out letters of invitation and I got one, probably because of my work in the 4-H Club. I'll get to stay in the dorm and meet lots of other kids."

"That's neat. Really neat." Tallie tried to be enthusiastic. "When do you leave?"

"Friday. On Saturday and Sunday, they have get-acquainted events planned. Things like a tour of the campus and the town, the pig barn, and the cow barn where they have a cow with a window in one of its stomachs, and the experimental crop stations, the arboretum, and then a dinner at the student union. There's lots more stuff to do after that and all week long. I can hardly wait. I've got my clothes all ready to pack."

"I hope you have a good time, Mary John. I really do."

"I will. Then she paused feeling a little sorry for Tallie. I'll miss you, but when I get home I'll tell you every little detail."

"I'll miss you, too. I'll be busy though. I'm making some more of those rock figures to sell. See you when you get back."

Tallie said goodbye, pulled a nail file from a jar of pencils by the phone and sawed the chipped places on her nails.

Aunt Jenny brought in the flowers and placed them on the kitchen table and a couple of places in the living room. She passed Tallie several times. Tallie kept sawing on her nails. Finally, Aunt Jenny reached across Tallie to pick up the Bible.

"Let's go out on the porch and see if we can't catch some of the breeze," Aunt Jenny suggested.

"Mary John's going to some university to stay in the dorm for a week with a bunch of other kids her age. They're going to tour the area and look at a pig barn and a cow's stomach, and some experimental crops. She said tell you, so I am."

"Good for her." Aunt Jenny noticed Tallie was still sawing and digging at her nails and let it pass. She took up the Bible and read, and when she looked up again, Tallie was still sawing, this time on her toenails. She went back to reading and gave a chuckle.

Tallie looked up. "What's so funny?

"God parted the Red Sea for the Hebrew children. I guess not all of them could swim either!"

"They probably never had a chance to learn. Pharaoh probably kept them too busy carrying water and chopping Johnsongrass."

"Could be. Could be the Nile was full of crocodiles. Enticing places can have dangerous things under the surface,"

Aunt Jenny suspicioned the cause for all the nail sawing Tallie was doing and knew it was serious when Tallie scarcely ate supper.

Tallie couldn't name what was happening to herself, but she was caught up in the notion that she was ugly and unpopular. Sitting before the mirror to brush her thick, auburn hair, she opened a drawer and found a jar of cold cream, some face powder, and a bottle of Cornhusker's Lotion. Finally, an answer to help the ugly. She made another decision and went to bed happy.

Chapter Eleven: Silver Beauty, Smelly Brillo, Green Smurf

The next morning, Aunt Jenny asked Tallie to bring the truck around. They were going to the rental house to remove Claude's things and take them to the filling station in town. Once again, Tallie was the driver and parked the truck under the shade of the large pecan tree.

Aunt Jenny saw the unused fruit jars in cardboard boxes on the back porch which they loaded into the truck before going inside the house.

"Look," Tallie said, noticing some ripe peaches on the trees to the south of the house. Shouldn't we pick those? Claude won't be here to do it."

"We can. He wouldn't do it if he were here, but first things, first. I'm going in the house."

The screen door screaked when Aunt Jenny opened it and remarked about it being busted out. The lovely, old hardwood floors were scarred and dull. Wallpaper yellowed and spotted. Over the bay window was a saggy, torn, fly-specked lace curtain. Aunt Jenny choked back some tears. The whole place smelled of abuse. Beer cans and whiskey bottles lay here and there.

"P-U—Pew!" Tallie shouted.

Aunt Jenny walked into the kitchen and stepped into a crusted-over pile of vomit. That did it. The tears flowed. Tallie couldn't stand to see her aunt break down and sob. She had never seen her cry. It stunned and hurt worse than anything thus far in her life.

"Why don't you pick some peaches, Aunt Jenny. "I'll clean that mess up. " Tallie offered.

"Nope. You go pick. I'll do what I told Claude I'd do." She sniffed and wiped her eyes.

Claude's clothes amounted to three uniforms from the filling station, an outdated suit, a few shirts and some faded jeans which Aunt Jenny packed as carefully as she would have packed a new, silk suit. He had very few dishes, one pan and a skillet which she washed and wrapped in newspaper. There was a cheap .22 hand gun in a kitchen drawer. She unloaded it and put the shells in an envelope underneath some magazines in a box separate from the one containing the gun.

An old, oscillating fan, a few tools and automotive supplies from the shed showed more respectful care than anything in the house. When it was all on the truck, she walked around the house to see how Tallie was coming with the peach picking.

"If these trees had been tended and the weeds kept down," Aunt Jenny said, "we could be picking a whale of a lot of peaches. It's still a wonderment to me that these old trees keep bearing, and sad to see things I've loved and tended go to ruination."

"There may not be as many, but they sure smell good," Tallie said, "and they're about to itch me to bits."

"When we get back you need to wash your arms. It's time to wrap this job up anyway."

Tallie crawled out of the tree and carried two pails of peaches to the truck—the very dusty truck.

"While we're in town, I'm going to the car wash and clean up this truck, inside and out, if you don't mind." Afraid she might hurt her aunt's feelings, she added, "Driving with the windows down sure lets in lots of dirt and I know you've made more trips to town because I'm here than you normally would."

"Wouldn't hurt, but it won't stay clean too long," Aunt Jenny warned.

As soon as they finished delivering Claude's things to the filling station, Tallie drove to the car wash where she sprayed and scoured every inch she could reach while her aunt waited inside the truck.

"What prompted the sudden cleaning streak in you?" Aunt Jenny asked, seriously interested in the matter.

"Other people's cars. They look cleaner than ours, that's all. Your house is spotless. Why not your car?"

" I only wash it once or twice a year because of the dirt roads.

You did a good job. Claude used to service and clean my truck more often, but that has been a while. Let's go by the grocery store. I need some fruit pectin for those peaches," Aunt Jenny said. She was getting better, Tallie could tell.

Alice Fursby was standing by the produce counter picking through all the bags of grapes when she spied Aunt Jenny and pulled her aside to tell her the latest scoop. Tallie slipped off to another part of the store to make some special purchases of her own and promptly hurried out to hide them under the seat of the truck. When she re-entered the store, Alice and Aunt Jenny were still yakking, apparently about the Henrys. Tallie walked up closer and quietly listened.

"Well, Ceidra and her mother were at the drug store yesterday talking about those South American countries and she said they were fascinated by some ancient city there."

"Which city would that be, Alice?" Aunt Jenny asked.

"I can't remember, but it's real famous. It sounded something like 'mashed peaches'. Anyway, Mrs. Henry is going to show her slides at the next meeting of our garden club. Isn't that simply exciting? And gracious of her! I'm the chairperson, you know, and I think it will be a wonderful change from all the usual programs other ladies put together."

"I'm sure it will be really nice, Alice. Maybe you can make a dessert from mashed peaches to keep the theme, so to speak. "

"What a great idea! I'll think about that. Well, toodle-oo, you two." And after a pinch to Tallie's cheek, Alice was off to the checkout stand.

"What is the deal about mashed peaches?" Tallie asked.

"I'm guessing Mrs. Henry and Ceidra have been to Machu Picchu in South America. Alice couldn't be sure, but then Alice's geography grades were seldom above 'C' level."

Tallie laughed genuinely for the first time in days.

"That's an old joke, Missy, but it's sure fits Alice's geography grade. Let's get on home. We've got our own peaches to do. "

By suppertime, hot jam was cooling in jars, and a peach cobbler sat on the cabinet. Tallie had hauled water for the house, the bath tank, the chickens, as well as pushed the Georgia stock plow through the garden. The ground was hard and fairly dry except where they had dug holes and filled them with water next to the plants, and she did it all with gloves on.

Tallie shook the dirt off her clothes and hung them on the hook by the bathtub. Sparingly, she filled the tub and poured in a small amount of bath oil Mary John had given her for her birthday. She sloshed it around good, then eased into the fragrant tub of water.

Pure luxury--a bath in four inches of water. She smiled a little. At home, she showered every day and ran the water for ages like it was nothing. It sure is different when you have to haul it yourself, she thought. She scrubbed hard at the mud stains on her feet recalling Aunt Jenny telling about a time when the well went dry forcing her to haul water from town in big milk cans and how the water smelled and tasted of dead fish. Tallie wondered how her aunt had managed it all by herself. She scrubbed and scrubbed, but gave up on her hopelessly stained feet and pulled the plug. She felt good about the water draining into a container to be reserved for other uses. She stood and rinsed in the least amount of water possible, thinking that tomorrow she would do some more scrubbing—scrubbing of a different sort.

~~~~~~~~~~~~~~

The next morning, Tallie waited until she was sure Aunt Jenny was concentrating on canning peaches and answering phone calls from the neighbors about wolves before she took off on business of her own.

She ran all the way to the rental house, but hesitated on the porch a few moments. The place was spooky and sad, but the sad part won over the spooky. She went inside and set to work with a mop and broom.

"At least, you're going to smell better," she said aloud.

Up went the windows to let in the fresh air. Next, soap and water were poured on the floor and eventually swept off the back porch to the few sprigs of grateful bermuda grass. Wax was applied to the wooden floors with old rags tied to her feet. While it dried, she picked the rest of the ripe peaches and hurried back home before her aunt got too suspicious.

After lunch, Aunt Jenny lay down to rest. Tallie slipped out the back door, ran down the hill, again and spent two more hours in the kitchen cleaning the appliances and cabinet tops. Too late, she realized she should have cleaned them prior to doing the floors. Live and learn. She mopped the kitchen again.

Grabbing time here and there, she had the house presentable by Friday. At least, the crust was off the place, and it didn't stink any more. Tired as she was, she got the rock figures finished and ready to mail to Mr. Black. Her favorite one was the rural mail carrier. She held it for a moment, then wrapped it quickly and placed it in the box.

"You like that one, don't you?" Aunt Jenny asked.

"Yep." Tallie waited to see if Aunt Jenny objected to 'yep'. There was no response.

"It's hard to give up something you've put your heart into. I know. It's like a quilt I made and gave to someone only to see later that they'd thrown it in the garage for the dogs to wallow on. I'd spent months making that wedding ring quilt-on my fingers. Not one machine stitch in it."

"What did you do?"

"What could I do? A gift given is a gift given. You have to let it go. Although, I did commence to study about it and decided there are two kinds of poor folks. Some are poor for lack of money, but others are poor because they flatout have poor ways, inside and out. I guess you could say they're a sorry, sort of poor."

"I loaned a girl a piece of paper at school one time, and she sat there and drew all over it instead of doing her lesson. When she was tired of drawing, she wadded her gum in it and threw it in the trash."

"What did you do?" Aunt Jenny asked.

"Nothing. It made me mad, that's all, and I've never loaned her anything else."

"When people mistreat your goods, they've mistreated you. Your property and your labors are part of yourself, an extension of yourself. Aunt Jenny's eyes lit up and she pointed her finger right at Tallie's nose. That girl took your goods and a slice out of your well-being right along with it. The paper is gone, but you can get your well-being back by not staying angry. I've heard it said that staying angry at a-body is like letting them live in your house rent free while they wreck it. They're off somewhere else and you are still letting the memory do damages. They are like the end-time locusts. Devour and move to the field while you are left on the sidelines wounded from it."

" You got that right. But I think I would have slapped her if we hadn't been in class. That was my last piece of paper."

"You can rest assured about this: You're God's property. If you're offended, He's offended. Anyone taking advantage of you has the serious attention of God who gave you your life and supplies. If they offend you in any of that, they've offended Him, and He'll tend to that little thing.   Aunt Jenny pushed herself up from the chair. Speaking of tending to things, I think I'll see if there is a tomato or two and some okra. I may stir them up in a little of Janet's butter with an egg and some green onions."

"You're kidding!"

"You wait and see if I'm kidding, Missy."

She wasn't. When they sat down at the table that evening, Aunt Jenny slid the strange stuff onto a platter and asked her to say a blessing over it. Tallie thought it looked like it needed blessing.

"Lord, thank you for this food. (And I hope she hasn't ruined it.) We ask You to bless it to our health. (And that may be a challenge.) Amen."

Cautiously, lest she get it for breakfast, Tallie took a small portion figuring to fill in the gap with peach jam on bread. With some trepidation, she took a bite and found it wasn't awful, but neither was it very good.

"Do you make this often?" Tallie asked.

"No. Never made it before. What do you think?"

"It's different."

"That's for sure. Those famous chefs put everything but the dish rag in eggs. It's called a frittata. Alice Fursby watches them on TV and tells me all about their fumblings in the kitchen. She says eating different things educates the palate."

"This is educating, all right." Tallie looked up and noticed a little sag come over her aunt and added, "I think I'll have some more." The sag disappeared. "How about you?"

"I reckon if a-body is hungry enough, it isn't too bad." Then her aunt laughed. Let's finish this up, and good riddance. We need to get our things ready for the Trade Fair tomorrow. I'm going to take some of that jam. What about you?"

"All I have are three extra rock figures. A fisherman, a surveyor, and a lady with a basket of eggs. I'm going to make signs for them. How do you spell surveyor?"

Aunt Jenny sat up straight and squared her shoulders.

"Surveyor," she said. "S-u-r, sur; v-e-y, vey; O-r, or; S-u-r-v-e-yor. Surveyor. One who measures land."

"Good grief! You sound like an auctioneer."

Aunt Jenny grinned.

"That's how we learned to spell when I was in school, by syllables. Good spellers in my day could really rattle it off. It got to be a real contest to see who could rattle it off the fastest." .

"Did you ever win?"

"Sometimes. Usually, Pastor Hay's daddy won. He had a tongue on a hinge and it paid off. He was in the state legislature for a while after he graduated." She returned to packing the jars of jam silently recalling how close she came to being Jenny Hay back then, and again, years later.

Tallie finished her signs and slowly climbed the stairs to bed thinking that she used to have whole days with nothing to do. Sleep came quickly.

Aunt Jenny read the paper wondering why Tallie could be so tired so early. Wondering, she slipped up stairs and looked at her sprawled diagonally across the bed. Whatever in the world have you been up to, child? She wondered. Picking a few peaches can't make a-body that tired. I wasn't asleep when you took off today. Then she raised her hands over her and covered her with a 'quilt' of silent prayer.

Tallie speedily did her Saturday chores to have plenty of time to dress. Today, things were going to be different. First, basin bath in perfumed water. Second, hot pink nail polish, applied on toenails and fingernails. Finally, the fun part. Tallie opened the dresser drawer and took out her secret purchases. Dark tan make-up base, peach blush, emerald green eyeshadow, and two eyeliners, one black and one sparkling green. All those went on easily enough, but the black mascara went on in hunks, marked her cheeks when she blinked, and smeared when she tried to wash it off. It took a while to repair the damage.

Next came the combs– the finishing touch. She untied her hair from its ponytail, lifted it dramatically high over her right ear and fastened it with combs she had found in the dresser. The left side of her hair flew free and sometimes fell across her face just like that girl she had seen on the cover of a beauty magazine in the grocery store.

"Eat your heart out, Ceidra Henry," she said aloud. The big city girl is in town!"

Aunt Jenny was loading goods in the truck when Tallie placed her rock figures next to the sack of okra. Aunt Jenny stepped aside, looked at Tallie, then looked again, long and straight. Tallie acted as casual as she could.

"Those were your Great Aunt Tallie's combs," Aunt Jenny stated. "They're bone. Hand carved antiques handed from her family clear back to Scotland. She wore them on her wedding day. Those sets are real pearls. No telling how old they are."

"Does that mean you don't want me to wear them?"

"Why don't you save them for tomorrow when you feel a little better."

"What do you mean, 'feel better'? I feel fine. I feel mighty fine!"

"Your color looks right sallow to me."

Tallie, unsure what sallow was, said, "You can't even see my color. I've got on makeup."

"Is that a fact! I thought you were getting bilious. I take it you've made up your mind to go into town that-a-way."

"Why not? It is the latest look," she said, wondering what 'bilious' was.

" Please take those combs back upstairs." Aunt Jenny shook her head and got in the truck.

Tallie respectfully removed the combs and took them back to their storage spot in the old vanity dresser. She then tied that side of her hair with a piece of hot pink yarn and latched the door before she returned to the truck. She rolled the windows up, almost to the top, to keep her hair from blowing and to keep the dust out. Aunt

Jenny grimaced and fanned herself with exaggerated motions all the way to town. The fanning would keep her dry on the front side, but she feared what the backside would look like when she got out of the truck— which she checked upon arrival with a sigh of relief.

The first customer was Doc Gilbert who looked at Tallie like she might at a specimen, then asked, "Are you feeling well?"

"I'm feeling JUST fine. Are you?" She might have said more but Aunt Jenny poked her in the back.

He kept looking at her with disbelief. "Haven't I seen you somewhere before?"

Tallie was red in the face in spite of all the makeup. Aunt Jenny all but shoved Tallie aside explaining– once again– that Tallie was her nephew's daughter who drove her to the hospital that stormy night.

Doc Gilbert mumbled, "Oh. Right." Her handed his melons to Aunt Jenny to be sacked, commenting on how well she looked for her age, laying it to the bounty of her vegetable garden which was why he bought his produce from her, etc.

Tallie turned her back on them and set up her rock figures wondering how a doctor could be so dumb.

Aunt Jenny had numerous buyers for her produce, but no one was very interested in the rock figures. Tired of standing around, she decided to wander around and show off her new face.

"Hey,!" a little voice said, but Tallie kept walking. "Hey, you?" it said again. "You're the one that had that old snake book, ain't ya? You was trying to sell it and everone's already read the dumb thing. Gee! That was really dumb. Are you still trying to sell it?"

"No. I decided to keep it." Tallie turned around and looked at the little boy, hoping he would go away.

The little boy stopped in his tracks and his eyes got big. "What is all that black and green stuff on your eyes?" he fairly yelled. It ain't for a parade, is it? It ain't Hallowe'en yet, is it?' You look like a green Smurf," he giggled.

Others were turning to stare at her. Some were giggling.

One man called out,"Hey, folks. Little Donnie has found hisself a green Smurf! "

Tallie walked as fast as she could, but he followed her calling, 'Smurf! Smurf.' You're 'pliking' you're a Smurf, but a real Smurf is blue.

" You're so dumb you don't know a Smurf is b_ue!"

People began to turn and view the commotion. Tallie turned and stared the little fellow right in the face. Through a phony smile and gritted teeth, she very quietly said, "I am nct play-liking I'm anything. How old are you? she asked. He said he was five and held up the fingers to match. Well, I was six when I was your age, so go find your mother or I'll find her and tell on you."

While he stood there trying to process all of that, Tallie pushed her way into the thickest part of the crowd. Safely away from her little tormentor, she slowed down to parade her new face passing slowly by the stalls of vegetables, melons, peaches, aprons, woodcrafts, and antiques. People paused their activities to look as she passed. Tallie was satisfied people looked at her much _onger than usual. She cut through the building and entered the parking lot on the way back to her booth.

"Hey, hey, sweet cakes," a male voice drawled.

Tallie didn't not look around but was consc_ous of two men leaning against a parked car.

"Aw, Brill, she's just a kid," the other man said.

"She sure ain't made up to be no kid," Brill countered. He caught up with her, grabbed her arm, jerked her around to face him.

"How old are you anyway?" he taunted.

"Old enough to sleep by myself. Now let go of me!" Tallie squirmed trying to free herself, but he held her fast.

"Are you old enough to sleep with me? "That's what I want to know." He laughed at the abashed look on Tallie's face.

Her skin began the elevator crawl. She was afraid, and he sensed it. He liked that she was afraid, just like those dogs that chased her back home. He laughed again, bigger, emitting fumes of beer and exposing rotten teeth. She kicked his shin as she wrenched free from Brill's sweaty grip and ran from the parking lot, zig-zagging through the pavilion to her aunt.

"Where on earth have you been, Missy? I sold all your rock figures already."

"I was just looking around and got held up."

"Yonder comes Mrs. Henry. She'll be wanting some melons and

jam. Hand me one of those nice gift sacks I made, will you please? They are in that big basket under there."

Tallie looked for the sacks, glad to have a moment to compose herself for the test that was on its way. Ceidra Henry was with her mother and looking as cool as a raspberry popsicle in a breezy sundress of the same shade.

"Aunt Jenny." Mrs. Henry held out her arms and sweetly greeted her long-time favorite old person. How well you look even on this hot day and in spite of your recent stay in the hospital."

"I'm as hardy as Oklahoma Johnsongrass and real glad to see you girls are home again. We missed you both. "

"I missed you, too, Aunt Jenny," Ceidra said and reached across the counter for a quick hug and Aunt Jenny called her precious and precocious, whatever that was."

"Sure is nice to be back," Mrs. Henry continued. "Fun to go but nice to be home, and I'm looking forward to some of these good melons. Oh, and look at that WON-der-ful peach jam!"

Aunt Jenny looked for the sacks. "Tallie, where in the world? Come out from under that counter and meet these folks."

Tallie endured a real wrench of fear but stood up anyway. Ceidra's perfectly shaped eyebrows heightened just a little, but Mrs. Henry's eye brows flew right up to her widow's peak. Aunt Jenny's face stayed subdued while she introduced Tallie as her niece, and a little about Tallie's parents. Tallie knew they were barely hearing anything her aunt said. Mrs. Henry could not take her eyes off Tallie, but Ceidra's were scanning the crowd when they eventually came to rest. Tallie tracked her line of sight to a distant part of the pavilion, resting on Tom Sawyer. Ceidra patted her mother's arm, whispered something, and left.

Tallie hardened. She picked up a squash and said, "How would you like some squash, Mrs. Henry?" I believe we have plenty left. Here. Take one. This one is free. They're really good at clearing the bowels after eating so much foreign food abroad. Squash lasts a long time in the refrigerator and is a very exciting vegetable. It's native to our local Indians. Did you know that? Wards off evil spirits, too, according to our natives."

Mrs. Henry's eyebrows flew up again, but only for a moment. She smiled as graciously as possible.

"I do believe you are quite a wealth of information," she said and thanked Tallie politely as placed the overgrown squash in her mesh shopping bag. We'll drive out your way as soon as possible, Aunt Jenny," she said. Then she nodded to Tallie and left.

Aunt Jenny stood with one hand on her hip and one on the counter.

"Lord have mercy!" What on earth was all that rigamarole about?" she asked.

"Nothing."

"Nothing, my foot. You'd better give me some answers."

"They acted like I was a freak or something."

"You look like one." Aunt Jenny took a handkerchief from her purse, spit on it, and began to scrub Tallie's face. That black stuff is 'smyeered' all under your eyes and plumb down onto your cheeks." Tallie squirmed.

"Hold still'" Aunt Jenny commanded.

"You're embarrassing me," Tallie painfully whispered.

"And you're embarrassing me. Your face looks like a map of the Dismal Swamp. I can't get it all off. Go along on to the restroom and scrub that stuff off. And hurry up if you intend to make it to the post office before noon."

Tallie found a bar of foul smelling, gray colored, grainy soap. By the time she got all the makeup off, her cheeks were sore and nearly matched the washed off neon pink lipstick. She thought of Ceidra's face which didn't seem to require much make-up to be beautiful. There was nothing on the market to make her as beautiful as Ceidra. She sighed and went to help load the truck.

"Good. You look like yourself instead of like you were hit in the face by some country's freshly dyed flag," Aunt Jenny said.

"Thanks a lot."

Her aunt laughed, and added, "Well? You did. Let's get some gas for the truck after you mail your package. And when we get home, we need to get something cooked for Sunday dinner and check on the hens. One's nesting."

~~~~~~~~~~~~~

"Do you know anyone named Brill." Tallie asked as she drove them toward home.

"Lah, yes, I do. Brillo Nudd How did you find out about him?"

"He was hanging around the pavilion today."

"Brillo Nudd. I sure didn't expect him back so soon."

"Some name," Tallie remarked.

"Right you are. Poor old Mrs. Nudd was one of the first to have a TV in this town, all though I did wonder how she came by it, God forgive me. She watched TV all day long, and wound up naming all her kids from things she heard in the commercials. There's Halo, the oldest girl. Then came Ivory, the second girl. Brillo is third and the only boy, and Camay is the youngest girl. All those kids named after cleaning products and not a one taking their names to heart, except maybe Halo. I don't think Mrs. Nudd was very familiar with any of those products before she got the TV."

"What is Halo?"

"It was a popular shampoo at one time. Halo Nudd turned out to be pretty good at typing and bookkeeping. Her typing teacher took an interest in her, got her to clean up, and when it was all said and done, Halo got a good office job over at Fort Sill. I was real glad for her, but Brill is another story. He never took a-hold of nothing——just rattled around in life like a lug nut in a tin can."

"Probably just bored. Normal people really do get bored sometimes." Tallie added.

"If bored is a hole needing filling with purpose and hope, he is sure enough bored. Bored has gnawed holes in him, body and soul. The Bible says as much."

"Where is that in the Bible?" Tallie's tone was one of incredulity.

"First Peter. Fifth chapter if I recollect. The adversary prowls around like an old lion hunting someone to gnaw on."

"Really. Holes in the soul? Aren't you imagining stuff?"

"Not to my understanding. A lion sinks his teeth into his prey and shakes his head to tear out a chunk. The devil gnaws like that—a hunk at a time and leaves holes. Our trick should be to go after the gnawer. Challenge the hateful thing. Some make the mistake of trying to keep the holes puttied with remedies of fun, food, drink, work, even denial. Don't you see? While he's chewing, he's pushing the poor chewed-on soul to go take his prescribed remedies."

"You make it sound awful."

"You bet it is, but the Lord restores souls. The Twenty-third Psalm says He does."

"How does He?"

"I can't say exactly. I do know He operates using Light and Word. Maybe He takes aim with a beam of light and says, 'Be restored!'"

Tallie smiled. "That sounds like a laser gun with ultrasound."

"HA! Maybe that's it. That's good thinking."

Tallie thought some and began to giggle. Aunt Jenny looked at her expecting an explanation. So Tallie said, "A soul is either holy and unhole-y, or it is hole-y and unholy."

"That's the whole truth and the hole-truth," Aunt Jenny laughed and continued to laugh until they both laughed uncontrollably at their puns.

"Lah! Aren't we silly?" Aunt Jenny said, wiping her eyes. It was good to enjoy the sound of Tallie's laughter, knowing that laughter and tears are both signs of healing, but laughter is the more enjoyable side of it.

Tallie stopped the truck at the mailbox and handed all the contents to her aunt.

Two of those letters were of particular interest to Aunt Jenny. One was from Jorbison-Black Operating, and the other one was from her cousin Mildred Hargus of Dispatch, Oklahoma. Mildred didn't write often, but when she did, it was always a fat letter requiring extra postage. Aunt Jenny smiled.

"Who is that fat one from?" Tallie asked.

"My cousin, Mildred, the mayor of Dispatch, so to speak. She's, let's see, 74 and got herself one of those electric typewriters so she could write things down until she has enough written to make it worth a trip to the post office. A-body has to sit a spell to read it all. She said her handwriting isn't what it used to be." Aunt Jenny tucked it into her pocket to read later.

Tallie gathered up her belongings and went into the house ahead of her aunt to head upstairs to stow her away.

Aunt Jenny took her time collecting her containers before slowly climbing the steps into the house. She walked through the kitchen to store things on the back porch, slipped out of her shoes and sat down at the kitchen table with a drink of water from the refrigerator. The house was so quiet.

"Tallie?" she called.

"In here." Tallie's soft high voice came from the front room. Aunt Jenny pushed herself up and went to see what she was doing. There stood Brillo Nudd with a knife at Tallie's back.

"Easy, old woman. I don't want no trouble outa neither of ya'."

"What DO you want, Brillo?" Aunt Jenny spoke quietly and sounded slightly annoyed.

"Cash money, old woman. You ought to have plenty from the Trade Fair."

"I spent most of it at the gas station."

"You get back into that kitchen and get your purse," he ordered.

Aunt Jenny sat down in her rocker instead.

"There's a little over eight dollars in my purse, and I've walked all I care to walk today. What do you want cash for?"

"None of your business. And guess what? I hear you're getting big lease money and I'm betting you cashed a big'un at the bank today."

"I'm going to pray some brains for you, Brill. You ought to know I don't keep cash around from the last time you prowled my house."

"Yeah? Get your purse, old woman. I won't leave without all you've got this time."

"You go get it yourself, Brillo. I'm tired."

Brillo stiffened and yanked Tallie closer to himself.

"I'll cut'er. I swear I will." He glared and pressed the point of the knife against Tallie's back.

Tallie flinched. "I've got some money," Tallie said, faintly.

"Where is it?" he demanded.

"In the upstairs bedroom."

"All right!" He started toward the stairs.

Aunt Jenny stood up.

"Don't you even think about it, Brillo Nudd. Don't even DARE go up there with her. You'll never be the same if you do."

"By you?"

"Do you want to find out? Do you want worms to eat you from the inside out? Or snakes crawling up your pants legs as you sneak around in the dark of night? If she wants to give you her money, let her go up there by herself. Listen to me! If I don't pray for brains and mercy for you, you could very well have snakes or worms or whatever God dishes up come upon you. You know that, don't you?"

Tallie quivered. "I'll get it. Just don't hurt us."

Brillo pushed her toward the stairs and grabbed Aunt Jenny by the hair with his knife at her nose and in a low growl to Tallie said, "Get it. You've got thirty seconds before I do her face a favor and carve this ugly beak off it."

Tallie was back almost instantly with a hundred-dollar bill.

"That's more like it," he said.

He snatched the bill from Tallie and Aunt Jenny and forced them into the hall closet. They could hear him laughing after he slammed it shut and locked it. The next sound they heard was of a motorcycle at the back of the house. Finally, silence.

"Is he gone?" Tallie whispered. She clung to her Aunt Jenny's arm.

"I imagine."

"How are we going to get out of here? Break the door down?" Tallie asked.

"Watch." Aunt Jenny rattled the door and it opened. "That door latch never was any good," she said, walking straight toward the telephone. "He flung us into the briar patch," she laughed, but he took my purse."

"You can't call the sheriff," Tallie said. "He cut the phone line with his knife."

"Well, if that don't beat all! Get the truck and we'll drive over to Hay's place and call."

Tallie went to the front door and looked out.

"We won't have to. Look down the road. I'll bet that's the sheriff in front of that cloud of dust. I still have his pager upstairs, and when I was up there, I punched it."

"Praise the Lord for that good thinking, Missy."

Sheriff Sawyer came to a rocking halt in front of the porch. He dragged a handcuffed Brillo Nudd from the car and yelled, "Aunt

Jenny? Are you all right? I caught this person speeding down the road with your purse hanging off his cycle "

"I'm very well," she said, walking to the edge of the porch for her purse, ignoring the presence of Brillo Nudd.

"Has this boy caused you any other harm?"

"He's disturbed the peace," she replied. "And a-body has to try hard to do that out here."

Tallie could not stand for her aunt to play down the danger that they had just endured. "He did a lot more than that! He held me with a knife at my back, took at least $100.00 from me and threatened to cut off Aunt Jenny's nose and.."

"That's, B and E. Robbery and assault with a deadly weapon, driving a vehicle without a license, and a few other charges such as resisting arrest, Nudd," the sheriff declared, looking him square in the face. "You're in a heap of trouble. You're not too smart are you, boy?"

"Oh, but he is going to be," Aunt Jenny said. I'll ask God to give him some brains and a new attitude to boot," .

"I'm taking you in, Nudd," Sheriff Sawyer hissed with such vehemence Tallie held her breath expecting the sheriff might beat the stuffings out of Brillo any second.

"Wait a minute, Sheriff," Aunt Jenny said. "Get him knelt down and I'll pray over him."

Brillo jerked this way and that in protest. "I ain't kneeling for nobody, least of all for that righteous, old heifer."

"You've been asked by the lady to kneel, son," the Sheriff commanded and kicked the back of Brillo's knees causing him to hit the gravel and Aunt Jenny commenced to pray.

Tallie sat down on the porch figuring the prayer could take a while.

Aunt Jenny praised God for this, that and the next thing and asked finally, for common sense and a Godly attitude to be given to the poor, gnawed soul kneeling before her; that he would accept those blessings and not end up in confusion or be eaten with worms like King Herod was when he set himself against Godly things. She prayed he would not have to live naked in a pasture and graze grass like Nebuchadnezzer who ignored the Lord, nor be bitten by a plethora of snakes like the errant Hebrew children in the wilderness. Then she closed her prayer and told the sheriff that she wanted to talk to him at church tomorrow. Tallie watched Sheriff Sawyer load Brillo Nudd into the car and drive away. I must have the craziest aunt in Oklahoma, she thought to herself—and the next day at church, she was sure of it.

"If you don't," Aunt Jenny said to the sheriff, "Brillo Nudd will sit down there and plot and gloat and get meaner past the point of no return."

"I'm sworn to take care of people---not put them in danger. He isn't one bit above using that knife or anything else he could grab," the sheriff admonished.

Aunt Jenny stiffened her back and instructed the sheriff that Brillo could hoe with cuffs and hobbles on. If we don't take this chance, he could continue on like he is and do no telling what all to any number of people, don't you see?"

"I'll think about it," Sheriff Sawyer said.

"You bring him on out about nine in the morning. You can chain him to that cottonwood tree in the back, if that makes you feel any better. I feel strongly about this, Hank."

Sheriff Sawyer wrinkled his forehead and looked upwards as if he hoped to see and answer on the brim of his white Stetson. There was none.

He sighed and said, "If I did allow that, I'd have to send Hooper out to stand guard and I'd have to come check on them and bring both of them back at night and all."

"Good. Good," Aunt Jenny smiled. "We got us a plan. You can have him back before supper."

Hank Sawyer wondered if he let her talk him into things against his better judgment.

Tallie was uncomfortable with the idea. She poured a glass of lemonade and went out to listen to the music which was just beginning. Oscar Ogle and Floyd Fursby could play anything with a string on it, Tallie decided, and today they were switching from mandolins to banjos to fiddles as fast as they could while Will Thompson and Sam Bliss blew harmonicas. Geneva Sawyer was playing the accordion. Everyone seemed to be able to play something. Tallie recalled that Pastor Hay played piano, guitar, and spoons– whatever that meant. George Hooper played juice harp or did he say Jew's-harp? He was hard to understand, not having four upper front teeth nor two below those.

Tallie knew most of the families now. Mr. Bliss was a barber and he and his wife had twin girls. Floyd Fursby and Will Thompson both ran farmer-rancher spreads. Mr. Wrothmeyer was a very elderly man who used to have a shoe and saddle shop. There were the Widkins. He farmed and worked for the highway department some. Mrs. Widkins taught second grade and was hoping to have her baby before school started again.

Tallie thought she was carrying a whole litter of babies as big as she was. Even Mrs. Widkins herself said she'd spin around like a coke bottle if she were to fall down. Tallie noticed Joyce Parks, a secretary for the rural electric company, came to church alone, a divorcee with no family close by. Dwight and Ruth Jenkins owned Gates Plumbing and Appliance where Tallie bought the bathtub. Noodle and Hub Gant were sitting on the church steps. They owned the Dairy Whiz drive-in on the south end of town.

Noodle was not her real name and no one else knew what it was, either. Tallie thought surely her real name would be better than Noodle, whatever it was. Alice Fursby said Noodle was probably called that because she liked noodles as a child. Harvey Boyce said she was good at 'noodling' for catfish which, Tallie found out, was to catch them by hand from the holes and caves under the banks of rivers. Weird? Yes, but anymore, nothing surprised her about this place.

Harvey Boyce was a checker at the grocery store and always managed to sit next to Joyce, the divorcee, at Sunday dinners, but Joyce never appeared very interested in Harvey. Harvey was good looking and definitely smitten with Joyce. Joyce, however, didn't show much interest in him. Tallie decided she might be afraid to take his last name.

Sometimes Jim and Mary Tall Trees came to church even though they lived in town. He was a tall, handsome, Indian of some sort and a professional referee, so they were out of town a lot on weekends.

Mrs. Tall Trees had long, shiny, brown hair down to her waist which was pinned up on the sides with big silver combs.

George Hooper, whom the sheriff was going to send out to guard Brillo Nudd, was always at church. He and Mrs. Hooper had five, blonde headed girls, all under the age of five, Two were twins. To Tallie, they all looked like little wads of white dough with raisins for eyes and invisible white hairs on their little heads. They were so fair you could not see their eyelashes or eyebrows at all. Two were always crying at the same time, and all of them had runny noses. Mrs. Hooper looked so pale Tallie thought she looked more like a thin rag hanging on the clothesline than a human.

Mr. Hooper grinned a lot showing a gap where front teeth used to be. He was a handyman and drove the bus for the school. Once during church testifying time, Mr. Hooper told how he used to have an awful temper and liked to fight. It had cost him jobs and his debts piled up right along with his temper. He said he began to rack up more days in Sheriff Sawyer's jail than he did at work, but that was a few years ago. The sheriff had put him to fixing up the jail since he was in it so much, then got him to repair stuff at the courthouse, and even taught him to read using the Bible. Mr. Hooper said that is how he got his head and his hands squared away for the Lord which was why he was so happy and grinned a lot, teeth or not.

If Mrs. Hooper was glad, it sure didn't show yet. She acted like going to church was another chore to do on Sunday. Tallie looked over at her. She was standing under a tree holding the baby while another thumb-sucking child held on to her hairy leg. Two of her kids were throwing handfuls of sand at each other and the fifth was asleep on a rag blanket clutching a half-eaten jelly sandwich.

Tallie decided if Mrs. Hooper hadn't gotten much out of church, it was probably because she was always wiping spit-up off her shoulder or having to take one of the kids to the bathroom or two of them outside to finish crying. Tallie briefly wished she could do something for Mrs. Hooper but couldn't think of anything, except send her some iron tablets. The two Hooper kids playing in the sandy drive ran to their mother when a car approached.

It was a silver sports car. Ceidra! And Tom was with her. She saw him kiss Ceidra's cheek before he opened the door. Tallie instantly decided to re-enter the kitchen to help clean up.

Aunt Jenny handed her a warm, soapy dish rag to wipe the table and chairs where the little Hooper children had eaten. Gunk and goo was all over that area. Meanwhile she went out to listen to Ceidra play.

The music had started up and there was a new sound. Tallie glanced out. Ceidra was playing a silver keyboard and playing it very well. Tallie bent down and scrubbed harder on the chairs. She grabbed a cup from the table and sent grape juice all down the front of her dress just as the screen door opened. It was Ceidra and Tom coming in for dessert.

Tom stared at Tallie. "This is Tallie Koums," he said.

"Yes, I know. I met her yesterday, she said while eyeing the large purple stain. "She certainly is a colorful person." Tom's eyes cut directly from Tallie to Ceidra.

"You know what I mean, Tom," Ceidra said, "an interesting addition to our summer."

"Well, if it isn't Ceidra!" Alice Fursby came out of the pantry with her arms open wide for a hug. "Come over here and tell me all about that Peru place you visited. I do hope your mother is rested and all so she can address the garden club after the Floral Parade. We've planned a lovely float this year, a throne decorated with silver sage and lavender. Your colors. And of course, Tom was elected to be your escort. I think the parade will be a great success as usual. Absolutely everyone is excited about the theme I selected, Wild Flowers from Wonderful Places."

Tallie stood as far away as she could and mopped at the grape stain on her dress not caring what Ceidra had to say about some dumb parade or anything else, or was that a lie to herself?

"Beats chicken manure," Tom whispered as he passed her with two pieces of cake.

"Shut up," she hissed.

He laughed on his way to rescue Ceidra from Alice Fursby. Tallie went back to cleaning the tables and went to find her Aunt who was talking to Mrs. Widkins about pickle making. Moments later, Aunt

Jenny's eyes polled the premises and decided to get up, indicating her move into the expected polite rituals of departing.

"Well, I've thoroughly enjoyed myself," she called to no one in particular, " but I'm about ready to hie for the homestead. Oscar and Floyd, you boys simply out-do each other! Ceidra, you get better and better. I expect to see you light up the music world with your great gift."

"Thank you. You are so sweet, Aunty J. I'm planning on studying various keyboard instruments in New York after I graduate next summer."

"I'm glad," Aunt Jenny said, "and you should come on back next Sunday and practice on our congregation some more."

Tallie picked up the food hamper and followed her Aunt purposely letting the screen door bang behind her.

Later that evening, Aunt Jenny sat on the porch with her feet in a pan of cool water reading her letter from Mildred Hargus, her cousin from Dispatch, Oklahoma, chuckling now and then.

"What's so funny?" Tallie asked.

"Mildred. She sits on the porch and manages the affairs of her town like a mayor."

"Is she the mayor?"

"Not by election of the town folk, but she runs the place all the same. Very little happens there without her praying over it or expressing her Godly opinion, needs be. That's what is known as occupying. We're told to 'occupy' until He returns.

"Really, Aunt Jenny. That's a little much."

"Okay, Missy. What's paining you? Out with it."

"Nothing."

"Nothing? That's a blooming fib. You scrub the varnish off the tables after dinner, tell Tom to shut up, barely speak to Ceidra Henry, and you haven't said anything but boo-hiss-sic-em since we got to home."

"What am I supposed to say? There's nothing to say and there is nothing the matter."

Aunt Jenny crossed her arms.

"I know there is, and I think you're jealous of Ceidra for starters."

"Ha! Her? Why should I be jealous of her? I don't live here and I don't care about her or her little, silver car, or her silver keyboard, or the silver sage throne Alice Fursby is decorating for the little precocious precious princess."

"And you aren't jealous? You need to face the truth about yourself and take responsibility for how you are reacting. You may not be responsible for your circumstances, but you certainly are for your reactions. And you—."

"Don't give me any longnose lectures! I'm not in the mood for any more rocking-chair sermons. I've had it with her and I don't want you telling me what is wrong with me when none of you can begin to see that she is nothing but a silver-plated stuck-up snob, milking all of you for adoration and compliments. Tallie's eyes filled with tears. "And you, of ALL people, suck up to her just like that old frizzled-headed Alice Fursby."

SWACK! Aunt Jenny slapped her across the face with her wet foot-washing rag and went into the house.

Tallie shrieked and ran from the porch down the path to the well and cried and cried. No one had ever hit her before. She cried so hard she got the dry heaves. All she could think about was how ugly she felt compared to Ceidra, and how untalented compared to everyone else, that Tom and everybody else was goofy about Princess Ceidra-ella—the whole stupid, backward bunch of them. Even Aunt Jenny took up for her and slapped me for exposing their precious snot wad.

" I'm sick of this place. I hate it here. I don't belong here," she said aloud. She wailed and added, "...or anywhere else! No one would care if I melted and ran through the cracks!" The dry heaves came on again and she threw up for real.

Tallie wiped her month and kicked dirt over the mess. Then she pumped some water and washed her face between dry sobs and heavy sighing which stopped abruptly at the sight of a long, silver Lincoln pulling into the drive.

"Yoo-hoo? Aunt Jenny?" Someone called. Tallie looked closely at the couple discerning whom she assumed to be Mr. and Mrs. Henry. They were carrying something. Aunt Jenny opened the door for them. Tallie washed her face some more and waited a bit before slipping around to the back door. All three of them were talking in turn in low and serious voices. The only word Tallie heard clearly was "Ceidra" and not caring to hear any more about that subject, she slipped in the back way and up to bed. It seemed she had scarcely gotten to sleep when something poked her in the back. It was Aunt Jenny with a serious face and a wooden spoon.

Chapter Twelve: Mr. Hooper's bat, Hell Hound's revenge, Tallie's Report card.

Aunt Jenny poked her again with a wooden spoon.

"You stay in your room today. You need time out, and I don't want you anywheres near that Nudd boy, do you understand?" Aunt Jenny set down three hot buttered biscuits and spiced apple juice and left.

Tallie ate, fluffed a pillow and lay down. I don't mind this little deal. Room service and a day off? Suits me just fine, she thought and nodded off.

Loud voices awakened her. Tallie went to the window to see what was happening. Brillo Nudd, chained to a tree, was chopping Johnsongrass with that dull hoe. Tallie knew it was dull because she'd used it last and had decided it was one that never was and never will be sharpened. She giggled watching him fling and flail at the Johnsongrass in the hard, dry dirt.

Aunt Jenny was at the clothes line singing, hanging out t-towels and straining rags. But when Nudd let out some colorful interpretations of Aunt Jenny's ancestry, she yanked her bonneted head toward him, pointed at him with her forehead and squinted her eyes. To Tallie her aunt reminded her of Old Janet, head down and imaginary horns ready. At the same time, Mr. Hooper rounded the corner of the house with a bucket of water and stopped slap in his tracks. He looked at Aunt Jenny for her 'yeah-sick-em' nod, but by then Aunt Jenny had gathered herself.

"Brillo Nudd," Aunt Jenny said, "I'm fixing fried chicken and peach pie for the noon meal. Now you're welcome to share it, if the Lord gives you any brains between now and then. Otherwise, Mr.

Hooper will give you some of that water and a raw squash or two to gnaw on for your meal."

Nudd spewed a scorching string against Aunt Jenny's squash and her bossy ways. Aunt Jenny reached into her bosom while looking straight at Nudd, took out a tissue, tore it and stuffed it into her ears before she turned back to the clothes line, singing all the louder:

Have you been to Jesus for the cleansing power?
Are you washed in the blood of the Lamb?

The louder Brillo cursed, the louder she sang. He could curse loud, but not as loud as Aunt Jenny could sing. Mr. Hooper stood there by the water bucket, looking back and forth between them. Brillo left off cussing about squash and took up cursing people, places, and things totally unknown to Tallie. Aunt Jenny kept singing to the rhythm of Brillo's blistering outbursts. It seemed to Tallie that Mr. Hooper was uncertain what to do next, but finally, he picked up a baseball bat (where that came from, Tallie had no idea) and walked to the edge of the Johnsongrass patch where he set down the bucket of water and backed away from it just a little.

Brillo stuck his face into the water, drank, and cursed Mr. Hooper. Then he sucked up some more water and spit it right at him. Mr. Hooper backed up to avoid the spew, and that's when Brillo slung the hoe at him. Mr. Hooper caught the hoe and spit an impossibly long stream of tobacco juice through the great gap in his upper teeth which splatted Brillo right in the top of his forehead and hair.

"When you want water I've carried, you'll p'litely ask," Mr. Hooper added and threw the hoe back to Brillo. "Get to work. Now!"

Brillo cursed and threw the hoe at Mr. Hooper again, who quickly ducked, picked it up and went to the far side of the Johnsongrass patch. Brillo crouched down and watched like he was expecting Mr. Hooper to make some sort of move.

Aunt Jenny wasn't singing anymore. She stood there holding the empty laundry basket on her hip with one hand over her mouth. Mr. Hooper looked at the hoe and then at Brillo Nudd. He shook his head, sorrowfully, and began to chop the Johnsongrass in Brillo's place. Aunt Jenny took a deep breath and returned to the house.

Brillo relaxed and began again. "That's more like it. That old cow has quit her squalling and you're doing the kind of work you was born to, you toothless bag of skin. Can't read, can't write, so you hoe, right? The only thing you can do is get them ugly schmoo kids borned, right?"

Mr. Hooper looked up from his work to stare at Nudd, and Tallie could tell he was nearly over the edge. He let go a nasty stream of tobacco juice at Brillo, deliberately but scarcely missing Nudd who jumped left. Hooper spat another stream to the right, messing up the shady spot where Nudd had been seated. Tallie slipped away from the window and dressed. She hoped someone had remembered to search him for any hidden knives.

Aunt Jenny opened the door and picked up Tallie's breakfast dishes. Pausing in the doorway, she looked at Tallie.

"Something wrong?" Tallie asked.

"You tell me," Aunt Jenny said. "That's the one reason you're in here."

"You're mad at me for telling you what's what with your Ceidra-ella, right?"

"Hardly. You'd better think on it some more," she said and left.

The smell of fried chicken floated all over the farm. Tallie's mouth watered and so did Brillo Nudd's. When the back porch screen banged, Tallie looked out the window again. Aunt Jenny carried a plate of food and handed it to Mr. Hooper. Mr. Hooper looked at the heap of wonderful food and thanked her. When Aunt Jenny was out of sight, he handed it to Brillo and walked to the garden where he took out a pocket knife, cut one tomato, and began to eat.

Brillo called Mr. Hooper a cheek-turning-Jesus-monkey and a few other things between bites of succulent fried chicken and hot rolls. Tallie wondered about all that for a moment, but Aunt Jenny was coming up the stairs, so she left off wondering and looked forward to her own plate of chicken. Aunt Jenny set down a plate containing a boiled egg, two cold weiners, and a glass of water.

"Well? What do you have to say?" Aunt Jenny asked.

"Did the chicken fall off the plate?"

"Have you thought about the condition you've let yourself get into?" Aunt Jenny asked.

"Condition? What do you mean 'condition'? I yelled and you

slapped me. I'm sorry I yelled, so let's forget about it, okay?"

"No. You sit right here and recollect the last few days, and you look at exactly what happened just as if you were somebody else, and you look at how you reacted. When you can name what's gnawing on you, we'll talk. There's a pencil and paper in that dresser drawer. I'll be back in an hour to see about you."

"I've got to go to the bathroom," Tallie announced.

"There is a slop jar under the bed. Call it a chamber pot, if you are finicky."

"No, I can't use—" but Aunt Jenny left and locked the door. Tallie could not help but finish protesting. "I've never had to squat on one of those things in my life! It's barbaric!" she yelled at the door.

As the urge got urgent, Tallie pulled the pot out from under the bed. It was white enamel with pink pansies on the sides and on the lid. "Gross!" she whispered." This is like going in your mother's dishes."

Tallie pushed the jar back under the bed and washed her hands using the old pitcher and bowl on the night stand. Thinking that there would be a quicker end to the confinement if she could come up with something on paper to satisfy her aunt, she reached for the writing supplies and thought while eating her cold lunch. She knew that whatever she wrote would have to be good. But nothing came to mind.

Sounds from downstairs indicated that Sheriff Sawyer was there to eat up the fried chicken and to check on his maniacal prisoner. How can Aunt Jenny be so bent out of shape over me, she wondered, when she has a real live criminal chained to a tree in her backyard. She says something is gnawing on me. I suppose she would call it a hole-in-the soul syndrome. HITS disease. Oh, great! She has me thinking like she does.

Tallie continued to wonder about what to write, finally admitting jealousy and loss of temper, but she could not decide why she lost her temper. Mr. Hooper didn't lose his temper. Except maybe once, when he spat that tobacco juice, but the way he spat was more like a warning than anger, she decided.

Brillo was the only one going nuts from anger, and Mr. Hooper probably isn't jealous of him. No one really sees that Ceidra is a silver-plated snot. She has everyone fooled—even the people I thought were smarter than I am. They can't see that, and that scares me. That has to be the bottom line, she thought, and banged on the door until Aunt Jenny came up to look at her writing.

"That is an honest report, but not the bottom line," Aunt Jenny said. Then she underlined the words 'scared' and 'thought'. "Listen, Missy. All emotional hoo-haws come from fear of something. Fear is at the root of all failings. Inordinate fear will run the show. YOU need to decide what or who you want running the show. That is the deciding point right there. Right there is where we are responsible. We are required to make wise choices in our reactions. Don't let fear rule you."

Tallie threw her pencil down and asked, "Then what were you afraid of when you slapped me with that nasty foot rag of yours?"

"Rejection, Missy. Fear that you think I'm too old to know what's what. Fear that you rejected my worth and the worth of my friends and my good way of life. All the fears I know of boil down to fear of rejection. But that is a life-long study and I don't have time to teach you all about that."

"I'm not afraid of rejection. Shoot. Who cares? Let the world go jump in a lake. I could care less."

"That's all smart talk and a dead give-away. Missy. A great fog of foolishness. You do care. That is exactly what the evil one wants to do, isolate you, make you lie to yourself, distort the truth and then he goes to work gnawing on your soul."

"The hole-in-the-soul. HITS disease," Tallie muttered.

"Right. Good thinking, for once."

"So what's the cure?"

Aunt Jenny sighed within herself. How could she sum up a lifetime's worth of study in twenty-five words or less?

"Be smart enough to stop long enough to know what is drumming you down into the dust. Call the thing by name and plan a good way to avoid it or to run it out of your territory. For instance, when you go to the barn, you think to yourself, "That is fresh cow manure and I do not want to step in that. Recognition of the thing is the first step. Jesus named the thing he came against and then took the necessary actions for restoration. Right action is the second step and steps do vary. Jesus often used a quote from the Bible. He started out by saying " It is written", but one time he used a whip. I can't give you a set pattern for that, but I would be careful about taking up a whip."

"Then why did you slap me?" She asked, simultaneously realizing the nasty foot rag was her version of a more merciful whip.

"To get you to cough up the pus in your craw. To reinforce the fact that bad manners get bad bad rewards. To clear the air—for both of us. Love isn't always compliments and hugs."

Tallie thought about Mr. Hooper spitting that stream of tobacco. She wondered if that might have been to draw Brillo's cussing on himself and away from Aunt Jenny. Or was he trying to keep from beating the tar out of Brillo with the baseball bat?

"Well?" Aunt Jenny prompted. "Didn't that slapping make you cough up all that poison?"

Tallie wondered if Aunt Jenny knew how much she had "coughed" up, including the vomit.

"What really counts, Tallie, is how we handle what comes in and out of our territories. Like a-while ago, Hank Sawyer had been down to the old house to get Claude's mail and he said someone had done a pretty good job of cleaning on it. Now that is love. You know that must have been an onerous job."

"The oven was the worst part! I mean, you know, when we were there I saw how yucky it was."

"I don't recall seeing it, but I can imagine it was caked and crusted with cockroaches. Poor old Claude." Aunt Jenny shook her head and took hold of the doorknob.

"Can I come out now?" Tallie asked.

"Not yet. You stay here until the sheriff comes back for that Nudd boy. And keep this door locked. I don't trust him any further than that chain around his leg."

When Aunt Jenny left, Tallie looked out the window again. Brillo and Mr. Hooper were standing by the water bucket.

"Why don't you answer when I talk to you, you old scab?" Brillo took a drink of water and stared at Mr. Hooper waiting for a response. Mr. Hooper looked at Brillo, bored like. Then he took the dipper from Brillo, put it back in the bucket, picked up the hoe and poked Brillo in the back with it.

"Watch it!" Brillo said and grabbed the hoe.

Mr. Hooper sat down on a tobacco-free spot under the shade tree and pointed to the Johnsongrass patch with the baseball bat. Brillo hacked half-heartedly at the grass and Mr. Hooper began to read from the New Testament he drew from his shirt pocket while tracing the words with his finger. Once in a while, he would look at Brillo and check the chain.

"You're wasting your time reading that pie-in-the-sky-book. I ain't listening. Brillo said. There was no response from Mr. Hooper. Brillo then walked closer to the shade tree.

"There ain't no God. There's no pie now and there's no pie later, that is unless you grab it for yourself, bus-barn brains!"

Mr. Hooper pocketed the New Testament, picked up the baseball bat and eased around the tree to keep a better eye on his prisoner who continued to spout his vitriol.

"There ain't no God, Man. I found that out a long time ago. Like a fool, I told God to do something and He didn't. I'll show you there ain't none. Brillo threw down the hoe, raised his arms and yelled, God, if You are who that stupid book says You are, say something to us so we can hear You."

Brillo waited with his ear aimed at the sky. Then he laughed. "See?" and yelled again. "I'll make it easy for You since You can't talk. How about a little demonstration? I ain't afraid of You. Hell, You ain't even up there! Take a big swing at me, God," Brillo chuckled and picked up the hoe and shook it skyward.

He continued to chuckle and hit some licks at the Johnsongrass, until his jocularity wore off. Then he made a few big whacks deep into the tall grass. The dirt was softer there, he faintly noted. He whacked again, this time, right into a nest of little baby snakes that fled in all directions like lightning, some running right up his britches leg.

Nudd screamed at the top of his lungs shaking the snakes off his feet and legs. Mr. Hooper ran to help, scooping the snakes away with his bare hands.

"Kill 'em! Kill 'em!" Nudd yelled between high pitched quivery screams. His eyes were wide open with fear, he pee-ed his pants and jumped up and down in one place, drooling and softly wailing in a high pitch.

Mr. Hooper took hold of Brillo. The jumping stopped but the flailing and wailing didn't. Mr. Hooper drew back his lean arm and knocked Brillo Nudd flat on the dirt, picked him up and dragged him easily by the armpits to the shade of the tree. Mr. Hooper sat down beside him and began to read the New Testament again.

Aunt Jenny appeared with two pieces of peach pie. "What was all that racket about?" she asked and saw Brillo on the ground.

"Nudd had a fit, but he's resting now. He learnt that sometimes, us Christians is called to be the arms and legs of Jesus. You want that I should wake him?"

"Maybe you'd better."

Mr. Hooper shifted his tobacco to the other jaw, took a half-dipper of water and dashed it into Brillo's face. Brillo jerked and coughed and sat up slowly.

"Miss Jenny has brung us some pie, boy." Mr. Hooper wiped the water off Nudd's face with his bare hand.

"He's washed up now, Miss Jenny. I reckon he can have some pie." Mr. Hooper looked shyly up at her and poked Brillo's shoulder.

"Well, what do ya' say, boy?" Mr. Hooper prompted.

Brillo paused, looked at the Johnsongrass then to Mr. Hooper and finally up at Aunt Jenny.

"Thanks, Miz Jenny," he mumbled.

Aunt Jenny nodded and left them alone.

Mr. Hooper washed the tobacco out of his mouth. Using a fork, he scooped his slice of pie into his hand and from where Tallie watched, it looked as if he ate it in two bites. He wiped his hand on the back of his britches and reached into his pocket. Brillo caught the New Testament Mr. Hooper pitched at him. "You read out loud and I'll chop. I'll chop as long as you read loud and plain."

Brillo nervously looked around to see who was in hearing distance, then he drew a deep breath. "I don't read too good," he admitted.

"Yore a-fixing to learn. You know the letters, don't you?" When Brillo nodded, Mr. Hooper said, "Spell them letters if you can't call the word."

"Where do I start?" Brillo asked, thumbing through the book

"Start with the red writing. Them's Jesus's words."

After the sheriff collected Mr. Hooper and Brillo Nudd, Tallie went downstairs following the fragrant path and the sound of chicken being fried. She gladly set the table and the mashed potatoes.

"Come here," Aunt Jenny directed, "I'll show you how to make cream gravy."

She began by pouring the chicken grease into a metal can and measured one-fourth cup back into the skillet. To that she added one-fourth cup flour and some salt. As that browned, she peppered it and stirred it with an egg turner until it turned a light tan color. Next, she slowly added two cups of rich milk, stirring all the while until it was well mixed. Then she let it gently boil down until it had a film on the top and bubbles the size of owl's eyes. "That's the way to make gravy," Aunt Jenny said, "and anything else is wallpaper paste, to my notion."

"I thought this chicken would be all gone," Tallie remarked at supper.

"I didn't fry all of it. I saved some for us. I just fried enough for the men folk, including the telephone repairman."

"Mr. Hooper didn't eat any. He ate a tomato out of the garden and gave his plate of food to Brillo Nudd."

Aunt Jenny laid down her napkin. "Is that a fact!" Then she smiled. "He did that, did he. Well, what do you know about that."

Tallie realized that Aunt Jenny had not eaten any chicken either and wondered if her aunt was fasting or just making sure she had enough for everyone else.

Aunt Jenny silently recalled the first time Sheriff Sawyer had set Mr. Hooper to chopping the Johnsongrass. He was bony, thin, and mean. He'd fight anyone over the least thing. Hank was getting so tired of locking him up. His frail, little wife needed him at home–not in jail. The last straw was when Doc Gilbert went to deliver Mrs. Hooper's fifth.

Hooper grabbed the doc and said, "If you deliver me another one of them girls, I swear I'll whup your tail. I need some boys to help me work."

Doc told him to get out of the way, that Hooper would get whatever came out, and when Doc Gilbert told him he had twin girls, Mr. Hooper blacked Doc's eye and cracked two of his ribs before one hefty nurse could throw a blanket over his head while the other called the sheriff. Apparently, Doc managed one good lick. Hooper woke up in jail with four front and two lower teeth missing.

A car came into the drive. "Oops, I forgot to tell you that the Henrys were coming out this evening," Aunt Jenny said on her way to the door.

"Are we too early, or too late?" Mr. Henry called. He helped his wife out of the car.

"Too late for supper, but just in time for peach pie," Aunt Jenny answered. Let's sit out here on the porch."

Tallie cleared the table and helped slice the pie, relieved that Ceidra was not with them. She carried the pie to the porch and asked about Ceidra anyway, even though it was an effort.

Mrs. Henry said Ceidra had been invited to Tulsa to spend the fourth of July.

"Oh, I almost forgot," Mrs. Henry said. A sales rep left some samples of cosmetics. I thought maybe you and Aunt Jenny might like to try them and let us know what you think. This package is designed for young girls, and this one for us older girls. We would appreciate an honest assessment of this new line."

Tallie thanked Mrs. Henry, knowing full well the reason for the gift. She peeked at the interesting looking bottles and jars. They smelled good even without opening them.

Mr. Henry swallowed the last bite of pie and when Tallie left to take the cosmetics inside, he asked Aunt Jenny if she had had time to think about what they talked about last night.

"I did. And I called my cousin, Mildred Hargus, over in Dispatch. She and I prayed. I didn't say any names of course, but we studied it out and talked again this morning. Mildred said there was a large revival that Pastor Hargus would be helping with. Some big convention at the Baptist Church in Fairview. Mildred suggested that Ceidra could easily be the guest musician for a week. Why don't you offer her that choice. Perhaps she won't be so apt to run off to Dallas to do that other thing she has in mind."

Mr. Henry asked his wife what she thought about the idea.

Mrs. Henry smiled, saying, "Why not try? I just hope she'll agree. I can't stand the thought of her going off to model and mess around in Dallas all by herself at her age. If I could get my hands on that modeling agent, I'd—I'd, no telling what I'd do," said Mrs. Henry. "I'm afraid she'll get exposed to too much too soon. She's too young and too many nice things to look forward to, like that audition as pianist for the touring choir at the university. She's even been asked to study music in New York. Juilliard. It has a good reputation.

Tallie had returned to hear the part about the college. "You mean Ceidra will be in college next year?"

"She'll be graduating early. At her school, you can move up a level if you pass certain tests with high enough scores," Mrs. Henry explained.

"Oh, how nice!" Tallie replied, fighting off a blinding flash of jealousy. "I'd sure like to be that smart."

"It has its drawbacks. Smart is one thing; wise is another." Mrs. Henry said.

Tallie couldn't imagine a drawback, but Mrs. Henry was certainly convinced. Silence followed, so Tallie decided to take the water buckets and fill them, realizing the Henrys needed to be alone with Aunt Jenny.

When Tallie was beyond hearing them, Mr. Henry asked Aunt Jenny what she thought would happen if Ceidra hopped off to Dallas instead of taking the guest pianist position.

"Either way, she'll come through okay. Cousin Mildred and I have a definite peace about it."

"Do you think Pastor Hargus knows Ceidra is a Presbyterian?" Mrs. Henry asked.

"I doubt it. But I do know Luff Hargus who's to do some of the preaching won't care. It's a revival. Thus, heathens and denominations of all kinds will be showing up by God's own doing, Aunt Jenny reasoned, causing the Henrys to laugh heartily."

When the Henrys left, Aunt Jenny got Tallie aside and told her to let go of any ill will toward Ceidra and to start praying for her.

"Pray?' Is she in trouble?"

"Not yet that I know of, but get those prayers said this evening.

Preventative covering is of great importance right now. And tomorrow, we'll go to town and pledge allegiance to the flag in front of the post office. It's the Fourth of July celebration."

"OH yeah, that's right. " Tallie said.

"Shall we go decked out?" Aunt Jenny asked.

"Sure!"

"Then get that cosmetic case out and practice a nice looking face so that you don't shock anyone tomorrow."

"I will, but only if you will, too," Tallie said.

"Why not? That'll be funny since I've never worn anything but powder, and it will give Alice Fursby some new talking material.

Tallie giggled. "Do you like her?"

"Of course I do, and I make sure she has me to talk about. That keeps her from doing any serious damage to someone else. She likes visiting and likes people. That's a talent, but the Old Deluder can twist information into gossip right quick just like he'd like to twist everyone's talents. Alice's, Ceidra's, mine, and yours, too."

"Mine? I don't have one."

"Sure you do. Whatever comes out of you naturally is your talent. Alice thinks you sing good, but there are other things that come out of you naturally such as making those figurines. Even Mr. Hooper can repair things as well as swing a mean bat, naturally."

"What about Brillo Nudd? That stuff coming out of him naturally was X-rated."

"That boy goes to great lengths to get a quick quarter without busting a sweat. There has to be a talent in there somewhere. Speaking of sweat, I'm going to get a bath. With all those men on the place today, I wore a full slip under my dress and the perspiration ran down my back all day. OH, hey! There is a letter for you on the buffet,"

Dear Tacky Tallie, Ha! A joke.

I am having a lot of fun. Sorry you are missing out seeing me this summer. I got a D in English and history so Mother decided I should improve my mind so I'm sitting here in the dumb libary by myself all day. So I called Bellisa and she came and its been totally rip-roaring trying to drive that old lady libarian insane with made up book titles and made up call numbers. I'm going, "can't you find anything?" and then these two nerdy boys walk in and Bellisa and me waited until they went to hunt something, and we sprayed their heavy backpacks with cologne. Really heavy with it. We thought it would make them sick, but decided they must like it becuz they waved at us. Like we would ever pay them any attention and we laughed so hard. Not outloud. I couldn't afford to get thrown out of there. I'm in major trouble already for staying out till two. Anyway, me and Bellisa she is my new best friend are going out for cheerleader so we practiced in the restroom for two hours. We locked the door so no one else could get in. When we left we locked the stalls up from the inside. HA. Isn't that funny? I bet you are laughing your head off and wishing you were here. Tomorrow, I get to go back to the pool if I don't get thrown out of this libary today. I hope my tan didn't fade. Oh yeah, I streeked my hair. Neat. Everyone thinks I look super great. Gotta go. I probably won't write any more, I've been too busy. Call me when you get back. You can come over and watch me and Bellisa practice for cheerleader tryouts. I like her alot. Gotta go, see ya! Amy

Tallie threw the letter in the trash.

"BOO!" Aunt Jenny said, peeking around the door.
Tallie laughed and stared. "You look nice! Hey, really! That make-up looks nice on you."
"It's your turn, Missy. Aren't we silly?"
"No. Wasting cologne on backpacks is silly."
"How's that?" She asked, but Tallie waved off an answer.
Aunt Jenny held up a mirror to see herself again, wiggled her lips and giggled. "I look like a 'possum in a pokeberry patch. Wrinkled and gray and with a red mouth."
"Is there really something called pokeberries, or did you make that up?" Tallie asked.
No, it's a real berry used to make dye and ink at one time. Revolutionary soldiers used to write love letters to their wives and sweethearts. It makes a cherry red ink and makes 'possum lips red, Ha. So! Get ready, Sawed-Off Corners, here we come in our 'possum lipstick!"

~~~~~~~~~~~~~
Hot as it was that Fourth of July afternoon, everyone who was able was on the courthouse lawn in Sawed Off Corners. Aunt Jenny and Tallie walked around surveying the people and the sights.

The VFW men were selling lemonade under an oversized red, white and blue umbrella. In the town square's gazebo was a musical contest. Several acts were standing by with all sorts of instruments. At the moment, The Presbyterian Church choir was performing "God Bless America" behind a little girl all dressed up like the Statue of Liberty holding a foil-covered flashlight.

The Lions Club was cooking hot dogs and barbecue. Noodle and Hub Gant were running a sno-cone operation. The sheriff's office was sponsoring a pellet gun shoot. The Flower and Garden Club had a dessert booth and all the desserts garnished by flowers, real or homemade, but edible.

The sanitation department maintained a recycling center and if someone reported that you threw trash on the lawn, they would put you in a bamboo cage and someone would have to come bail you out.

There were other events: The baseball throw, Get the American flag painted on your cheek, A perambulating clown dressed up like Uncle Sam. You could pose for polaroid pictures with him for a dollar each. Tallie paid for two pictures of her and Aunt Jenny on either side of the Uncle Sam clown.

"There is a lot more going on than I expected," Tallie said.

"The town is raising money for an ambulance and a defibrillator to go in it– if your heart stops. That is why we're having such a turnout. A major percentage of the profits go for those things which are badly needed."

"I thought you were only coming in to say the pledge in front of the post office."

"It's the main thing, and I'll get to it dreckly. The postal workers make you say the pledge before you get a drink of cold water at their booth. Then, if you want a cup with ice, you pay 25 cents or even more if you want to donate. The funeral home is giving out free fans, and the Henry's have free pill boxes for adults and balloons for the kiddies just for coming to the celebration.

"Over yonder, the school teachers have desks set up to give tests about Independence Day. It costs a dollar to take the test. A straight "A" report card is good for a little American Flag, or an ear of buttered corn from the Lions Club's booth. You want to try?"

"No thanks. I take enough tests at school," Tallie said.

"Well, let's go say the pledge and get a cool drink anyway, Aunt Jenny suggested. I love to hear the little kids say the pledge. They're liable to say most anything. I believe the best I ever heard done here went something like: I pledge a smidgen to the flag and to the republic for itchy' hands."

Tallie laughed with her aunt then asked, "Who said that?"

Aunt Jenny sighed and rose from the bench in the shade. "Brillo Nudd. I guess a smidgen was all he ever had and I know he was well acquainted with the itch."

"Jenny Raider!" It was Alice Fursby prancing as fast as she could in her red, beaded sandals, red summer bag, and straw hat with a stars-n-stripes scarf tied as a the hatband with long tails flying behind her; all of which was aimed at drawing attention and favorable comments. She usually responded to the comments saying she wanted Floyd to find her in a crowd.

"Jenny, if you have time, be sure and...   "Alice's eyes opened wide as her mouth. "What is THAT?" She exclaimed.

"What is what, Alice?" Aunt Jenny asked with raised chin and eyebrows.

"If that don't beat all! You're wearing lipstick, and (she peered closer) eye stuff! Why you've even got on rouge. The whole nine yards! What brought all this on?"

"My man friend," Aunt Jenny replied.

At that remark, even Tallie jerked to attention and watched Alice Fursby draw a sharp breath with her hand over her heart, mouth agape.

"Well, don't you think I look nicer, Alice?"

"What MAN friend?" Alice demanded.

"You answer my question first," Aunt Jenny said. "Don't you think I look nicer?"

"You look nice, Jenny, now what is this man-friend business?"

"Actually, Alice, there are other reasons I'm wearing this besides a man. Haven't you read about protecting your skin from ultraviolet rays? As much as I'm in the sun, even a bonnet isn't enough."

"Bonnet, schmonnet! What MAN?"

"Tallie and I wanted to dress up especially nice for the occasion."

"Is there really a man friend or are you getting that Old Timers' disease?"

"There is a man, but I'll tell you about it later. Right now, I'm going to say the pledge and get a cool drink."

"You always did like taking your time to tell me anything. You always keep things to yourself, like some perishing lady of mystery. Sakes alive! Make-up at your age."

"My daddy said a little paint is good for all old barns."

Alice clearly wanted to push the man thing to conclusion, but someone on a bull horn called for Alice Fursby to return to the Flower Garden booth. Tallie wondered if Alice supplied the horn and ran off from time to time just to hear her name called on it. She softly chuckled at the thought. It was a clever trick to have oneself paged and committed the idea to memory, just in case.

"I've got to get back to our booth, but you can count on seeing me later, Jenny."

Tallie looked up at her aunt, "What man are you talking about?"

"Why Mr. Henry, of course. I wouldn't want to drag his name into this unless we turn out to be good advertising for him, don't you see?"

After the pledging, they stood in the barbecue line waving their newly won little flags and joined the Thompsons, Hays, and Doc Gilbert at a long table. Mary John was there as was Banta and waved Tallie to sit with them.

Tallie spent most of the lunch time listening to Mary John tell about her stay at Oklahoma State University. She was right in the middle of telling about a famous chef when a loud motorcycle roared around the courthouse square. The driver stopped and revved the motor several times before he turned it off. A gangly man from the courthouse crowd walked toward the biker.

"Dear Lord, have mercy! That's Claude Worth walking toward that biker," Aunt Jenny exclaimed.

"It's Claude, all right," Doc Gilbert avered. "I'd better go find the sheriff."

"...and Mr. Hooper." Tallie suggested.

"What's going on?" Mary John asked Tallie.

"I'm not sure, but if that biker is who I think it is, those two are definitely not friends. Claude accidently wounded a biker in the rump with a booby trap, and that biker is probably the one that has been hunting Claude ever since."

"This could be a bummer," Mary John said. She took hold of Banta's arm for comfort.

They all watched Claude stop about six feet from the biker and plant his feet in a wide stance like a gunslinger in an old movie. The rider got off the bike slowly, revealing 'Hell Hounds' written in fiery styled letters across the fuselage of the bike. Claude said something that no one could hear. The biker ran his fingers through his hair and gave a reply. When Claude began to speak again, two men exited a blue sedan parked a few feet from the bike and walked toward Claude and the Hell Hounds rider.

Sheriff Sawyer appeared, seemingly from nowhere, to join the men in the street. His white stetson hat was low over his forehead. He loomed in height over the other men. His hand was on his waist close to his gun. He nodded to Claude first, then said something to the biker who nodded and pulled a billfold from his back pocket and showed it to the sheriff. All those men formed a huddle and did some more talking, but not a word of it could be heard by Tallie or anyone else at the table.

"Sheriff Sawyer is checking the biker for an operator's license, I betcha" Banta said.

"Do you think Sheriff Sawyer will arrest him?" Tallie asked.

"Not unless there is a reason, " Banta said.

Tallie was hoping the sheriff would clap the cuffs on the biker and arrest the men in the blue sedan, too. A big clean-up operation all at one time. Instead, the sheriff was bringing all three of those thugs over to the table Tallie realized.

"Oh no! They are coming over here." she said.

"Sheriff Sawyer wouldn't do it wasn't safe," Mary John assured her.

Claude Worth, however, parted and went off in another direction, but the rest followed the sheriff to the table.

"Folks," the sheriff said, "This here is Bud and Speck", as he pointed toward the men who had exited the blue sedan. And this here is Roland, alias 'Rat'."

The men at the table mumbled polite responses or nodded at them, and moved over for them to sit down.

Momentarily, Claude came back to the table with a tray of lemonades. Aunt Jenny got up to help serve it, but Pastor Hay laid his hand on her shoulder and told her he would do the serving today.

"Now," said the sheriff, "let's go through this one more time, slowly. Claude, you start."

"Doc over there called a hospital in Oklahoma City and had me admitted up there, only he didn't want me to do the driving on account of my being so,uh, you might say 'sick'. Bud and Speck are hospital volunteers who came to get me. When I got in the car with them, I told them I needed some things out at Aunt Jenny's place.

I really wanted my keys. I don't like to leave my car anywhere, nor like to be without it. In fact, I didn't think I needed to be in no hospital, neither. I guess if I could have found my keys in her house, I'd have never went to the hospital. Doc knew that I reckon. Anyway, these old boys took me on and while I was up there, they said I needed to do something about making up for my past or I'd pickle myself to death or land in a nursing home with somebody else wiping my rear. Sorry. Anyway, they said I had to settle up. So I called some places where the Hounds usually went and put out the word that I wanted to see the main dog about some unfinished bidness."

The sheriff stopped Claude and pointed to Roland. "Your turn," he said. Roland ran his fingers through his thick, black hair. His forearms displayed tattoos of snakes.

"Roland", he chuckled. Still sounds like someone else's name to me. I'm still used to Rat." He shifted in his chair. "For starters, we don't have a gang anymore. Haven't had one for two or three years now. A couple of the guys are doing time, the rest of them are dead. Me? I guess I'm lucky. I tangled with a big black dude called Jesse Wash one night.

"I was alone, sleeping under bridges and lifting a little food from the 7-11 store. I'd decided to go west and hook up with another gang somewhere. I was hungry and short on gas one night when I saw this old Ford pickup on the side of the road. It was past midnight. I figured someone was sleepin' in it. It should have been easy pickings, but not off Jesse Wash. He pulled me through the window like I was Kleenex, held me like a vise, tied me up, threw me in the floorboard, and laid the Scriptures on me for two days. And to make a long story short, Jesse turned me over to some tough Christian bikers and, brother, I do mean tough. They took me on. Tied me to them, literally; wouldn't let me go until they were sure I would serve the Lord. I do now, from my bike, picking up strays like myself and pointing them to a ranch we have where they rest and heal. It's a working ranch in Kansas where guys can live and work until they decide to leave. I finally was able to repurpose myself.

" So, I was working at a place one night that I used to hang out in. The bartender gave me the word that this Claude dude was looking for me. That's why I'm here. Like I told you in the street, I'm out of the revenge business, but I figured I'd better face this dude by myself, even if Claude prefers charges against me for my past crimes. That's about it, Sheriff."

"I'm not wanting to get revenge on anybody, Neither," Claude said. "I just want to get this straightened out for good. I don't want you or any of your guys torching me or my car or anything I'm affiliated with. I'm willing to pay for the damages I did with the booby trap, or go to jail for it if I have to."

Sheriff Sawyer tilted his hat back. "How much would you say Roland aka Rat robbed from your station back east, Claude?"

"Maybe five-hundred dollars, all totaled."

"What about your bike and wound, Roland? What was the cost on that?" the Sheriff asked.

Roland thought for a moment, then said, "Oh, I'd say about five-hundred dollars," he said, trying not to smile.

"Well, that evens you two up, I reckon, but Roland," Sheriff Sawyer said, rising from the table, "you need to step over to my office, and I'm purely sorry Son, but you have something coming to you. You might want to brace yourself."

Roland's slight smile fell and he drew his eyebrows close together. Claude suddenly looked frightened again.

"Claude," the Sheriff said, "do you have something else to say?"

"Yeah. Roland, or Rat, or whatever they call you, I'm sorry. I'm really sorry, Man. I only wanted to settle with you. I didn't mean to get you in deeper with the law."

"No sweat, Man. I told you, I'm out of the revenge racket. I reckon I got coming to me."

The Sheriff nodded toward the jail. " Let's go, Son."

Bud and Speck said something to Claude and drove away in the blue sedan. Doc's pager went off causing him to stand up. "It's been interesting," said Doc, "but I expect that's either someone with firecracker burns or Mrs. Widkins is about to domino."

"Seems like I've heard of Jesse Wash before," Aunt Jenny said, "but for the life of me, I can't recall just where. But then, when you get as old as I am, all names sound familiar," she laughed.

"What do you think will happen to the biker?" Banta looked to his dad.

"I have no idea, son."

Mrs. Hay stood up and said, "Banta, are you bringing Mary John home now, or are you all going to sit out here in this heat some more?"

"I'll have her home later if that's okay."

"Mrs. Hay," the Pastor said, "let's stop by the hospital and see if Joe Widkins is pacing the floor. And as for you two kids," he said looking at Mary John and Banta, "don't let me find your names in the newspapers tomorrow."

Pastor smiled, but it was a friendly warning nonetheless. Tallie and Aunt Jenny were left with Claude.

"Thanks for storing my things," he said to Aunt Jenny, "and if you'll let me have my keys, I'll get my car and my junk from the station and bug out of here."

"What do you plan to do with yourself?" Aunt Jenny asked.

"Bud and Speck have some job interviews for me. I'll be paying my back rent when I get some cash coming in."

Aunt Jenny handed Claude the keys and wished him good luck.

"Thanks for your help, too," he said to Tallie.

"What help?' I don't remember doing anything for you."

"I finally figured out it was you yelling those prayers through the screen door. I needed them, kid."

Aunt Jenny gave Tallie a curious look and Tallie shrugged it off with a smile. Claude shook their hands and left.

"Let's go, Missy." I want to wash this goo off my face and soak my bunions. I get tired of town pretty quick."

Tallie eased the truck onto the highway and pushed it up to thirty miles an hour. In the rearview mirror, she saw something coming up fast. A big Harley motorcycle whizzed expertly around their truck and someone waved.

"LOOK!" Tallie yelled at her aunt. "That's Roland the Rat on that bike, and that's Brillo Nudd sitting behind him."

Aunt Jenny leaned forward and squinted hard. "Sure enough and praise God!" she said and laughed. "The Sheriff said he hoped Roland could take what was coming to him."

Tallie pulled off the highway onto the county road toward home sorting out the confusing details of the recent events.

"There were two blue sedans", she reasoned aloud to her aunt. The professors drove one and Bud and Speck drove the other one. That means that Claude was in the blue sedan with Bud and Speck he lied to about saying he needed to pick up a few things, and that makes Claude the one prowling your house hunting his keys, but didn't steal anything, right?"

"Makes sense. I think Sheriff Sawyer gave Brillo Nudd a choice of some kind and he chose to go with Roland to that Kansas ranch. That means Nudd has made a good choice for once and got the brains I prayed for. Hallelujah." Aunt Jenny said and meant it.

"Your prayers were answered fast, " Tallie said.

"Some are. Some take a long time, and there's some I may never live long enough to know the answer to. But the scriptures say that all prayers of his children are answered 'Yes' and 'Amen'.

Tallie decided to let that last remark pass for now and changed the subject.

"You know what?" Tallie asked.

"What?"

"When I first saw that biker, I was afraid you'd have him out here chopping Johnsongrass first thing in the morning."

Aunt Jenny chuckled. "Do you want to milk or cook supper when we get home?"

"Both," Tallie replied, "You're getting so old you have to wear paint like a barn."

"Bite your tongue, Missy."

"Okay, I'll milk and you can cook. You cook better than I do," Tallie replied.

After supper, they sat on the porch enjoying the quiet. Tallie was deep in thought, planning characters to make from her rocks. Aunt Jenny was soaking her feet in Epsom Salts water with her head back against the rocker. The sound of the telephone caused them both to jerk upright. Tallie answered it.

"It's for you," she called through the screen.

Aunt Jenny grimaced and wiped her feet hastily.

"Alice Fursby! How could you think such a wad of nonsense? I was referring to Mr. Henry."

Tallie giggled. What a day! Suddenly she thought about Tom Sawyer. She had not seen him at all.

~~~~~~~~~~~~~~

The house was cleaned from top to bottom by mid-morning, having started at 6 A.M. while it was cooler, and while they had on lightweight nightgowns.

"It's hot. It's too HOT to THINK. There's not a breeze stirring anywhere!," Aunt Jenny declared.

She plopped down by the phone and dialed. "Yes, This is Jenny Raider. Tell Dave to bring me one of those air conditioners, the kind that sits in the window and makes your house as cool as the drugstore. If he can get it in for me today, I'll take it. If he can't, I might change my mind. In fact, bring two of them. I have upstairs rooms that could use a little cooling off as well. No, I'll pay cash on delivery. Thanks. I appreciate that."

Tallie hung over the stair rail and suppressed an urge to shout, but couldn't. "Hal-lay-loo-OO OOO-yah!"

By two o'clock that afternoon the air conditioners were installed. Aunt Jenny drew up a chair right in front of the one in the living room.

"That's wonderful. It was so hot last night, I could barely sleep," she said. "I can remember when the drugstore was the only place in town that was cooled by frigid air. The hospital, the dry goods store and the cafe had water coolers. If a-body had curly hair it would straighten it, and if you had straight hair it would curl it. Am I getting silly? Maybe that make-up made me silly. What do you think, Tallie?"

"You have a furnace; why not an air conditioner?"

"I'll tell Alice Fursby that very thing if she finds out what I bought, and you can rest assured she will find out."

Tallie wanted to suggest getting water piped in from the well, too, but decided her aunt would get around to that one day.

"I'll see how much my 'lectric runs and maybe this fall, I'll check into some plumbing."

Tallie kept a serious face and said, "If you keep the house at 80 or so it won't cost too much and it will be lots cooler than 95 in here or a 100 when you're canning."

"If Claude pays me, and I think he will; and if I get Aunt Tallie's house rented and the lease money keeps coming, I should be able to have a little simple plumbing put in. Besides, if we had a bad winter, some of the folks might think they'd have to come fetch water for me. Why, I'd be remiss, too, if I passed on and didn't do a little something to add to the value of this place? It is just like God to make me turn loose of that old bathtub just so I'd smarten up, don't you think?"

"I know He wouldn't tell me where it landed," Tallie said and went to answer the telephone.

"Mom!...Yes, we're fine. It's so hot here, but Aunt Jenny bought some new air conditioners and had them installed today. Yes, two of them....How's Daddy?...Great...Oh...I suppose so. I've been really busy...How? On the fifteenth?...No. I'm glad, in a way...But that isn't very long from now...Yes, she's right here. It's Mom," she said. Tallie handed the receiver to her aunt and went to the porch.

The heat felt good— like a cleansing. She picked up the hoe and dug around Aunt Jenny's flowers, walked to the garden and pulled a few stray weeds and ended up drawing water for the chickens. They were sitting in the shade again with their mouths open. Even old Jube was quiet.

She pumped the horse tank full and dipped her head in up to

the shoulders. It felt good—the hot sun and the cool water. The dirt smelled good. The weeds smelled good. The few pillowy clouds were lightning white and the sky a forever sort of blue. She breathed deep and let the tears fall.

She never dreamed it would be hard to leave such a boring place, the place where she was twice-born, the nursery room of her soul. She wiped her eyes and made a decision.

Saturday at the Trade Fair, Aunt Jenny sold butter and eggs, melons and okra. Sheriff Sawyer came by and filled them in on the details of Brillo Nudd and Roland, but mainly to give Tallie her $100.00 and Aunt Jenny's $8.34 from the purse he had kept for evidence.

"I saw your Mrs. at the dessert booth on the Fourth," Aunt Jenny said, "but I never caught a glimpse of hide nor hair of Tom."

"Tom was up to Tulsa. Ceidra called him to take her to a 4th celebration at a big band concert and to prowl a few T-town sights as she called it. It made Geneva plenty nervous with him out driving alone on a holiday, but there comes a time when you have to turn loose of them kids and hope they can find their way home again in one piece and no exotic diseases."

"That's a fact. But I also know you've worked enough wrecks that it must have made you a little edgy, too, right?"

"Yes'm, but he's home with all his pieces and parts and Ceidra made it to Dallas without a hitch."

Aunt Jenny looked up sharply. "Dallas, you say? Hm-m."

"Let me have a couple of those melons, please Ma'am, while I'm here. How much?"

"Ten cents apiece," Aunt Jenny said. The sheriff laid down two dollars and left with two melons.

"You never could count anything but votes, could you, Hank?" she called after him and began to pack up the booth alone.

Tallie had gone to mail her rock figures, and on return, suggested they get a hamburger at the Garden Club snack bar before they left town.

Aunt Jenny chewed slowly on the hamburger as well as on the

fact that Ceidra had gone off to Dallas. She decided to tell Tallie about her concern.

"I guess Mrs. Henry is in a snit," Aunt Jenny said. Ceidra sure can pull off some stunts."

"Maybe she won't like it and will come back in a couple of days."

"Maybe. But I know it's going to be alright, eventually. I know, that I know that. But how long 'eventually' is, I don't know, and that is the hair in the soup."

When they got home, Tallie insisted Aunt Jenny turn on the air conditioner and perhaps call the Henrys. She hurried back to unload the truck and get a shovel from the barn.

Satisfied that her aunt was tied up with the Henrys, she took 13 little pecan trees wrapped in a wet bag from the truck. They were about two feet long. Perfect, she thought, for her thirteenth summer. It satisfied her to think that some day, someone would eat from the trees she was planting.

A horse whinnied. Tallie looked toward the driveway. It was old Brownie with Tom Sawyer in the saddle. He reined up.

"What's happening?" Tom asked.

"I'm trying to decide just how far apart to plant these trees."

"Here, I'll help you. You put the markers and I'll dig." Tom took the shovel.

"What are you doing, just exercising Brownie?"

"Yep. Did you go to town on the Fourth?" Tom asked while he dug holes.

"We had a nice time, and it was an interesting day. How was your holiday?" She asked.

"Phony party, a band that was more loud than talented. Tom waited but Tallie didn't ask anything else. He shoveled some dirt over the roots of the little pecan and continued.

"I like to come out here sometimes. I was over at Hay's and Pastor said Brownie needed some exercise."

Tallie grabbed up a large bucket of water and poured some over the roots. Tom dug another hole, looked at Tallie who remained silent, so he continued."

"Pastor also told me what happened about Brillo Nudd and then on the fourth. Some couple of days, huh?"

"It was wild there for a while. The best part was seeing Nudd ride out of here," Tallie said.

"How come you're planting all these trees at this time of year?"

"For one, I'm named after a tree planter. And secondly, I have to plant them now because I have to leave on the 15th. The pastor and Mrs. Hay are taking me to the city to catch the plane home."

"I see. That's not far off is it." Tom said.

"Nope. Not long."

Tom quit digging, walked to the barn lot and returned with a burlap sack half full of cow chips which he began to crumble and work into the soil.

"This should help them get started good," he said.

Tallie thought it was remarkable that he would crumble it with his bare hands so matter-of-factly. She could imagine what some of her St. Louis friends would say and do if they could see him. She knelt and placed the last tree in the last hole and patted the dirt around it.

Tom hung his wrists over the shovel handle.

"Are you glad to go home?" he asked.

"Yes and no." She kept rearranging and patting the dirt on the last little tree. I miss my folks, but I—I—I hate to go off and leave her. I'll think about her and wonder.... Tallie's voice gave way to a muffled choking and then a quiet but pitiful little wail. Tom reached down and pulled Tallie up from the ground and held her.

"I know. I know," he said. "I'm the same way. I'd never tell anyone else that, but I like being here and I think about her a lot."

"Thanks," Tallie said against his chest.

"Yeah, she's something."

"TAL—LEE!" Aunt Jenny called.

Tom let loose of Tallie and smiled a little.

"Out here!" She answered.

"Who's here?" Aunt Jenny called, coming around the edge of the house. "Why, it's Tom!" She answered her own question. "And what is this? What on earth are you two up to now? Trees!"

"Pecans. Thirteen of them to commemorate my 13th birthday and the year of my born-again birthday. Mostly to carry on the legacy of planting to remember like Aunt Tallie did."

Aunt Jenny put her hands on her hips and smiled. "No one forgets why they planted a tree. I'll be here remembering, and maybe Tom too, right?"

"Yes ma'am," he said thinking that he'd be out to keep them watered and weeded.

"Can you stay to supper?" Aunt Jenny said.

"My car is at the Hay's. I'd have to take Brownie back first."

"Go right on. And take Tallie with you. She might enjoy a horseback ride. I'll have something on the table in a hip-hop, so don't take too long, you two."

Tom put Tallie in the saddle and told her to hold on. He led Brownie to the barnyard shed so that he could put up the shovel then washed up at the well, taking a hidden bar of soap from under the horse tank.

"I didn't know that was under there," Tallie said.

"There may be lots of things you don't know," he said and swung himself up into the saddle behind her, put his arms around her waist and clucked Brownie into a gentle walk.

Brownie's easy gait and the squeaking of the leather were pleasant. She felt safe sitting in front of Tom and comforted by his slow, even breathing across the top of her hair.

~~~~~~~~~~~~~

Back in St. Louis, Tallie sat in class and thought about her summer at Aunt Jenny's, especially about being twice born, and the planting of the trees and the horseback ride. She looked again at the English assignment on the blackboard. "Highlights of My Summer", three pages, or four hundred words. How could she tell even the highlights in so few words? And just how much of that summer did she want to share with whom? Then suddenly, she decided it was none of her teacher's business what this particular summer had been about and proceeded to tell about another summer, since the assignment didn't specify any particular summer.

~~~~~~~~~~~~~

Back in Sawed Off Corners, Aunt Jenny waved Tom off to town to register some very special letters at the post office. When she was sure he was out of sight, she whistled all the way to the barn for a bucket of store-bought fertilizer.

"Hee! Lord, You are so funny. Who'd ever guess," she said strewing the fertilizer, "that this little patch of Johnsongrass is really hallowed ground, Your burning bush of Sawed Off Corners.

What I went through trying to chop it out when I was twelve! But I must remind You, I never intended to set such a big fire to get rid of it. I was only twelve and it seemed much easier to burn it out than to chop it out.

"When the laundry on the clothesline caught fire--oh, I never was so scared. The thought of it still made her shiver. She paused and laughed again.

"And then the only thing left standing in the whole, burnt, backyard was that everlasting Johnsongrass, the very thing I wanted to burn up. Thank God for Aunt Tallie. That's when Aunt Tallie said You must have intended something special for that grass patch and to leave it be. She said she was so glad I had not gotten burned and hugged me close, but Mama sure was mad.

"Okay,maybe Mama was just scared. But she took action. She insisted I find a way to pay Aunt Tallie back for all the diapers she had brought up to wash in Mama's new wringer machine and had hung on the line. Aunt Tallie said she would ask the Lord to bless us all because of that old stubborn grass patch since none of us could chop it out.

"So who'll be next?" she asked. She thumped the last grain of fertilizer from the bucket? Hmmm? Well, you can tell me later. Right now I'm glad to be back to normal. I got tired of calling St. Louis after ten o'clock just so Tallie couldn't hear my reports to her mom. I'm purely sorry I ever agreed to do that.

"Yes, I'm going to enjoy a few days of peace and quiet or until You decide to trot some new Moses into our little weed patch, since you won't let me retire.

"Say," she added, "where did You throw that old bathtub? She paused. Nothing. You really enjoy Your little secrets, don't You. I hear You laughing. Well, I do. Don't I have an ear to hear? Anyway, thanks for the peace and quiet of this day. I'm enjoying it."

.......and so were some baby bass out in the pond swimming

around and under that old, bent up bathtub safe from turtles and other prey.

Down in Dallas, Ceidra sat in a modeling agency and read the contract several times. Some of the phrases could be taken to mean two different things. Finally, she told the secretary that she would have her lawyer look it over prior to signing. The nervous secretary snatched the contract from Ceidra and told her that if she needed to consult her lawyer first, maybe they would all be better off if she would look elsewhere for employment.

"I think you are exactly right," Ceidra answered and went to call her dad.

St. Louis: "Your report card came today, registered and special delivery," Tallie's mother said.

"Report card? It is only the first week of school."

"Look on the dining table. You'll find it." Tallie found a thick envelope from Sawed Off Corners and inside there really was a report card.

Patience=D and improving. Self starter=A Hard worker=A Ingenuity=A Sharing=A Merciful=B Self control=C Talent=B (must sing more) Honesty=A

Spiritual standing=Positive (let her tell you)

Love,

Aunt Jenny Raider

"What is this supposed to mean?" Tallie asked.

"We sent you to summer school, Sweetie. Your dad and I decided it was time. He went through it when he was fifteen. You didn't know that, did you?"

"No."

"I wouldn't ask him about it either," her mom said. "If he wants to talk about it, he will."

"I can understand that," Tallie said, remembering her English assignment. In the same envelope was an unopened packet marked 'For Tallie Koums'. She opened it wondering what it could be? Maybe something she left at her aunt's house.

There was a deed to Great-aunt Tallie's house and lands with full mineral rights, minus rent and/or grazing leases to be paid to Aunt Jenny Raider for administering the trust in the landlord's absence. The last page in the envelope was a letter.

Dear Tallie,

You must come back home, now and then and see after your place. I told you I had other things to consider about leasing the land for drilling. You. I've done what Aunt Tallie wanted. I made sure her little namesake could stand up to hard work. Learn how to do with less or more. Be counted on to take responsibility, a solid overseer appreciative of her earthly inheritance as well as the one to come. With that being so, her place was to be yours. Your folks didn't know that. You can tell them, if you care to. I miss you and look for you to come through that old screen door one of these days. Here comes Tom to take this to the post office. Poor Tom. His dobbers are down today. Boggy Creek beat them in the finals 5 to 3. He comes once a week to water your trees. And Mr. Hooper was made head driver and superintendent of the Bus Barn.

I heard you have permission to get your ears professionally pierced next week for the birthday present they didn't send in the mail. The jewelry box with 3 pairs of earrings. Real gold earrings, real pearls, and real green emeralds. Oh My goodness. How beautiful they will be on you. And the combs of Aunt Tallies will be for your hair one fine day.

P.S. Alice Fursby was wearing lipstick at church last Sunday. Isn't that a lick?